THE MARY PLAIN
OMNIBUS

THE MARY PLAIN
OMNIBUS

Gwynedd Rae

containing

MOSTLY MARY
ALL MARY
MARY PLAIN IN TOWN
MARY PLAIN ON HOLIDAY

illustrated by

Irene Williamson

ROUTLEDGE & KEGAN PAUL
LONDON, HENLEY AND BOSTON

The Mary Plain Omnibus
first published in 1976
by Routledge & Kegan Paul Ltd
39 Store Street,
London WC1E 7DD and
Broadway House,
Newtown Road,
Henley-on-Thames,
Oxon RG9 1EN and
9 Park Street,
Boston, Mass. 02108, USA
Printed in Great Britain by
Lowe & Brydone Printers Limited,
Thetford, Norfolk
Contains Mostly Mary, *1930*
reprinted fifteen times
All Mary, *1930*
reprinted fifteen times
Mary Plain in Town, *1935*
reprinted fifteen times
Mary Plain on Holiday, *1937*
reprinted twelve times

ISBN 0 7100 8437 4

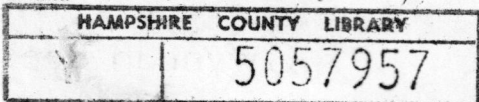

THIS IS FOR THE MAN BECOS HE WAS SO KIND MARY PLAIN

CONTENTS

THE BEAR FAMILY TREE

ALPHA AND LADY GRIZZLE'S FAMILY

Big Wool *grandmother to* Mary.

BIG WOOL'S FAMILY

Young Wool (*dead*) *father to* Mary.

Friska *aunt to* Mary.

Bunch *uncle to* Mary.

Forget-me-not }
Plum } *aunts to* Mary, *but younger than she.*

FRISKA'S FAMILY

Marionetta }
Little Wool } *cousins to* Mary.

Harrods. *A cross bear with no relations.*

and

Mary (*called* Plain). *An orphan.*

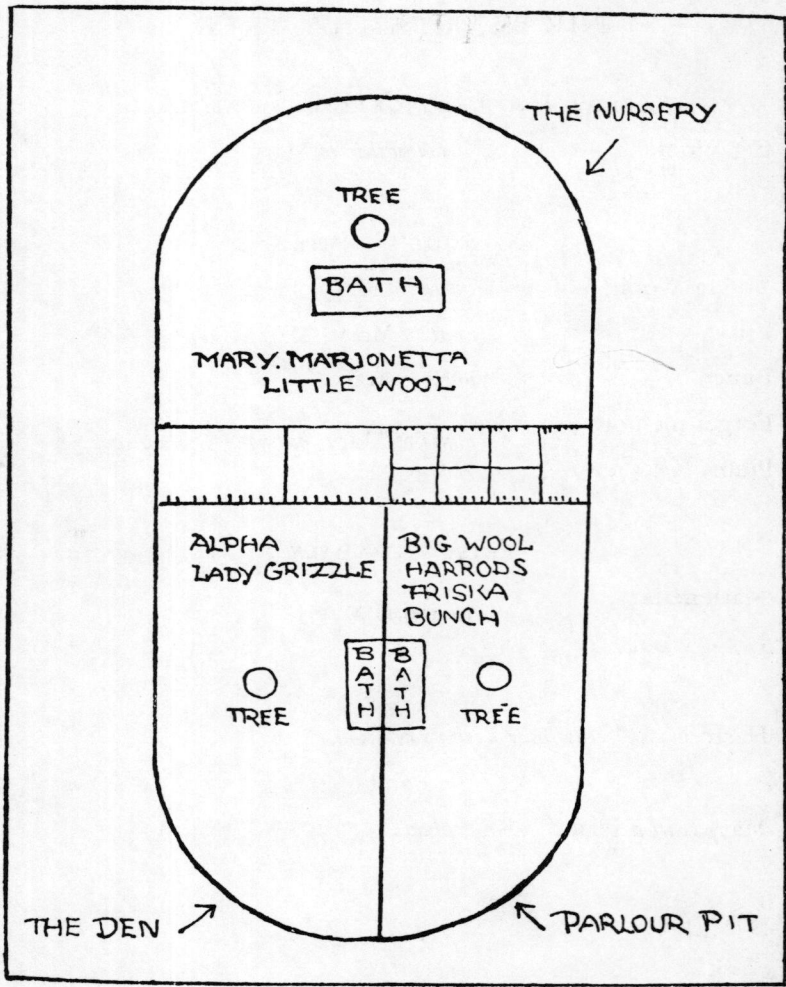

THE NURSERY

TREE
○

BATH

MARY. MARJONETTA
LITTLE WOOL

ALPHA
LADY GRIZZLE

BIG WOOL
HARRODS
FRISKA
BUNCH

TREE
○

BATH
BATH

TREE
○

THE DEN →

← PARLOUR PIT

The Home of the Bears

MOSTLY MARY

CONTENTS

THE INTRODUCTION

WHICH IS *MOST* IMPORTANT

THE following is a story about my friends, the Berne bears, who are *real* bears, and not just Teddies.

A few years ago I was obliged to spend most of the winter months at Berne and I began to look around for some interest. I found it at once in these bears, who live in a pit there, and who were, from the very first, an immense joy and amusement to me.

I must explain in a few words their history.

An old legend runs that, as far back as 1191, a certain duke built himself a fortress to protect himself from his enemies, and this same fortress gradually grew into a small fortified town.

One day, hunting near by, he killed a bear, and named the town after it—Berne—now the capital of Switzerland, which still has a bear as its coat of arms.

It was as long ago as 1513 that the Bernese first kept some bears captive in a pit, and ever since, all through the centuries, they have done the same.

They are extremely proud of these beasts, and at

3

all times and in all weathers you will see an affectionate audience leaning over the wall, feeding them with carrots, biscuits or figs.

There were nine bears when I was there, and they were divided into three pits, which I have called The Den, Parlour Pit and the Nursery. I have also drawn a little plan to make it easier to understand about their home.

I would add that, though I have written this small book, I know nothing whatsoever about the bears' real lives and habits; only, through my many visits to them, they have become my friends, each with their own separate character. So I have written down some things about them, and I feel sure that some of the many children who love bears, will agree with me that they might easily be true.   G. R.

CHAPTER ONE

IN WHICH WE GET TO KNOW THE BEARS

MARY was six months old. She had rather pointed ears, and she lived in Nursery Pit, with her twin cousins, Marionetta and Little Wool. The twins had nice black coats, but Mary's was a kind of browny grey, but she did not mind much, for, as she said to herself sensibly, " At least we can't get mixed up."

Mary was not sensible about many things, but this was one of the few exceptions. Being an orphan, she had had to bring herself up, more or less, and she had on the whole made a fair success of it. Of course, she was usually in some kind of trouble, but she was quite used to that, and supposed that orphan bears were born different from the rest, so that was why she was always just a little less lucky than the others.

The twins' mother, Friska, lived next door in Parlour

Pit with her mother, Big Wool, her brother, Bunch, and Harrods, a cross old bear who was called this because she was the kind of shaped bear one usually sees on a stand in a toy bazaar.

Friska was a nice sensible bear, very good-tempered and a great help to her mother. She was quite different from her brother. He was lazy and greedy and thought Bunch much the most important person in the world.

Big Wool had done her best to break him of these bad habits when he was a cub, but she gave it up in the end, for it was mere waste of breath and did no good at all. As far as looks went she could not help being rather proud of him, for he had a lovely dark coat which stood out in a thick ruff round his neck, which was most becoming—but his manners were a great sorrow to her.

In Parlour Pit, as in both the others, there was a big fir-tree in the middle, with branches all broken off to stumps where the bears had climbed, and on the side of the pit was a big square bath full of running water, where they drank and had their baths on Wednesday afternoons. There were also big iron doors which ran up on chains, leading to the sleeping-dens, but these were always kept shut during the day, as it was a very strict rule that no bear was allowed to go to his den for a midday rest, however tired he might be. He just *had* to make the best of the pit-floor.

In Den Pit, which was the last of the three, lived Alpha and Lady Grizzle. They were so old that they could not climb their tree, which was the only one that still had beautiful shady green branches—just what they needed to rest under when the sun was too warm to be really comfortable. They were so ancient and wise that all the other bears were in awe of them and they were kept quite separate from the rest, having their own dens to sleep in ; and only once a year, on St. Bruin's Day, which is the great bear festival, the younger ones all went to visit them and took them some small present.

One sunny morning in early autumn, Friska was busy getting all the bowls clean and ready for breakfast, which would be brought at any moment. She licked them all with great care, and then gave them a final polish round with her paw. She sighed when she came to Bunch's bowl, it was always so clean—no stray bits of meat or bran to provide a rather empty bear with a little courage till breakfast time arrived.

Just as Friska finished the last bowl she heard Job undoing the chain on the door. For a long time the bears had not known his name, and they had always called him " the kind breakfast and supper man "— rather a long name for one person. One morning he was having a lot of trouble raking up the straw to make their beds, which were in a great mess. Mary happened to be in the corner, looking rather self-conscious and hoping no awkward questions would be asked—for the truth was that she and Little Wool had had a splendid pillow-fight the night before.

However, he only grumbled a bit as he poked it into place, and said " You're more trouble than a whole pack of children, and it's a lucky thing my name's Job," and Mary heard and ran off to tell Friska what his real name was.

Breakfast was, somehow, a very hungry meal—at least the bears thought so. Through the day they had plenty to eat, for so many grown-ups and children came to visit them, and threw them carrots and biscuits, or any other odds and ends they had collected and brought in a paper bag. But they found it a long time to wait from supper-time till breakfast—especially Bunch, who got restless towards daylight and began to twist about and mutter in his sleep, which was rather disturbing to the older bears, who were not quite so tight asleep as the babies.

Directly after breakfast, Big Wool clapped her paws and said "Now then, all of you in a row—quick!" And all the bears hurried to their places—first Harrods, then Friska, Bunch, and soon in sizes down to Mary, the babiest of them all.

"Faces!" said Big Wool, and every bear licked its paws and smoothed the fur on its face.

"Ears!" and then all the paws moved busily from mouth to ear, smoothing and patting. All but Mary's, who found the whole toilet business a great bore and thought that ears, especially, should be left in peace.

"Mary!" said Big Wool sternly. Mary gave a quick lick and pat and fiddled half-heartedly with an ear—just till Big Wool looked away again.

"Chests!" and this was the part that Mary quite enjoyed—for it meant straining back one's neck to reach

and Mary would see how far back she could lean without going over, and it nearly always ended in her going just a little farther than she could.

As soon as this was over, Bunch would hurry to the door, so as to be the first to reach the tree. He was very selfish about the tree and did not like any other bear to come on to it. Not that any of them wanted to, but Bunch pretended to himself that they did, for it made a far better game. Sometimes he would come down to the bottom of the tree and stand with his two front paws still on the lowest branch, looking very ready for a quarrel, and, if any of the others come within a few feet of him he would rush up the tree again, making a most lovely Bunch noise through his nose. It was a kind of loud, snuffly roar and he kept it specially for this occasion.

He was an intelligent bear altogether, for he had chosen

that branch, just in front of and level with the carrot-
stall because he knew that anyone buying carrots and
turning round, would find him in a beautiful position
exactly opposite, clapping his stiff paws for the first one.

He also knew very well that only the heavy carrots
reached him there, the small ones fell short, so, though
some people were bad throwers and he missed a good
many, when one did reach him, it was sure to be a nice,
big, juicy one, well worth the catching and the eating.
Big Wool had warned him many times that he would lose
his figure if he ate so much, but he just shrugged his fat
shoulders and ate all the more. Bunch was like that.

Only the heavy carrots reached him there

CHAPTER TWO

ALL ABOUT SCHOOL AND RATHER SHORT

SCHOOL was held very early, before the iron doors were let down and the bears separated for the day.

Friska rattled the chain on the door which was the signal for the cubs to come running to their places. They sat in a row along the edge of the bath, which made an excellent bench, and Friska stood in front of them with a long stick in her paw. Not that she ever used it, but there was always the feeling that she might.

Only the three little ones had lessons, and Mary thought with longing of the time when she would be so big and clever that she would have nothing more to learn.

One day the twins were having rather an argument as to which had been at the top of the class when lessons had ended the day before. This never worried Mary, for she had never been even in the middle, so she was standing under the wall and chatting to a robin who had been pecking near the railings up above.

Friska looked up and saw the sun was getting very near the tree tops which meant it was late, so she gave a sudden deep growl. " To your seats, please." At the same moment she leant forward and gave Mary a poke with her stick, which made her jump and then scramble off to her seat as quick as quick.

By this time the twins had changed places so often that they had worked their way to the end of the seat, and, when Mary, still looking over her shoulder at Friska's cane, reached her place below the twins, she sat down—just beyond where the seat ended ! The cement was very hard and Mary had a quick temper, and before anyone had time to do anything she was up again and flying at the cubs in a fury, she pushed them deliberately backwards into the bath.

They gasped and gulped and climbed out like drowned rats, looking the picture of misery, for the sun had not had time to warm the water, and it was not Wednesday, their bath day, anyway.

Now, Friska was a wise bear and, though she knew it had all been a mistake at bottom, she felt she could not let it pass. So she ordered her two cubs to run up and down in the sun to dry themselves, at the same time telling them that because they had argued so much, they should have no sugar after supper.

Then she called Mary to her and said, " I expect you are sorry, already, that you have been so unkind to your little cousins, but——"

" No—I'm not at all," said Mary rudely, for she was still very sore.

" But," went on Friska firmly, " you will be far more sorry when I explain to you that it was all a mistake. They had no idea that, while quarrelling, they had moved so far up the seat and had left no room for you. Also—— "

" I —— " began Mary.

" Also, also, also," said Friska very quickly so that Mary could not interrupt, " even if they had done it on purpose, it wasn't at all right to push them into the water—especially after the bad cold Little Wool had last week. So, although I know you only did it because you were hurt and angry, I am going to send you into the corner for ten minutes, so you will have time to think over how sorry you will be if, through your fault, Little Wool gets pneumonia."

Mary went off quite happily. She had no idea what pneumonia was, but she did not in the least mind if Little Wool got two of it. Nor did she feel ashamed when she heard him sneeze, but lay down on her back and started the game she had invented with her four paws, which passed the time splendidly.

"Come along, you two!" called Friska. "You must be nearly dry now. Sit down quietly and attend to your lessons, or you'll find yourselves in the two other corners—besides having no sugar."

"Yes, mamma," they said and sat down with their paws folded demurely.

Friska began the first lesson.

"A for—?"

"Alpha!" said Little Wool.

"Good! C for —?"

"Carrots," said Little Wool again.

"Right! Come along, Marionetta. Don't let your little brother do all the answering. F for —?"

"Figska!" said Mary unexpectedly from her corner. The paw game had begun to get a bit dull and she was sitting up and listening.

Friska took no notice. "F for —?"

"Food!" said Marionetta at last.

"P for —?"

Marionetta looked at Mary and then said "Punishment!" very loud.

"Pig!" flashed Mary and stuck out her tongue. But when Friska turned round to see if she had heard aright, Mary had her back to her and seemed very interested in a crack in the wall—so she thought she must have been mistaken.

"S for —?"

"Sugar," moaned the twins. Mary turned round quickly.

"S for Stout," she said deliberately and then felt

rather frightened for she knew well that **Friska was** very anxious *not* to grow stout.   Friska looked at her and Mary held her breath.   Then after a long moment she turned back and continued.

" G for —— ? "

" Good," said Mary quickly, much relieved.

Now all these interruptions were not helping the class so Friska decided they should end.

" If Mary is now going to be good," she said, " she may come and join in the lessons."

Mary came, running, and sat down.

" W for —— ? "

" Wuffle," said Mary.   The other two giggled.

" What," said Friska coldly, " is a wuffle ? "

" I thought perhaps you could tell me," said Mary innocently.

Friska decided to let this pass, as she felt perhaps she ought to know what a wuffle was.

" M for —— ? "

" Me ! " said Mary brightly.   " Me *and* Mary, Mary *and* me—both of us."

There was no denying the truth of this, so Friska cleared her throat and said, " We will now have some arithmetic.   How many carrots make a bunch ? "

" Eight," said Marionetta.

" Nine," said Little Wool.

" It all depends," said Mary and was right.

" Ten in season and six out of season," explained Friska, " and don't forget.   How many bears are there in this pit ? "

" Four," said the twins.

" Three," said Mary.

" How many did you say, Mary ? "

" Three, Auntie," she said modestly.   " I felt perhaps I ought not to count myself as I'd been naughty." And at that moment, to Friska's great relief, Job called down that she must hurry into Parlour Pit, as he was going to let the doors down—so that ended lessons for that day.

CHAPTER THREE

OF HOW MARY FOUND HER MISSING NAME

MARY was sitting on the side of the bath hugging herself. She was so terribly happy that she would gladly have hugged somebody else, but as there were only the twins handy and she knew they would hate it, she had to do the best she could with herself. Being an orphan, and the others being twins, Mary sometimes could not help feeling a little lonely; for though they were all very friendly on the whole, the others naturally played together and not always games for three. So she had a good deal of time to think in and she had spent quite a lot of it over her name.

Her name was a great sorrow to her. She felt that it was so very short, and this had made her, each time she thought about it, rather sad—though she had far too much pride to show it.

Little Wool had two names and Marionetta, though she had only one, had at least a good long one; but

Mary—just Mary—seemed such a very small name to have. She had often wondered whether, as she was the youngest bear, there perhaps had not been enough names to go round; but she had never quite liked to ask.

And on this afternoon a most wonderful thing had happened, and she could never remember being so glad about anything before.

She had a special friend, a kind lady, who wore a fur coat rather the colour of Mary, who came and gave her carrots and really seemed to take an interest in her jumping efforts, for she was the only cub that could jump and she was very proud of it. Well, she had been standing looking wistfully up at the lady, with Little Wool and Marionetta beside her, when she saw her friend lean over the railings, and, as she dropped a nice pink carrot, say " *Isn't* Mary plain ? "

Mary was so startled that she let the carrot lie un-noticed at her feet, and Little Wool pulled it to him with his paw and gobbled it up. But Marionetta had heard and said in an excited voice, " Mary, did you hear ? That lady called you ' Mary Plain.' Is it your name ? " Mary pulled herself together.

" Yes," she said, " didn't you know ? " Then she walked away casually, and hoped they wouldn't notice how her heart was thumping in her side.

Directly the twins had moved away a little, she hurried back to her friend and did three of her very best jumps running to show how grateful she was. She felt somehow taller, and less lonely already, and the more she thought of it, the more excited she got inside, till at last she felt she must do something to work it off, or she would burst. So she suddenly ran up and gave Marionetta a soft box on the ear and cried "Can't catch me!" and then of course Marionetta had to show she could, and there followed a tremendous game of "Catch" round and round the pit—dodging round the bath and behind the tree into the corner, till at last Mary was caught, because Little Wool had joined Marionetta explaining that it was quite fair and not two against one, as they were twins. Mary, panting hard, had no breath and no real wish to contradict them, so she waited a moment, and then said she'd be "He."

Off they went again, tearing after each other while all the people looking over the wall laughed and clapped.

It ended in a very flat way for Mary—and not for the first time. Just as she was going to catch her, Marionetta gave a big spring and scrambled up the tree, leaving poor Mary down below, looking longingly up at her, for Mary could not climb the tree. Nor could Little Wool for that matter, which was a comfort, but Marionetta could, and showed off abominably over it.

Nothing, however, could really make Mary feel unhappy that day—she felt too bubbly inside—so she and Little Wool had a rolling match and Mary won, and it was great fun, and before they knew where they were it was time to go to bed.

Except in the case of the two very old bears, all the sleeping dens connected inside, and though there was one for each, the three cubs nearly always crept into one and snuggled up together. They took it in turns to be in the middle and on cold nights they rolled up so tightly that they looked like balls of wool.

On this night Mary could not settle for a long time, she kept being so happy about having two names, that it made her very wide awake. She turned this way and that and through her head ran the happenings of this most thrilling day. She started at the beginning and went over them all again and when she got to where Marionetta had sprung up the tree she began to puzzle, as she often had before, how she did it.

It was such a smooth tree till far further up than she could reach—only some flattish bumps that you could not catch hold of. So, till she could be tall enough to reach the first branch, how could she ever hope to get up the tree? Then, quite suddenly, she had a brilliant idea.

She thought: " When I want a carrot, I jump for it, and if I jump enough times, I get it. So if I want very badly, as I do, to get up that tree, I shall get up if I jump enough, because jumping always gives me what I want." Which, though it sounds a little muddling, was quite plain to Mary. So she decided she really must put it to the test, and while she was wondering why she had never thought of it before, she fell sound asleep.

Luckily Little Wool had a nightmare towards morning and he gave Mary such a violent kick that it woke her. She was just going to be very angry about it, when she remembered that to be woken early was just exactly what she wanted; so she got up and crept carefully out into the Nursery.

It was still almost dark and she felt very grown-up at being up all alone—and oh ! she wanted so dreadfully to be able to say to Marionetta, " I can climb that tree too—so there ! "

She crept up to it and then, with a heart full of hope, she stood up beside it and started jumping.   She jumped till her breath came in short pants and her front paws felt too heavy to lift.   Then she took a little rest and started again—always with eyes uplifted, waiting for the blissful moment when she would find herself on that branch. How comfortable it looked !   The thought gave her fresh strength.   She made no effort to touch the tree— just jumped.   But, alas, after a little time more, she ached all over and her hind legs were shaking and she felt bitterly disappointed.   At last she had to acknowledge it just was not any good.   Here she still was at the bottom of the tree, very tired, very hungry, and no better off than before.   She was, indeed, tired out, and without knowing it she fell asleep there and then, and Big Wool found her a few hours later.

" Whatever is this cub doing here ? " she said and woke her.

Mary sat up and rubbed her eyes and Big Wool said, " Why, my dear child, how did you get here ? "

" I—I c-can't think," stammered Mary, very embarrassed, for it had all flashed back on her.

" Perhaps you walked in your sleep ? " suggested Big Wool.

" Yes—perhaps I did," said Mary gratefully, and so it was settled.

CHAPTER FOUR

WHICH BELONGS CHIEFLY TO BUNCH

MARY PLAIN was not the only bear who had a special friend, but Bunch's, as was fitting, was a man, known as the " Owl Man," because of the dark rings he wore round his eyes.

He and Bunch had many long talks together ; in fact he was the only person that Bunch talked to much at all.

He was frankly unfair about the carrots, for he gave *much* the most to Bunch. This after all, as he was his particular friend, was forgivable, but the other bears felt that he might at least have pretended to be a little interested in them from time to time, just for politeness's sake, especially as practice had made him a dead shot. Very few carrots fell below ; and anyway, they did not have quite the same sense of enjoyment in eating Bunch's " misses," as the carrots they had themselves caught with some skill.

The Owl Man had not been to pay a visit for two

days, so Bunch was very pleased to see him come round the corner, one afternoon. To his surprise, instead of walking straight up to the carrot-stall as usual, he turned aside just before and leant over the wall, looking a little odd.

"Good morning, Bunch!" he said.

"Good afternoon," said Bunch.

"There's something I want to ask you."

"Oh?" said Bunch.

"And I'm hoping very much it will meet with your approval."

"Oh?" said Bunch again.

"It's a little difficult to explain."

"Oh?" said Bunch and yawned—which was neither encouraging nor polite—so the Owl Man took the bull by the horns and said, "Do you like milk?"

"No," said Bunch. This was a very large lie, but he was tired of listening to all these rather dull remarks and wished the Owl Man would get on with the buying of his carrots.

This answer was obviously a blow, and the man looked very disappointed.

"You're quite sure about it? Not even condensed?"

"No!"

"*And* sweetened?"

"No!" Bunch was determined to be difficult, so the man got just a little annoyed.

"Well—I'm sorry," he said bluntly, "for I was hoping you'd get down off that tree and come and stand underneath me here, and let me pour some NICE —SWEET—SUGARY—*STICKY* milk down your throat " (here Bunch licked his lips) " but I realise that nothing will budge you from that blessed tree of yours, so I shall just give it to the other bears, who—who have more sense," he finished with some heat.

Bunch suddenly had a great wish to break his rule and get down—just for once—but no, it would not do ; once might lead to many times. So he forced himself to say, coldly, " I prefer carrots."

" Oh—but———" said the Owl Man, " I'm sorry to say I've come without my purse, so I can't buy you any carrots and it's milk or nothing ! And I am going to start now ! " And he unscrewed the top of the tube.

As he said this Bunch's legs started to come down of their own accord, but he stopped them quickly and pretended he'd just wanted to change his position a bit.

This was serious. He had not at all understood that the milk was to be *instead* of the carrots, and it had never occurred to him that he would not get his bunch as usual. How very careless of the Owl Man to forget his purse ! And he looked away quickly as he saw a long white stream pouring into Friska's eager mouth. He felt that it would have been kinder of his late friend, at least, to have chosen a spot a little further away and not directly opposite him. He tried hard to keep his attention fixed on a distant tree, but " sugary," " sweet," " sticky " and other equally attractive words would float disturbingly into his mind, and his lips seemed curiously dry that afternoon.

It was nearly over the next time he looked, and what a mess they were all in—covered with white sticky stuff —really a disgusting sight. And it was so bad for the coat, he felt sure ; in fact he got so worried over the harm it might do his mother's coat, for she seemed in the worst state, that he seriously thought of getting down and offering to clean it for her. After all he was her only son, and perhaps he had not been quite thoughtful enough of her lately. He was wavering like this, when he saw the Owl Man preparing to go, so that decided him to stay where he was, for the present at any rate, till he was out of the way.

The man was wiping his hands on his handkerchief and Bunch hoped very hard that the stickiness would not come off. He finished at last and to Bunch's surprise, instead of going, he leaned over the wall and smiled at him.

" Well, old chap, did you really think I was going away without giving you anything ? But I couldn't resist teasing you ! It's quite true, I have left my purse behind and I can't buy you any carrots, but how would some sugar do instead ? I happen to have a lump or two in my pocket."

Now Bunch had meant to be very offhand and not at all ready to make friends again, after the thoughtless way he had been treated that afternoon, but at the sound of that magic word " Sugar " he could not, for the life of him, control his ears—they just *would* prick.

" Come along ! " went on the Owl Man. " Cheer up ! Let's shake hands on it and be friends again and here goes the first lump—as a sign of peace ! " And he threw a square white lump right into Bunch's mouth, which happened to be open, and by the time the fifth lump had disappeared Bunch had lost all his soreness and they were fast friends once more.

When his friend had gone, Bunch turned his attention once more to his mother. Though she had been licking away as hard as she could and Friska had very kindly helped her, she was still in a great mess. Just as he was wondering how she would ever get clean again, Big Wool settled the matter herself by deciding to take a bath, so Bunch's mind was relieved, and he arranged himself comfortably on his branch and soon forgot all about her.

Big Wool was really very glad of the excuse for a bath, for she enjoyed bathing hugely. She was so big that, when she got right into the bath, the water over-flowed all over the sides, and she splashed such enormous splashes that everything near by was drenched. She washed very thoroughly, all four paws, while she floated on her back, and then she put her head under the running spout of water and got that well rinsed.

Friska was not afraid of enjoying a game when her cubs were not there to see her, and she became quite jolly and full of fun. She would go up to Big Wool and chaw her neck and tease her, till Big Wool would pretend to be angry and plunge out of the bath after her and they would lumber round and round the pit like two big babies. There was a big wooden ball in the pit, and Big Wool had great games with this, tossing it about in the water, hiding it with one paw, and then finding it with the other. Sometimes she would throw it out of the bath and then heave herself out after it and fetch it back. Once it rolled right into the corner where Harrods was lying and trying, as usual, to go to sleep.

Now Harrods was a disagreeable old bear; no one really liked her for she was jealous and cross, and always spoilt the fun—and besides she had a horrible squint. Bunch and Friska were continually getting into trouble with her, and Big Wool was the only one who could manage her at all. When the ball rolled past her and Big Wool came after it, Harrods sprang up snarling, and looked as if she would attack her if she went any further.

Big Wool pulled up short when she saw her face. " I've lost my ball, Harrods," she said politely.

" Grrrrr," growled Harrods.

" I believe I saw it roll this way," went on Big Wool.

" Gr——, Gr——," growled Harrods.

" Oh yes—there it is—I'll just get it." But Harrods barred her way, with teeth bared, and paw uplifted.

Big Wool stood still and then she said, quite quietly, " Do you like cake ? " and, as she spoke, Harrods put her paw down and moved on one side, and Big Wool went forward and got her ball, with no further fuss.

Now the explanation of the curious hold Big Wool had over Harrods is this—

A long time before, when Friska was quite a cub, she was having a birthday (bears always have two birthdays every year) and she was very excited because her mamma had told her she was going to have a party that evening, and there would be a lovely surprise.

Friska was a particular favourite with Mrs Job, who kept the carrot stall, so when she heard she was having a birthday, she had very kindly made her a lovely cake, with pink iced sugar and three candles—fixed in a little wooden stand, sitting on top—and sent it to the bear, by her husband, that morning.

Big Wool was delighted and hid it carefully under the straw in her den till the evening, so it would be quite safe. Job had promised that, as soon as the den doors were opened after sun-down, he would stand it in the middle of the floor in Big Wool's den, which was the biggest, and would light the candles.

Just as they were all getting ready, Friska, who was having a wrestling match with Bunch, fell over and bumped her head very hard against the wall. She was a little over-excited, which was natural, so wasn't quite as brave as usual, and Big Wool had to come and rub her head for her.

As soon as she stopped crying, her mother hurried off to see if all was ready. She went into her den and could hardly believe her eyes. The cake had gone—entirely disappeared! Only the candles were left burning in their stand and behind them stood Harrods, licking her lips. Big Wool could have cried, only she was far too angry—so angry that she did not dare trust herself to speak, so she just gave one terrible growl at the thief, who shrank back into the corner, ashamed.

Then she had to think quickly how to make the party fun without a cake, so that poor Friska's birthday would not be quite spoilt.

She had no other food. The only thing to do was to make the most of the candles, so she went to the door and said in an excited voice. "You can come in now, Friska, and look at the lovely stars we have caught for your birthday."

Friska came bounding in, walked round the table and then stopped and sniffed. Perhaps she couldn't help being just a tiny bit disappointed that there seemed nothing to eat.

But just then Big Wool cried, " Oh what a lucky girl to have such a lovely party ! Three bright stars, all especially for Friska—*Such* a treat ! None of us ever had stars for our birthdays before ! " And she made them all join hands, all except Harrods, who had slunk away to hide her shame in her own den, and they hopped round and round the tree singing, " Oh, lucky Friska ! Oh, lucky Friska ! " till Friska began to think it *was* rather a nice thing to have stars for presents after all ; and when, at the end, Big Wool led her up and showed her how to blow them out, she was quite sure of it.

Big Wool must have had a very straight talk with Harrods that night, and threatened to expose her, for ever since that day, whenever Harrods is being tiresome, Big Wool has only to say, in a certain tone of voice, " Do you like cake ? " and Harrods behaves at once.

CHAPTER FIVE

WHICH IS WHITE WITH SNOW

THE days were getting shorter and shorter and sometimes it was very cold. One morning Mary ran to the door and gave a cry.

" O, Twins, come and look ! The ground is all covered with white ; do you think a cloud has tumbled down ? "

The twins rushed out to see, and when they too had said " Oh ! " a great many times, they looked up and saw that the trees were white, too, so decided it could not be a cloud.

" Could it possibly be sugar ? " said Mary hopefully. " Shall I try ? " and she bent down and licked the strange white stuff. " No," she said disappointedly, " it's not, and it doesn't taste of anything but wet."

Their cries had brought Big Wool and Friska to the door and they had been standing behind them and listening with amusement to their conversation.

Big Wool said, " Why, that's snow, cubs ! Didn't you know ? "

" The twins didn't," said Mary rather unfairly.

Then the older ones showed them how to roll the snow up into balls and there followed the morning of their lives, such splendid games, for the snow was quite four inches deep, and they didn't feel the cold in their nice fur coats.

Marionetta chased Little Wool with such a big snow-ball that he fled out of her way, and, in his hurry, tripped and fell backwards over the edge of the bath, but imagine his surprise, when, instead of the wetting he expected, he found himself lying *on* the water, in the middle of the tank. Was he dreaming, or floating, or what had happened ? He called to Marionetta cautiously, " Do you mind just feeling the water at the edge of the bath ? "

Marionetta did so. " Why, I can't put my paw in it," she said. " It's quite hard."

" You're sure it's hard there, too ? "

" Quite ! But how funny ! Are you *on* the water, Little Wool ? "

" Yes, I am. And I'm going to get off ! " But this didn't prove to be quite so easy as he thought, for every time he got carefully to his feet, they somehow left him. Try as he would, he could not stop them, and there he was, flat on his back again. He got rather hot and bothered, especially as Mary Plain had joined Marionetta, and they were both standing beside the bath, and shouting with laughter.

" It doesn't *feel* funny," said Little Wool, as he reached

the ice with a bang for the tenth time. " Can't you two suggest something, instead of standing there laughing ? "

" I can't help it," gasped Mary Plain. " Do you really want to get off ? Because if you'd just go on trying to get up a few times more, it's such—such *awful* fun ! " she finished hysterically. But Marionetta was a twin, and so, though she couldn't quite stop laughing however hard she thought of dead beetles and empty breakfast bowls, she leant over as far as she could reach and said, " If you stretch out your paw as far as you can, I think I could pull you off." And she did. Little Wool didn't feel very dignified being pulled along on his back, but he didn't really much mind what happened, as long as he got on solid ground again.

Later on they made a huge snowball bigger than themselves and Mary Plain cried, " Oh, it's like a man."

" But without eyes and nose," said the twins.

" I know," shouted Mary and she went and stood under a kind-looking old lady and jumped, and for each jump she got a dried fig and laid it at her feet. When she had collected three, she picked them all up and, running back, fixed them in the snow-man's face for two eyes, and a nose ; and then the twins rushed off and got a carrot, which did beautifully for a mouth.

Presently Mary got tired of playing with the snow-man, who was beginning to melt, for the sun was very warm, and she noticed a stone lying near the bath, which was long and rather pointed. She picked it up and sat down on the side of the tank and began dragging it up and down the edge of the ice. To her surprise it made a lovely mark, so she started to write, and as she did not know how to spell many words, she drew pictures of them instead and this is what she wrote :—

[eye] AM A SMALL [bear] [eye] LIVE IN A

PIT [and] YU CANT [eye] MUCH OUTSIDE
XCEPT [bushes] AND A LOT OF [people] WHO
ARE VERY KIND [and] BRING US [carrots] [and]
ooooo2 EAT [and] ⅕ TIMES 4 A G[box] TREAT
VOME [jug] I HAVE A [cake] ALWAYS
ON WENDSDAY [and] SOME [clock]s ON OTHER
DAYS W[bird] THE [sun] IS SHINING
[and] WE [watering can] SIT AND GET DRY. I HAVE

A 🛏 OF 🖌 AND 👁 HAVE A 🥣 OF MY
OWN 2 HAVE MY BREAKFAST 8 ONCE
WE MADE K 😊 8 HE WAS VERY
ROUND 8 HE TURNED 2 🌱▁
& I WAS SAD 8 THIS IS ALL T🍵 i HAVE
TO SAY XCEPT THAT. MY NAME IS
MARY PLAIN

Mary sat back and looked at it, and was pleased. She strolled over to the twins and said, " I've written a book on the bath, about me. I don't mind your reading it, if you want to very badly, just for once.

The twins rushed to look. " But it's half pictures ! " they cried. " How clever of you to make pictures ! "

" Oh, it's quite easy," said Mary, trying to look modest. " Would you like me to write a book about you ? "

" Oh please ! Oh yes," they shouted. So Mary wrote

LITTLE WOOLS 👀 A D 🚤 AND HIS
✎ IS P 🖌

Little Wool jumped up and down with excitement and cried, " What have you said about me, Mary Plain ? " Mary told him, and he said, " Oh, is it ? " and stuck out his tongue to see.

"Now me, now me," cried Marionetta, so Mary wrote

MARIONETTA 12 $\frac{3}{4}$ TIMES PID
AT HER ABC DEF GHI

and when she told her what she had written Marionetta was not at all pleased and said " I'm not."

" I said, ' sometimes,' " said Mary.

" But I'm not *ever*, I'm very clever, and I shall write it underneath."

" Do," said Mary and handed her the pencil. Marionetta took it and held it ready to write just off the ice, but, after she had wriggled it to and fro a few times she threw it down and said, " No, I don't feel like it now."

" Just as you like," said Mary, and was secretly very pleased, for she knew perfectly well that Marionetta did not know how to write.

She waited till she moved away and then wrote

MARIONETTA IS A †

but it did not matter, for when the twins looked at it later on, they decided it was a picture of Bunch.

The next two days were not such fun, for the sun had shone so hard that the lovely white snow had turned to muddy water. They had quite an amusing time paddling which, however, had sad results for poor Mary Plain, who woke up next morning with a swollen face and bad toothache. She spent a very miserable day, curled up in a ball in a patch of sun, which had dried a corner of the pit, and she didn't want to play, or catch carrots, or anything.

That evening, as soon as the den doors were opened, the twins ran to tell their mother about it. Big Wool was with Friska and when she heard, she took Mary into a corner and looked at her mouth. Then she patted her very kindly on the shoulder and said if she'd just open her mouth quite wide, she'd pull the tooth out in a second, and the pain would stop, but Mary backed away and shut her mouth tight, and wouldn't let Big Wool even look at it again.

Then Friska had an idea, and said excitedly, " I know a lovely plan, it's like a game. We fasten a bit of thread to the tooth, and Mary sits down, and then we tie the other end to the door-handle, and we go out and slam the door after us hard, and out comes the tooth, before you can say ' Jack Robinson '."

Mary did not think *her* part sounded much like a game and said so, but Little Wool jumped up and down and said " Oh yes ! Do let's."

" If little Wool thinks it would be such fun," said Mary, " why shouldn't he have it done first—he's biggest ! "

" But Little Wool hasn't got toothache, and you don't pull out teeth unless they are bad," explained Friska, and Little Wool breathed again.

After a great deal of discussion, Mary let them tie the thread on to the tooth and then attach it to the door.

" And now," said Friska brightly, " we'll all go out and bang the door, and when we come back the tooth will be gone."

But it wasn't, for every time they pulled the door to, Mary ran with it, and each time they rushed back to look, there she was, standing just inside, with the threads still on and the tooth still in.   They tried it seven times and then gave it up and untied the thread.

Friska was a little out of breath, and she sat down on some straw, and said " Well, I'd really be ashamed to be such a little coward, and I'm sure my cubs would be braver.   You wouldn't mind having a tooth pulled out, would you, Little Wool ? "

" N'–No," said Little Wool, whose nerve had been shaken.

While they all sat round and wondered what they'd better do next, Mary said suddenly, " It's better ! " And everybody sighed with relief and hurried off to bed.

CHAPTER SIX

WHICH BEGINS WITH MARY AND ENDS WITH BUNCH

SOMETHING brown came shooting out of a den door into the Nursery, giving the twins, who were playing there, a great fright—for at first they did not see that it was Mary.

We must go back to early that morning. Mary as usual was the first up, and she wandered out into the Nursery, sniffing and snuffing along the ground, and presently she saw that the door leading into Big Wool's den was partly open.

Big Wool had not been seen for two whole days, and the cubs had been told not to make too much noise as she had a headache.

Mary, seeing the door open, thought she would go and ask her how she was, so in she went. At first it was so dark that she thought it was empty. Big Wool was not there, and she was just turning to go when she espied two little round balls, covered with brown fur, lying on some straw. Mary was fond of exploring, so she advanced and poked one of them with her paw.

"Grrr——," said the ball. Mary backed away hastily. "Grrr——," said the ball again, and Mary retreated still further and then stood, with head on one side and ears pricked.

"I beg your pardon," she said politely.

"Grrr—— Grrr——," said both the balls together.

"Y–yes—of course," said Mary—and fled.

Once safely in the Nursery again, she could not get get them out of her mind—such a queer noise for a ball to make—and she'd never seen a furry ball before. It was all most mysterious and she didn't much like it. But like it or not, after a few moments curiosity got the upper hand and she crept back to look again.

This time, just as she reached the odd things, Big Wool rose—immense and unseen in the gloom—and with a terrible roar she seized Mary by the scruff of her neck and hurled her out without a word of explanation.

Mary landed against the wall, having flown through the air for a space of ten seconds. First she saw stars and then she was sick and after that she felt a little better.

The twins rushed up, full of enquiries and sympathy.

"Gracious, gracious!" they exclaimed. "What has happened and why did you come out like that?"

"It wasn't on purpose," said Mary, as she leant back and closed her eyes. The pit seemed to be going up and down in a curious way.

She remained quite still for a few minutes and then she sat up and said bitterly, " I never did like Big Wool."

The twins stared, for their grandmother was always particularly kind to the smaller ones and they were all very fond of her.

" Perhaps you aren't feeling very well ? " suggested Marionetta kindly.

" Perhaps not," agreed Mary—and was sick again.

She was still feeling rather upset when Friska came running in, a little later and said, " Oh, cubs ! Such a surprise. You've got two new little aunts ! Isn't it lovely ? "

So that was it !

" Would you like to come and have a peep ? Big Wool says you may—and Mary too. Poor Mary's nose will be out of joint now." Mary felt it hastily. She was quite ready to believe that far more than her nose was out of joint.

" Aren't you coming, Mary ? " asked Friska.

" No, thank you," said Mary, " I like it here."

Friska was rather surprised, but there was no accounting for Mary's moods, so she trotted off with a cub clinging to either paw.

Mary did some thinking when they were gone and when they came back she said, " Then won't I be smallest any more ? "

" No, of course not."

" But if they are the twins' *aunts* how can they be smaller than me ? "

" Because they are Big Wool's babies, don't you see ? "

Mary didn't. It was all very muddling, and altogether sickening. She had always been youngest and she didn't see why she shouldn't go on being it, and her head ached anyway. So she decided to find a nice corner and have a sleep to see if that would make everything come right. She had great faith in sleep as a mender of ills—so much so, that when she woke later, she sat up and said. " And am I still not the youngest ? "

There was no one there to answer, for the twins were right at the other end of the pit. So Mary lay down again and yawned. Her head was better, so that was good, and she rolled over and there within a few inches of her nose, lay a ball. Goodness, what a lot of them there were about to-day ! But this was a paper one. Mary played with it idly, and then she noticed some writing on it, and soon she found she knew one of the words written there, which was Bunch. She scrambled up and trotted to the twins.

" I say, look here, you two, I've found a ball with ' Bunch ' written on it."

They all looked at it, and found it was made of lots of paper rolled together and all with writing on.

" Let's keep it and ask Mamma about it when she comes back," said Marionetta. " We're to have a holiday to-day so she could read it to us."

" Yes, let's ! " said the others.

Now ever since Mary had got two names she insisted

on being called both of them. The twins knew this and whenever they wanted to tease her, which was quite often, they would join hands and hop round her, singing :

> " Ma-ry, Ma-ry,
> Mary, Mary—P.
> How we won-der
> Whatyournamecanbe ! "

and it never failed to stir her to anger.

They were full of impatience, on this morning, awaiting Friska's arrival, so that she could read them the story about Bunch, so, for lack of something better to do, they began this " Mary " song.

Mary knew herself to be in a strong position, as she had the ball in question tucked under her right arm, so she said, " Mary who, did you say, Little Wool ? "

" Mary, Mary P." sang Little Wool joyously.

Mary looked up at the wall and then took out the ball and looked at that. " I daresay I could throw it over the wall—if I stood on the edge of the bath on tiptoe," she said thoughtfully. The twins stopped dead, and Mary turned to Little Wool with a sweet smile, " *What* did I hear you say my name was, Little Wool ? "

" Mary Plain," said Little Wool earnestly, " Mary Plain."

" I hope you'll remember that," said Mary.

" I'm quite sure I shall, " said Little Wool, with an anxious eye on the ball.

Mary went on looking first at the ball and then at the wall a few times—just to keep the twins in suspense, and then Friska came in and they all rushed up to her and begged her to read them what the ball said. So she unrolled it and read, and this is what it said:

THE POEM ABOUT BUNCH

I went down on Friday, just after my lunch.
" May I ask you some questions ? " I asked my friend, Bunch.
His answer was vague—" Pray, *have* you a carrot ?
For I've not had a mouthful since dawn."

I threw one, and said, " Could you tell me, at length,
What you use for your coat, for its beauty and strength,
And "—" Lick," he said shortly, " but *have* you that carrot ?
For I've not had a mouthful since dawn."

I said, " Surely sitting cramped up on that tree,
Must give you lumbago and pains in your knee ? "
" Appalling," he groaned, " but *have* you a carrot ?
For I've not had a mouthful since dawn."

" If you suffer so sadly, then why do you stay ?
What is it that keeps you in torment all day ? "
" Food ! " he said frankly. " Pray, *have* you a carrot ?
For I've not had a mouthful since dawn."

I remarked his companions looked hungry below,
" Now help me decide to which this one shall go."
" Me ! " said Bunch, promptly. " Oh, *have* you a carrot ?
For I've not had a mouthful since dawn."

I dangled a carrot invitingly low,
And pretended I would, and then did not quite throw,
" I'm waiting," sighed Bunch. " Oh, *have* you a carrot ?
For I've not had a mouthful since dawn."

" I'll throw it," I answered, " if you'll whisper to me
If you'd rather 'twas biscuits, or cabbage, or tea."
" Hang ! " said Bunch rudely. " Oh, *have* you a carrot ?
For I've not had a mouthful since dawn."

I explained his digestion quite soon would resist,
That the time might arrive, when he'd *have* to desist.
" Never," vowed Bunch, " Oh, *have* you a carrot ?
For I've not had a mouthful since dawn."

" Mark my words," I went on, " it will soon go on strike ! "
A remark, I'm afraid, that he did not quite like,
He replied, in tones icy, " Pray, *have* you a carrot ?
For I've not had a mouthful since dawn."

I then did my best to impress him, with vigour,
That he'd better take care, or he'd soon lose his figure.
He stifled a yawn, " Pray, *have* you a carrot ?
For I've not had a mouthful since dawn."

" Your greed, Mr Bunch ! " I exclaimed with some heat,
" Would really require super-courage to beat."
He brightened a little. " Oh, *have* you a carrot ?
For I've not had a mouthful since dawn."

I threw him the last. " Oh, Bunch, how you lie !
To speak but the truth I beseech you to try."
He swallowed with haste—" Pray, *have* you a carrot ?
For I've not had a mouthful since dawn."

As my steps bore me homeward, the sun shone in splendour,
And after me floated, by distance made tender,
The plaintive lament, " Oh, *have* you a carrot ?
For I've not had a mouthful since dawn."

"Oh!" said the twins, "fancy, Mary Plain, a poem about Bunch!"

"Oh!" said Mary Plain, "fancy, twins, a poem about Bunch!"

And, though Friska was much older, she too could find nothing better to say than, "Dear, dear, dear, a poem about Bunch."

"I wish it was about me," murmured Mary. But nobody heard.

CHAPTER SEVEN

HOW MARY FLEW

MARY was having a difficult time getting to sleep again. She had collected all the words beginning with A she could think of, and she had counted backwards as far as she could go (which was up to 5) several times, and then she had thought of all the things she would do next day—but nothing seemed any good. In despair, she was just beginning to think of the things she would *not* do next day, when she heard a scratching noise at the door. The door was always left partly up at night so that the bears could get out into the pit if they wanted to, but there was a plank leaning across the open space to prevent the cold getting in.

At first Mary thought it was a burglar, and she was going to wake Friska, but then she decided it was too

small a noise for a burglar to make, and she would be
very brave and find out what it was, quite by herself.
So she went to the door and leant down and said, just
to be sure, " Are you a burglar ? " and a little voice
said—

" No.   I'm Cock Robin."

When she had pushed aside the plank, sure enough
there was her friend Sir Cock.

" Hallo," he said.   " I had a kind of feeling you'd
be awake, and I wondered if you'd care to come for a
fly with me.   It's a lovely night and not too cold."

Mary was very surprised.   "But I can't fly," she said.

" O, that will be quite all right.   I'll sprinkle you
with some shrinking powder I have and in two minutes
you'll be the right size to ride me comfortably."

" Will it hurt ? " asked Mary anxiously.

" Of course not.   If you'll look under the third
feather in my left wing, you'll find a little blue packet,
tied with a hair.   That's right—thank you."   And
he undid it and threw some yellow dust on Mary's head.
She could never decide, afterwards, exactly what happened, but the next moment Cock Robin looked so very
big that Mary felt a little nervous of him.

" Now," said he, briskly, " just stand on the doorstep and you'll be able to reach, I think, and, if you feel
a bit strange at first, just hang on to my neck feathers."

Mary did as she was told, expecially the hanging on
part, for, as they rose into the air, she did indeed feel
very odd.   After a few seconds she got used to it, and
she began to look around and enjoy herself.   It was really

great fun to be sailing over the tops of the trees, almost as high as the moon, and what a lot of things there were to see in this wonderful outside world ! For Mary had never been out of the pit, and she had only seen the same trees and the same bit of sky every day.

Presently Cock Robin said, "On the way back, I thought we'd stop in at my nest a moment ; I'd like you to meet my wife, and then we've been invited to a meal at Berrrumperbotch Chalet. Of course you know Miss N, the lady who lives there ? She wears a fur coat."

"N for what ? " asked Mary.

"Ssh ! N for Nothing," said Sir Cock.

"Then must I call her Miss Nothing ? " asked Mary.

"Psst ! " said Sir Cock, and he looked anxiously at the tree they were passing, to see if anyone had overheard. "Don't let me ever hear you say that again. Her name is Miss N and don't ask any questions."

Mary sighed. She would have liked so much to know why. She thought privately that Berrrumperbotch was an odd name for a house, but she supposed Miss N must have some good reason for calling it that, and anyway, it would be delightful to see her.

They flew over a lovely green field, and here the sun was shining and the moon seemed to have disappeared.

Soon they came to a dear little pink house standing in a garden. Cock Robin flew first to a big rose bush near the gate, where he lived with Lady Cock, but, as she was rather busy with three brand-new babies, they didn't stay long, and moved on to the house.

Berrumperbotch Chalet

" Why, it's just the colour of carrots," said Mary, as they walked up the path.

" It *is* carrots," said Sir Cock, " and now, let me tell you one or two things, before we go in.   First, be sure to walk in backwards ; Miss N prefers it.   And, let me warn you, that whenever she says ' Wheazle ! ' whatever you are doing, you must get up, turn round three times, and then bow.   If you are hard up for something to answer, just say, ' Oh, what fun ! '   That always pleases her.   You know, she is just a little funny in the head, poor thing, because her sister was dropped by the nurse when she was a baby, but nothing much, nothing much."

Mary would have liked to ask a great many questions, but she had not even time for one, as, at that moment, they reached the door, and a voice called—

" Good-bye, good-bye, come in, don't."   And she turned round as she had been told and began to back in.

It was a little difficult getting over the doorstep, but Mary managed it all right.   Then she stood up, and there was her friend of the fur coat, and yet she was not quite the same.   She was so very small and had queer eyes and legs.   Mary didn't like to stare ; indeed she had no time, for the little lady hustled forward and opening a door, said, " Just step into the bathroom, and I'll run and dish up the pebbles," and she gave them a push into a room, which had a table in the centre, and a pile of umbrellas against the wall.

Mary looked round the room and underneath the table, but could see no sign of a bath, and before she

could ask Sir Cock what it all meant, Miss N hurried
back with a large dish, heaped with every kind of pebble
—square ones, round ones, large ones, small ones, and
all of different colours.

" Wet or dry ? " she asked Mary.

" Dry, please," said Mary, who didn't want any at
all.

" Draw me some milk, please, Cock," she said next,
" not too warm." And Mary watched Sir Cock go
to the corner and turn on a tap, and, to her amazement,
out came beautiful white milk, with which he filled the
jug.

" Pull up that umbrella, bear, and make yourself
comfortable," and Mary fetched an umbrella and did
her best to get settled on the handle. Miss N handed
her some pebbles, but before Mary could say " Thank
you," she snatched them away again, leant forward and
said " Wheazle ! " very suddenly.

Mary almost fell off the umbrella, turned three times,
made a bow, and sat down again, feeling very giddy
and said " Oh, what fun ! "

" He, he, he," laughed the little lady, and then she
dropped her voice, looked round the room, and said
softly, " Have some flies' wings on toast ? "

" No, thank you," said Mary, hastily.

" Very thinning, you know, only not too much, or
you know what happens to your ears, and how ugly
you'll look with no ears." Mary began not to like this
place very much. " He, he he," laughed Miss N,
" my father always had sandwiches of flies' wings when

we went on picnics—very warming you know, and you need warmth, sitting on a cloud, for they're apt to be damp, very damp." She looked at Mary fiercely. "You understand that we never had another picnic after he was swallowed by the moon? No, we somehow lost heart after that—my poor mother felt it very much. What do you think, bear?"

Cock kicked Mary under the table, so she said, "Oh, what fun!" which didn't seem quite the right answer. But it didn't matter, for Miss N clapped her hands and said "He, he, he!" Then she got up, laid her finger on her mouth for silence, tiptoed to the door, looked out, closed it, and then went to the corner and beckoned mysteriously to Mary. Mary went, unwillingly, for she was feeling rather upset by this time. Miss N drew her close to her, till her mouth was touching Mary's ear, and then shouted, "Wheazle!" so loudly, that Mary jumped. But she remembered her manners, turned round three times, and bowed. "Well, well!" said Miss N impatiently and clapped her hands. "Oh, what fun!" said Mary drearily.

At this Cock Robin got up and said he thought they had better be going (and Mary felt sure he was right) so Miss N said, "Do have a cup of treacle before you go, just to cool you; it's so refreshing and it's boiling on the stove. Will you please get it, Sir Cock, because, you know—the fire—my legs—you understand."

Mary glanced down and saw that her legs were made of sticks of barley-sugar. Of course she did not dare go near the fire, for fear of their melting, poor thing.

How awkward it must be, and how did she manage when there was no one there to help her? But she could never remember noticing about her legs before, and she had often seen them through the railings.

Cock Robin came back, holding the cups, and, at that moment, Mary sneezed.

"Ah, now you've done it," said Miss N. "If anyone sneezes after moon-set I'm bound to melt."

"Melt!" said Mary. "Do you mean your legs?"

"No, me—all of me." And, as Mary stood there full of astonishment, she saw that Miss N's face was changing; her eyes, always odd, were now definitely figs: her mouth was a carrot and her figure was white and round.

"Why, you're the snow-man we made the other day!" said Mary, but already the snow-man was melting rapidly, and it only just had time to say, "Ah, your ears, your ears!" before it all disappeared.

Mary's paws flew to her ears and sure enough, they had gone! "Oh, oh, my ears, my ears!" she shouted. "Oh! my ears, my ears!"

"Come, come, what's the matter?" said Friska's voice, and Mary found herself being shaken to and fro. She opened her eyes and there she was—back in her own den. How had she got there? She rubbed her eyes, but when she looked again, Friska was still there, so she must really be at home.

Then she felt for her ears. Yes, they were both there, so that was all right too. She sat looking very bewildered, wondering what it all meant.

Friska said, " You'd better come along and have your breakfast, and that will wake you up, or perhaps you aren't hungry, and don't want any ? "

" Oh, yes, I do ! " said Mary, jumping up.

As she went through the door and saw the steam rising from her bowl, she smiled and said, happily, " Oh, what fun ! " and, for the first time, she meant it !

CHAPTER EIGHT

FULL OF PLANKS, POLES, PUNISHMENTS AND
MARY PLAIN

As soon as the morning brush up was over, Mary hurried away. There were several things she wanted to find out. She had thought it all out during breakfast, and she really could not believe it had been only a dream. It was all so real, and she had been wide awake when Cock Robin fetched her.

Of course, there was the question of her ears. They were back again, but then she could not remember anything about the journey back, so, for all she knew, they had grown again on the way, or, possibly, Sir Cock had bought her a new pair. In any case, these were very comfortable, and that was all that mattered.

The first thing she set out to do was to see what came out of the tap which she'd noticed in Big Wool's den. If it was milk, then the tap at Miss N's was quite an ordinary one, but she somehow felt milk didn't usually come that way. While she was thinking about this she arrived at the den. The balls, or aunts, were now a little larger, but they still lay on the straw and did nothing but squeal, so Mary was not very interested in them any more, and only just glanced at them as she went in.

She found she wasn't tall enough to reach the tap, so she pushed a barrel underneath and then climbed up on it and tried to turn the tap handle, but it was very stiff, and pull as she might, she couldn't move it. Then, just as she was giving up all hope, she gave an extra big pull, and it gave way, so suddenly, that Mary fell off the stool, and out rushed a stream of water. Mary picked herself up and waited a few moments, to see if it would turn to milk, but it didn't, so she got up again to turn it off. Alas, this seemed to be just as hard as getting it to start, and after a short struggle, she gave it up, and said to herself " I don't expect there *can* be much more water there, and then it will stop," and she got down, went out and forgot all about it.

This was one of the mornings when the twins were playing games for two, so Mary amused herself by rolling over and over between the wall and the den door. She did it very fast, with her eyes shut, and the second time she reached the door, she felt it was rather damp, so she opened her eyes and got up, and there was a long stream of water running into the Nursery.

This was serious, and Mary felt she must do something about it, so she ran along till she came to the door to Friska's den, where she and Big Wool were sitting, and said, " I think you had better go and see in your den, Big Wool. I can't quite turn the tap off, and it's dripping a little."

Big Wool sprang up, thinking of her babies and the colds they might catch, and hurried along to see. When she got there she found an absolute pond of water, with the tap full on, and she had a terrible fright. She pushed the handle back first and then rushed to her babies, and found them still on their bed of straw, which was floating about on the water. Luckily they were only a little damp, and she moved them quickly into the next den and fussed over them till she got them quite dry.

Mary had been watching from the door, but when she saw Big Wool's face she thought it was time to disappear, so she went out to look for somewhere to hide. The Nursery did not seem any good so she crept into her own den, got as far under the straw as she could and shut her eyes, hoping, if she found her asleep, Big Wool would not like to disturb her, for she had a feeling she would be looking for her very soon.

She was right. She heard Big Wool go out into the Nursery and say in a furious growl, " Mary Plain, come here immediately ! " Then, when Mary did not come, she began looking for her. Mary heard her come in at the door, and kept her eyes very tight shut and hoped she didn't show. But the straw was rather transparent and Mary made rather a big lump, so she was found almost at once.

Big Wool seized her by the neck and shook her on to her feet, and her eyes were blazing as she said, "How dare you do such a wicked thing—how dare you ? How would you have felt if my babies had been drowned, by your fault ? "

"Glad," thought Mary, but she didn't dare say so aloud.

"You are more naughty than I should have thought possible, and why didn't you come at once and tell me you couldn't turn the tap off?"

"I forgot," said Mary sulkily, for Big Wool gave her a fresh shake after every sentence, and it was not at all pleasant.

"Oh! You forgot, did you? Forgot that those two helpless little cubs were lying there, in greater danger every moment! Well! You'll have plenty of time to think about it, for I shall lock both doors and you shall stay in here all day long, quite by yourself, and that may teach you not to forget, another time." And with another shake, she let Mary drop on the straw and rushed out, locking the door behind her. Mary rubbed her neck ruefully. Those horrid cubs, what a nuisance they were! This was the second time she'd got into trouble through them; and she had not done it on purpose. She wished to goodness Big Wool would not have babies. It seemed to make her lose her temper so very easily.

Well here she was, so she would have to make the best of it. She got up and looked round to see what she could do. She began building a straw house, and that kept her very busy, till it all fell down on her and buried her, and that did not seem quite such fun. Then she found a piece of string tied on to a post, and trying to get it off took up another half-hour. But after that, there did not seem anything left to do, so she began to

feel very bored, especially as she could hear Little Wool
and Marionetta laughing, outside in the Nursery.

If only she could get out! She went and tried the
doors, but they were fast shut. Big Wool didn't do
things by halves.

The only other place was a little window, high up
in the wall, with the sun shining through it. What a
dreadful pity it wasn't lower down, and she taller, but
it was so high up that even Big Wool could not have
reached it, so Mary could only give a big sigh and turn
her back, so as not to see the sun inviting her to go out.
She walked over to the wall opposite, where three
shelves were built, and for lack of something better to
do, she started climbing up them. When she got to
the top one, she saw a big beam over her head, so she
swung herself up on to this, and then found she was so
very high up, she hardly dared to look down. Instead,
she looked along it, and there, at the other end, right in
front of her, was the little window. After all, she could
reach it! How too exciting!

She crept very carefully along the beam till she
got to the end, and there she found the window was
unlatched, so all she had to do was to push it open and
then she was looking down into the Nursery which
seemed a good way down below. She was just going
to call out to the Twins, who were playing with their
backs towards her, when she saw a long plank tilted
against the wall, just below the window sill. What
wonderful luck, and she would give the twins such a
surprise! So she climbed out, and sat on the top of the

plank, and just before she let go of the sill, she called out,
" Here I am ! "

As the twins swung round, they saw her come shooting down the plank, with ears flying.

" Why, Mary is it really you ? But how did you
get out ? We were told you were locked tight in."

" So I was, but I was tired of myself ; so I climbed
up to the window and got out, and oh ! it's lovely
sliding down the plank, and I must go and do it again.
Come on, Little Wool, I'll show you how."

They had a wonderful time, climbing up a rain
pipe and coming down by the plank, one after the other.
Indeed they made so much noise that, in Parlour Pit,
Friska said to Big Wool, " Do you hear those cubs of
mine ? They must be having a very exciting game."

And Big Wool answered rather grimly, " I hope
Mary hears them too." She little thought that Mary
was herself, at that moment, leading a glorious sliding
party on the other side of the wall !

Mary could not help getting a little anxious toward
evening, for she knew she would get into fresh trouble
for having escaped. Six o'clock came at last, and the
doors were pulled up. Mary lingered in the Nursery
behind the others, but in a few moments, Marionetta
came running back and said " Big Wool wants you at
once in her den." Mary heaved a heavy sigh.

Big Wool was standing just inside the door. " Come
here, Mary," she said sternly. " You were in disgrace
this morning, but you are far, far more in disgrace

Climbing up a rain pipe and coming down by the plank

to-night. I am not going to try and talk to you, as it does no good. I therefore intend whipping you."

"I don't care," said Mary quickly, in case Big Wool should think she were frightened.

"Don't be rude, Mary, you need not speak, for I've no wish to listen to you. Come here." And poor Mary went forward and found herself, the next minute, lying across Big Wool's knees and being well spanked by her stiff paw. It hurt a good deal but Mary's feelings were more hurt, for she had never been whipped before and she felt so very undignified. It was over at last, and Mary had not made a sound. "Now go," said Big Wool, and Mary went, limping a little, and hoping that the twins would never know what had happened. When she got to the Nursery door the twins came flying up to her and said, "Oh, Mary, come on, have one more slide—just one more before bed-time."

"No, thank you," said Mary and turned away.

"You must, you must, it's such fun, and we'll all come bumping down together!" Mary shuddered. "I'd rather not, thanks."

"Oh, but why? You've liked it so much before all day. Why do you suddenly not want to?"

Friska, who had been listening and knew all about Mary's punishment and felt rather sorry for her, said, "Mary's tired, cubs, don't worry her; she's going off to bed at once."

And Mary went, gratefully.

Next morning, however, she had quite recovered

and, directly after school, was ready to do some more sliding.

She ran to the plank. " Why, it's gone green in the night. How funny ! " she cried. " Come on, Little Wool ! I'll come down first and you next." And she scrambled up the pipe and sat down on the plank. "I'm off," she said, and let go of the sill—but she wasn't. Instead of shooting down like a flash, there she was still at the top. " I'm off ! " she said again, and gave a little jerk—but no ! She still wasn't. And, what was more, she couldn't if she wanted to ; she was stuck— stuck tight on to the plank.

" Oh, twins, I'm stuck ; I can't move ! " she cried. " Oh, come and pull me off; what can be the matter ? It was so slippery yesterday and now the green has spoilt it all."

Little Wool had, by this time, climbed up on a level with the window sill, and he leant over and pulled ; but pull as he would, it was no good, and, struggle as she might, there she still was. As luck would have it, just at that moment along came Bunch's friend, the Owl Man.

He did not often come and see the cubs, and, naturally, they were very anxious to make a good impression, so Mary whispered " Stop pulling, and get down quick, till he's gone," and then she crossed one leg over the other and tried to look as if it were quite usual to be sitting on a steep green plank.

" Hallo, Mary Plain ! What are you doing up there ? " he called.

" Just sitting here for a bit."

" Come down and do some jumping for me."

" I'm too tired," said Mary.

" Too tired at this time of the morning ? Why ? "
Mary yawned a very big yawn and said, " Just because."

' Well, well, well," said the Owl Man, " I think it's
a very odd thing for a cub of your age to feel tired at
this time of the morning—very queer. Are you sure
you feel quite well ? "

" Perfectly, thank you," said Mary politely, and wished
he would go.

But he didn't. He just stood and stared.

" Wouldn't you like to go and see Bunch ? " suggested Mary.

" I've been," said the Owl Man. " I say, that plank's
been painted ; it wasn't green last time I was here, was
it ? "

" No," said Mary, with a great deal of feeling.

" I thought not," said he, " the paint's a good colour
—a nice shade of green."

" Could you tell me," asked Mary, " is paint sticky ? "

" Rather ! When it's wet ! " and then suddenly he
understood, " By Jove ! " he said, " you aren't stuck, are
you ? "

" I should just think I am," said Mary.

" I *am* sorry," said the Owl Man. " Have you been
there long ? "

" Hours ! " said Mary, who had been there exactly
ten minutes.

" Then we must get you off as soon as we can. I wonder if I got a good long stick, if I could reach you and pull you off."

" Oh, please," begged Mary. He went off, and in a few moments came back with a long pole, and leaning over the wall, stretched as far as he could and Mary just managed to get hold of the other end.

" I am afraid it will hurt a bit, but it's the only way," said the Owl Man, and pulled.

" Ow ! " said Mary, but she was off, and though she felt most uncomfortable behind, she was truly grateful to the Owl Man, who was as nice as could be, and gave her so much sugar, that Little Wool, who had been watching all the time, wondered if it would be worth getting stuck himself.

Later on that day, Mary, who had forgotten about it, was dancing round and round for a carrot a little girl was holding out for her. " Why, look ! " cried the child, " she's got a green back ! Oh, doesn't she look funny ? "

Poor Mary tried to look, but could not manage it, so she called Marionetta and said, " Am I green behind ? "

" Yes, very," said Marionetta, and then, thinking to please Mary, she repeated, " Very green indeed."

Mary backed into a corner and sat down and there she stayed the whole day—refusing all invitations to jump or play. Nothing would move her till the doors were up at six, when she sidled along, with her back to the wall, into her den. Job heard about it when he brought the supper, and he very kindly washed all the green off with some special stuff, but though it rather burned and pricked, Mary was most grateful, and promised him she would never again slide down a plank. " At least not a green one," she added to herself.

CHAPTER NINE

IN WHICH MARY BEHAVES HER VERY BEST

Job walked into the dens one afternoon and pulled up one of the doors leading into the Nursery.

"Come here, Mary Plain," he called, " I want you."

Mary came running and so did the twins, for never before had they seen Job come there during the day, and they couldn't imagine what he wanted.

When Mary was sent for, it usually meant she'd got into fresh trouble, so she said half-anxiously, " I haven't been sliding down the plank, and I'm not a bit green. See ? "   And she turned round.

Job laughed. "You're a funny one," he said. " But I want you in here to give your coat a good brush, for you've been invited out to tea."

Mary's eyes grew round.

"Me—out to tea ? Who with ? Where ? Oh why ? "

" Why not us ? " said the Twins.

" I can't say, I'm sure.   Perhaps two cubs together would be too many ; and as to who, it's a kind lady who is interested in you all, but she sent the invitation specially to Mary.   Come along now, we must hurry up and get off or we shall be late."

Mary stuck her chest out as far as it would go.   She was the youngest, and had been invited out to tea, and nothing so dreadfully exciting had ever happened to any of them before.   It even made her feel a little sick.

" Good-bye, Twins," she said grandly, and waved her paw.   " I hope you won't miss me too badly but I daresay I'll be back some day.   I'm sorry you weren't invited.   But I'm gladder it was me," she added to herself.

Job brushed her till her coat was lovely and smooth and she tingled all over, and then he put a collar round her neck, with a chain to it, which Mary didn't much like, but he explained that bears always had to wear them when they went out to tea, and especially in trams. They climbed up some stairs and came out of a door at the top, and Mary, looking through the railings, could see the twins in the Nursery down below, looking very dull and sad.   She called down, " My coat is all shiny and now I am going in a tram—so good-bye ! "   This was just to cheer them up a little.   The twins didn't know what a tram was, but they longed to go in one.

When the first one came rattling up and Mary was told to get in, she felt a little nervous, but Job got in first and seemed quite used to it, so she plucked up

courage and followed him. A man came along and Job
said, " One and a half, please."

" Bears fourpence," said the man.

" But she's under seven months," said Job.

" Bears twopence extra," said the man firmly, so
Job sighed and Mary sat down feeling terribly important
at being extra. While they were going along Job
explained to her that she must be careful to remember
her manners. Shake hands with her right paw, say,
" thank you " and " please."

" Back or front paw ? " asked Mary.

" Front, of course ; and you must stand up nicely
when you are introduced to people."

" What's ' introduced ' ? "

" It's saying ' How d'you do ' to someone you don't
know, and being told their name."

" I see," said Mary, who didn't in the least. " Do
I have to walk in backwards ? " she went on, while
vague memories of Berrrumperbotch Chalet stirred,
" and do we have pebbles to eat ? "

" Gracious me ! " said Job, " what is the cub thinking
of ? You'll probably have cake and biscuits, and milk
to drink ; but remember you must never eat anything
until you are asked."

" How asked ? "

" Well, till someone says, ' Do have some cake or
biscuit.' And then you say. ' Yes, please ' and take
some."

" Of course," said Mary.

They changed trams once, just opposite the big

fountain with the bears carved on it. Mary caught sight of them, and started jumping up and down and pulling Job towards them.

"Oh, Mr Job, there are the Twins. I must go and speak to them." Job pulled her back sharply and looked quite startled; he began to think she was a little odd in her head, what with talk of eating pebbles and now seeing the twins. Then he saw what she was looking at and said, "It's not the twins, and don't go pulling and jumping like that and making a scene."

"What's a scene?"

"What you're doing—making people look at you."

"But don't they like looking at me?" Just then the other tram came up, so Job didn't have to answer.

Nearly all the streets in Berne are arcaded, with shops under the arcades, so you can do your shopping on rainy days and walk nearly all over the town, without getting wet. A great many people have flats over them and the family Mary was going to visit lived in a large one on the second floor.

When they got out of the tram they turned a corner, and went in at a big door and got into a lift, and when Job pressed the button they began to go up, and Mary thought it was most thrilling.

"Have I flown?" she asked, as she stepped out. But Job only laughed and pressed a button in the wall, and this time it didn't make them move, but it made a funny tingling noise through the wall.

The door was opened and a man with shiny buttons on his coat said, "Will you come in, please?" Job pushed Mary in, in front of him and took off her collar, and then he whispered, " Don't forget—the right paw ! "

They had to walk down a passage so Mary said " Right, left, right, left," to herself all the way, so as to be sure not to forget. Only somehow she must have got muddled on the way, for when she got into a room at the end, which seemed to be full of people, she held up the paw, which she thought was the right. Job pulled it down and hissed—" Wrong paw, Mary. Mind your manners."

A tall lady in grey came up and said, " How do you do ? " and shook her paw.

" How do you do ? " said Mary. " I came by tram, twopence extra."

" Oh, she is charming," cried the lady to several others who were standing by her.

" No, not charming ! " said Mary. " Plain—Mary Plain." Then she was suddenly surrounded by lots of ladies, who wanted to pat and stroke her, and seemed really delighted that she had come. Mary began to feel a great success. One lady said, " I do think she's a lamb." So Mary said, " No, I'm a bear " and that made them laugh a great deal, and they patted and stroked her all the more.

" Well, now—how about tea ? " asked the Grey Lady. " Are we all ready ? "

" I am ! " said Mary.

" Jill hasn't come," said another lady.

" Never mind, we'll begin without her. Hark, there's the bell. I expect that's her."

It wasn't her, but it *was* the Owl Man, and Mary beamed. He shook hands with her and then bent down and said, " How's the paint ? " But Mary looked round anxiously to see if anyone had heard and then said, " Hush, that's a secret."

" Rather," said the Owl Man.

" If you're all ready, come along to the dining-room," said the Grey Lady, and then turning to Job, " Will she be all right, if you leave her with us ? "

" Quite, I'm sure, madam ; and if you should want me you can give me a call," and he went off to find the man, Thomas, who had opened the door to them, but, as he passed Mary, he said in a low voice, " Now, Mary, manners ! "

Mary was led to the table and shown a chair next to the Grey Lady.

" Come and sit down and we'll begin," she said. " I expect you are getting hungry ? "

" I am," said Mary frankly.

" Well, you must eat all you can. Let me help you on to your chair." But Mary drew back suddenly.

" No, thank you—I like to stand," she stammered, with her eyes fixed on the chair which was of very bright green leather.

" But you can't possibly reach."

" Oh, yes, but I don't want to, thank you."

" Let me just give you a jump up. You'll be far more comfortable."

" No, please—I mean thank you, oh dear, oh dear," said Mary getting more and more worried and then, all at once, she remembered the Owl Man was there, quite close to her ; so she pulled him into the corner and when he bent down, whispered " Is it paint—please ? "

He might have laughed, but he didn't. He just patted her on the head and said, " No, I promise you. Here, I'll give you a lift up," and with that, he swung her up and landed her with a bump on the chair, and she wriggled with happiness.

There on her plate was a lovely piece of cake and, beside the plate, a big bowl of creamy milk.

Mary had to sit on her paws she was so afraid she'd begin before she was asked.

The Grey Lady said, " I hope you like cakes ? "

" Yes, yes," said Mary, " oh *very* much."

" That's right ! Then I hope you'll enjoy it."

" I am *sure* I shall," said Mary.

" It's a home-made cake and very good," went on the lady, wondering why she didn't begin.

" It looks *too* lovely," said Mary, with a little gasp.

" There is some sugar icing on that piece—perhaps you don't like it ? " said the Grey Lady, getting very puzzled.

" Oh—I do—I do ! " sighed Mary, and sat tight on her paws that would try and get out. If *only* someone would say what she'd been told to wait for, so she could begin.

Just then a girl with a red frock leant forward and said, " Do have a little cake ? " and Mary adored her for it, and said, " Oh, thank you, I will ! " At last she could eat it.

She had a great many cakes, and she was just finishing off a beautiful pink sugar carrot, when the door opened, and in walked the Fur-Coat-Lady and everybody said " Hallo, Jill." Mary was delighted and scrambled down and went to meet her. " How do you do ? " she said. " I came by tram, twopence extra."

" Did you indeed ? " said the lady. " Well that must have been fun ! "

" It was," said Mary and sighed happily.

By this time she was really very full of cake and sweets and she had drunk all the milk she wanted, which was a great deal, so perhaps it was a good thing when the Grey Lady said, " Let's go back into the other room, for I promised baby should see Mary after tea."

Back they all went and presently the door opened and a little tiny girl came in. Mary didn't know how small little girls could be and she hoped she wouldn't be at all like the aunts. But she turned out to be very nice and they made friends at once. The Owl Man suggested the baby having a ride on her back and Mary said she wouldn't mind, just for once. So they lifted her on and Mary walked very carefully round the room. All went well till she caught sight of a large sugar carrot, which someone had left hanging over the side of the mantelpiece, when habit proved too strong for her and she stood up and jumped.

When the baby had been comforted, Jill asked if they would like to play a game of " Pop goes the weasel." Mary immediately turned round three times and then bowed, and every one looked very surprised. That

Mary walked very carefully round the room

reminded her of something she'd wanted to find out for some time, and while they were thinking of another game, she had a good look at the Fur-Coat-Lady's legs and feet, and they weren't barley sugar at all, but just legs, which was a great relief and meant that it really must have been a dream after all.

They settled on "Hide and Seek," and the Owl Man hid Mary in a beautiful place under the sofa, but the minute he left her, she started shouting, "I'm here, I'm here" till they found her, which was almost at once, so they changed the game to "Here we go gathering nuts in May"—but though Mary kept a sharp look out, she never saw a sign of a nut from beginning to end, so she thought it a very dull game. Then they finished up with "I spy" and Mary always got caught because, instead of trying to get home, she was busy looking for the "Ice pie." After that, the Grey Lady rang a bell and a man came to the door, and she said, "Will you bring some milk and biscuits please, Thomas?" He did and Mary thought Thomas a most delightful kind of man. Then Job came in and said it was time to go home and he whispered, "Be sure to shake hands nicely and thank her for having you."

"No—no—just bow," whispered Mary, who was standing with her arms very straight down.

"I said 'Shake hands'," said Job sternly and gave her a little push forward. So Mary went up to the Grey Lady and said, "Thank you for having me." When she held her hand out, Mary knew she would have to shake it, so she lifted her paw—and out tumbled five biscuits which she had tucked under her arm !

The lady was very surprised, because she thought Mary had been given enough tea. However, as she was so nice, she didn't say anything, but stooped to pick them up. But, when Mary moved to help and six more tumbled out from under the other arm, Mary began to think perhaps it wasn't quite usual to take other people's biscuits away from a party and she'd better explain, so she whispered, " It was for the Twins I wanted them." And the lady smiled and said, " Of course—I ought to have thought about it," and she told Thomas to get a big paper bag and fill it with biscuits.

Mary smiled happily and shook hands again, and said, " Thank you for having me," and then waited, as if she expected something.

Job came forward, after a moment and said, " Come along, Mary, are you dreaming? We must be off home." And they went—Mary clasping the paper bag tightly.

" Why did you wait like that after you said good-bye ? " asked Job curiously.

" I was waiting for the lady to thank me for coming."

" It was very kind of her to ask you."

" Wasn't it kind of me to go, then ? " asked Mary. But Job didn't seem to know.

CHAPTER TEN

ST. BRUIN'S DAY—AND THE LAST

THE GREAT DAY had come at last. After breakfast Big Wool stood up and cleared her throat and said, in a very serious way—

"Bears! This is St. Bruin's Day, and I hope we all realise, *all* realise—Mary," she said, for Mary didn't seem to be listening quite attentively, "how great an occasion this is. We shall take very special care with our toilet this morning, and at six we shall meet again to have a final brush up." (Mary sighed loudly.) "In the meantime, I ask you all to pass the day in a fitting manner." She was so pleased with the last sentence, that she gave a little cough, and repeated, "in a fitting manner." "I think that is all I have to say—except that, when we all meet this evening before waiting on our—on our—ancestors," said Big Wool, getting a little muddled, "you will, of course, all bring with you the slight offerings you have put aside."

This brought Mary to full attention. Gracious Heavens! She hadn't got an offering. Last night she'd had one—a beautiful pink juicy carrot with the leaves still on—how juicy it had been she was, alas, in a position to know only too well—for, to stop a queer " asking " feeling in her waist, she had eaten that carrot in the small hours of the morning.

Only now did she realise what a terrible thing she had done. There wasn't the slightest hope of getting another such carrot. It was the biggest she'd ever seen and it was pure luck that it had fallen to her share, so beautifully—just the day before St. Bruin's Day, and she had been so proud and pleased and guarded it in a corner all day. Oh dear, oh dear, she must have been mad, and indeed she had been half asleep.

She collected frantically all the morning and at mid-day retired to a corner and examined her store.

One faded carrot stalk, two very small figs, half a biscuit, and an empty milk tin ; oh—and a cork.

She sat down and eyed them sadly. She was quite certain the carrot stalk and the figs wouldn't do and she felt sure that neither Alpha nor Lady Grizzle would appreciate half a biscuit, especially as she knew for a fact that Marionetta had a whole one she'd saved from last week. No ! It was between the tin and the cork. Suddenly she pounced on the tin—a hole in it ! If the cork would fit ! Her paws shook with excitement as she tried to persuade the cork into a hole half as big as itself—but presently she threw them both away in disgust.

Then she thought of developing a frightfully sudden cold, so she went and stood just under the wall which divided the Nursery from Parlour Pit, and sneezed for ten minutes. But, alas, they can't have been very good imitations for she distinctly heard Big Wool say to Friska, " Listen to those cubs. They must be playing at doctors, for one of them is pretending to have a cold." So that was no good.

Then she thought of breaking her leg, and her eyes got quite misty with tears of self-pity, as she pictured herself being carried into the presence of the two ancients by Friska and Bunch and hearing them explain, " This poor little cub has broken her leg, but she is so extremely brave about it, in fact we have never seen anyone quite so brave before." They would be so dreadfully sorry for her and so proud of her courage, that they would forget to expect a present from her.

Yes—the leg idea seemed far the best, but just as she was wondering what was the best way to set about it, a strange kind of whistle made her look up at the railings above. At that very moment she saw a little boy there open his mouth to speak, and out dropped something which fell into the pit, close to Mary. He seemed most upset at having lost it and wanted to climb over to fetch it, but his mother didn't seem to want him to do this. Mary thought to herself, "If he's so unhappy at losing it, it must be something rather important—perhaps a tooth," and she picked it up and had a look. It wasn't a tooth at all. It was round and small and shiny, like silver, and had a hole in the middle, but, though she licked it, it didn't have any taste. However she'd decided it must be a kind of sweet, for the boy had it in his mouth. At any rate, that settled it.

She'd take it to the two old bears, and if they didn't like
it she couldn't help it—it was the best she could do,
and at least it was shiny.   So she went and hid it under
a loose stone in the corner of the pit, to keep it quite
safe till the evening.

"What *are* you going to do about your present?"
asked the twins, later on, for Mary had told them about
the carrot.   "Won't you be very frightened to go without anything?"

"But I've got something," said Mary casually.

"Oh, what?"

"Something, I said."

"Oh, but do tell us what."

"No, it's a secret," and she kept it all day.

As soon as the doors were up, all the business of
getting tidy had to be gone through again, and Mary
was heartily sick of it, and very thankful St. Bruin's Day
only came once a year.   At the end they all stood up and
recited the poem they had been learning in school all
that week, to be sure they had it quite right.   It went
like this :

> "Many happy years we wish to you,
>   May carrots and dried figs your pit-floor strew,
>   We hope that happiness will with you stay
>   Till we all meet on next St. Bruin's Day.
>
>   By Friska."

"Be sure not to forget to say 'by Friska,' will you?"
said Friska anxiously—she was so very proud of having
written the poem—and they all promised to remember.

Then Mary slipped off and flew to the corner where she had hidden her present. She felt quite anxious as she lifted the stone, in case anyone had stolen it, but it was still there safe and sound and she breathed a sigh of relief and popped it into her mouth. That was where the small boy had kept it, so obviously it was the safest plan to do the same. She was so quick that no one had noticed her absence, and she got back just in time to hear Big Wool say, " Now, are we all ready? And don't forget to bow! " And it began to be rather exciting.

Mary felt her heart going pit-a-pat and she stood up very straight and tried to turn her feet out. Unfortunately Little Wool spoke to her just as she was stepping over the doorstep into Den Pit, and she caught her paw and fell in flat on her face. However, Friska, who was in front, picked her up quickly and smoothed her down, so no real damage was done.

It is true she had *very* nearly swallowed her present, but, as she had not *quite* done so, it did not matter.

Now the cubs had heard these two old bears talked about a great deal and they had been told they were very wonderful and wise and knew everything there was to know, and as they had heard all this and yet had never seen them they seemed all the more mysterious. When Mary's turn came she determined to make a very good impression.

Alpha was sitting on the edge of the bath to receive them and Lady Grizzle stood just beside him.

"You now," said Friska, who was standing at the side and telling them each when their turn came.

Mary stepped forward and made a really beautiful bow. Then she took a deep breath, opened her mouth and out came, not the expected poem, but a piercing whistle. Mary looked very surprised and so did all the others, and they looked round to see if anyone else had come into the pit. But no one had, so Mary tried again and the same thing happened, so then she knew it must be herself. This time, however, she was determined to get through the poem, so she went on, whistling bravely till Friska, who saw Alpha was getting angry, came and pulled her away. She whispered to Bunch to go and say the poem again, and to go on saying it till she told him to stop, so as to keep Alpha busy. Then she led Mary into the farthest corner and said, "Don't you feel very well, Mary?"

"Wheee——" whistled Mary.

Friska started. This was serious. She had heard of people losing their voices during a bad cold, but never of their making a noise like this, and besides, Mary had not had a cold. She put her arm round her and said kindly, "Tell Auntie where it hurts, Mary dear?"

"Wheee——" went Mary.

Every time she made this extraordinary sound, Friska looked anxiously to see if Alpha had heard, but Bunch was saying the poem in such a loud voice, that she did not think he could have.

"There, there, there," she said, soothingly. "I'm

sure it will soon be better," and she rubbed Mary's tummy gently. But Mary shook her head violently and pushed her paw away. "Wheee———. Wheee———. Wheee———!" she whistled earnestly. Friska said, "Sch" again, and then looked at her helplessly. It was so like Mary to go and get unwell on this most important day, and such an odd kind of illness, too. She might at least have chosen a silent one, or one that could be understood and cured like a sore throat or a tummy-ache.

Just then Big Wool hurried up and Friska drew her on one side and explained. "I know," said Big Wool, capably, "a firm hand. Leave her to me!" and she nodded her head knowingly. Then she came to Mary, clapped her paws sharply, and said, "Come, come, Mary, enough of this nonsense! Just stop making that noise and behave yourself. I can't imagine what you———" "Wheee———" interrupted Mary. Big Wool stood and blinked and then she turned Mary slowly round, while she felt her carefully all over. But she could not find anything wrong.

Now Mary was getting rather tired of all this fussing, so she decided she would go and give Alpha his present and give up trying to say the poem again, and she started off towards him. Directly Big Wool and Friska saw where she was going they rushed after her and each taking a paw they led her firmly back into the corner. "Wheee———!" said Mary, trying to explain, but Friska put her paw over her mouth and said, "Sch! Sch! Quiet, Mary, quiet." And Big Wool stroked her in long soothing strokes down her back, which Mary hated, but she could not speak, so she had to bear it.

"Shall we take her home?" suggested Big Wool, but at this Mary whistled so loud and so long that it took them some moments to silence her. When she was quiet again, Friska beckoned to Big Wool and said in a low voice, "Perhaps she'll take a sudden turn for the better?" But Big Wool shook her head. "I doubt it, I doubt it," she said, "it looks to me very bad."

While they were talking, Mary took the opportunity to escape again, and this time she got to within a few feet of Alpha before Friska caught her and dragged her back again.

"Oh dear, oh dear, what *can* we do?" she said to Big Wool. "We can't go on like this. What do you suggest?"

Mary turned away and putting her paws behind her back, she kicked the ground a bit, to show she did not know they were talking about her.

"How about a slice of cake?" said Big Wool, and Friska trotted off briskly to fetch one. When she brought it back, Mary felt suddenly so terribly hungry that she forgot all about the little thing in her mouth and took a huge bite of cake. Then she choked and choked and they had to pat her on the back and finally shake her by the heels and, as they did this, out dropped something which fell with a tinkle on the ground and rolled away.

"Let me go, let me go," shrieked Mary, kicking for all she was worth, and Big Wool was so surprised at hearing her speak again that she let go rather too quickly and Mary fell with a thud on to the floor. But she scrambled up, rushed to pick up the little disc, and before anyone could stop her, she had flown across the pit to Alpha's seat. Now Bunch was just saying the poem for the thirty-second time, in a rather hoarse voice, and Alpha was so sick of it, that he was almost glad of any interruption—even Mary.

She was a little out of breath when she reached him. " Here is your present, and oh please take it because it's so little and I am afraid of losing it and I do hope you'll like it," she said, all in a rush—and laid it on his knee.

Alpha looked at it. " Is this a practical joke ? " he asked sternly.

" Oh, no," said Mary, " it's a kind of noise and you keep it in your mouth."

Alpha did not look as if he believed it, but he placed it in his mouth all the same, and sure enough out came a low whistle. He took it out hastily. " Is that me, or is it still you making that noise ? " he asked Mary suspiciously.

" No, sir, it was you," said Mary.

Alpha looked again at the round thing in his paw, and putting in into his mouth he blew, and out came another splendid whistle. A slow, broad smile crept over his face, and he sat down and blew and whistled and whistled and blew for several minutes, looking more and more pleased.

Then he beckoned Mary to him and patting her on the shoulder said, " Well, well, my cub, you have brought me a most interesting present, and I am very pleased, very pleased."

So Mary's gift was the greatest success after all, and, when they went away that evening, they left Alpha sitting happily under the tree, blowing the whistle as loud as he could.

It had been altogether a rather tiring day, and when they got home the bears found they were all very ready for bed. Just as the cubs had got tucked up all together, Little Wool said,

" Wasn't it awful when Mary wasn't well ? "

" Mary who ? " asked Mary, sleepily.

" Mary Plain," said Little Wool.

ALL MARY

CONTENTS

CHAPTER ONE

IN WHICH THINGS BEGIN TO HAPPEN

MARY sat on the side of the bath, being important. On her knee was a square blue envelope, and she was stroking it with a paw that shook a little. She had never had a letter before.

Job the keeper had dropped it over the side of the pit a few minutes earlier and called, " Mary Plain, here's a letter for you." Just like that !

Mary had played up beautifully. She had strolled across to where the letter lay on the floor of the pit and picked it up. " Why, so it is," she said, and her voice only gave the tiniest shake. But her cousins danced up and down in front of her, both talking at once.

" What's the writing on it, Mary Plain ? Does it say it's for you—and how can you tell ? "

" Because it's written on it," said Mary, who could

read her own name quite nicely.   " See, ' Miss Mary
Plain.' "

" Yes, yes," urged the twins.

" What lives in Nursery Pit," went on Mary, inventing wildly.

" Aren't you going to open it ? " asked Marionetta.

Mary was stroking the envelope and thinking.   If
there was one thing she hated, it was to own she could
not do a thing, and she knew quite well that she would
not be able to read the writing inside.

" I thought perhaps I'd let Friska read it first," she
said slowly ;   " it would be such a treat for her."

The twins stared.   Mary was not in the habit of giving
Friska treats.

" But it's your letter, not hers," they said.   " Oh
come on, do—do—open it."

Mary gave in, and after rather a struggle, for her paw
seemed too fat to fit under the flap comfortably, she got
the envelope open and drew out a big sheet of paper.

Mary cleared her throat.   " I'm afraid I can't read it,
twins.   You see, it isn't my kind of writing at all."

Just at that moment Friska came out of the den door,
so Mary called, " Please could you come and read this
letter for me ?   It's rather bad writing and I can't
understand it."

Friska at once put on her lesson face and hurried over
to the cubs.

" Let me see," she said.   Mary handed her the letter,
and she read aloud :

" ' Dear Mary Plain,

" ' I would be so pleased if you would come and pay me a visit——' "

" What's that ? " interrupted Mary. " Is it more than a penny or not so much ? "

" A visit is not anything to do with money," said Friska excitedly, " it's a stay—a stop—a-a—well—a go-to."

" Like when I went out to tea, do you mean ? " asked Mary, helpfully.

" Yes, but hush, listen what it says next," said Friska, her eyes running down the paper. " Dear, dear, why I can't believe it—I don't ——"

" I'm listening," said Mary. But Friska went on reading the letter to herself, till Mary said again, rather angrily, " I'm still listening and it's my letter."

" ' I live just outside Berne,' " read Friska, " ' and I have a lovely big garden where you can play ball and a lake where you can swim, and I think you would be very happy here.

" ' I have asked the Owl Man if he would bring you out in his car when he comes to-morrow, so have your luggage and yourself ready at three. We shall have such fun. With love,

from the Lady in the Fur Coat.' "

If bears could go pale, Mary would have gone. Instead she took a deep breath. " To-morrow," she said, " that's next to to-day, isn't it ? "

Friska nodded. She and her twins were all staring at Mary. The twins had that rather " not liking Mary

very much " feeling that they had had when Mary was
asked out to tea and they weren't.

" And what is luggage ? " asked Mary next.

" Oh, luggage," said Friska vaguely, " well—just
luggage.   You know."

" But I don't," said Mary.

" Well, I haven't time to explain just now," said
Friska hurriedly.   " Now, how do you spell visit ? "

However, Mary was far beyond spelling that morning,
so she said, coaxingly, " You'll have to tell me the first
time, Auntie, then I'll know."

" V–I–S–I–T," spelt Friska, " and when it's more
than one visit, what would it be ? "

Mary didn't know.   " Yes, come, come, you know as
well as I do.   What does one add on ? "

" S," said Little Wool.

" Good boy.   Well, Mary ? "

" Svisit," said Mary brightly.

Friska groaned.   " Mary, Mary, you know as well as
I do that's wrong.   Think of a word you know—pit.
Now what is it with an S added on ? "

" Spit," said Mary.

" Oh, Mary Plain," cried the twins in shocked voices,
" what do you mean ? "

" This," said Mary, and spat.

Friska gave an angry growl, and was just stepping
forward to box Mary's ears when she heard the chains
rattle, and she had only just time to get back into Parlour
Pit before the doors came down.   And then Mary

suddenly saw a familiar hat up above, and there was the Owl Man.

" Good-morning, Mary," he called down.

Mary waved with both arms. " I'm going on a svisit," she said, " and it's a stay, and a go-to, too. And I'm very pleased, and so are the twins, only not quite so pleased as I am, are you, twins ? "

" Well, it isn't our visit, you see," said Little Wool sadly.

" Nor our stop, neither," added Marionetta.

They both looked so dreary that Mary's heart smote her.

" Just go into that corner for a moment," she said, " both of you. I want to ask the Owl Man a private ask." The twins looked rather suspicious but went. Mary looked up at the Owl Man and said :

" What's luggage ? "

" Well, it means things you bring with you on a visit."

" Hurrah ! Then the twins are my luggage," said Mary, clapping her paws.

" Oh, but," said the Owl Man hastily, " not that kind of thing, I meant things you need."

" But I need the twins," said Mary.

" But they haven't been invited. You see, the kind of things I meant were your bowl and your brush. Bears aren't things—they're bears. And you can't take bears on a visit unless they're invited, and the Fur-Coat-Lady hasn't invited the twins. She hasn't room for them."

" They could squeeze up quite small," said Mary wistfully.

" Now, look here, Mary, we must get this quite straight. The twins are delightful but they are not you, and they are not special friends of the Fur-Coat-Lady."

" Am I, then ? " asked Mary.

" A very special friend indeed," said the Owl Man.

Mary was impressed. She backed with dignity to the bath and sat down rather straight and stiff with her arms folded.

" I tell you what, though," said the Owl Man," when I come and collect you to-morrow, I'll bring a box full of surprises for the twins. Cakes, and sugar and figs, for you to give them when you go away. How will that be ? "

" Lovely," said Mary happily.

" And look here, Mary. It's a great compliment to be asked to stay with the Fur-Coat-Lady, and you'll have to be on your best behaviour, you know."

" Am I on it now ? " inquired Mary.

" Yes, I should think you were."

Mary got up, looked behind her, and found she was sitting on her letter. She settled herself carefully on it again.

" I'll try not to forget," she said.

" That's right. Now I must be off, but you'll be ready at three to-morrow, won't you ? And I won't forget—you know what," and he winked at Mary knowingly.

Mary winked back gravely.

" I suppose I couldn't stop being a bear and be a thing instead ? " asked little Wool, who had a hopeful nature.

Mary shook her head. " I'm afraid not. I heard Big Wool say the other day, ' Once a bear, always a bear.' "

The twins looked rather disappointed, but on the whole they were really very good about it, and whenever Mary felt specially sorry for them she remembered the basket, and that made her happy again. After all, she thought, you couldn't always tell what a svisit would be like—especially when you had never been on one before. But a box with sugar and cakes ! Well ! It was a box with sugar and cakes !

CHAPTER TWO

IN WHICH MARY GOES SVISITING

It took a long time for next day to come, at least Mary thought so.   She had a very restless night, and wriggled so much that the poor twins got little sleep.

" Oh, Mary Plain, can't you keep quiet ? " groaned Little Wool.

" You'll be sorry when I'm gone," said Mary.

Little Wool knew this was true, so next time Mary kicked him, he just bore it.   At last it was daylight, and Friska came in to tell them it was time to get up.

" Now, Mary," said Friska fussily, " Big Wool wants to see you for a minute, but first you must get nice and tidy.   Mr Job said he would give you a good brushing, but he wants me to see to your ears and face," she finished importantly.   " Are your ears clean ? "

Mary bent her head down obediently, but she moved her ears up and down very quickly, so Friska couldn't possibly see.

" Keep still, can't you, Mary ? " she said.

" I'm not moving," answered Mary.

" No, but your ears are," said Friska.

" I'm sorry—perhaps they're a bit excited to-day," said Mary.

" Perhaps you are, you mean," said her exasperated aunt, giving it up as a bad job. " Now, come along and say good-bye to your grandmother. She wishes to say a few parting words."

Mary's heart sank as she trotted off to Parlour Pit. There was nothing Big Wool liked better than making speeches and they were always so dull.

" Well, Mary," said Big Wool kindly, " I hear you are going on a visit. Now, remember, you must be on your best behaviour all the time, my child."

" The Owl Man told me," said Mary.

" Oh, he did, did he ? Well, I hope you will not forget. And you must be very polite. Always shake hands with your right paw—which is your right paw, Mary ? "

" The one that isn't my left," said Mary cleverly.

" And don't forget to say ' please,' and ' thank you,' and ' how do you do,' " continued Big Wool.

" But what do I say if they don't ? " asked Mary.

" Don't what ? "

" Do."

" That, I am afraid," said Big Wool, with dignity, " must depend. But in any case I trust that you will do us credit."

" I'd try, if I knew what it was."

" What what was ? " asked Big Wool.

" Credit."

Really, how Mary did catch one up ! " Well, it's a little difficult to explain," said Big Wool, " so never mind."

" I won't," said Mary.

" Won't what ? "

" Mind."

Altogether the conversation was not getting on very well, so Big Wool gave Mary a pat on the head.

" Well, run along now, and don't forget what I have told you."

" No, I won't," promised Mary, as she went off to the Nursery.

Friska had polished her bowl till it shone, and Job gave her a thorough brushing, and then he made a

beautiful paper parcel of the bowl and brush, and tied a label on it with *Miss Mary Plain* written on it.

Inside the parcel Mary tucked her precious letter.

"Now," said Job, "just you keep still for once and don't go and ruffle your coat, or the gentleman won't take you along when he comes. He won't want any untidy bears in his car, I'll be bound."

This sounded very alarming, so Mary sat all the morning on the side of the bath with her parcel beside her and found it the longest morning she had ever spent.

The twins did not have much of a time either. For whenever they began to enjoy themselves Mary, from the bath, would say, "You'll be sorry when I'm gone." And that, of course, ended the fun.

At long last three o'clock came, and with it the Owl Man. He leaned over the wall and called, "Hallo, Mary, are you ready?"

Mary jumped up. "Oh," she said, "I've been here so long keeping smooth for you that it's nearly to-morrow."

The Owl Man laughed.

"Well, let's get off at once," he said. "I'll call Job and he'll bring you up—and this down." And he held up a big basket all bulging with surprises. Mary was delighted, and went and stood close to the door with her luggage in her paw. Then she heard the key rattle in the lock, the door flew open, and there was Job, with the basket in his arms.

"Twins," called Mary, "here is a huge treat for you. It's instead of my svisit." The twins came rushing up, their eyes sparkling with excitement.

" For us, Mary Plain ?   Where does it say it's for us ? "
asked Little Wool.

There were a few odd marks painted on the basket,
so Mary, who was awfully good at inventing, pointed
at them and said, " Here, do you see ?   It says, ' For
two left-behind bears ! ' "

They were both so excited that they quite forgot to
say good-bye to Mary, so she gave a little cough and
said, " I'm going now."

" Are you ?   Good-bye ! " said Marionetta in a cheerful voice, still walking round and round the basket.

" You'll be sorry when I'm gone," said Mary reprov-
ingly.   But the twins did not hear, so Mary went.

Job put on her collar and lead : he said bears never
left their pits without them.   The Owl Man met them
at the top of the stairs and led Mary to a big red car
which was standing in the road.

" Is this a tram ? " asked Mary.

" No, it's called a car," explained the Owl Man, as he
helped her into the front seat and put her parcel in behind.

" Are you looking forward to your visit ? " he asked,
as he got in beside her.

" Not just now," said Mary anxiously, " I'm looking
backwards at my luggage.   I'm so afraid the label will
blow off, and then we shan't know it's mine, shall we ? "

" Would you rather have it in front ? " said the Owl
Man.

" Oh, please ! " said Mary, so he lifted it over and
put it by her feet, and Mary kept touching it with her
toe to see if it was still there.

The Owl Man pressed a button, and the car gave a soft growling noise.

"Is it angry?" asked Mary nervously. "Doesn't it like me being inside?"

"Oh, yes, it's very friendly with bears," said the Owl Man. "That's just the noise it makes when it's going to move. Now, we're off!" and sure enough they were.

Another button made a loud hoot when the Owl Man pressed it, and Mary jumped. "Was it us?" she asked. And the Owl Man said yes, and she could do it next time.

When the next time came and the Owl Man said "Now," Mary bent forward, but she was not expecting the corner, and in a second she had shot down the seat and bumped into the Owl Man.

"I'm sorry," she said, "but it's a very slidy seat."

"I know," he said, and, pulling up at the side of the road, he lifted Mary on to a cushion and tucked a rug round her. "There," he said, "now you'll stay put."

Mary kept a sharp look-out to see if any of the cars they passed had bears in them, but none had. She asked the Owl Man about it, and he said, "No, as a matter of fact, Mary Plain, you're a very unusual kind of bear," and Mary felt as proud as proud.

The drive was most exciting, up hills and down hills, and then along straight roads, so fast that the wind blew Mary's pointed ears up on end.

"Doesn't the wind taste nice," she said, "all cold and prickly!"

Once, on an empty road, the Owl Man let her help to steer the wheel.

At last the car began to go slower and slower, and presently they turned in at a gate, and after a little bit they came to a white house with green shutters. Mary looked at the shutters hard—she was not very fond of green things. As they drew up by the big door, out came the Fur-Coat-Lady, and she was all smiling as she helped Mary out.

"Is it because of me you're smiling?" said Mary.

"Indeed it is. I'm so very glad you've come," she said, "and I hope you are too?"

"Oh yes," said Mary, "and we've come a long, long way, and I blew the wheel and steered the horn, and the Owl Man says I'm rather an unusual kind of bear."

"I should think you were," said the Fur-Coat-Lady, laughing. "Now, let's go in."

"Oh, my luggage, my luggage!" cried Mary. "I must have my luggage!"

"All right, all right," said the Owl Man, as he got it out, "I believe you must have some diamonds tucked away in that precious parcel. Here, wait a second while I take your collar off."

"I expect you'd like to wash your paws and then have some tea?" said the Fur-Coat-Lady.

"I don't want to wash my paws, but I'd like some tea, please," said Mary, who was always frank. "I'm very empty down here." She patted the empty part. "Please, could I have a carrot or a biscuit?"

"You shall have as many and as much as you

The drive was most exciting

want, and now at once," said the Fur-Coat-Lady.

" I think I'm going to like this svisit," said Mary, as she followed her friend into the dining-room.

There were quite a lot of people there. Mary felt quite shy. She clung to the Owl Man's hand, till the Fur-Coat-Lady said, " Won't you come and sit here by me ? " And then she had to let go of it. But when she saw him go down to the other end of the table she ran after him and said, " Please, I want to sit next to the Fur-Coat-Lady, but couldn't I sit next to you too ? There's room on both sides of me."

" Rather," said the Owl Man, and followed her back up the room.

Mary had left her parcel beside her chair, but when she got back she found it gone.

" My luggage—my luggage—" she began.

" Look here, Mary," said the Owl Man, " you can't have luggage at the table, you know, it's not done. It's there, quite safe in the corner, and after tea you can have it."

But it just wasn't any good arguing. Mary hurried off into the corner and began wrestling with the string. The Owl Man followed her, " Look here, Mary Plain," he began, " what about that best behaviour ? "

" That's just it," said Mary, looking quite frantic, " that's just it ! Oh do, do, open this string for me, please ! "

The Owl Man saw there would be no peace till she got her way, so he cut the string. In a moment Mary had opened the parcel, got out her letter, and carrying it back to the table, she spread it carefully on her chair and then sat on it, beaming. Every one looked very surprised. " Whatever is that you are sitting on ? " asked the Fur-Coat-Lady.

" My best behaviour, of course," said Mary. " The Owl Man said I must always be on it here. That's why I had to unpack at once."

" You absurd cub," said the Owl Man, patting her on the head, " and now, for heaven's sake, get on with your tea ! "

" I will," said Mary—and did.

CHAPTER THREE

GOING TO BED IN A MARY WAY

AFTER tea the Fur-Coat-Lady suggested that it might be a good thing to sit down quietly for a bit.

"Well, if you don't mind," said Mary, "I think I'd better run about, I feel rather fat."

"Very well, then," said the Fur-Coat-Lady, "Sandy shall take you out and show you the garden."

"And who is Sandy?" asked Mary.

"Sandy is my nephew," she answered.

"This is him." And she put her hand on the head of the small boy, who had come up beside them and was staring at Mary, who still held her letter clutched in her hand.

"Don't you think you'd better let me have that letter?" asked her friend. "It will be rather a nuisance while you're playing, won't it?"

Mary looked worried. "But I promised I'd always be on my best behaviour you see," she said.

"But supposing you behaved nicely, that would do just as well," said the Fur-Coat-Lady. Mary looked relieved and handed over the letter. "It *is* getting rather rumpled," she said.

She and Sandy started off together. The garden was lovely. A big lawn with trees growing out of it came first.

"I have a tree where I live," said Mary grandly.

"Have you?" said Sandy. "Do you ever climb it?"

"Oh, yes," said Mary, "when I feel climby."

"Do you feel climby now?" asked Sandy.

"Yes," said Mary. "Let's race; you up that side and me up this. One, two, three, go!" But it was not much of a race, because before Sandy had hoisted his plump person on to the bottom branch, Mary was at the top.

"Hallo!" she called down. "Why are you so slow?"

He looked so helpless that Mary came hurrying down to give him a helping paw. They both got pretty high up, and then Sandy said he felt swimmy and he would rather get down.

"How can you feel swimmy when you're not in the water?" asked Mary. But Sandy only knew that he did. Mary bundled down first, and because she was very happy and very full of tea she decided to give Sandy a treat and play the game she and the twins always played when they were happy, so she waited till Sandy was on the branch next to the bottom, and then she chawed his leg.

" Ow ! ow ! " yelled Sandy.   " What are you doing ? Go away ! " and he kicked at her.

" Only being friendly," said Mary in an offended voice ;   " don't you like having your leg bitten ? "

" No, I do *not*," said Sandy, looking very cross.

" And I'm not at all sure I like biting it either," said Mary, " it's so pink and bare.   Why haven't you got hair on it, like mine ? "

" Because boys don't, and it's rude to make personal remarks," said Sandy.   " Let's go down to the lake." Mary stood on the edge and stared.   She was just going to say, " What a huge bath ! " when Sandy said, " That's the lake."

" I have a lake at home too " said Mary, not to be outdone.

" Have you got a boat on yours ? " asked Sandy.

Mary had no idea what a boat was, so she said, " Pardon ? "

" Have you got a boat on yours, I said ? " repeated Sandy.

" No," she said, " I haven't—but it's only because I don't want one," she added.

Next, Mary was introduced to the see-saw, and here she had to give up competing.   " I suppose you've got one of these too ? " said Sandy.   And Mary, flying up on her end, shouted, " No, but oh, I only wish I had ! "

She chawed his leg

" What kind of a tree is that ? " she asked, pointing above.

" That's a yew tree," said Sandy.

Mary walked slowly up to the Fur-Coat-Lady, who was sitting on the terrace with the others. She pointed to the tree and said, " Sandy says that's a me tree—a Mary tree." The Fur-Coat-Lady looked at Sandy and raised her eyebrows.

" I told her it was a yew tree," he explained.

" Fancy that," said the Fur-Coat-Lady, " and do you know, Mary, that the tree over in the corner is called a plane tree, so I have two trees in my garden named after you ; isn't that a funny thing ? And now I am afraid it's your's and Sandy's bedtime. Say good-night, and I will show you your room."

Mary looked very depressed, so the Fur-Coat-Lady said, " Remember, the quicker you get through the night the sooner to-morrow will come." Mary had not thought of that, so she cheered up and said good-night all round, and followed her friend into the house. They went into a big empty room, and at once Mary fell flat on her back.

" I didn't know ice was ever brown," she said, as she picked herself up.

" Poor Mary ! Bad luck ! It's not ice really, but it's nearly as slippery, and you must walk very carefully." With great care Mary got across the room with only one more tumble, and then they went upstairs and along a passage to a room at the end. It had a big window looking on to the garden and, against the wall, a very large bed with a roof on it, held up by four pillars. On the bed was a huge rug. In the corner was Mary's bowl and on a table her brush. Mary walked over to the window and leant out, and there was the terrace just below.

"Hallo," she called. "Just look at me up here!" The Owl Man called back, "Pity there's not a green plank—eh, Mary?" And he and Mary had a secret laugh together.

"Well now, Mary," said the Fur-Coat-Lady, "I hope you'll be very comfortable and get to sleep quickly," and she patted her on the head. "Good-night—sleep tight!"

As soon as she had gone Mary began to look round. She looked hopefully at her bowl, but that was empty. Then she tried to brush her coat, but she could only reach the front of herself, so that wasn't much good. Walking about she came to a door she hadn't noticed before, and when she had opened it there was a small room, all white, with a big white bowl in it, bigger than Mary. Her eyes fell on two bright silver things at the end of the bowl, and she walked over to have a look at them. Why, they were taps! Like the one in the den at home. Mary turned one on, and out came some water which made a hissing noise, and all the room got full of cloud.

"How funny!" she thought, "I wonder if it's wet water or not?" and she bent over to see.

"Ow!" yelled Mary, shaking her paw; then like a flash she was out of the room and tearing down the

stairs.   She was in such a hurry that she forgot all about
the brown room, so she crossed that on her back, and
then scrambled out of the window and rushed on to the
terrace.   " Oh ! oh ! the water's bitten me, the water's
bitten me ! " she cried, hugging her hurt paw.   The
Owl Man sprang to his feet.

" Hot water, by Jove ! " he said, " she must have
turned on the tap in the bathroom."

" Oh dear ! " said the Fur-Coat-Lady, " I forgot to
lock the door.   Poor dear Mary ! " And she took
Mary away and made her a lovely white cotton paw
with grease inside, and it soon began to feel better.   Once
again they went back to the bedroom and the Fur-Coat-
Lady saw Mary comfortably settled on the bed.

Directly the door closed Mary got up.   What to do
now ?   She wandered round and found near the window
a wide flat kind of string just asking to be pulled, so
Mary pulled, and there was a loud clatter and suddenly
the room was nearly dark.   Mary did not like that much
and tried to pull it up again, but she only had one paw
and could not manage it.   She felt her way to the bed
and then began wondering what was on top.   The only
way to find out was to go up and see.   With her three
good paws she got up one of the pillars quite easily, and
she had just hoisted herself on to the roof when the door
opened and there was the Fur-Coat-Lady.   Mary lay
flat on her face and looked at her over the edge.   " You
don't know where I am, so there ! " she called.

" I do not," said the Fur-Coat-Lady.   " I can hardly
see a thing, why is it so dark in here ? "

"Perhaps it's night," suggested Mary, with an eye on the window.

"Perhaps it's this blind," said the Fur-Coat-Lady, and she pulled it up. She looked round. "Where-ever are you, Mary? In bed?"

"No, on bed," said Mary, from the top.

"Mary, Mary," said the Fur-Coat-Lady, "that's not at all good—what about that best behaviour?"

"Is it naughty to be on the bed instead of in it?" asked Mary.

"Yes, it is at this time. You ought to be in bed and sound asleep. Now, come down at once. I can't think how you got up with a bandaged paw."

"With the other three," said Mary, sliding down the pole.

"I hoped I should find you fast asleep," said the Fur-Coat-Lady.

"But you didn't," said Mary.

" No, I didn't, but now, Mary, you must really settle down. Shut your eyes, and count ten——"

" But I can't," said Mary.

" How much can you count ? "

" Five every day and seven on extra clever days," said Mary.

" Well, that's something," said the Fur-Coat-Lady. " You count up to five and then go back to one and do it again and you'll see, before you can say ' Jack Robinson,' you'll be asleep."   And with a wave of the hand the Fur-Coat-Lady went away.

" One, two, three, Jack Robinson," said Mary quickly, and then waited. Nothing happened.   " Jack Robinson," she said again, but she was still awake, so she gave up trying and got up again.

She opened the door a crack and a lovely dinnery smell came pushing in. She sniffed it and then began to follow it down the passage.   It pulled her all the way downstairs and into the room where they had tea, and there were all the people sitting round the table, eating. Mary stood in the doorway.

" *I* haven't had any supper," she said.

Everybody jumped. The Fur-Coat-Lady looked helplessly at the Owl Man, but he had his face buried in his napkin and his shoulders were shaking.

" But surely you couldn't be hungry, Mary? " she said.

" But I am," said Mary.

" You had such a very big tea," went on the Fur-Coat-Lady, " and you're really far too small to be sitting up to dinner."

" I wouldn't mind about the sitting, as long as I had the dinner," said Mary, willing to please. And at that the Owl Man said, " It's no good, Jill—she wins," and he pulled up a chair for Mary. So Mary wore a napkin and ate some soup and custard, and then the Fur-Coat-Lady said she simply must not stay up another moment.

" I can take myself upstairs," said Mary, " and thank you for the dinner," and off she went. She went up to her room, and rolled up in the rug on the bed, but it got into lumps, so she kicked it off and lay on the bed without it. That was chilly and lonely, so she picked it up again, lay on it, and began to think about the twins. And as she thought about them, and how warm they all kept, snuggled up together at night, she began to miss them very badly. And the more she thought about them the more unhappy she got, till at last she could not bear it any longer. It didn't take long to find the people on the terrace. By this time they were all getting quite used to seeing Mary appear, and only the Owl Man murmured, " Again ? "

" I've come to say good-bye. I'm going home," said Mary. " Please, will you fetch your car and take me home ? "

The Owl Man had a good look at her, and then he put his arm round her and said, " Now, now, Mary, this won't do at all. You can't come on a visit and then behave like this."

" Do you think the twins are happy without me ? " she asked in a wobbly voice.

" I think so," he said, very kindly, " you see, they have each other."

" That's just it," said Mary, " I've only got me."

This was terribly true. The Owl Man thought hard and then he said, " Now, look here, Mary Plain, I know you're a sensible little bear, so just make up your mind to make the best of being here to-night. By to-morrow, after a good long sleep, you'll feel quite different, mark my words." He got up. " Now, Jill, we're going off to bed, Mary and I, and I'll see to her getting settled, don't you worry. Just a touch of home-sickness, I expect," he added in a low tone.

" But I only ate a little supper," said Mary, " only it presses here," and she pointed to her chest.

" I know," said the Owl Man sympathetically, " it's a beastly feeling."

When they got upstairs he went into the room next to Mary's. " This is where I sleep," he said, " and now I'm going to open the door between our rooms, so you won't be able to feel lonely even if you try, and then I'm going to sit by you till you go off to sleep. I know it won't be long, for you're really very tired." He brought a chair and put it beside her bed. " That better ? "

" Much," said Mary. The Owl Man rolled up the rug into a nest, and Mary curled into a ball while he sat down close by the bed.

" I wish you were *my* friend," said Mary.

" But I hoped I was," said the Owl Man.

Mary shook her head. " You're Bunch's," she said.

" But surely I can be yours too ? "

Mary shook her head again. "You can't be two friends," she said.

She thought hard for a minute. "I suppose you couldn't be my cousin?"

"I'm afraid not," said the Owl Man.

"Nor my aunt neither?" asked Mary.

"No, I certainly couldn't be that," he said. Mary sighed.

"Well, what could you be? Couldn't you think of something if you tried very hard?" The Owl Man did.

"I'll tell you what," he said, "if I can't be your friend, I don't see any reason against my being your partner, do you?"

But Mary was fast asleep.

CHAPTER FOUR

IN WHICH MARY BEHAVES AS A SVISITOR SHOULDN'T

MARY was awakened next morning by a tickling feeling
in her nose that was nearly a sneeze.

She sat up, and first she had a look at her paw. It
was quite mended, so that was all right. Next she
slipped off the bed and ran to look out of the window.
All the sky was pink and gold and it must be next day
already. She padded across to the door, but when
she turned the handle she found it was locked. So she
went instead to the other door, which led to the Owl
Man's room and was half open. Peeping in, she saw
the Owl Man was still in bed, and she crept nearer to
have a look at him. How funny and undressed he
looked without his owl's eyes! and every time he
breathed he made a queer rattling noise in his throat.
It would be a pity to wake him, thought Mary, as she
tip-toed away.

Her window was wide open, and when she looked out

she found that a long round pipe passed just close to the sill on its way down to the ground. It did not take long for Mary to slide down it, and there she was on the terrace.

Looking round, she saw some small houses peeping over a hedge that ran beside the lawn, so she decided to have a look at them and started off towards them. Coming to a small gate she pushed it open and found herself in a square place, with a good many doors round it. Some were big doors and some were little doors, and some were just doors. Before she could decide which to try first, a swishing noise behind her made her turn round quickly : sitting on the little gate she had just come through was a very large bird with long thin legs and curly tail feathers. It was fluffing out its wings, and when it had shaken them well it stretched its head up and Mary saw it had two red beards, one under its beak and the other on top of its head—a queer place to wear a beard.

" Cock-a-doodle-doo ! " said the bird loudly.

Mary jumped.

" Quite well, thank you," she said in her politest voice. She was not at all sure she cared about this stranger and she wanted to keep on the right side of him.

" Cock-a-doodle-Dooooo ! " repeated the bird.

" Quite well, thank you," said Mary again.

This duet went on a few times more and then Mary got bored. After all she couldn't stand there all day saying ' Quite well, thank you,' so she gave a little bow and turned away.

And then another noise started in another direction. It got louder and louder, and suddenly round the corner came a troop of ducks. Now, Mary had never seen any ducks before, and as it was early morning, these ducks were greatly wanting their breakfast and were all quacking their hardest. They seemed so hungry, and advanced with their beaks so wide open that Mary, in a panic, wondered if they wanted her. She backed against the wall and tried to feel brave and hoped they wouldn't notice that her left leg was trembling a little.

" G–G–Good-morning," she said nervously.

The ducks were now in a large circle in front of her, all out-quacking themselves. As Mary spoke the largest duck stepped forward.

" What are you ? " it said, in a quacky voice.

" Only a bear," said Mary.

" A bear ! "—and the duck said it in such a way that Mary flattened herself still closer against the wall.

" Aren't bears allowed here, then?" she asked, in a very small voice.

" How should I know ? " said the duck rudely. " I tell you I never heard of a bear before, so how can I say whether you're allowed or not ? And why have you got a fur coat on, this hot day ? "

" I haven't," said Mary, " it's me."

All the ducks laughed quacky laughs, and Mary got a little angry.

" I was told," she retorted, " that it was rude to make personal remarks." The ducks looked rather uncomfortable, and Mary began to feel braver. After all, she was much the biggest.

" I should like to pass, so would you please stand back there ? " she said. Not a duck moved. Then Mary had a brilliant idea. She dropped down on all-fours, lowered her head, and advanced very slowly on the ducks, making the growliest growls she could. At the first growl the ducks fled, and by the sixth growl not one was left—only a few frightened quacks came echoing back. Mary breathed a sigh of relief.

The cock had gone off the gate, and, closing it carefully behind her, Mary walked down a path close to the hedge. Presently she came to an archway leading into another garden, but she was not very interested in it, because she suddenly felt so terribly empty that nothing mattered very much except how soon it would be breakfast time. However, as she came through the arch, what should she see but a carrot stalk sticking up out of the ground. What a funny way to find a carrot ! Perhaps this was a different kind and didn't have the pink

end that tasted so good. Mary gave it a pull to see, and, sure enough, up came a long pink tip.

. . . Half an hour passed, and then Mary went back

to the house, walking very slowly. She had never felt
less like running in her life. She was extremely uncomfortable inside, and she had begun to feel perhaps she
ought not to have got up so early, so when she arrived
at the house she climbed quickly up the pipe and into her
room. Just as she dropped inside the Owl Man came
out of his room and said, " Hallo, Mary, what are you
doing ? " And Mary leant against the sill, yawned, and
said, " Just seeing what a lovely day it is."

" Isn't it ? " said the Owl Man.

" But I feel rather sleepy," said Mary, "and I think
I'll go back to bed again."

The Owl Man looked very astonished—but Mary was
often surprising, so he said, " All right, you tuck up
again till I've had my bath, and then we'll go down
together."

Down in the dining-room Mary was put on a chair
and a napkin tied round her neck.

" And what will Mary have first ? " asked the Fur-
Coat-Lady.

" Nothing, thank you," said Mary.

When Mary said, 'Nothing thank you,' the Owl Man
felt her head to see if it was hot, and the Fur-Coat-Lady
took her into the corner and asked her to put out her
tongue. Then Mary was brought back to her chair and
they tried again.

" No, thank you," she said. " You see, I've had one
breakfast and I'm really very full."

" Had one breakfast ? I should think she has ! "

said a voice from the window, and there on the terrace was a very angry gardener.

"Why, Wilhelm," said the Fur-Coat-Lady, "whatever is the matter?"

"The matter, madam, is," said Wilhelm, "that young visitor of yours has pretty well cleared my carrot-bed—that's what the matter is."

"Weren't they for me, then?" asked Mary.

The Fur-Coat-Lady sighed deeply. "I am so sorry, Wilhelm, that this has happened. You see, our visitor isn't used to visiting, so doesn't quite understand about things."

"She understood what carrots were," said Wilhelm bitterly, as he went off shaking his head.

"I shall not understand them again," said Mary, "they have given me a pain."

"I think perhaps it would be better for you to go and sit quietly on the terrace, while we finish breakfast, Mary," said the Fur-Coat-Lady; so Mary went. Presently they all came out and joined her.

"How about a picnic this afternoon?" said the Owl Man. "It's such a heavenly day, and we could all get into two cars."

"All right," said the Fur-Coat-Lady. "I'll go and see about the food, and we'll start at half-past eleven."

Mary had no idea what a picnic was, but as long as it included food she was sure she would like it—which showed she had had recovered from the carrots.

"What an exciting week," said Sandy, "for to-morrow is my birthday, and we are having a party and a conjuror!"

"Is it a kind of cake?" asked Mary.

Sandy burst out laughing. "No, it's a man who does all kinds of tricks," he explained. Mary lost all interest at once.

Sandy was still talking about his birthday.

"I have another birthday soon," announced Mary, "and I shall be one."

"Two, you mean," said Sandy.

"No, one," said Mary firmly.

"How can Mary have a second birthday and only be one, Aunt Jill?" asked Sandy.

"Because, my boy, bears have two **birthdays every** year."

"I wish I was a bear," sighed Sandy.

CHAPTER FIVE

WHEN Mary had been brushed, she and Sandy had a good game of ball, and then, when it was nearly time for the motors to come round, Sandy said he must run up and get tidy. Mary was tidy already, so she waited about in the hall till Sandy came down again. He had a green thing hanging over his arm.

"What's that?" asked Mary.

"My bathing dress," he said.

"When do you wear it?" said Mary.

"When I bathe, silly," said Sandy.

"Does everybody wear them?" said Mary.

"Of course," said Sandy.

"I—I left mine behind," said Mary; "what can I do?"

Sandy whistled. "Perhaps Aunt Jill has got an extra one; shall I run and see?"

"Oh do!" begged Mary. So when the Fur-Coat-Lady came down she brought a beautiful pair of red and white striped bathing drawers which she handed to Mary. Mary hung them over her arm and then, as she heard the cars arriving, she ran out to see which was the nicest to go in.

As she was wondering, two large baskets were brought out and placed on the steps, smelling simply delicious, and Mary's mind was made up at once; she would travel with the smell. Presently the people all came out and the Owl Man moved the baskets close to his car, so Mary went and stood beside him.

"Coming with me, Mary Plain?" he asked.

"Please," said Mary.

The Owl Man opened the door at the back. "In you get, then."

"But I'm not luggage," objected Mary.

"Not luggage! What on earth do you mean?"

"Isn't the back only for luggage?" said Mary.

"Rather not," said the Owl Man, "it's for bears," and he lifted her in, "and for boys," and he jumped Sandy in, "and for baskets," he finished, plumping the two baskets on the floor.

The drive was very like the last one, up and down hills and things flashing past them, only it was much bumpier sitting at the back.

Just when she began to wonder if they were ever going to get there, the car stopped and out they all bundled. They were beside a large lake, and all round it were woods full of birds singing.

" Shall we have lunch at once ? " asked Jill, and every one said, " Yes "—so they did.

They all sat on the ground and had lovely things to eat. Mary's bowl was full of meat and potatoes, but it did not stay full for long. Mary still felt a little hungry when she had finished, especially when she saw the other people were still eating, so she turned her head away so as not to see, and when she looked back her bowl had been filled up again—this time with biscuits and figs.

" Like to try some ice-cream ? " asked the Fur-Coat-Lady, giving her some in a spoon. Mary gasped. " It's friz me all the way down my inside," she said.

After lunch Mary behaved very well, and helped pack away all the things. Then she said, " And now where are the nics ? "

" The nics ? " said the Fur-Coat-Lady, surprised.

" Yes, what we're going to pick," said Mary.

" Oh, you lamb ! " said the Fur-Coat-Lady, and every one laughed so much that Mary felt suddenly shy. So she went up to the Owl Man and said, " Do you think the twins are happy without me ? "

" Help ! " said the Owl Man, springing to his feet, " something must be done at once. Come along, Mary Plain, you and I will go and find something else to pick as there don't seem to be any nics about to-day." He and Mary went off, and found some funny fluffy-topped things called dandelions, and the Owl Man showed Mary how to blow the fluff off and tell the time.

" When I was a small boy," he told her, " I used to find a whole lot of these where I lived."

"Didn't you be small here, then ? " asked Mary.

"No, I lived in a place a long way off, called England."

"As far as we came in the car ? "

"Much, much farther ; and you couldn't get all the way there in a car, because you have to cross the sea."

"The A B C I suppose," said Mary.

"No, not that kind of sea. It's like an enormous lake, so big that when you are in the middle you can't see anything but water all around you."

"And you don't get tired swimming ? " inquired Mary.

"Oh, you don't swim. You go in a big boat, big enough to take hundreds of people." As Mary could only count up to five she had no idea how many a hundred was.

"Could I come, please ? " she said.

"Perhaps, some day," said the Owl Man, " one never knows. Here, how about picking some of these red flowers to make a nice bouquet for the Fur-Coat-Lady ? " Presently they had a lovely big bunch, and Mary took it back to the Fur-Coat-Lady. She gave her best bow and said, " Here's a bucket for you, dear Fur-Coat-Lady," and the Lady was terribly pleased and so was every one else.

Several of the party now said they were feeling awfully sleepy and would like forty winks. It was rather dull, but it was not a very long rest after all, because Mary and Sandy were both bad resters and their wriggling disturbed the others.

"How about a swim?" said the Owl Man, sitting up and yawning.

"A good idea," said the Fur-Coat-Lady, "we'll go and get ready." Mary watched carefully to see what the others did, and found they all chose a different tree to undress behind. So she chose rather a nice pine tree, but Sandy shouted, "You aren't very private, Mary Plain, I can see you sticking out on this side of the tree."

Mary moved a bit. "Is that better?" she asked.

"No, now you're showing on the other side," he cried.

Mary drew herself up straight and made herself as tall as she could. She hardly breathed, and felt terribly thin. "Aren't I private yet?" she called.

"No, you're bulging both sides at once," was the discouraging answer.

"But why?" wailed Mary, who could do no more.

"Because your tree is too thin or you too fat. Find a bigger one."

Mary then ran behind an enormous oak, and this time she was private as private.

The Owl Man started down to the lake. When she heard him, Mary came out from behind her tree. Her arms were through the two legs and the drawers hung in a lump on her chest.

"It doesn't seem to dress me behind at all," she said anxiously, turning round. The Owl man bit his lip. "Look here, old girl," he said, "you've got them on wrong side up—I'll show you. There, that's better."

"It fits better this way up, doesn't it?" said Mary.

" It's a perfect fit," said the Owl Man, " isn't it, Jill ? "
He turned to the Fur-Coat-Lady, who had joined them.
The Fur-Coat-Lady looked at Mary's shape—very
sticking-out behind—and said, " It's quite the most
perfect fit I ever saw."

Mary proved an excellent swimmer.

" Can I ride on your back ? " asked Sandy. He
climbed up, and Mary swam out a good way, and then
Sandy got rather heavy, so she emptied him into the
lake. Luckily the Owl Man was near by, for Sandy could
not swim.

" I'm sorry," said Mary, when Sandy was sitting gurg-
ling and spitting on the Owl Man's shoulders, " but I
thought every one could swim. And yesterday you
said you felt swimmy up in the tree, so, of course, I
thought you could."

" That was altogether a different kind of swimness,"
said Sandy.

When they had all got dressed again the Fur-Coat-Lady
suggested a game of Oranges and Lemons. Mary's ears
pricked, it sounded the kind of game she liked. The
Fur-Coat-Lady and the Owl Man made the arch and
all the others marched round, singing. When Mary
got her head chopped off and they whispered, " Oranges
or Lemons ? " she said " Both, please." The Owl Man
said she must choose one or the other, so she thought
for a moment, and then said, " Oranges, please, and will
you please take the skin off, because I don't like its taste."
Altogether a dull game, Mary thought, when they had
finished explaining.

Mary swam out a good way

Then the Fur-Coat-Lady looked at her watch, and said if they were going to have tea before they started home they must begin to see about a fire. So every one went and collected all the bits of wood they could find, and the Owl Man made three long bits of wood stand up on end and hung the kettle of water on them, and soon it began to sing. Mary was very interested.

"Is it happy?" she asked.

"I expect so," said the Fur-Coat-Lady. "Now if you'll tell me as soon as the kettle steams, that means it's ready to make the tea."

"Yes," said Mary, who had no idea what steam was. All the same she felt very useful as she stood waiting for it to happen. Nothing did happen for some time, and then some smoke came out.

"There's **a** cloud come out of its nose," she said excitedly; "is that steam?"

"That's right," said the Fur-Coat Lady, and she got up and made the tea, and Mary was very happy indeed, especially about the cream buns.

Then it was time to go back, and they got home quite late, and found a man waiting for them on the doorstep.

"Why, Bill," said the Fur-Coat-Lady, "wherever did you turn up from?"

"I've been here since just after you left," said Bill. "I'm over for a week and thought I'd run down and see you. Hallo, who's your friend?"

"Miss Mary Plain. Mary, this is Mr Bill Smith."

"How do you don't?" said Mary, who was rather tired after her picnic.

" Bless my soul, but I don't believe I do don't, do I ! "
said the man, and everybody laughed. Mary laughed
too, but only for a little, for she felt very sleepy. She
wandered off, and presently she found herself in the room
where they had breakfasted and she began looking about
for a snug corner to curl up in and have forty winks.
Near the door she found an open place in the wall with
two deep shelves in it, and on the bottom shelf was a
bag of biscuits. It might have been specially prepared
for Mary. She climbed in. Then she got a great

fright, for suddenly it was quite dark inside, and she
was dropping down, down, down. It dropped so fast
that only part of Mary seemed to drop too, and then with
a bump it stopped. Mary tried to find a door but there
was none, so she decided she might as well have her sleep.

The only trouble was that the bag of biscuits took up rather a lot of the shelf. Soon, however, there was plenty of room. Mary curled up and fell sound asleep beside a very flat paper bag.

Meantime upstairs some one said, " Where's Mary ? " and no one seemed to know. The Fur-Coat-Lady began looking in the rooms downstairs, the Owl Man ran up to see if she was in her room, and Sandy ran round the garden calling " Mary, Mary,"

They all met again on the terrace, rather out of breath, and all of them said, " Well ? " and every one answered, " Not a sign of her anywhere."

" She can't have gone far," said the Fur-Coat-Lady ; " what time is it ? "

" Half-past seven," said Bill, looking at his watch.

" And we came in at 6.30," said the Owl Man with a groan. " Plenty of time to disappear in."

" Especially when you're Mary," added the Fur-Coat-Lady. " What can we do ? "

" How about the lake ? " said the Fur-Coat-Lady. " She wouldn't go out in the boat alone, by any chance ? " So they all rushed down to the lake. But there was the boat and no sign of Mary. Then they all went back to the house, and every one looked very worried.

" You see, we shouldn't have taken her off her lead," said the Fur-Coat-Lady.

" I'm afraid not," said the Owl Man, " but she seemed perfectly at home."

He looked at his watch. " 8.30. I think I'll get the car and run along the road," he said. " She's such an odd little creature—perhaps she said, 'I wonder if the twins are happy without me,' and there was no one there to answer, and so she started off home. Yes, I'll go and get the car."

"Wait a minute," said the Fur-Coat-Lady. "I absolutely insist on your having something to eat before you go. It's a cold supper because the cook is out, so it won't take a minute to get it up. Come along into the dining-room."

The Owl Man followed her in, and the Fur-Coat-Lady went over to the lift and pulled the rope. "Bother," she said, "this lift's gone wrong again."

"Let me try," said the Owl Man. He gave a strong pull and the lift began to move. "It's coming now," he said, "but whatever can there be for supper? It's as heavy as lead."

"Just cold beef and meringues," said the Fur-Coat-Lady.

But it wasn't meringues—it was Mary.

CHAPTER SIX

HOW MARY DID HER BEST TO HELP THE CONJUROR

MARY slept quite late next morning; in fact the Owl Man had to give her a poke to wake her up.

"How about some breakfast," he said, "or do you want more sleep?"

"No," said Mary, "I think breakfast would be much nicer than more sleep." So off they went downstairs.

"By the way," he said, "you must be sure to say 'Many happy returns of the day' to Sandy when you see him."

"Why?" said Mary.

"Because it's his birthday," said the Owl Man.

Sandy was standing near the window when they went in, and Mary went up and said, very nicely, "Many happy returns of the day, Sandy."

"Thank you," said Sandy.

"And are these the returns ? " asked Mary, pointing to a table piled with presents.

"Those are all my presents—aren't they lovely ? " said Sandy, in an excited voice.

"Perhaps they are, under the paper," said Mary ; " aren't you going to look ? " So Sandy unpacked them and found they were all just the very things he wanted most. Especially the gramophone !

"Now, I really think you must get on with your breakfast, Sandy," said the Fur-Coat-Lady. "You can go back to your presents afterwards. Come along." So they all sat down at the table.

There was nothing wrong with Mary's appetite this morning, and nobody had to ask her to put her tongue out. When the Fur-Coat-Lady said, "What first, Mary ? " she said, "Thank you, I'll start at the beginning and go on to the end."

"And don't forget the middle," said the Owl Man.

"I won't," promised Mary, and kept her word.

"Tell us some more about this business that's brought you over here, Bill," said the Owl Man.

"Well, it's to do with this big show at the Crystal Palace that's to come off next week. The idea is to give people who own any odd animals a chance of showing them."

"What sort of animals ? "

"Well, anything you like—from performing fleas to elephants—excluding horses, dogs, and cats. I believe there are a fair number of entries already, among them some tame slugs and a baby hippo trained to the tight-rope. Any unusual pet can be exhibited."

"That's me," said Mary, "you said I was unusual, didn't you, Owl Man?"

"I did," said the Owl Man.

"And you're certainly a pet," added the Fur-Coat-Lady.

"I say," said the man called Bill, and he started talking to the Owl Man in a low voice. As he talked the Owl Man stared at Mary in an odd kind of way. Mary felt rather uncomfortable.

"Have I come unbrushed?" she asked, trying to see her own back.

"No, no, you're all right," said the Owl Man, but he still looked so queer that Mary began not to like it at all.

"Do you think the twins are——" she began. The Owl Man stopped looking queer at once. "I'm quite sure they are, Mary. And now if you've finished your breakfast, I'm sure the Fur-Coat-Lady wouldn't mind you going out into the garden."

"Of course not." So Mary ran on to the lawn and did a bit of jumping, just to keep in practice, and when she had finished the Owl Man called her to him.

"Do you remember my telling you about my home, Mary Plain?"

"Yes," said Mary brightly, "over the B—a long way off."

"Not quite right! Over the sea. Well, how would you like to go there on a visit?"

"To-day?" asked Mary.

" No, not to-day, but quite soon."   Mary felt a little giddy.

" Do you mean I'd be your svisitor ? " she said.

" Yes," said the Owl Man.

" But won't Bunch be angry ? "

" I don't see why he should," said the Owl Man; "as a matter of fact he'd be too old to go."

" I'm nearly one," said Mary in a grown-up voice.

" Yes, I know, but I think she'd be allowed, don't you, Bill ? "

" I do indeed," said Bill.

" Well, Mary, it's for you to say.   You must decide if you'd be happy ; no one can tell that but yourself." So Mary went into the corner by herself and said, " Mary Plain, would you be happy to go on another svisit with the Owl Man ? " and Mary Plain answered, " Yes, Mary Plain, I should."   So that settled it.

Then Sandy carried the gramophone out under the trees, and he and Mary played soldiers.   There were some lovely marchy tunes, and Sandy taught Mary how to march, and how to stand at the salute when they sang " God Save the King."   Mary even learnt to say " God Save the King " with a strong Swiss accent. Then it was lunch time, and afterwards Sandy and Mary were sent up to rest for an hour, so as to be quite fresh for the party.

" Run up and lie down, Sandy, there's a good boy, and put on a clean white shirt and your new corduroy breeches, for you must look festive for the party," said the Fur-Coat-Lady. "The children are coming at three, so mind you are ready by then."

"Must I look fes— what you said too?" said Mary.

"Yes, of course," said the Fur-Coat-Lady.

"Then shall I put on my bathing costume?" said Mary.

"I am afraid it wouldn't be quite suitable," said the Fur-Coat-Lady kindly.

"It's all the clothes I've got," said Mary, her voice rather quaky.

"I tell you what," said the Fur-Coat-Lady hastily, "I've got some lovely wide blue ribbon and you shall wear a big bow of that. How would that be?"

"Where would I wear it?" asked Mary.

"Round your neck. You will look very gay."

So when Mary came down at three, she wore a beautiful satin bow just behind her left ear, and every one said she was the smartest bear they had ever seen.

Lots of children came, and they were all most interested in Mary. She had to shake hands so often that her paw began to ache.

"My how-do-you-do paw is tired," she said to the Owl Man, "what can I do? Shake hands with my back one?"

"Why not your left?"

"Because Big Wool said it must always be a right one," said Mary.

"I think a very good bow would do as well," said the Owl Man resourcefully.

They all played hide-and-seek to begin with, and then

had some races. Mary came in third in a three-legged race and won a large red ball, which was very exciting. After that came tea—and such a tea! A huge white

iced cake stood in the middle of the table with seven candles burning on it, and by each plate was a pile of crackers.

Mary did not know about crackers, and when they began to go off she put her paws up over her ears. "Do you think the twins are—— " she began.

The Owl Man was standing behind her and said, "Come, come, Mary, that won't do. Why, look at all the little children pulling away at them—they'll be calling you 'cowardy custard' next! Now, you hold tight on to the other end and pull hard, and perhaps you'll get a cap or a present."

The next minute Mary was wearing a most becoming little sailor hat on one side of her head, but though she pulled a few more, she was not really happy till cracker time was over.

Then came the most thrilling part of the whole party. They all went into the big slippery room, and there were lots and lots of chairs, and at the end a platform, and on the platform was a very friendly man dressed in grey. He was called a conjuror.

" Good-evening, young ladies and gentlemen," he said. " It is a great pleasure to see so many little people here this evening, and I hope we are going to have a pleasant time together. But, you know, it isn't very easy to have a nice time all by oneself, and as I shall be wanting a little help now and again, I hope some of you young gentlemen will be willing to lend me a hand."

" I could lend you my paw," said Mary, but every one said " Ssh ! "

The friendly man did a great many wonderful things. he made twelve silk handkerchiefs come out of a ball, and shook them into a flag. He showed them an empty box and then blew on it, and when he opened it again there was a lovely flower growing in it ; and then he made a real live rabbit come out of a top-hat. Every time he had finished doing one of these wonderful things, the children clapped, and he came forward and bowed, and every time he bowed Mary got down off her chair and bowed back.

" Now," said the man, " I will do a little thought reading. I am going to place a blackboard on the platform. Then I am going to ask some one to come and blindfold me with this thick silk handkerchief. I shall then be able to see absolutely nothing. I shall sit on this chair, and then I want one of you young ladies or gentlemen to come up and write a little poem about yourself on the blackboard, and go quietly back to your seat. I will then remove the handkerchief, and when I have read the poem I will tell you who has written it. Now—if some one would be so kind as to fix this scarf? Thank you, sir."

"There, ladies and gentlemen, I am now quite blind," and the man gave a little bow from where he sat.

Mary bowed back, as usual. She felt very sorry for him all wrapped up in the black scarf.

Then the Owl Man crept up on to the stage and wrote in printing letters. "I'm small and fat, and I wear no hat," and crept back to his place. The children were all laughing—they felt sure the conjuror would never guess. But he did! He walked up to the board, looked at it hard, and then turned and pointed straight at the Owl Man; "I think I am not mistaken in saying that that gentleman in horn spectacles has written this," he said. Every one clapped very hard because of his cleverness. They blindfolded him again, and then Sandy went up and wrote.

"I'm not a girl, I'm not a man,
So just you guess me if you can."

And again the man guessed right. Then a short little girl had a turn, and she had to be lifted up to reach. She wrote,

"If you can guess me,
You'll be clever, d'you see."
But he did.

Mary was tremendously excited. She ran and pulled the Owl Man's sleeve. "I want a turn," she said, "couldn't I?"

"Rather," said the Owl Man.

"I've got the poem (Mary pronounced it 'pome') but I can't write it," she explained. So the Owl Man went up with her, and she whispered him to write,

"I am an unusual bear.
And I don't mind telling you once again,
One of my names is Mar
y, and the other's Plain."

"Is that the right kind of poem?" she whispered anxiously, and "Rather," said the Owl Man again.

This time the conjuror looked very hard at the board before he said, "Of course it will be extremely difficult for me to guess who this poem is about—extremely difficult."

"Can I help?" asked Mary from her seat.

"If you would be so kind." Mary was helped on to the platform.

"Now, about this first line, 'I am an unusual bear.' What would that mean?"

"That means a bear," explained Mary kindly.

"Oh, I see—a bear. That's good. I'm glad you were able to tell me that. And next—'One of my names is Mar'?"

"Yes, that's quite right," said Mary excitedly, "the first one *is* Mary."

"Excellent—we're getting on like a house on fire. And the last line—' And the other's Plain ' ? "

"It's the second name," said Mary, jumping up and down, "and now, can't you guess ? " The man looked doubtful and shook his head, and Mary could not bear it any longer.

"It's me," she shouted, "it's me ! I am Mary and a bear and Plain and it's me."

There was a roar of clapping and laughter all through the room, and the conjuror took Mary by the paw and they both bowed and bowed.

The next thing was that the man held up a gold watch and asked every one to have a good look at it. Then he put it in a little box on the table and locked it with a key, which he handed to a big boy in the front row to keep safe.

"Now, I suppose no one can guess where that watch will be found ? " asked the conjuror.

"I can," said Mary unexpectedly.

Every one turned and looked at her, and the man gave a little laugh and rubbed his hands together. "Well, well," he said, "if this young—er—lady——"

"Bear," corrected Mary.

"I beg your pardon—if this young bear—Miss ? "

"Mary Plain," said Mary.

"Thank you, if Miss Mary Plain can find that watch she'll be a wonder."

"I am unusual, you know," said Mary modestly,

" but I'd like to be a wonder too. May I try ? "

" By all means," said the conjuror, but you could see from his smile he felt a little sorry for her.

Mary climbed down from her seat, went straight to the Owl Man, put her paw in his left-hand pocket— and held up the gold watch. " There," she said.

There was tremendous clapping and shouting, and Mary had to be helped on to the stage again to do more bowing. And Sandy called, " How ever did you guess, you clever Mary Plain ? " Mary was just stepping off the platform, but she stopped and said, " Because I saw the conjuror put it in the Owl Man's pocket before tea." Loud and deafening applause followed Mary as she left the platform.

Now Mary did not realise it, but she was tired out. She did not go back to her seat ; she wandered behind the platform and had a look round. There were a few things like handkerchiefs and hats about, and in the corner a big red and white striped barrel. "Just like my bathing costume," thought Mary, and it made her feel very friendly towards the barrel.

Meantime the conjuror was getting to the end of his programme. He told the children he would now show them his best trick of all—the last and the best.

" Do you believe in fairies ? " he asked. All the little girls said " Yes," and the little boys tried to look as if they didn't.

" Well," he said, " the first thing I am going to show you is an empty barrel," and he rolled the red and white barrel on to the middle of the stage.

"Now this barrel is perfectly empty," he said, giving it a tap with his magic wand. "Come in," said a faint voice. The conjuror stopped a moment and looked towards the door. Then he continued, "This barrel is completely empty," and he walked right round it, tapping as he went. Two or three times he thought he heard "Come in" again, but he took no notice.

"Now, though I have assured you that there is nothing in this cask, you would no doubt like me to prove it to you. As the saying goes, 'seeing is believing.' So I will remove the lid and show you it is full of—emptiness!"

"But it's full of me!" said Mary, popping up through the hole, with a very ruffled head and her pointed ears and blue bow all standing up in an excited kind of way. "Why did you say it was empty?" she asked indignantly. When Mary appeared the poor conjuror had sat down rather suddenly, and he looked quite white.

"Because I thought it was—because I was absolutely dead certain it was," he said in an exhausted voice.

"But I thought conjurors could guess everything," said Mary, "and you are a conjuror, aren't you?"

"I'm beginning to doubt it," said the man.

The great excitement caused by Mary's appearance in the barrel began to die down, and one or two children called out, "Where's the fairy? We want to see that fairy." The conjuror stood up.

"And so you shall, young ladies and gentlemen—if some one would—" he pointed helplessly at Mary, who was still sticking up out of the barrel.

"Certainly," said the Owl Man, and, jumping on to the platform and lifting Mary out, he carried her to the back of the room.   There, with the Owl Man's arm firmly round her waist and the Fur-Coat-Lady holding one of her paws tightly, Mary was safe.

And it was a lovely ending to a lovely day.   For the conjuror, after showing them the now really empty barrel, pulled in a box, and stood the barrel on top "so they could see better."   Then he tapped on it with his wand and cried, "Abracadabra ! ! " and out came a lovely little fairy with blue eyes and curly hair.   In her arms she held a basket made of silver, and in the basket were lots of coloured paper parcels.   These she threw among the children, and they caught them, and inside each parcel was—well, just you guess !

CHAPTER SEVEN

IN WHICH MARY SENDS OUT SOME INVITATIONS

THE day after Sandy's birthday the Owl Man had to go away, and as Mary was to go to England with him so soon, it was decided that he should take her back with him to Berne.

" But I'm quite sure the twins are happy without me, and I'd rather stay here, thank you," said Mary when she was told. " You see, I'm liking this svisit so much," she said.

" But you'll be going on another next week," said the Owl Man, encouragingly.

" It might not be as nice," said Mary, sighing.

The Owl Man sighed too. It was sometimes a little difficult to please Mary. Several times during her stay she had wanted to go and see if the twins were happy, and now that she had a chance of going, she was determined to stay.

The Fur-Coat-Lady tried to help. "You'll come again some day soon, I hope, Mary, and you have got a lot of things to tell the twins about, haven't you?" Mary brightened; she hadn't thought of that.

"And I tell you what," said her friend, "how would you like to take back a big box of cakes and biscuits and things, and then give a 'welcome home' party to all the bears?"

Mary's eyes shone. "Would it be my own party?" she said.

"Of course, your very own. You would have to send out the invitations and sit at the head of the table, like I do here."

So when Mary went off with the Owl Man she was much comforted by the thought of the large box on the back seat. She really had quite a lot of luggage. Her bowl and brush and her bathing costume and sailor hat and bow made one quite large parcel. Both that and the box were labelled *Miss Mary Plain*, but the box had *Private* written on it too.

Before she had realised it, there they were back at the pits.

Mary looked round. Everything seemed just the same as when she had gone away all that long time ago. She felt terribly travelled as she got out of the car and shook hands with Job, who had come forward to meet them.

"Hallo," he said, "where's your collar? Lost it?"

"No, here it is," said the Owl Man, "but she hasn't worn it since she left as there seemed no need. She has been very good on the whole."

"Which whole?" inquired Mary. Both men laughed.

"Isn't she a one?" said Job. "I'm bound to say we've quite missed her here."

"Well, you'll be missing her more soon," said the Owl Man, "for I'm taking her over to England next week; I've come up to-day to make all the necessary arrangements," and he told Job all about the show.

While they talked, Mary ran across to look through the railings into Parlour Pit.

Harrods was lying in the corner asleep, as usual. Bunch sat on his branch, and Friska was over on the other side of the pit playing with an empty milk-tin.

And Big Wool? Well, Big Wool was just under Mary, doing her best trick. She was lying flat on her back, holding her front paws with her back paws and sticking out her tongue as far as it would go. Though very becoming, it was not a dignified position to be found in by your grand-daughter, and directly Big Wool saw Mary she lumbered to her feet and hoped she had not noticed her.

"What are you lying on your back like that for?" asked Mary. Big Wool pretended not to hear. She gave herself a shake, looked up, saw Mary, and started. "Well, well," she said, "back again, Mary? Fancy that."

"Yes I am," said Mary, "but I want to know what you were lying on your back like that for?"

"Just for a rest," said Big Wool.

"Is it a rest to hold your toes like that and hang your

tongue out such an extra long way?" said Mary.

Big Wool had time to wish Mary had stayed away before she changed the subject.

"When did you get back?" she asked, and then she called to Friska that Mary was back. Friska hurried up.

"Good-morning, Friska," called Mary, and, "good-morning, Bunch." Friska waved her paw, but Bunch took no notice at all; perhaps he was a little jealous at seeing Mary so friendly with the Owl Man.

"So you're all still here," said Mary, looking down on them.

"Where else could we be?" asked Friska.

"Oh, I only thought some one might have invited you on a svisit as well," said Mary.

Big Wool, Friska, and Bunch all tried to look as if they wouldn't go on a visit if they were asked, but only Bunch succeeded.

"Now, Mary," said Job, coming up behind, "you must go back to your own pit, I can't let you stand about like this or I shall be getting into trouble." So Mary shouted, "Good-bye till I see you again," and went off.

The Owl Man followed her. "I must be off now, Mary Plain. I've got a lot of things to settle before we go. One day I shall have to take you to the barber's, by the way, and have your coat trimmed."

"Trimmed with what?" inquired Mary.

"Scissors, of course," said the Owl Man.

Mary had a vision of herself with scissors sticking out all over her. It seemed a bit odd, but the Owl Man had said " of course," so perhaps bears going to England always wore scissors. Anyhow she'd wait and see before she said she'd rather not.

" Meantime, you'll keep her well brushed, won't you, Job ? " said the Owl Man, and Job promised he would, and Mary was sorry, because she hated being brushed.

" Well, *au revoir*, Mary. Be good," said the Owl Man.

" Aren't I always, then ? " asked Mary.

" More or less," said the Owl Man, laughing. " Now, I really must go." He gave Mary a final pat on the head and then went over to Parlour Pit and had a few minutes' chat with Bunch about sugar. Then he jumped into his car, waved to Mary, and was off.

Mary turned and peeped through the railings of Nursery Pit, and there were Marionetta and Little Wool. Directly she saw them, Mary realised how much she had missed them. They were playing a climbing game, and Little Wool was balancing in a very unsteady position on a branch which hung over the bath.

" Boo ! " said Mary, through the railings. There was a loud splash, and then a second one, as Marionetta joined Little Wool by mistake.

" It's Mary Plain," shouted Little Wool, as he clambered spluttering out of the bath. " She's come back ! "

" Yes, I've come back," said Mary. " Wasn't it good of me ? "

Before the twins could answer, Job pulled Mary away from the railings and said she must really hurry down. On the way Mary told him about the party she wanted to give next day, and Job promised he would keep the things all safely put away till then.

" You look just the same," said Little Wool, walking slowly round her. " Visits don't change you at all then ? "

" Only inside," said Mary. " I've got lots of things inside that you don't know anything about, you see."

" Carrots ? " said Marionetta enviously.

" Carrots ! " said Mary. " *And* figs, *and* biscuits, *and* cakes, *and* porridge, *and* potatoes, *and* CREAM BUNS ! ! ! ! "

" What are they ? " asked Little Wool.

" They are round and you bite them and cream spills into your mouth," said Mary.

Little Wool licked his lips.

" And did you eat cream buns all the time ? " he asked.

" Most of it," lied Mary, " and when we weren't eating we were doing terribly exciting things."

" Oh, what ? Do tell us," begged the twins. So they all three sat down in a shady corner, a twin on each side of Mary, while she told them all about everything she had done, and quite a good deal she hadn't.

" And now you are going away again," said Little Wool. " Why couldn't Marionetta and I go instead this time ? "

Mary shook her head. " You see," she said, in a very confidential voice, " it's because I'm unusual."

" What does that mean ? " said Little Wool.

Then all three sat down in a shady corner

" I don't know," said Mary, " but I'm it. That's why I'm going away on another svisit."

The twins sighed. " Never mind," said Mary, " I'll tell you all about it when I get back. And there's to be a party to-morrow."

" A party ? " cried the twins brightening up at once. " Whose ? "

" Mine," said Mary, " but it's to be a surprise, and I shan't tell you anything about it till it happens, so don't ask questions."

" I'll try," said Marionetta.

" Could I ask just one ? " said Little Wool.

" Is it a very big one ? " said Mary. Little Wool shook his head.

" Ask," said Mary.

" Will there be cream buns ? " said Little Wool, in a hoarse whisper.

" No, you may not," said Mary.

" Mayn't what ? " said Little Wool.

" Ask one question."

" But I have, and you said, ' Yes '."

" That was a mistake," said Mary. " I wasn't think-ing. But now I must write the invitations."

" What are invitations ? " said Little Wool.

" Oh, they're ' askings,' ' Will you comes,' that you send to people before a party. I've got some paper that the Fur-Coat-Lady gave me ; I'll run and get it."

The paper was spread on the floor, and Mary lay on

her front and wrote with a red pencil and an anxious
expression.   She wrote it in " Mary writing " :

The twins were full of admiration over the letter.

" It's a beautiful letter," said Marionetta.

" It is rather," acknowledged Mary.   " Now, Mr Job
must take it to them so I can hear whether they can
come."

" Mightn't they be able then ? " asked Little Wool.

" You never know," said Mary.

" Why ? " said Little Wool.

"Oh, well," said Mary, "Harrods might have broken her leg, or Friska might have caught a chill."

"What is a chill?" asked Marionetta.

"Don't you *know?*" said Mary, who had no idea herself.

"No," said Marionetta.

"Then I shan't tell you," said Mary.

"Do you catch it in your mouth?" asked Little Wool.

"Sometimes, in your swallow," said Mary.

But none of these alarming things happened. Job delivered the letter. The envelope was addressed like this,

> To BIG WUL.
> To Frizcca.
> To Mr Bunsch.
> To Haruds.

and its arrival caused great excitement in Parlour Pit.

Big Wool was eldest, but Friska was the best reader, so she read it out loud. Bunch refused to come down from his branch, so the others had to stand underneath, and Friska read in a very loud voice so he could hear. When she had finished Big Wool scratched her head and said, "Is it proper for a small bear to give a party for us big ones?"

Friska looked very dashed. She had been thrilled at the idea of going.

"What do you think, Bunch?" she said looking up at him.

"I don't think," said Bunch. And that was all they could get out of him.

"So we shall have to decide," said Friska, looking anxiously at Big Wool. Big Wool thought for a bit, and then she said, "Perhaps it would be a shame to disappoint the cub."

"Especially just when she has got back," said Friska eagerly. She was simply longing to go.

So it was settled that they would all go, and Friska wrote a letter in real bear writing, which, as you know, can only be read upside down.

Dear Mary Plain,

We would all like to come, so we will, thank you,

Big Wool,

Friska,

Bunch,

Harrods.

Friska had to borrow some notepaper from Job, and when the letter was written he took it to Mary.

"What does it say, oh, what does it say?" said the twins, looking over her shoulder. And Mary read aloud,

" ' Dear miss Mary Plain this letter is from **Big
Wool** and Bunch and Harrods and me to say we shall
be most delighted to say yes to your very very very
kind invitation to your party we think you are the
kindest bear we have ever heard of and I am proud
because you are my niece and Bunch is proud because
you are his niece and Big Wool is proud because you
are her granddaughter and Harrods would be proud
too only she is asleep with heaps and heaps of kisses
and five hugs from all of us.' "

" Why five hugs ? " said Little Wool. " There
aren't five of them, are there ? "

So they all counted up to see how many there were,
and they found there were only four. Mary thought
hard for a minute and then she said,

" One hug from each of them, and I expect the other
is for me to give myself because of the party."

" Of course," said the twins.

CHAPTER EIGHT

MARY'S PARTY

THE next day went very quickly on the whole. In the evening up went the doors, and Job called Mary to see how he had arranged the party. The twins longed to go too, but Mary said they must go into the corner and keep their backs turned till she came back or there wouldn't be a party at all.

On the table were piles of figs and cakes, and carrots, and in the centre the largest heap of all was made of cream buns.

An empty bowl was by each place, and beside it Mary put a small paper parcel. Then she said that if Job wouldn't mind going away she would get ready herself.

Mary shut the door, and at the same moment a procession from Parlour Pit arrived.

First came Big Wool, holding Harrod's arm and walking carefully in step. Next came Bunch, but there wasn't much step about him, for he kept turning back longingly to his tree. Last of all came Friska. She had to be last because they thought Bunch might be troublesome. So Friska was prepared, and every time Bunch turned back she gave him a little butt with her head and said, " Buns, Bunch," and that sent him on again. Once in Nursery Pit Friska locked the door and hid the key.

By this time the twins were so tired of the corner and keeping their backs turned that they were definitely peeping, and directly they saw the others arriving they backed out of their corner.

" Where's Mary ? " asked Big Wool. " Why is she not here to receive us ? Or is it a mistake, and isn't there a party at all ? "

At this, Bunch made off towards the door, but Friska let him go because she knew he couldn't get out.

" Oh, yes, it's a party," said the twins, " and Mary's gone in to get it ready, and she said we must stand with our backs turned to the door till she told us we needn't or there wouldn't be a party at all."

All the bears hastily turned and faced the wall, and when Mary opened the door she saw six obedient backs.

" Good evening," said Mary.

All the backs turned quickly into faces, and all the faces stared and stared at Mary.

For Mary was in full dress. She wore her bathing drawers, and the sailor hat perched over one ear, and round her throat, being unable to tie a bow, she had wound the blue satin ribbon. But it was the drawers that held them spellbound. Friska, especially, thought she had never seen any one look so smart before.

"First a red stripe, then a white," she murmured to herself. Her eyes travelled upwards and fell on the ribbon.

"Oh, Mary," she said, "is your throat sore?"

"Not at all, thank you," said Mary, "I am only wearing my party bow."

"I beg your pardon," said Friska. Mary bowed.

"Will you come in?" she said. "The party has begun."

She went and climbed on to her stool. It was a tall stool and made her sit quite a lot higher than the others, which was very satisfactory. Big Wool sat on her right and Friska on her left. Bunch sat as near the cream buns as possible. Mary said, "Will you pass your bowls for milk, please?" Big Wool's was the first to arrive.

"How many lumps?" said Mary.

"Three," said Big Wool, with great restraint.

"Three for manners and four for a treat," said Mary.

When Bunch's turn came he said, " Three for manners and twenty for me," but Mary took no notice and gave him the same as the others. Every time she put the sugar into one of their bowls, she popped a lump into her own mouth just to be sure it wasn't turning into salt.

Just at first no one spoke much, but when some of the piles had got lower Mary told them all about her svisit.

"I can speak English," she said, and she told them about " God save the King," and how they must always stand up and salute when it was said. After a few practices they all learnt to do it very well, and now and then, during tea, so as to be sure they wouldn't forget it, Mary said, " God save the King " and they all had to stand at attention.

" And did you always wear those beautiful clothes ? " inquired Friska.

" No, only bathing and at parties."

Friska looked horrified. " Not bathing, Mary. You didn't get those stripes wet, did you ? "

" Oh, yes," said Mary, " you see, it's a bathing costume. Everybody wears them."

" But wasn't yours the smartest ? " asked Friska.

" Much," said Mary.

Now Mary had been so busy talking and pouring out that she had really eaten much less than the others, and she had not yet had one single cream bun. She had counted Bunch eating five, and now only one was left, and Bunch had his eye on it. Swallowing his last mouthful as fast as he could, he put out his paw to take it.

"God save the King," said Mary quickly. Back Bunch's paw had to come, and up to his head it had to go.

It was the rule that no bear could lower his paw from the salute till Mary took her own down. All had their eyes fixed on Mary except Bunch, who had his fixed on the cream bun. Still with her hand at the salute Mary said,

"And please pass me that cream bun. I have not had one yet——'God save the King!'" she ended quickly, as she saw Bunch's paw begin to move. So Mary got her bun, and Bunch watched her eat it gloomily.

"Why," said Mary, "you haven't any of you opened your parcels yet."

They had been so busy eating that they hadn't even noticed that they had parcels, so now there was a great crackling of paper and exclamations of delight. For they were very nice paper caps—just the right one for each bear.

Big Wool felt this was the time for a slight speech, so rapping on the table she stood up.

"Bears and cubs," she began, "I think you would all like me to offer our thanks to Mary Plain for giving us such a—er—pleasanterable party. I have enjoyed it, I am sure we all have enjoyed it."

"And Bunch has just enjoyed the last carrot," wailed Little Wool.

Big Wool glared. "Silence, there," she growled, and Little Wool made himself as small as possible.

" We are glad to welcome Mary back," continued Big Wool, " and at the same time, alas ! we have to bid her farewell. For she is again to go out into the world. One never can tell—one never can tell. The outside world is very big, and Mary is very small, and she is going a long way off. I repeat, as I repeated before, ' You never can tell.' " A tear trickled down Friska's nose. " But, though we cannot tell, we can always hope, and we do hope, and we must go on hoping that our hopes will come true."

Here Big Wool sat down, leaving every one a little uncertain as to what they had hoped.

" And now shall I show you a conjuring trick ? " said Mary.

" Please, please," cried all the bears.

Mary took from a small box by her side two tin watches. First she walked to where Little Wool sat and, removing his sunbonnet, hid the watch in it, and replaced the cap on his head.

" Ow ! " said Little Wool, " it's tickling my head."

" Ssh ! " said Mary sternly.

Then going back to her place she opened the box, put the second watch inside it, and closed down the lid.

" Now," she said, " I shall say a magic word over this box, and then I shall ask one of you to tell me where the watch inside has disappeared to. Now, ready ! "

All the bears held their breath.

" Cabra ! " said Mary, who could only remember part of the word.

A complete silence reigned, broken only by Bunch,

who, at the point of suffocation, was forced to take a deep breath.

"Cabra!" said Mary again, and dropped behind the table with the box. A moment later she reappeared, still with the box.

"Now," she said, "I will show you this box is empty —quite empty."

She opened it and held it up. The bears gasped; the watch had gone, completely. It just wasn't there.

"Marvellous!" said Friska, in a throaty whisper. "Marvellous!"

Mary bowed. All the bears bowed back.

"Now," said Mary, "not one of you can guess where I shall find that watch, can you?"

Dead silence.

"Very well," said Mary grandly, "I will show you." She marched down the table, removed Little Wool's bonnet, took out the watch and held it up.

"There!" she said triumphantly. "There is the watch!"

Lots of "clever Marys" were shouted, and Mary bowed.

"The party is now over," she said, "so good-bye."

The bears at once began to leave.

Big Wool asked if she might have a word in private with Mary, so together they went into a corner. Big Wool cleared her throat and said.

"I only want to say, Mary, that I trust you would not consider appearing in the Pit during the daytime in those clothes. I should not at all like you to draw attention."

"What is a tension?" asked Mary.

"Well, it means making people notice you," explained Big Wool.

"Oh, but I like people to notice me," said Mary.

"Yes, yes," said Big Wool, "I have no objection to their noticing you yourself, but I should not care for them to notice the costume—at least, not on you."

"But the Fur-Coat-Lady said it was a perfect fit," said Mary.

"That may be. But it is not fitting to wear even a perfect pit in a fit," said Big Wool, getting a little muddled.

Mary was getting a little muddled too, so it was a good thing that Job came along just then and said it was bedtime, and would they please hurry to their dens.

"Did you like my party?" said Mary, as she and the twins snuggled up together in the straw.

"Yes," said Little Wool, "wasn't it exciting when you found the watch you had hidden in my bonnet? Is it very grown-up to give a party, Mary Plain?"

"Yes," said Mary, "especially in a bathing costume."

CHAPTER NINE

ABOUT THE BARBER AND THE WAGON-LITS

PUNCTUALLY at eleven o'clock the next morning the Owl Man came to take Mary to the barber's. She was feeling a bit nervous inside, but she tried not to show it.

It was not far to the barber's, and the tram stopped just opposite the door. There was some writing on the glass of the door, and the Owl Man said it was " English spoken," which meant the barber could talk English. Mary said it to herself all the way upstairs.

" I know English already," she announced.

" Do you ? " said the Owl Man. " How much ? "

" English spoken," said Mary.

" Good ! What else ? "

" God save the King," said Mary, at the salute.

" Splendid, splendid ! " said the Owl Man. " You'll get on like a house on fire, I can see."

As Mary got near the top of the stairs, the idea of being trimmed upset her more and more. " Will it

173

hurt much ? " she whispered, tugging at the Owl Man's arm as he opened the door of the barber's room.

" Hurt ?   What could hurt ? "

" The scissors," said Mary, " being trimmed with scissors. Will they stick them into me all over ? "

" Good gracious me ! " said the Owl Man, " it's not that sort of trimming. The kind of trimming they do in barbers' shops is cutting."

Mary thought to herself that sounded even worse, and she wore a very anxious expression as she was lifted on to a revolving stool and a large white cape was tied round her.

The barber picked up the scissors and said, " I will now proceed. I think we had better have a bit off the ears to begin with, and then pass on to the body."

Mary clapped her paws over her ears. " No, no, not my ears ! " she cried, struggling to get off the stool and getting more and more entangled in the cape. " Don't let him cut my ears, please, Owl Man ! "

" Steady, Mary, steady ! " said the Owl Man. " It's only the long hair on your ear he wants to cut off, so it will be nice and smooth and smart. You don't want to go to England and have people say how untidy Swiss bears are, do you ? " And he went on talking like this till Mary quieted down, and then the barber very kindly clipped a bit at the back of her head, just to get her used to it, and Mary found she didn't mind a bit.

She really looked very sleek when he had finished. She gazed at herself admiringly in the glass.

" Couldn't I have a little white path down my head

like yours ? " she asked the Owl Man, but he assured her that the best bears didn't wear paths.

" It wasn't so bad after all, was it ? " said the Owl Man when they were on their way home.

" No," said Mary ; " shall we go again this afternoon ? "

" I think once is enough for one day," said the Owl Man.

The twins rushed up when Mary got back to the Pit.

" I've been barbered," she said, " aren't I smooth ? "

" Your coat's all flat like the floor," said Little Wool.

But it didn't stay flat for long, because Mary started a race round the pit, which is very unsmoothing to fur—especially when you get two cousins on top of you.

It seemed like a dream to think of going away that very night, and Mary wondered if it could really be true, because she went to bed with the others exactly the same as usual. The only difference was that she solemnly shook hands all round, and Big Wool told her to be good and mind her manners, and Friska begged her to keep up her counting and not forget all her Swiss, and Bunch said he'd be obliged if she'd bring him back some English cream buns—largest size.

Mary was tight asleep when she felt a shake and heard Job say, " Come along, Mary, time to go—wake up ! "

She had been tucked in warmly between the cubs, and it felt very chilly to be taken out.

" Wake up, Mary," he said again as he slipped her collar on ; " if you don't look sharp the Owl Gentleman will be off without you."

The Owl Man was waiting in a taxi, Mary was lifted in, and almost before she could wave to Job she was off. Mary had never been in a station before, and she thought it a very big and rather frightening place. When they stood on the platform and a huge black train came thundering in, she got really upset and, bracing all four legs firmly, she refused to budge. In vain the Owl Man pulled and argued. Mary just said, " I would rather stay in Berne, thank you." Finally, he was so afraid the train would start without them that he picked Mary up, and tucking her, kicking, under his arm, he landed her in the corridor—just as the train started. Mary promptly fell flat on her back, as she was not expecting it. · " What a rude train ! " she said, as she picked herself up.

The Owl Man was rather hot and bothered by the scene on the platform, and he hurried Mary along to their compartment, which was the last in the carriage. But Mary took one look and refused to go in. " I will not, I will not go in that box ! " she screamed.

It was the first time she had ever been really naughty, and he knew it was partly fright, but he felt the quickest way to bring her to her senses was to leave her alone, so he went into the compartment and said, " Very well— you can stay outside, all alone, till you can behave yourself," and he slammed the door.

Then he sat on the edge of his bunk and mopped his forehead and wished Mary were safely back in her pit.

The growls stopped directly he shut the door—only a succession of bumps went on outside, which was Mary falling down because she had not got her train legs yet. Presently even the bumps stopped, and at first the Owl Man was glad, and then he began to feel a little uneasy. You never could tell what Mary would think of doing next, and he wondered what she was up to.

He did not wonder long ! A piercing shriek sent him flying to the door, and as he opened it he heard something like this : " Fire ! Wild animals !—(shriek)—in my compartment—(shriek). Zoo ! (shriek). Fire ! (shriek)," and down the corridor came an old lady. Her grey hair streamed behind her, and she held a worsted petticoat high above her thin knees. With her mouth wide open she advanced on the Owl Man. " Zoo ! Fire ! Help ! " she screamed, as she flung herself into his arms. " Save me, oh, save me ! Zoo ! " The Owl Man held her up and patted her soothingly. " There, there," he said, " there, there, I beg that you will not distress yourself, Madam. I can assure you that the small bear is perfectly harmless. Mary, Mary," he called.

Mary emerged from a door at the other end of the corridor, and directly the old lady saw her she started screaming again, and hid behind the Owl Man.

Another door opened and a man's head popped out. " What is all this confounded noise ? " he asked.

" Save me ! Wild animal ! Help ! " shouted the old lady from behind the Owl Man. Turning his head, the man saw Mary approaching, and he banged the door to.

The others had now reached the farther end of the corridor, for as soon as Mary appeared the old lady had begun pulling the Owl Man backwards, and though she was not young, there was nothing old about her pull.

"Will you kindly let go of my coat?" said the Owl Man, who was getting rather annoyed. "It's ridiculous to make so much fuss over a small harmless bear—a perfectly friendly bear."

"I don't wish it to be friendly with me," panted the old lady.

By this time Mary was level with their compartment door. The Owl Man pointed at it and said, in a voice of thunder, "In you get, Mary, in double quick time, or you'll be sorry!" and Mary, with one look at his face, obeyed like a lamb.

The Owl Man closed the door, with the old lady still fastened on behind him like a tail. Then he shook himself free, and tried to be polite, because after all, Mary was his bear.

"Now, Madam, if you will permit me, I will accompany you back to your own compartment. I am more than sorry this should have happened."

Then he returned to his own compartment, and found Mary sitting on the edge of the bunk looking rather sheepish.

"Well, Mary Plain," he said, "I hope you are proud of yourself."

"Whatever was the matter with that old lady?" asked Mary. "I only thought it was your door, and when it wasn't, I said I was tired of being in the corridor, so could I sleep in her bed with her?"

The Owl Man, tired as he was, had to smile, but he quickly put on a stern face again and said, "Now, see

— *looking rather sheepish*

here, Mary Plain, you have given me a whole lot of trouble——"

"Was it a trouble when the old lady hugged you?" asked Mary in an interested voice. "I thought it was kind to hug."

"Don't interrupt me, please, Mary. As I was saying, you have given me a lot of trouble, and if this happens again, back you go to Berne by the next train—understand me?"

"I do," said Mary.

"Either you behave from now on, or home you go—*at once!*"

Mary stared at him.

"Are you angry?" she inquired. "Your face is all red."

"I should think it would be, and yes, I am angry—and it all depends on you how soon I stop being angry—see?"

Mary saw. Sometimes she could see quite well, and when she was told to get up into the top berth and go to sleep, she went without a word.

In the middle of the night the Owl Man was disturbed. He heard a movement and switched on the light, and there, in the air, were a pair of furry legs—kicking wildly. Mary was suspended from the strap of the upper berth.

"What in the world are you doing, Mary?" he asked.

"I want to get down because I'm thirsty," said Mary, "but I've lost my way. Where has the staircase gone to?"

The Owl Man helped her down and gave her a drink, and very soon all was quiet again.

Morning came, and together they had breakfast, and Mary had a whole thermos of milk to herself.

"Will that be the only night in the train?" she inquired, as they spun across Paris in a taxi.

"Yes, thank goodness!" said the Owl Man, and Mary could see from his face that he was glad.

CHAPTER TEN

WHICH IS STILL ABOUT THE JOURNEY

The Owl Man had taken seats in the "Golden Arrow" because fewer people travel by that train and he thought it would be less crowded.

The attendant showed them to two corner seats, and they were really quite private. Mary was very impressed by the chairs, and stroked them admiringly. The Owl Man explained about its being velvet, as he lifted her on to hers.

Mary felt very grand.

"Am I a hostess, then?" she asked.

The Owl Man smiled and said, "That's right, and I am the party."

"Are you all the party I've got?" said Mary, looking rather disappointed.

"I'm afraid so, you'll just have to make the best of me," said the Owl Man. "Now, look here, I'm just going to get a paper, so sit still till I come back, there's a good cub."

From her seat Mary could see all the way down the carriage, and just as the Owl Man disappeared, a lady came through the door at the farther end of the carriage. So there was some more party after all.

Mary slipped off her chair and went forward with paw outstretched.

" I'm so glad you've come," she said, " because the Owl Man doesn't make a very big party all by himself."

The lady was so surprised that she dropped one of the wraps she was carrying, and by the time she and Mary had both tried to pick it up, and had bumped their heads together and then said, " I beg your pardon," several other people had arrived. Mary was busily greeting them when the Owl Man came back. He saw Mary's chair was empty and his heart sank, and then he saw a little crowd at the other end of the saloon, and felt sure it was because of Mary.

He was quite right.

" And I made a pome and I have a bathing costume," she was saying, " and do sit down. There's lots of chairs and they're all blue velvet, and blue is my best colour, and then red and then yellow."

The Owl Man hurried up.

" I'm so sorry," he said apologetically, " I do hope she hasn't been a nuisance, but I just ran out to get a paper."

" Not at all," said a charming young lady in a very blue hat, " she's been most entertaining. It isn't often one has the chance to travel with a bear, you see."

" Thank heaven ! " said the Owl Man fervently.

" Is it tiring ? " asked the young lady aside.

The Owl Man didn't answer, but he just rolled his eyes up and the young lady seemed to understand at once what he meant.

" Now, come along, Mary Plain," he said, " you must come back to your corner now, and sit still. You know you aren't supposed to run about all over the carriage like this. I've only paid for those two chairs in the corner and that's all that belongs to us."

" But didn't you pay for this lady's seat ? " inquired Mary.

The Owl Man looked a little embarrassed and shook his head.

" Oh," said Mary, " and she's my party ! "

At this both the Owl Man and the young lady burst out laughing. Then the Owl Man took Mary firmly by the paw and led her back to their seats, and luckily lunch was brought in just then, so Mary was kept busy for some time because she said "Yes, please" to everything all the way through.

After the pudding, the Owl Man went into the passage to find a book he wanted which was in his suit-case, and when he came back he could hardly see Mary, for she was hidden behind a pile of things she'd said "Yes, please " to. There was a basket of fruit, cheese, biscuits, butter, a cup of coffee, liqueur, two large cigars, and several boxes of cigarettes and matches.

" Great heavens ! Mary Plain," exclaimed the Owl Man, " what in the world have you been doing ? "

" Just saying ' Yes, please,' " said Mary.

The Owl Man had to collect the attendant and explain

how difficult it was for Mary ever to say " No, thank
you ! " and the man was a kind man and understood
about bears, and said he would take the things all away
again, which he did.

And then Mary had a sleep. When she woke up she
found the lady in the blue hat had moved to a chair near
the Owl Man's and was talking to him in a low voice.

" And then I looked over the edge of the pit," she
was saying, " and there was a large bear lying on its
back, holding its toes and hanging its tongue out."

" Big Wool resting," said Mary, sitting up.

" Hallo, awake again ? " said the lady. " Big Wool
is a splendid name for a bear, I think : and then there
was a black one in a corner asleep, and a brown one
wandering about looking rather dull."

" Harrods was the asleep one," explained Mary, " and
Friska only looks happy when it's lesson time."

" Really ! She must be very clever."

" Yes," said Mary, " she teaches me. I can count up
to five," she added modestly.

The young lady opened her eyes wide. " Well, isn't
that marvellous ? " she said. " Now, I wonder if
you can tell me the name of the last bear in that pit.
He has a big ruff of fur round his neck, and he sits on a
branch of the tree and claps his paws."

" Bunch," said Mary, " waiting for carrots."

" Or sugar," said the Owl Man. Mary looked at
him.

" You always keep some special Bunch sugar in your
pocket, don't you ? " she said wistfully.

And then a lovely thing happened, for the Owl Man said, " Open your mouth and shut your eyes and you shall have a nice surprise," and when Mary had done both these things there were two lumps of sugar in her mouth. They all laughed, and then the lady continued.

" Afterwards I went to another pit, and there were two very, very old bears with not many teeth."

" Lady Grizzle and Alpha," said Mary respectfully ; " they are very old and clever and we only see them on St. Bruin's Day, so I don't know them well."

" That's most interesting," said the lady, and hoped Mary would tell her about St. Bruin's Day, but instead she said eagerly,

" And where did you go after ? "

" Well," said the lady slowly, " I went on a bit and then I came to another pit."

" Yes, yes," said Mary, beginning to wriggle in her chair. " Go on, go on ! "

" And in that pit there was one small bear having a bath, with a black coat."

" Little Wool," said Mary. " Go on, go on ! "

" And another brown one climbing the tree."

" Yes, yes," said Mary in an agony of expectation, " and go on ! "

" Let me see, *was* there another ? " said the lady, who was rather a tease.

Mary's face fell, and she sat quite still.

" Oh, of course," said the lady, " now I remember, there was a browny-grey bear with pointed ears, a little smaller than the others, who did the most beautiful jumps."

"Me, me," bounced Mary, "that was me!"

The young lady fell back in her chair. "You? You? But I don't believe you can jump!"

So then Mary had to get down off her chair to show her that she could, but unfortunately she had forgotten about the train, so she landed rather flat on her face. The Owl Man picked her up and gave her a rub, and the lady said she did hope it hadn't hurt much.

"Just my dinner place, a little," said Mary, stroking it.

"Do you think it's going to be rough?" the lady asked the Owl Man as she got up to go back to her own seat.

"Well, it's not very hopeful. The papers say 'sea rough to very rough.'"

"Isn't she a good sailor?"

"I trust so, but she's never crossed before. We must hope for the best!" He smiled and bowed as the young lady went off.

Calais was most exciting. They walked up a steep plank on to the boat and Mary could see all the water underneath.

"Is that the C?" she asked.

"That's right," said the Owl Man, holding her paw tightly.

When he got on board the first thing he did was to say, "Is Steward Saunders here?" Saunders was a great friend of his, whom he had known in the war, and he always looked after him very nicely. He found the

Owl Man two chairs in a good position on the upper deck and got them settled.

At first Mary walked about a bit. She peeped round the corner and then came back and said, " There's a very untidy gentleman round the corner."

It was a rough day, so the Owl Man knew at once what she meant, and said, " Yes, and it's very, very wrong to be untidy on the deck ; you must always go to the side of the ship."

Mary listened gravely. She played about for a few minutes and then she came running back to the Owl Man.

" I feel——" she began.

The Owl Man hurried her to the side of the boat.

" Am I going to be untidy ? " inquired Mary, much interested.

" That's a question you alone can answer," said the afflicted Owl Man, " but I sincerely trust not." They went on leaning over for a bit and nothing happened, so they went back to their seats.

Mary hummed a little song and then said, " I feel——" In a twinkling the Owl Man was back at the side of the boat with a sympathetic hand on her forehead.

" Why do you hold my head ? " asked Mary.

" Don't you like it ? " said the Owl Man.

" No," said Mary.

The Owl Man took his hand away. Mary gazed downwards.

" Does any one live in the C ? " she asked.

" Only fishes," said the Owl Man.

" And what are their names ? " asked Mary next.

" There are such heaps of different kinds," said the Owl Man. " There is sole, and trout, and hake, and salmon, and halibut, and cod, and——"

" Do cods wear bathing costumes ? " interrupted Mary.

The Owl Man chuckled. " No, you see, all fish wear slippery skins especially made for the water."

" Cods, too ? "

" Yes, all the same."

" I should like to meet a cod," said Mary.

Just then Saunders came up. " Getting on all right ? " he asked.

" Yes," said the Owl Man. " Had one or two frights, but nothing came of them. I think the great thing is to keep them interested talking and give them no time to think."

" That's right," said Saunders. " I've just got to

run down and see about some luggage in the hold. Shall I take her along and relieve you a bit ? "

" Thanks," said the Owl Man. " You'd like that, wouldn't you, Mary ? "

" Yes, please," said Mary.

But before they went down Saunders had to take a message, so Mary went with him and visited the Captain in his little glass box with his enormous wheel. He had a kind face, and when Mary told him she was quite used to driving the Owl Man's car he let her drive the boat for just five seconds, and that is probably the first and the last time that the *Canterbury* has ever been steered by a bear.

Then they went down a lot of stairs, and at last they got to a square place piled full of luggage. Near by was a huge heap of bags, and Saunders told Mary that every bag was full of letters going to England, and then he was called away and Mary was left alone.

She waited for a bit and then began climbing about the pile of bags, and then she got tired of waiting, so she curled up between the top bags and fell fast asleep.

And she didn't wake till she felt herself suddenly being violently upset. For a moment she was upside down, and then a bag slipped and she was right side up again—wedged between two bags of letters which were hugging her very tightly.

All around her and the bags was a huge net, and inside her was a queer rocky feeling.

At first she wondered if she was in a dream, and then she thought she must be flying, and when she looked over the edge her heart stood quite still, for it was true. She was flying—high, high up in the air, and far down below she could see the boat with little people moving about on it. Above her head was a huge iron kind of bird which held the net in its claws. In fact, Mary couldn't look up or down without hating it, so she closed her eyes very tightly instead and was glad of the affectionate bags.

Though it seemed simply ages to Mary, it was only a few seconds that they were up in the air, and then they began to drop, down, down, swinging backwards and forwards, as they went, a perfectly horrid feeling. And the end was the most alarming of all, for the net just opened itself, and out fell all the bags—and Mary.

Luckily she had been at the top, so a good many bags fell first and made a sort of mattress for her to fall on when her turn came.

As she picked herself up and stood up in the middle of the bags, several men who were standing round began rubbing their eyes. Could they be mad, or was that really a live bear standing there ?

Mary stared back and realised this must be England. One man with gold buttons down his jacket ran off and brought some more, and presently there were twelve gold-buttoned men all standing in a row and staring at Mary.

" God save the King ! " said Mary, saluting smartly.

All the men stood with their arms very stiff down at their sides and nobody spoke. There was a pause,

" English spoken," said Mary pleasantly.

The fattest man stepped forward at once and said, " That's a good thing, for now perhaps you'll be able to answer a few questions."

But to Mary it sounded like, " Thisaguthinfonopraps-yulbeabtoanserafuquesuns," because she could only understand Swiss.

She shook her head and said, " I am afraid I don't know those kind of words, but will you please find the Owl Man for me, because I want him."

And then it was the men's turn to shake their heads. And just when they were all trying to decide what to do, the Owl Man hurried up with Saunders after him. He looked quite white.

" Mary Plain ! " he exclaimed, " where in the name of thunder have you been ? "

" I haven't been in any name," said Mary, " I've been in with those bags, and not on purpose, neither."

" She must have gone to sleep among the mail," said Saunders. " Then, of course, she got swung over in the net along with the bags."

" I did," said Mary, " but I don't want to do it again, please."

" I bet you don't," said the Owl Man, who had gone pink again with relief at finding Mary. " Well, all's well that ends well. Come on, Mary, hang on to me and don't let go for one single second."

The twelve buttoned men were still standing in a row staring, and still wondering if it were all a dream.

The Owl Man and Mary went into a long place with benches and more men with gold buttons standing behind them.   One of them asked the Owl Man if he had anything to declare.

" Only this bear," he said, pointing at Mary.

The man looked rather agitated, and had to go and talk to several other officers, and then he came back, had another stare at Mary, and said,

" That will be sevenpence halfpenny, please, sir."

" God save the King ! " said Mary.

This time they got into another train, and this time there were red velvet seats, and there was hot buttered toast to eat.   The toast was extra buttery, and so was Mary when she had finished, because her chest stuck out a good deal and was very inviting to butter.   The Owl Man had to use a whole handkerchief getting her clean.

" Will it be long now ? " she asked him.

" Long before we arrive, do you mean ? "   Mary nodded.

" No, only another hour," said the Owl Man.   Mary sighed happily.

" I feel———" she began.

" No you don't—nonsense, Mary ! " interrupted the Owl Man quickly.

" But I *do* feel glad I've come," said Mary, getting it out at last.   The Owl Man groaned.

" Is that what you've been trying to say ever since we left Calais, Mary Plain ? " he asked.

" Yes," said Mary, " but you never let me finish, did you ? "

CHAPTER ELEVEN

WHICH A BUS STARTS, AND THE KING ENDS

MARY had an excellent night. She slept in a tiny empty room opening out of the Owl Man's, in the small flat which was his home.

Next morning he said that he thought the first thing to do was for Mary to have a swim, as she was a bit grimy after the journey and she must be looking her very best for the show next day.

The Owl Man decided to go by bus, as his car had not yet arrived, so they went and stood at the corner of Baker Street for a No. 30 to come along.

When the bus drew up there was a slight difficulty about getting on, as the conductor said Mary didn't come under the heading of " small dogs under proper control." This was quite true, but Mary had her collar on, and, as the Owl Man pointed out, though she wasn't a dog she was certainly under proper control, and she was perfectly accustomed to travelling in trams and trains.

" But not in a bus," said Mary excitedly. But the Owl Man coughed very loudly, so luckily no one heard her.

" Orl right," said the conductor at last, " take 'er up aloft, but if there's any complaints, mind, off you gets."

So the Owl Man pushed Mary in front of him up the stairs. Upstairs Mary and the Owl Man were in the front seat, and Mary was enjoying it very much.

" Aren't I tall ? " she said, looking over the side. " Why, look at all those hats walking about ! " The Owl Man explained that it was because she was so high up, and that underneath the hats were the people that wore them.

No one seemed to object to Mary except one elderly gentleman who made a clicking noise with his teeth and murmured, " The Zoo is the Zoo—but bears on buses ! (Click, click.) "

The Owl Man and Mary changed buses at Hyde Park Corner, and a No. 9 took them to Prince's Gate, and from there they walked across the park to the bathing place.

Here a new difficulty arose. Mixed bathing was allowed at certain hours, but just now it was divided up into " Ladies " and " Gentlemen," and the man in charge was not sure which heading bears would come under. He decided to take no risks, and he went indoors and fetched a small board and on it he wrote, " Bears only," and stuck it in the water a little beyond the ladies' part.

There was rather a fuss when Mary realised she had forgotten her bathing costume, but the Owl Man told her bears were not allowed to wear them in England *ever*, so Mary was pacified.

All the ladies were very excited about seeing a bear bathe, but they were also glad there was a rope dividing Mary's section from theirs, and they stayed well on their own side of it and watched.

Now, being watched always went to Mary's head, and, finding a kind of bar between two poles close to the rope, she climbed up on it and did some excellent dives. The ladies clapped and shouted and Mary felt no end of a success, and did more dives. Finally she got so excited that she forgot to remember which direction to swim in under the water, and she came up right in the middle of a bunch of ladies, giving one of them a severe butt with her head.

" Ladies only ! " shrieked the outraged female, and all the others started screaming and shouting too. One of them sank with fright and had to be rescued by the attendant, and the Owl Man said Mary must stop bathing and come out at once.

So Mary plunged out, and she and the Owl Man walked home across the park, and Mary shook herself and rolled on the grass to get dry and ran races with herself and always won.

They passed one place where several people were standing and staring into a garden.

" What are they looking at ? " inquired Mary, and the Owl Man told her that was where the third greatest lady in the land lived, and that she was the King's grand-daughter.

" Like me and Big Wool ? " said Mary.

" That's right," said the Owl Man.

Mary ran loose in the park, but directly they got to the gates the Owl Man put her lead on again, as he did not want to risk mislaying her. The traffic was very bad at Marble Arch ; Mary did not at all like crossing the street, and several times the Owl Man had almost to drag her on. He was quite breathless when they got to the other side.

" You mustn't pull like that, Mary Plain," he said, " you'll have us under one of those buses if you're not careful."

" I don't like it," said Mary. " All the motors and buses are running after me and trying to catch me, and I don't like it."

" Well, this afternoon we'll go and collect my car, and then, thank goodness, there will be no need to go out in anything else," said the Owl Man.

After lunch and a rest they set out again, this time by Tube. Tubes are very hot places, and the Owl Man noticed that Mary got quieter and quieter, so when she said, " Do you think the twins are happy without me ? " he got out at the next station, which was Oxford Circus.

Once out of the Tube, Mary forgot all about the twins. They walked down Regent Street towards Charing Cross, and Mary stopped to look in nearly all the shop windows. One shop had a stuffed bear in it, and Mary tried to talk to it, but she didn't know about windows so she walked straight up against the glass and got a bad bump. The Owl Man explained that though you could see through glass you couldn't walk through, and also that the little brown bear couldn't talk because he was a dead little bear.

"But he looked at me, and I *think* he winked," said Mary.

The Owl Man said, "Come on now, Mary," and pulled, but Mary stood with all four legs braced and refused to budge.

The Owl Man knew the only thing to do was to draw her attention away, so he said in an excited voice, "Why, I do believe that's the Fur-Coat-Lady," and, though he knew quite well she was in Switzerland, he dashed down the street dragging Mary with him.

And Mary was so delighted at the thought of seeing her dear Fur-Coat-Lady that she ran too. Safely out of sight of the bear the Owl Man stopped running, and said he was afraid he had made a mistake, and it wasn't her after all.

"Then can I go back and see the little bear again?" said Mary, beginning to stiffen her legs again, but the

Owl Man said, " No, we'll go in here and get some tea. Wouldn't you like a cream bun ? " And Mary unbraced at once and followed him in obediently.

In this shop she met meringues for the first time. She couldn't quite decide whether she liked éclairs or meringues best, so she had to have first one and then the other to make sure, and by the time she finally decided on meringues she had eaten twelve éclairs and thirteen meringues.

They then continued their walk, and when they got to Trafalgar Square Mary was very interested in the lions when they passed them.

" They are put there to guard Lord Nelson—that man who is standing on the top of the pole," explained the Owl Man.

" Is he pretending to be a bird ? " asked Mary. " And isn't he very lonely all alone up there ? "

" I never thought about it," said the Owl Man.

" I'll just run up and ask him, shall I ? " said Mary, making for the column, but luckily her lead was on, so the Owl Man pulled her back and said she would be arrested if she started climbing public monuments in London.

" What does 'arrested' mean ? " said Mary.

" It means that big blue gentleman with the helmet would come along and take you off with him."

Mary stared hard at the policeman standing close to the column.

" Isn't he kind then ? His gloves are very white," she said.

" I'm sure he'd be kind—policemen always are," said the Owl Man, " but when you break the law——"

" But I shouldn't break it, climbing it," interrupted Mary, " it's made of stone."

" Breaking the law means doing things you are forbidden to," explained the Owl Man. " And when you do that you get popped into prison."

" Isn't it a nice place ? "

" Well, I don't fancy you'd enjoy it much."

" Wouldn't there be no figs, or cream buns, or milk, or meringues ? "

" None, only bread and water," said the Owl Man.

" Then I shan't go," decided Mary, and gave up all idea of swarming up the Nelson column.

It took some time to collect the car at the station, and when at last they got away they were held up by a traffic block just outside. The Owl Man stood up because he heard some shouting, and then he saw that at the corner of the street a crowd of people were cheering and waving.

" By Jove," he said, " it's the King ! Up you hop, Mary," and he held her up on the side of the car, so she could see right over all the cars in front.

" God save the King ! " shouted Mary, and just as she spoke the King, who was bowing from left to right, did a left bow in Mary's direction.

" I called ' God save the King ' and he heard me," she said happily.

" How do you know ? " asked the Owl Man.

" Because he bowed a ' thank you ' at me," said Mary. So there was no doubt about it. He had.

CHAPTER TWELVE

THE SHOW

As the show was to open at twelve and all competitors were requested to be at the Crystal Palace by eleven o'clock, the Owl Man and Mary set off in good time.

She was looking in excellent condition, with her coat thoroughly brushed. The Owl Man had given her a tin of biscuits to take, in case there was any difficulty about her dinner. The biscuits made a rattly noise when Mary shook the tin, and the rattle made her wonder very much indeed what kind of biscuits they were.

As Mary had never been exhibited before, the Owl Man thought he had better explain about her being put in a cage.

" I would like to stop outside with you, thank you," said Mary firmly.

" But you can't do that, Mary Plain," said the Owl Man. " Why, you've come half across Europe for this show, and one of the rules is that all competitors have to be in a cage. Who knows? You might win a rosette!"

"What is that?" said Mary, who liked winning things.

"Well, some very important gentlemen go round and they have three little knots of coloured ribbons— white, green, and blue; and when they have decided which is the very best animal shown, they give it the white ribbon to wear; the next best gets the green, and the last best, the blue ribbon," explained the Owl Man.

The Crystal Palace loomed up above them as they climbed the last hill.

"Is that my cage?" asked Mary.

"No, that's the Crystal Palace. It's all made of glass, and inside is where the show is to take place," said the Owl Man.

They drew up at an entrance labelled *Competitors Only*, and the Owl Man helped Mary out. They walked through a gate and down a passage, and then the Owl Man noticed that Mary had not got the biscuit tin.

"Why, Mary," he exclaimed, "you've forgotten your biscuits!"

"Oh, no, I haven't," said Mary.

"But where's the box?"

"I didn't like the rattle the biscuits made," said Mary.

"How absurd!"

"So I stopped it," said Mary.

"Well, you'll be sorry not to have them when lunch time comes."

" But I couldn't eat them twice, could I? " said Mary.

" Oh, Mary, Mary! " said the Owl Man.

Then they were stopped by a man who sat behind a table and worked a turnstile.

" Is this a competitor? " he asked.

" Yes," said the Owl Man. So he handed them a beautiful pink ticket and they went clicking through the gate.

A tall thin man with a sad face was telling the different people where to go, but it was rather a muddle, because so many would ask him all at once.

A lady with a large flop-eared rabbit tucked under each arm was begging to know where she could put them down quickly, because they were so heavy ; while another very old lady, holding a cage with a parrot in it, clung to his arm.

" Would you be so very kind as to tell me where place Twenty-Seven is, please? "

" Please a poll—please a poll," said the parrot.

And before the man could answer up came some one else leading a young seal who didn't care about shows and was saying so in a very loud voice.

Mary drew close to the Owl Man. " Why does it make that rude noise ? " she asked, and the Owl Man, shouting very loudly so as to be heard above the parrot and the seal, said, " I can't think, Mary, but I wish he wouldn't."

" My poor Philip, so tired ! " said the owner of the parrot, " and I should like the poor dear to have a quiet sleep before the judge comes round."

" Good-morning, all ! " said Philip brightly.

" Honk," roared the seal, who was called Bertha.

" Shut up, Bertha ! " said its owner.

At last they all got sent off in the right directions, and then the Owl Man got a chance to ask where number Nineteen was.

" You come along with me," said the sad man in a gloomy voice, " I'll show you," and he led them to a corner where two big cages stood.

Mary did not like the look of the cage one bit, but the Owl Man talked to her very sensibly, and at last she consented to go inside.

The door was locked, and Mary stood close to the bars and said to the Owl Man, " Do you think the twins are happy without me ? "

But the Owl Man had been prepared for this to happen, and almost before Mary had finished asking he had popped a caramel into her mouth.

After the third caramel Mary felt quite resigned to the cage and began to look around her.

On one side was a small enclosure and inside was a zebra. Mary was very interested about the stripes and wanted to know if they came off in the bath.

And on the other side was, funnily enough, another bear.

He belonged to a man who took him round to country shows, where he begged for buns, and he was getting old and a bit stiff in the joints. He reminded Mary a little bit of Harrods, only his eyes were not quite so squinty as hers.

"Good-morning, bear," said Mary conversationally.

The old bear had a look at her and then sniffed and looked away again.

"I'm a bear too," said Mary.

The old one sniffed again.

"A Swiss bear," added Mary, and when she said that, the old fellow turned round and stared.

"My brother-in-law was Swiss," he said; "did you know him?"

"Was her name Harrods?" asked Mary, thinking of the likeness.

"My brother-in-law was not a she," said the bear; "*he* was called Hoodwink."

"No, I don't know him at all," said Mary. "Could he wink?"

The old bear turned an outraged back.

"Do you know what his name is?" Mary asked the Owl Man, and he told her it was Albert.

" How did you guess ? " said Mary.

" Because he's got a notice fastened on to his cage which says, ' Albert, Performing Bear ; Owner, Alf Jones.' "

" Have I got a notice too ? " said Mary.

" Yes ; yours says, ' Mary Plain, from the famous bear pits at Berne, shown by Mr Owl Man.' " Mary felt very proud of having a printed notice about herself, and asked if she could take it home with her after the show.

" Bunch hasn't got a notice about him, has he ? " she said.

" No, he hasn't."

" And he hasn't been to a show, has he ? "

" No, he hasn't."

" And he hasn't won a blue prize, has he ? "

" No, he hasn't—nor have you, Mary Plain," said the Owl Man, who thought Mary needed taking down a peg.

People were beginning to come round, looking at all the animals. When they saw, " Albert, Performing Bear," written up they all stood there to watch him perform.

And whatever Albert did Mary did a little better next door.

Presently, all the people that had been looking at Albert were standing outside Mary's cage, and laughing at her, and Albert was left quite alone, except for Alf Jones, who leaned against the cage and looked very glum.

You could see the judges getting nearer and nearer,

and the Owl Man wished they would hurry up and see Mary at her best.

Then a terrible thing happened.

Mary got hiccoughs. She stood quite still. " What is it ? " she asked, and the Owl Man told her they were hiccoughs and she must hold her breath.

" I'll—*hic*—try," said Mary, and she held it tight until her eyes began to bulge, and then she was sure it was cured, and she took a long breath to stop herself from bursting.

" They've gone ! " she said.

" Hurrah ! " said the Owl Man, much relieved.

" Yes, hur-*hic*," said Mary.

" Dear, oh dear ! " said the harassed Owl Man, " what terribly bad luck ! Can't you think of anything that would stop them, Mary ? "

" Shall I try a cara—*hic* ? " suggested Mary.

But that was no good ; she nearly choked. The Owl Man looked at the judges ; they had only to look at some guinea pigs and Albert before they arrived at Mary. He ground his teeth. It would be too much to bear if Mary said " God save the *Hic* " to the judge.

" Try making her jump," suggested an onlooker ; " give her a fright." So the Owl Man got down on his hands and knees, and then bounced up suddenly and said, " BOO ! " But Mary only said, " Aren't you feeling very well, Owl Man ? "

Then the Owl Man remembered about water being a good thing, and several people ran to get a glass of water, and all of them told Mary which was the best way to swallow it. And when she had tried all the ways she put the glass down and stood very still in the middle of the cage, wearing that questioning look that means, " Have they gone ? "

All the people stood as still as still—you could have heard a pin drop.

At last the Owl Man said, " Gone ? " and his voice was full of hope.

" *Hic !* " answered Mary. Every one groaned.

The judge was now on his way to Albert, and it seemed certain that Mary's chances were finished, when, after all, she got cured by a fright.

Bertha had wandered along till she was just opposite Mary's cage, and suddenly she found she could not see her master anywhere and made the noise that seals only make when they are lost. Mary nearly jumped out of her skin, and did jump right out of her hiccoughs.

Then the judges came, and Mary showed off beautifully, jumping, marching, dancing, and winking with the greatest skill, and the judges were delighted with her.

They asked a good many questions, and the Owl Man said a lot of kind things about her, and Mary pretended not to hear.

Then the head one said, " We have unanimously agreed that this young bear shall be awarded first prize."

And all the crowd cheered and clapped, and the Owl Man said, " Well done, Mary Plain ! " and Mary got over-excited and said, " Well done me ! "

Then the judge said, " I should like to pin the rosette

on myself," and the Owl Man said, " Certainly, sir," and unfastened the door.

Mary got out and came up to the judge, and he said, " Mary Plain, it gives me much pleasure to award you the first prize," and Mary saluted and said, " God save the King," which delighted the judge. He shook her warmly by the paw, and the crowd sang, " For she's a jolly good fellow."

Of course the prize couldn't be pinned on to Mary, because there was nothing but Mary herself to pin it to, so they tied it round her neck on a piece of string, and Mary was very proud and pleased.

Now, it is very nice for the person who wins a prize, but it is never such fun for the ones who don't.

Bertha said, " Honk, honk, honk-honk-honk," which meant that she had already said that she didn't like shows ; she had turned herself inside out and upside down doing tricks for the benefit of the judges, and she had not even won a blue ribbon. So this settled it— no more shows for her.

" Have you been to many ? " said Mary.

" Seven," said Bertha.

" But why aren't you wearing the rosettes you won ? " asked Mary.

" I—er—I—er—haven't got them with me," said Bertha hurriedly.

Meanwhile the parrot's cage had been covered with a green baize cloth. Philip had not even won the second prize, though, of course, he undoubtedly deserved the first. " Judging is not what it used to be," said the owner as she bent over the cage.

"Happy Poll, happy Poll," said Philip from under the baize, so his mother thought it was time to go home.

Only Albert was left. Alf Jones was heard to say something rude about " little foreign upstarts butting in."

" Am I a upstart ? " Mary asked the Owl Man.

" Certainly not ! " he said indignantly. " It's pure jealousy."

" And I don't butt, do I ? " said Mary.

" Certainly not," said the Owl Man again, and he led Mary off to find the car.

Half-way home Mary said, " Bunch didn't have a notice about him, did he ? "

" No, he didn't," said the Owl Man.

" But I did, didn't I ? "

" You did," said the Owl Man.

" Bunch didn't win a white rosette, did he ? "

" No, he didn't," said the Owl Man.

" But I did, didn't I ? "

" You did," said the Owl Man humbly.

" So there ! " said Mary Plain.

The Owl Man felt certain that he ought to take Mary down another peg, but when he turned to do it and saw her sitting beside him, with the rosette sitting on the very stuck-outest part of her chest, he just couldn't.

CHAPTER THIRTEEN

MARY SVISITS THE ZOO

" I THINK we'll go to the Zoo to-day," said the Owl
Man next morning ; " it will be our only chance, because
we start back to-morrow."

" And what kind of a place is that ? " asked Mary.

" Well, lots and lots of different kinds of animals live
there, collected from all over the world."

" Any Swiss bears ? " asked Mary.

" I don't know about Swiss ones, but there are bears
there all right," said the Owl Man. " Now, I'll go and
ring up the garage and tell them to send the car round."

When the Owl Man came back from the telephone
Mary was standing in the hall.

" I'm ready," she announced.

" I should jolly well think you are," said the Owl Man.
For Mary wore her white rosette perched on top of her
head with the string knotted under her chin, and the

placard with her name on it was round her neck. The string of this was rather short, and the cardboard stuck out like a little shelf over her chest.

The Owl Man rubbed his chin. " Why have you got those—er—decorations on, Mary ? "

" Because if I don't wear them no one will know that I'm a first prize bear," said Mary.

This was perfectly right. " That's true," said the Owl Man slowly, " but all the same I think I should take them off if I were you, Mary Plain. You see, after all, most of the animals there haven't had a chance to go to a show and win a prize, and it might make them feel rather badly to see you wearing a rosette."

Mary sighed, and took it off slowly. " If only I had my bathing costume," she said.

" Come on now," said the Owl Man briskly. " Once you get there you'll be so busy seeing and talking to all the different animals that you won't have time to miss your rosette or anything else," and he bundled Mary into the car before she could think of something more to wear.

The Zoo was terrifically exciting, and Mary's head whirled.

They went first to the monkey house, and Mary said she didn't like their old faces and the rude way they scratched themselves all the time.

Then they went on past the penguins, and Mary liked them a lot. They came hurrying towards them, holding up their black knickers like penguins always do.

One penguin, who wore a very smart tan and coloured

scarf, was standing beside a very small black and white penguin, and he was buffing him over the head with his wings.

"Why do you do that?" asked Mary.

"Because he doesn't want to be adopted," said the penguin, going on buffing.

"But must he be?" said Mary.

The penguin stopped and stared at Mary. "But, of course," he said. "His mother and father are both dead, and therefore he must be adopted, and I am going on buffing him till he wants to be."

Mary and the Owl Man moved on, Mary hoping very much that the small penguin would soon be willing.

They climbed a lot of steps, and there they were at the Mappin Terraces.

"You'll find some friends here, Mary," said the Owl Man. "This is where the bears live."

Mary stared at the two bears who were lying on the edge of the big space which separated them from the railing.

"They're a long way off, aren't they?" she said. And she shouted, "I've come a long way to see you, half in a train and half in a boat and half in a net."

"You can't be three halves, Mary," murmured the Owl Man.

"I *can* be," said Mary, "because I was."

Then one of the bears yawned, and Mary, encouraged by this sign, shouted, "What are your names?"

The yawny bear said, "We are called Brownie and Doris, and we are neither of us deaf."

" I have got two names," said Mary ; " would you like to guess what they are ? "

" No," said Brownie, " but perhaps the twins next door might like to know them."

" The twins ? " shrieked Mary, rushing to the next division.

" But it isn't," she said flatly, as she saw two large elderly bears lying asleep.

" Why, you didn't think he meant Marionetta and Little Wool, did you, Mary ? " said the Owl Man.

" But, of course ! " said Mary ; " he said the twins."

" But twins can happen more than once," said the Owl Man.

" I wish they hadn't happened here," said Mary, who was bitterly disappointed.

They moved on to the next lot. Of the three bears living here, the most interesting was " Tarpot " Nellie, who was called this because she had fallen into a pot of tar when she was a baby.

" I should have chosen a pot of jam if it had been me," said Mary as they went on to the Polar bears.

" What smart white bears ! " she exclaimed. " Have they had so many baths that they've come white ? "

The Owl Man laughed and said no, it was because they were a special sort of bear who lived in a country of ice and snow.

The keeper was standing near by, and he came up and told them about the Polars. They were called Babs and Sam and Elisabeth. He said they got fed

They went on to the Polar Bears

three times a day with raw meat and were very intelligent and clever, and if they would wait a minute he would run and fetch some meat and show them how they did their tricks.

He went off, and while he was gone Mary chatted to Elisabeth. At least, it wasn't quite chatting, because Elisabeth wouldn't answer. Mary asked her five times, each time a little louder, whether she liked being called Elisabeth, and she just took no notice at all.

" She must be deaf too," said Mary, giving it up, and just then the keeper came back.

" If you will step up here," he said, " you'll get a better view." And they went up some steps and on to a tiny platform, and the man had to lock the gate behind them, because lots of little boys tried to come on to it too. " Get off! You know you're not allowed here," he said roughly.

" Only us," said Mary, from the right side of the railings.

" Now, come on Babs," shouted the keeper, and he threw a large bit of raw meat into the water, and Babs dived in—a graceful, " leaving-one-foot-behind " kind of dive—and before the meat had reached the bottom she had caught it. Then the man shouted, " Now, Sam ! " Sam stood up and saluted.

" And how about Elisabeth ? " asked the Owl Man, and the keeper laughed and said he was afraid Elisabeth was a slow old thing and not up to tricks.

Next they visited the seals. One large black fellow was asleep on a rock, looking like a huge patent leather hand-bag stuffed full of things. But his wife, who was brown, was not sleepy, and she began making hungry noises close beside him and woke him up. He had long black whiskers, and he started honking like a motor horn, and they made a fearsome duet. So Mary and the Owl Man crossed over to the ostrich, who lived just opposite. It had its head buried in the sandy pebbles and looked very foolish.

" What is it doing ? " asked Mary.

" Hiding," said the Owl Man.

" But it's still there."

" Yes, I know, but ostriches are always like that; when they hide their heads they think the rest of them is hidden too."

" Shall I tell him he isn't ? " asked Mary.

" I don't think I should bother," said the Owl Man.

Next came the Lion House, and it was feeding time, and everyone who has been in the Lion House at feeding time knows what that means.

But Mary did not know, and she held the Owl Man's hand very tight, and was glad of the bars.

Next they visited Simba.

Simba had just been fed, and looked the picture of a very fine and extremely full lion. He was lying by the bars and licking his lips. There was a keeper near by, and as the Owl Man went over to talk to him Mary asked if she might go and have a little chat with Simba.

" Certainly," said the Owl Man, and slipped off her lead.

Mary approached the huge lion rather timidly, for the lion is the king of all beasts.

" Good-Morning, Sir," she said respectfully.

Simba turned his head slowly. " Good-morning," he said, " who are you ? "

" I am Mary Plain, an unusual first prize Swiss bear from the pits at Berne, and I am nearly one," said Mary, and hoped she had impressed His Majesty.

" You seem to be a good many things," said Simba good-humouredly.

" Yes," said Mary, " I have been unusual for a long time, but I have only been first class since yesterday— at the Show." She hoped very much that Simba would ask her about the Show, so she could tell him she had won a rosette, but Simba, it seemed, was not interested in shows.

" I have travelled a lot too," said Mary, " in a tram, and a motor, and a train, and a ship and—and—a net."

Simba's ears cocked slowly. Everything he did was slow and majestic.

" I have travelled too," he said.

" Oh, do tell me," begged Mary.

" Well it was a long while ago now," said Simba. " I belonged to a kind lady who brought me in a big ship to this country—England, I think it is called——"

" English spoken," said Mary, who was in a very showing-off mood.

Simba, however, did not speak English, and only said, " I would rather you did not interrupt me, please."

Mary stopped feeling showy-off and felt a very small bear indeed.

"I lived in a garden for a bit," went on Simba, "and then, one day, the lady brought me here, and here I have been ever since," he finished sadly. "For though she came to see me at first, she has not been for a long time now, and I think she has forgotten me."

Mary felt suddenly sick. The lady had brought Simba here—the Owl Man had brought her here, and he was talking to the keeper too. She sidled up to him and jerked his arm. The Owl Man looked down and saw that she was trembling.

"Why, Mary," he said, "whatever is the matter?"

"I don't think the twins are happy without me," she said in a wobbly voice, "and I want to go home at once —now, please, this very minute!"

The Owl Man looked very astonished and said she really must tell him why she felt like that.

"Simba," said Mary with a gulp. "He came with his kind lady, and she left him behind all alone, and he's been in that cage ever since."

The Owl Man saw at once what Mary was afraid of.

"Perhaps," he said, "but Simba wasn't just a visitor, was he? You run across and ask him." So Mary went back to Simba.

"Were you a svisitor?" she asked.

"What is that?" asked Simba in a surprised voice.

"It's what you are on a svisit—a stop or a—or a go-to," explained Mary.

"No," said Simba, "I've always been a lion."

Mary heaved a sigh of relief, and at that moment the Owl Man came up.

"Well, Mary Plain," he said kindly, "feeling happy again? I know just exactly what you were thinking of, you know."

"But you wouldn't, would you?" said Mary.

"Rather not," said the Owl Man. "Let's go and see the elephants."

On their way they passed the ostrich, still with its head sticking into the pebbles. Mary felt sorrier than ever about it. Then they went down under a bridge and up the other side, and there were the elephants.

Each elephant had its name written up over it, and the Owl Man read them out. Ranee and Heera Cully both took children out for rides, and there was a huge red saddle hanging from the ceiling, opposite Heera Cully's stall. He shot out his long trunk and blew at Mary, and she backed away.

"What is that he's blowing at me with?" she asked.

The Owl Man told her it was his trunk, and how it was like an extra paw to an elephant, and how he lifted his food up to his mouth with it.

"He wouldn't lift me, would he?" said Mary anxiously.

"Not he. You give him this bun and see him eat it."

Then Mary made a very long arm so as not to be too near and gave Heera Cully a bun, and he twisted up his trunk and popped it into his mouth, and it was very funny.

But all the time they were seeing the elephants, Mary was worrying about the ostrich. It did seem so sad he should think he was hidden when all the time he was there. If only some one would tell him about it he could be more careful.

The Owl Man began chatting to the attendant, and Mary edged nearer and nearer to the door, and the next minute she was galloping down the wide path that goes under the bridge on her way back to the ostrich.

But somehow she must have taken the wrong turning for when she got to the place where she was sure the ostrich was, there was only a buffalo.

" Could you tell me where the ostrich lives ? " she asked in a panty voice, for she was rather out of breath.

" What does it look like ? " said the buffalo.

" Well, it's made of heaps of curly feathers, and it's fond of hide-and-seek," said Mary. The buffalo shook his head.

" There's a wolf over there who is particularly fond of cheese," he said, but that was no help at all, so Mary set off on her hunt again.

How it happened it is difficult to know, but one small boy saw Mary and gave the alarm, " A little bear has got loose." And from all directions people came running towards Mary shouting, " Send for the keeper —try and stop it—catch it—hasn't any one got a rope ? "

Mary took fright and made off round a corner, and the faster she ran the faster the people ran after her. And the crowd got bigger and bigger, and half the people ran because the other people were running and had no idea what they were running after.

" What is it ? " gasped one pursuer, and another shouted, " A little bear has got loose," and then another said, " A big bear has got loose," and then it changed to " A dangerous bear has got loose," and by the time Mary swung round a corner by the sea-lion pond a hundred and fifty people were all screaming, " Beware of the man-eating bear ! "

By this time Mary was thoroughly frightened, and when she saw a keeper with a rope in his hand trying to cut her off from the side, she made a final dash for safety and swarmed up a telegraph pole.

There she sat in perfect security and looked down at her chasers, all clamouring at the bottom of the pole.

" If only you'd been a bit more nippy with that rope, Jack," said one keeper.

" Nippy yourself," said Jack crossly. He had run half a mile as fast as he could after Mary, and it was a hot day.

" She'll never come down now," said another keeper, called Fred, " she's taken fright."

" Till she's hungry," added Jack. And he was quite right.

Sitting up there Mary was safe ; but she was also empty, and though, when you have been chased, safety is a delicious feeling—emptiness is not.

Mary began to wriggle. She longed for the Owl Man and searched for a kind face among the crowd below.

Picking out a young man with a freckled nose who

was standing close to the pole, she said, with a choke, "Do you think the twins are happy without me?" But, alas! the man was no Swiss scholar, so he couldn't answer.

"What would you do if she came down?" asked Jack.

"Take her to the Lost Property Office. She doesn't belong to us; that's all we could do," said Fred.

Mary stared round miserably. "Could somebody fetch the Owl Man?" she pleaded, but nobody understood, so Mary hung on to the pole and went on being hungry.

"Tell you what, Jack," said Fred, "let's get all this crowd away and then put a plate of meat down at the bottom. I bet she'd come down after it and then we could rope her in a jiffy."

And Fred was right. When the crowd had been sent away they put a tempting dish just at the foot of the pole, and Mary sniffed and came, very nervously, a little way down. Then she took fright and scrambled up again, but soon the smell was too strong for her, and she slid down; this time nearer to the ground, and that meant nearer to the smell, and when she actually saw the lovely bits of meat with tips of carrots among it, she gave up all idea of "Safety first," and slid the rest of the way down.

Almost before she touched the earth she was neatly lassoed, and within a few minutes she was standing among a lot of umbrellas and hand-bags in the Lost

Property Office, while several hot keepers stood near by and mopped their faces.

They had been very kind and given her the meat to eat as soon as she was safely in the Lost Property Office, and Mary tucked into it busily.

Suddenly there came the sound of running footsteps, and one of the keepers went to the door. "Some one in a hurry," he said.

Outside was the poor Owl Man, so exceedingly red in the face that the keeper felt quite sorry for him. "Lost something, sir?" he asked kindly. "A bear," gasped the Owl Man. "A small bear. Seen her anywhere?"

"Yes, he has, I'm here," yelled Mary from among the umbrellas.

So the Owl Man went in, and they brought him a chair to sit on, and he sat and patted Mary and panted, and it was quite a little time before he could speak again,

Then Mary told him all about what had happened, and the Owl Man said that ended it once for all ; she should wear her collar and lead and be padlocked on to his wrist till they got back to Berne.

"But I felt so sorry about the ostrich," protested Mary.

"I'm the person you ought to feel sorry about," said the still-out-of-breath Owl Man, and he looked so red that Mary really did pity him.

When he had cooled off, and had a drink they went and found the car and drove home, and Mary was very quiet on the way. This was so unusual that the Owl Man asked her what she was thinking about.

"I'm thinking I'm very glad I haven't got a luggage like that elephant," said Mary. "I like paws best."

CHAPTER FOURTEEN

HOW BERNE WELCOMED MARY HOME

MARY set to work very seriously over her packing next morning, but even she couldn't take very long over one brush and one bowl, so she wandered in to help the Owl Man do his. But after she had packed a bottle of hair lotion among his shirts without a cork, the Owl Man said he thought perhaps he'd better do his own packing, and she could sit and talk to him while he did it.

So he put Mary on top of a chest of drawers safely out of the way, and she drummed her paws on the chest and decided, very kindly, to sing him a song, so he shouldn't be dull.

" I shall sing you a song," she announced.

" That will be delightful," said the Owl Man.

" It's a song about bears," said Mary.

" No, really ? " said the Owl Man.   Mary nodded.

" And it's *most* exciting," she said.

" As long as it doesn't distract me from my packing," said the Owl Man.

" Now," said Mary, and began.

But first she began too high and then she began too low, and then it took her some time to find the note she wanted in between.   But once she found it she wasn't going to risk losing it again, so she sang all the song on it, and this was the song she sang.

> " Once there was a bear called Alpha.
> Once there was a bear called Lady Grizzle.
> Once there was a bear called Harrods.
> Once there was a bear called Bunch.
> Once there was a bear called Big Wool.
> Once there was a bear called Friska.
> Once there was a bear called Little Wool.
> Once there was a bear called Marionetta."

Here she broke off for a second because she wanted to ask the Owl Man a question ; but because of her fear of losing the note she sang it at him all on the same notes.

> " Aren't you getting very excited ? " she sang.
> " Ter—ri—bly," sang back the Owl Man.
> " There's only the last verse left," sang Mary.
> " And once there was a bear called MARY
>   PLAIN."

" A—men," chanted the Owl Man.

" What men ? " said Mary, looking round.

"Nothing," said the Owl Man, "No men at all.   I like your song immensely, Mary Plain."

"Shall I sing it again?"

"Well, perhaps another time," said the Owl Man hurriedly.   "I tell you what, I've never shown you your presents to take back to the other bears, have I?"

"Me? Presents? Mine?" said Mary, and in her excitement she fell off the chest with a whack.

The Owl Man picked her up and took her into a room where there were eight brightly-coloured bowls all standing in a row on the floor.

They were really the loveliest bowls, and Mary danced up and down when she saw them.   Every bowl had its name on it, beginning with Big Wool on the biggest and so on down to the two smallest.   Mary examined each one and the Owl Man read her out the names.   When she got to the small ones, she said, "But who are these for?"

"For the aunts," said the Owl Man.

"And what are their names?" inquired Mary.

"Forget-me-not and Plum," said the Owl Man.

"I don't think Get-me-not's a nice name," said Mary.

"For-get-me-not," corrected the Owl Man.

"Yes, I know it's for Get-me-not, but I don't think it's a nice name," persisted Mary

"But her name is *Forget*-me-not," said the Owl Man.

"Who has she forgotten, and why has she got three names?" said Mary, in a jealous voice, but the Owl Man really didn't know, and left Mary to gaze at the bowls while he finished his own packing.

" You know, we are flying over to-day," said the Owl Man, as they were eating their lunch.

" On Cock Robin ? " asked Mary, remembering a dream she had once had.

" No, in an aeroplane," said the Owl Man ; " it will be a case of ' Mary Plain, in an aeroplane,' won't it ? " but he was sorry he had been funny, because Mary was so amused that she swallowed a potato the wrong way and had to be shaken by the heels to get it back.

They motored down to the place they were to start from, which was like a big flat field, and in the middle was a huge bird with silver wings, and it was the aeroplane.

The pilot was standing talking to some of the passengers, but directly he saw Mary he came over and spoke to her.

" Are you one of my passengers ? " he asked.

" No," said Mary, " I am Mary Plain."

" But you are one of his passengers, too, Mary," said the Owl Man.

" That's great," said the pilot. " Do you know, I believe this is the first time I've ever had the pleasure of piloting a bear across."

" Is it a pleasure ? " asked Mary.

" A very great one, I assure you," said the pilot.

" But I have flown before," said Mary.

" Have you indeed ? "

" Yes, once in a dream and once in a net," said Mary, and she told him about how she had got mixed up with the mail.

Mary had no flying clothes, so the pilot very kindly lent her a helmet, and when she had put it on it was time to start. Mary's short legs were a little inconvenient for getting into the plane, so she had to be lifted, and when she got inside there were little seats down the sides, and hers was the front seat of all.

A man came round and gave them paper bags, and Mary thought him most kind till she found the bags were empty.

" The biscuits have all gone," she complained to the Owl Man, who was sitting just behind her. It was a little awkward for him, because he did not want to tell her that the bag was in case she felt sick, for fear it should put it into her mind to *be* sick, so he said, " I think he just wants us to take care of it for him on the journey. Tuck it into the corner of your seat so it will be safe."

Directly the engines started Mary decided she would walk home. She had to climb down off her seat and go and shout in the Owl Man's ear to be heard above the noise.

" Nonsense ! " he said, " flying is the greatest fun," and he lifted her straight back to her seat. He felt a firm hand was the only hope, for a " Mary " scene in an aeroplane would be too much to bear.

Mary promptly got down again and came and shouted that she didn't think they were very friendly chairs with all their backs turned and only an empty bag beside you. The Owl Man was just going to be firm again when Mary said, " Do you think the twins are happy without me ? " so, instead, he said if she was very good she might sit on his little attaché-case by his feet, and Mary sat down and held his ankle for company and was much happier.

Now, however comforting a grey silk ankle may be, it isn't exactly exciting, so when Mary felt a tap on her shoulder and understood by the Owl Man's pointings that if she was on her chair she could see better, she nodded her head and consented to be put back again. Then she looked out, and there was the earth, so tiny that it didn't look like the earth at all, and while Mary was looking it all got blue underneath and it was the sea.

When they had flown over some more land, they began to go round and round and down and down, a little bit like when the lift went down, but not so bad, and then they could see little black dots moving below, and soon they were low enough to see they were men, and they had arrived.

" I like aeroplaning better than netting," said Mary, as she said good-bye to the pilot.

" That's splendid," he said, as he wrung her paw.

" Yes, I liked it all, except the empty bags," said Mary.

" Empty bags ! " said the pilot, looking bewildered.

So the Owl Man explained about Mary's appetite and how it never got tired, and the pilot said, " One moment please," and ran off.

In a minute he came back with two bulging paper bags, one full of biscuits and the other with bananas and peaches in it.

" I hope this will remove the blot on my escutcheon," he said, as he handed them to Mary.

"Thank you," she said, "bags look nicer fat than flat, don't they?"

"How soon before they are flat again?" murmured the Owl Man, but Mary was too engaged with a peach to answer.

The rest of the journey went very smoothly. Mary was drowsy after the flying and slept soundly all night, and when they woke up there was only just time for a hurried breakfast before they were at Berne.

Mary began to feel terribly excited.

The Owl Man's feelings were mixed. He was sorry to part with Mary, but, on the other hand, he couldn't help feeling relieved that he had got her back safely. Travelling with Mary was anxious work, and now that was all over; they only had to go a short taxi ride and Mary would be back in her pit and all his responsibility at an end.

But alas! for once the Owl Man was forgetting that Mary was an unusual bear—and not only that, for since she had been to the Crystal Palace Show and won first prize, she was also a famous bear!

The people of Berne, however, had not forgotten, and nearly all of them had come to meet Mary at the station.

When the train began to slow up the Owl Man went into the corridor to call a porter, and he saw, to his astonishment, that the whole station was one mass of bobbing heads and waving flags. Just opposite their carriage was a group of officials and behind them a band.

" Whatever's happened ? " the Owl Man asked the man nearest to the door. " Is somebody important arriving or something ? "

" Certainly, " said the man, " the famous bear is returning by this train, and the Burgomaster and Corporation have all come to welcome her home."

" Great heavens above ! " said the Owl Man distractedly, and rushed back to collect Mary.

There was no escape. The Owl Man ground his teeth. Of all the things that Mary had done to him this was by far the worst. But though he might wish himself in Timbuctoo, it didn't help at all, because here he was in Berne, and outside were all the inhabitants of Berne waiting for Mary.

" Now, Mary, listen carefully," he said in a hurried whisper, and as he spoke he slipped her rosette round her neck. " There are a lot of people outside—they have come to welcome you home, and with them are the Burgomaster and Corporation."

" And what are they ? " said Mary.

" Very important persons indeed, Mary," said the Owl Man, " and you must be as polite as you know how. Their coming to meet you like this is a very great honour."

" On who ? " asked Mary, as the Owl Man hurried her along to the door. Luckily the loud cheer that greeted her as she appeared in the doorway drove all other thoughts out of Mary's mind.

As she stepped on to the platform, holding very tightly to the Owl Man's hand, a roll on the drums and cries of

" Welcome home! Well done, Mary Plain!—Your country is proud of you—Long live Mary Plain!" went echoing round the station.

It was an alarming ordeal for a small bear to face even when the bear was as travelled as Mary.

The Burgomaster was a plump man with a boomy voice. He bowed low over Mary's paw, and he stayed so long bowing that she patted him kindly on the head with the other paw. Then she shook hands with all the Corporation, and then the Burgomaster cleared his throat and some one cried, " Silence for His Honour the Burgomaster."

He went on clearing his throat till every one was quite silent, and then Mary asked him anxiously if he thought he had caught a cold.

" Ssh, Mary," said the Owl Man, " Don't speak— listen." And the Burgomaster read.

" We, the Burgomaster and Corporation, together with these loyal citizens of Berne, have one and all gathered here to welcome you home, Mary Plain, and to tell you that we are proud that you should have brought such fame to your native town."

" I haven't got any fame, but I've got some bowls for the bears," said Mary.

" Will you shut up, Mary!" said the Owl Man from behind.

" I feel," boomed the Burgomaster, " that it is an immense pleasure and privilege that, as Burgomaster of this said city of Berne, it should fall to my lot to offer you our most sincere congratulations and to lead this great and, may I say, enthusiastic welcome."

Here he had to break off for a minute because the cheers broke out afresh, and Mary tugged at the Owl Man's hand and whispered, " I'm tired of this man."

" Hush, Mary, for heaven's sake ! " said the Owl Man.

The Burgomaster made a large gesture with his hand. " I think these honest people's voices tell you better than I can how proud we feel of you, and I will now, in the name of the city of Berne, present you with this medal."

Here the Burgomaster stepped forward and slipped a gilt chain round Mary's neck and on the end of it was a big flat medal, like a gold penny. Mary examined it. " Why," she exclaimed, " it's a picture of me, all in gold ! " And every one cheered some more, and just then a procession approached.

They were all the pastry cooks of Berne, and each one had tried to see if he couldn't make the best cake, and all the cakes were for Mary. The most exciting of all was a chocolate bear cake.

Then the Burgomaster said, if Mary would step forward, a car was all ready waiting to take her to the pits ; but just at that moment Mary caught sight of the Fur-Coat-Lady who had come to meet her too, and she was thrilled.

" Hurrah, and how-do-you-do, Fur-Coat-Lady ! " she shouted. " You must come here and help me choose which is the nicest cake."

" But you can't possibly start choosing now, Mary,"

said the Owl Man in despair. He knew how long Mary's cake decisions took.

" I shan't move till I have some of that chocolate bear," said Mary. Her legs began to brace, so the Owl Man knew she meant it ; they quickly chopped off some of the bear, and Mary, with her mouth quite full of head and her paw full of hind leg, consented to follow the Burgomaster.

It was not an ordinary kind of car, but a lorry, and in it they had built a platform, all decorated with flowers, for Mary to stand on.

When Mary appeared she was, for the first time, in full view of every one, and they began shouting and calling, " Speech ! Speech ! "

" I'm very sorry," Mary shouted, " but I ate the last one for my breakfast this morning."

" No, no, Mary," said the Owl Man. " ' Speech ' means that they want you to say a few words."

" Oh, words," said Mary, " I see." She thought for a moment and then she said, very loud, " Svisits—meringues—rosettes—netting—cream buns—King—bathing costume——" before they managed to stop her. Then they did some whispering. Mary nodded and started again.

" All of you," she said, " I am glad you are glad about me. Thank you," and she bowed deeply, and the Owl Man said she couldn't have done it better.

Then the procession started for the pits.

First the band, playing a welcoming march, then the Burgomaster and Corporation, and then Mary in her lorry. And all the people shouted and sang, and all the little boys threw their caps into the air, and flags were waved out of the windows, and Mary bowed and waved and saluted all the way.

When they reached the pits, Mary insisted on their driving the lorry close to the edge so the other bears could see her. When the bears heard the band and looked up—there was Mary, standing on the platform in all her glory, taller than any one else.

" God save the King," said Mary, saluting.

Big Wool saluted back, and Friska lost her head completely and curtsied to the ground, and even Bunch clapped stiff paws, and as for the twins—well, they nearly burst with excitement.

And then all the Corporation and the Burgomaster had to be said " Good-bye " to, and last of all the Fur-Coat-Lady and the Owl Man.

They stood by the entrance to Nursery Pit, and the Owl Man patted Mary on the head.

" Well, Mary Plain," he said, " I am glad to have got you safely back, and I am sad to say good-bye," and he really did look it.

Mary stared up at him, and then she turned and looked through the railings.

" Twins," she shouted, " were you happy without me ? "

" No," roared the twins.

Mary turned back. " So you see," she said, " I have to go back."

" Yes, that settles it," said the Owl Man. " Well,

good-bye, Mary Plain, we shall meet again soon, and in the meantime you'd better have a good sleep—you must be tired out."

She was indeed ; but a good sleep soon put her right again and made her feel as fresh as anything for the party she gave that night.

There were all the bears and all the lovely cakes at the beginning of the party, but at the end there were only the bears.

Then Mary presented the bowls, and they were all terribly proud and pleased, and Big Wool said, " Three cheers for Mary," and they gave her a bear cheer.

And all the people of Berne on their way home to bed stopped and wondered as they heard, far away, " Hip, hip, hoo-Mary—Hip, hip, hoo-Plain."

MARY PLAIN IN TOWN

CONTENTS

CHAPTER ONE

MARY GIVES AN ENGLISH LESSON

" Now, now, now ! " said Friska, bringing her stick sharply
down on the edge of the stone bath. " Little Wool ! Will
you please attend to me ? Marionetta ! "

The twins' heads came round to face their mother but their
eyes stayed sideways on Mary who was in a corner of Nursery
Pit, apparently in paroxysms of laughter. It was a good thing
she had her back turned because anyone, with half a glance
at Mary's face, could see it wasn't amused. Neither was the
laugh amused really, but then Mary wasn't laughing because
she was amused but because she wanted to annoy Friska.
And she did. If she could only have known how Friska's
paws itched to box her ears !

The same scene happened every morning. It had happened
every day since Mary, fresh from her svisit to England,
had refused to attend lessons unless they were given in
English.

Friska had been very fussed and upset. " But Mary," she

expostulated, " English is all very well when you are in English but—"

" England," corrected Mary.

" England," repeated Friska before she could stop herself. How dared Mary correct her !

" But," she went on, her voice trembling a little, " you must not on any account forget your Switzerland."

" Swiss," corrected Mary.

" Swiss," said Friska, again before she could stop herself and then, drawing herself up so as to be as much taller than Mary as she possibly could, she said, in her growliest voice, " I wish to goodness you had stopped in Engzerland ! "

Poor Friska, she was in a very difficult position.   She could, of course, appeal to Big Wool, the cubs' grandmother, and Big Wool would instantly put her paw down and Friska knew, all the bears knew, what a firm paw Big Wool had.   But that meant acknowledging that she, Friska, couldn't manage her own niece and a small niece at that and this she could not bring herself to do.   So Mary went on being disturbing in the corner, and Friska's paws went on itching to box her ears and the twins went on being inattentive on the edge of the bath until one morning Friska couldn't bear it any longer and, swallowing her pride, a big lump of it, she resolved to approach Mary once more.

She always came over into Nursery Pit for half an hour every morning to give the cubs their lessons before she herself was shut into Parlour Pit for the day.   So one day she said on her arrival, " There will be no class this morning, cubs, because I want to have a little chat with Mary."

The twins chased each other up the tree with whoops of

delight, while Mary followed Friska into the corner, wondering very much what the little chat would be about.

Friska cleared her throat. "Mary," she began, "first of all I would like you clearly to understand that the only reason I do not know any English is because I have never had any time to learn it." Here she stopped a minute just to wish that it had been French that Mary was making all the fuss about, for Friska knew quite a lot of French. She knew that 'oui' meant 'little' for instance, and that 'carotte' meant 'carrot' and that when someone said 'Bonjour' the answer was 'Encore.' "Now I feel it is a great pity that you should be missing all these lessons and one day you'll be sorry. Nobody wants to grow up stupid, do they?"

"Don't they?" asked Mary.

Friska hastily tucked her right paw behind her back. "No," she growled, "and what's more—you know it."

"But then I'm not stupid," said Mary. "How could I be, when I'm an unusual first-class bear with a white rosette and a gold medal with a picture of myself and a—"

"Yes, yes," interrupted Friska, impatiently, "but what I wanted to tell you was that I am not quite so busy just now and if you—well, if you would like to -er- well—talk to me in English, I will, of course, learn it very quickly. And then," she finished brightly, "we could all do our lessons together again."

"Certainly, Auntie," said Mary sweetly. "And what would you like me to teach you first?"

Friska tucked her second paw away.

"Please," she said, "recite my poem about St. Bruin's

Day." Mary might have been to England but at least she hadn't written a poem.

Now Mary only knew two sentences in English. One was ' English spoken ' which she had learnt from the door of a barber's shop, but she was awfully good at inventing. " Very well," she said, " will you please step into the schoolroom ? " and she pointed to the bath. Friska retreated a little further into the corner. She had not bargained for this.

" Oh no, Mary," she said, " I–er–I think it would be more—well—fitting to stay quietly here in the corner. No one will notice us here." Which was a silly thing to say to Mary who, above all things, liked being noticed.

" Just as you like," said Mary, " but no schoolroom, no English," and she walked away with her head in the air.

When she had walked as far as she could without running into the wall she turned and saw that Friska was already sitting on the extreme edge of the bath—right up at the end which was the top of the class. Friska hoped Mary wouldn't notice this. " Ha—Ha ! " thought Mary to herself, noticing at once. She strolled back towards the bath and said, quite kindly, " Shall we begin now ? "

Friska nodded. She was beyond words.

" Manyery happery yearsery we-pop wishery to-pop youery," said Mary, very fast indeed. Friska blinked.

" Are you quite sure that's right, Mary ? " she asked. " It sounds very odd to me."

Mary raised her eyebrows and tapped impatiently on the floor with her paw, exactly like Friska did when the cubs were slow at their lessons.

" Of course it's right," she said. " Do you think I could

make a mistake? Wasn't I five whole days in England? Aren't I an unusual first-class bear with a white ro—"

"Yes, yes," said Friska, who was sick of Mary's list and bothered if she was going to listen to it twice in one day.

"Very well then, go on," said Mary, a bit sulky because she hated her list being interrupted.

Friska swallowed.

"Many – happy – er – pop – years we – wish –to – pop – you," she said, "oh, and ery."

Mary pointed with her stick. "Kindly move to the bottom of the class," she said. Friska moved, with a nervous look up at the railings to see if anyone was watching her disgrace. There, by rights, she should have stayed but Mary enjoyed moving her up and down and if her English didn't progress, her body did, from one end of the seat to the other, till where she sat got quite hot and sore from all the sliding. At the end of the time she was so muddled and out of breath that she actually bargained with Mary.

"If you will come to lessons and do your very best to be good," she said, "once a week I will allow you to give the twins an English lesson."

"You, too," said Mary quickly.

"I said the twins," said Friska.

"Then, no," said Mary, starting to walk away.

"Very well, me too," said her aunt, who knew when she was beaten.

So that night Friska went to bed feeling rather nervous but hoping for the best and Mary went to bed, very chirpy, but hoping, hard, for the worst.

And if you should happen to pass the pits on a Wednesday

morning you will see the three cubs sitting sedately along the edge of the bath and you will hear them chanting the bears' multiplication table :—

  2 *smiles make* 1 *laugh.*
  4 *sneezes make* 1 *cold.*
  2 *much racing makes* 1 *tired.*
10 *licks make* 1 *clean.*
20 *carrots make* 1 *full.*

But on Saturdays, if you should happen that way, you will see a very different sight. The two cubs will be wriggling so hard that every minute you will wonder how soon they will fall backwards into the bath, and beyond them, still at the bottom of the class and still on the very edge of the bath, you will see Friska, still with an anxious eye on the railings above, while before them, brandishing her stick, her legs very wide apart, stands Mary.

" Now then ! " she shouts, as if they were all deaf. " All together ! "

" God save the King."

Which was the rest of the English that Mary knew.

CHAPTER TWO

MARY IS TAKEN ILL AND FRISKA IS TAKEN IN

ONE morning when Friska called the cubs to their lessons, Little Wool came running out of their sleeping-den and said, " Mary can't come, she's ill.   She can't stand up and she's very ill indeed."

While Little Wool was telling Friska this sad news, Mary, curled up on her bed of straw, was having a private laugh. The truth of the matter was that, ever since her visit to England, Mary had been a bit too big for her boots and wanted all the attention for herself.   Now that the baby aunts, Forget-me-not and Plum, were bigger, they were let out into Nursery Pit on fine days from eleven o'clock until three o'clock, and all the people of Berne leant over the stone wall and cried, " Aren't the baby ones sweet ! "   which annoyed Mary exceedingly.

So one day, she determined to be ill, because ill people just have to be noticed.   " They'll be sorry when I'm gone to bed," she thought to herself.

" Yes," said Little Wool again, " she's very ill."

" Tut, tut," said Friska as she bustled off to visit her suffering niece.

Mary, indeed, seemed to be far from well, judging from the groans she was giving ; every time they lifted her up, her knees seemed to fold up and down she went again.

" Put your tongue out, please," said Friska.

Mary obeyed gladly, shooting it out as far as it would go.

" It seems a little long," said Friska, uncertainly.   Then, " Whereabouts are you ill, Mary dear ? " she asked, hoiking her to her feet.

" All over," said Mary, folding up again.

Friska, thoroughly alarmed, sent for Big Wool, who arrived, looking very capable.   Friska rushed up to her ex- citedly.   " Mary's very ill," she said.   " She's ill in her legs and in her front and in her back and in her head—"

" Ssh ! " said Big Wool sternly, who considered Friska had lost her own head.   Friska sshushed at once.   " Leave her to me," she went on, starting to hoik, " I'll manage her.   Now then, Mary, upsy daisy ! "

But there was no upsy and very little daisy about Mary just then, who continued to fold up and to moan till Job, their keeper, arrived to send them all to their own pits for the day. Big Wool stepped forward and explained about Mary, and Job, giving her a quick glance, said to Friska, " You'd better stay with her—I'll give you something for her," as he hustled the other bears away.

Presently he returned with a hot sandbag, a bowl of water, two dry biscuits and a bandage.   " You can tie it on with this," he said as he went off.   " Very well," said Friska, not at all sure what she had to tie on to where.   While she was wonder- ing about it, Mary, who had had no breakfast and who had

"*I don't really think you need tell me how to manage a bandage*"

stopped folding up, wasted no time in wondering what to do with the biscuits.

Friska, meantime, carefully unrolled the bandage and then, picking up the sandbag, she popped it on to Mary's head and said bracingly, " We'll soon have you better, Mary dear ! " She always called people who were ill ' dear.'   " Just hold this against your head," and she handed Mary one end of the bandage and then set out to find the other end herself.   When she had found it she was a good way off from Mary.

" Do you know how ? " asked Mary, suspiciously.

" Really, Mary dear," said Friska, " I don't think, no I don't *really* think, you need tell me how to mandage a bandage ! " She began walking slowly round Mary and every time a loop went round Mary's head a corresponding loop went round Friska's waist till, at the end, they were so closely looped that, if it hadn't been for the bag on Mary's head, you couldn't have told which was which.

By this time, the heat had penetrated Mary's fur and was causing her great discomfort.

" It's burning me, my head's on fire, take it off ! " she shrieked.

" There, there," said Friska, who knew for a certainty that unless someone let them out they were both in the bandage for good.   " Be a good girl, there's a dear."

" I'm not a dear and oh, I wish I wasn't here," shouted Mary. " Take it off, I say."

" There, there," said Friska again just because she could think of nothing else to say.

But Mary, maddened at being burned and there-there'd, wriggled desperately to get free, and catching her foot in a loop of bandage brought them both to the floor, winding Friska completely. For a moment she lay making kind of dying noises, while Mary, not caring in the least if she died twice, went on being burned and trying to get loose. Then, having got her breath back, Friska, seeing the bowl of water close at hand, poured it over Mary's head. " There, Mary dear," she said. And it must be confessed the ' dear ' was nearly a spit !

At this moment the door opened and Job appeared. He stood and gazed at them with his mouth open. Friska lay on her back with Mary's head still attached affectionately to her front, the sandbag at a rakish angle over one eye. She was furious with Mary. Furious with her for being ill, furious with her for tripping her up, and furious with her for being so close.

" What's she listening to ? " asked Job, much interested. " Listening to what you had for breakfast ? "

"She's not listening to anything," said Friska with as much dignity as she could assume under the circumstances, and Mary. " It's—well—I tied it on—but we're tied too."

Job whipped out his knife, bent down, and in a moment they were freed. Friska got up, feeling her damp front and glaring at Mary. Mary started to glare back but Job soon put an end to that by producing an ugly-looking black bottle and a spoon.

" Open your mouth, Mary," he said. Mary took one sniff.

" Oh, but I'm quite well now, thank you," she said. " Extra well."

" I daresay, but we'll be making sure of it," said Job and gripping Mary between his knees, he seized her by the nose so that she had to open her mouth to breathe and poured a large spoon of warm castor-oil down her throat.

Which is what always happens to bears that pretend.

A day or two after this, Mary was sitting on the bath and thinking of how dull everything seemed to be, when suddenly she heard a voice say, " Hallo, Mary Plain ! "   Looking up, she saw her great friend, the Owl Man.   She hurried up the tree and out along a branch.   She always did this when he came so as to get as close to him as possible.

" You're not looking very gay this morning," said the Owl Man.

" No," said Mary, " I'm feeling un-gay."

" Everything rather dull, not much fun, eh ? " enquired the Owl Man.   Mary nodded.

" I thought so," he said.   " I know exactly what's wrong with you, Miss Plain.   You're suffering from swollen head. It's a nasty complaint."

Mary felt her head carefully all over.   " Whereabouts ? " she said.   " I can't see where."

" No, but everyone else can," said the Owl Man with a laugh.   " Now, there's only one cure for that and that is, get busy."

" Busy over what ? " asked Mary.

The Owl Man thought a moment and then he said, "How about those young aunts of yours ?   Couldn't you give them swimming or drill or lessons or something ? "

Mary brightened.   She definitely didn't like the aunts enough to play with them, but she did like them enough to teach them.

" I'll try," she said.

" That's right," said the Owl Man.   " It shall be a surprise
—a goodbye surprise for next Tuesday."

" Goodbye, did you say ? " asked Mary edging a little
nearer along the branch.

" Yes, I'm off to England next day," said the Owl Man.

" Didn't you want a svisitor this time then ? " asked Mary
hopefully.

" I'm afraid not, old girl," said the Owl Man.   " Some day,
perhaps.   Now, you get busy over that surprise."

So Mary worked hard all that week and when the Owl Man
turned up on Tuesday she paraded the aunts in front of him.

" Now, both together !   One, two, three ! "   And the aunts
sang in high squeaky voices (to the tune of *Polly put the
kettle on*) :—

Forget-me-not :	" Once there was a clever bear
Plum	clever bear
	clever bear "
Forget-me-not :	" Once there was a clever bear
Both together :	a clever bear."

Chorus. *Forget-me-not :*   " Now you try and guess her name
       Plum :   guess her name
                                      guess her name "

      Forget-me-not :   " Now you try and guess her name
       Both :   and guess her name."

The remainder of the song was sung as above.

                     " And she once went s'visiting
                                s'visiting
                                s'visiting "
                     " And she once went s'visiting
                           This clever bear."

                     " Now you try and guess her name
                                guess her name
                                guess her name "
                     " Now you try and guess her name
                           and guess her name."

                     " And she won a white rosette
                                white rosette
                                white rosette "
                     " And she won a white rosette
                         This first class bear."

                     " Now you try and guess her name
                                guess her name
                                guess her name "
                     " Now you try and guess her name
                         It's MARY PLAIN."

" Oh Mary," said the Owl Man, wiping his eyes, " I might have known I could bank on you,"

" How do you mean—bank ? " asked Mary.

" I mean bank on it's being a real Mary surprise," said the Owl Man.

" Was it very Mary then ? " asked Mary.

" Exceedingly," said the Owl Man.

CHAPTER THREE

MARY BETS A BET

RATTLE, bang! Down came the door of Lady Grizzle and Alpha's sleeping-den.

Bubble, bubble, bubble, went Mary.

Rattle, bang! This time it was Big Wool and her family who were locked behind their iron doors. Rattle, bang! And now the twins were safe for the night.

Bubble, bubble, oh thank goodness, bubble, went Mary.

Job sighed as the last door went rattling home. He was always glad to get them safely shut up for the night. Bears could give a lot of trouble and often did, especially since that Mary Plain had got back from England. The way she bossed those young cubs, Forget-me-not and Plum, teaching them to salute her and God saving the King. It was a wonder the other bears put up with her sometimes and yet, come to think of it, Mary Plain was the kind of bear one did put up with, whatever she did. He smiled as he let down the last door. Well, she was safe for to-night, anyway.

But she wasn't.

Bubble, bubble, oh do go, bubble, before I burst, went Mary, as Job went off home.

For a moment the little black disc with the two holes in it went on floating quietly on top of the water in the bath but presently, with an extra big bubble, it came popping up and turned into Mary's nose and behind it came the rest of Mary, very damp indeed. She climbed out of the bath and shook herself.

That morning she had bet a bet with herself. " Mary Plain, I bet you won't be able to hide and stay out in the pit all night, so there ! " And now she had won the bet and it didn't seem to matter very much. All that mattered was that she was extremely cold and wet. She climbed up the tree and sat on a branch where a moonbeam was shining. She had never been out at night before and thought what a pale sun it was, as she waited for it to dry her. But it didn't. Ten minutes later she was just as shivery and cold so she thought she'd better go to bed with the others after all. Also, she thought she would give up betting in future.

Climbing down, she went and stood outside the den where the twins slept with the baby aunts. How they would get her in she didn't stop to think, but she was sure they could if they tried. About a foot from the ground holes were pierced through the iron to let in some air, so Mary put her mouth against one of these and said, " Twins ! I'm tired of betting and I want to come in. I don't like it out here."

" Rrrrch, rrrrch," snored the twins.

" Aunts ! " tried Mary next. " Forget-me-not, do please let me in. Aunt Plum ! "

But Forget-me-not and Plum only answered " Rrrrch, rrrrch."

So she moved on to the next den door where Friska and Big Wool and the others slept and, standing outside, with little runnels of water running down her front and little shivers of cold running down her back, she tried again.

"Auntie! It's me! I fell in the bath and I'm wet." Pause. "I'm sorry for last time I was naughty." Pause. "And for all the times before. Do please let me in." Pause and then, very persuasively, "Nice, *clever* Friska." But the only answer she got was "Erruch zi bu, erruch zi bu," from Friska, who prided herself on snoring with a French accent.

Before the third and last door Mary's legs trembled a little and not only from cold. She gave a little bow and then said, "Sir, I'm the cub, sir, what gave you the little whistle you liked, sir, and I'm wet, sir. Could I come in, sir, please? I wouldn't take much room, sir." But the terrifyingly growly snores that came out sent Mary hurrying away.

Suddenly she caught sight of an unfamiliar lump in a corner of the pit—a big lump it was. Hurrying across she saw with delight that it was a bundle of soiled straw, tied together in the middle, which had been turned out of the sleeping dens when the fresh straw had been put in that evening. Just exactly what she most wanted. She climbed in, burrowing deep into the straw till it closed about her—a warm tickly nest. "I'm glad I betted, after all," she said and dropped off to sleep.

Because Mary was very tired she slept a long sleep and when she woke up she couldn't, for a moment, remember where she was. Then a piece of straw tickled her on the nose and sh~

remembered. Of course she had betted herself into the bath and then into the straw. But what a funny thing, the straw seemed to be moving! At least not so much moving as kind of trembling all round Mary. Very carefully, she poked her head out and found, to her amazement, that instead of one fir tree fixed in the middle of the pit, there were lots of them, all moving up to her and then moving out of sight beyond the straw.

Now Mary thought she knew a lot, but she had to confess she hadn't an idea, not a single idea, that trees could walk. " This is what comes from betting! " she told herself, as she pushed her head a little further out.

Then she understood. It wasn't the trees that were moving but she, herself, and the straw, because she and the straw were both in a cart. Listening carefully, she heard voices, a deep slow one and then a quicker one, answering. So she wasn't alone and Mary was glad about this for, devoted as she was to Mary Plain (and really there wasn't any one else she knew of that she was quite so fond of), she didn't awfully like being all alone with her—not for long. But, as Mary stared out of the straw, with one tufty bit sticking very becomingly behind her ear and saw the two backs that belonged to the voices, she knew one thing for certain. The two backs didn't know she was there or they wouldn't stay backs but would turn quickly into faces, which was what always happened when Mary was about. So she got under the straw again till she could settle what to do, and while she was settling, dropped off to sleep again.

She was awakened by a violent lurch and the next moment she was sliding downwards with the straw. First she was upside down and then she was downside up and then there was a bump and a bang and a noise of wheels rattling away.

Mary fought her way out of the straw and came out looking very ruffled and untidy with bits of it sticking all over her coat. She was standing at what seemed to be the end of a road with a wood behind her. Mary didn't much like being at the end of anything so she decided she'd rather go with the wheels.

" Hi ! " she shouted, but the wheels went on rattling away and though she ran to the corner and shouted " Hi ! " again, they were far out of sight, so Mary gave it up and came back to the straw again. She came back to the straw because it was the only thing she knew and just then she wanted rather badly to be near something she knew. She'd never been out alone before and she wasn't sure about roads that ended. She sat down on the straw, feeling extra small, and for Mary to feel extra small meant she was in a very bad way. To cheer herself up she started talking to herself.

" Now, Mary Plain," she said, holding her left paw tightly
with her right, " let's hold paws for company and talk a bit,
shall we ? "

" Yes," said Mary Plain.

" How are you feeling ? " asked Mary.

" Terribly hungry," groaned Mary Plain.   Mary knew only
too well how true this was, so she hastily changed the subject.

" I like straw," she said conversationally.

" Yes," said Mary Plain again.

" I like the smell," said Mary, very much hoping that Mary
Plain would find something more interesting to say this time
but she didn't, she just said " Yes " again.

Now, Mary's inside was feeling so like a big empty hole
that she took some deep breaths of air to fill it up a bit and the
air she breathed smelt of straw and the smell of the straw was
a smell of things you know very well, a homey smell—a
beary smell.

" Oh," said Mary, feeling smaller than ever, " do you think
the twins are happy without me ? "

But no one answered.   Not even Mary Plain.

CHAPTER FOUR

IN WHICH A BET LEADS TO A SVISIT

'Now, that's the very last time you bet, Mary Plain, and don't forget!" said Mary, as she got up off the pile of straw. She turned and looked at the wood. It was rather dark with a little green path under the trees which seemed to say "Follow me!" But Mary wasn't sure about woods either, and especially alone. She looked round to see if she could see any-one about, but there was still only the end of the road and the straw, so, facing the wood again, she squared her shoulders and, cocking her head on one side, said, "Mary Plain, I bet you you won't go into that wood," and marched off under the trees.

For a long time the path went on saying "Follow me" and Mary followed and then suddenly she saw, lying at her feet, what looked like a brown saucer upside down. Now, saucers usually mean food and Mary was terribly wanting food so she bent and picked it up and then she got the fright of her life. For out from under the saucer popped a tiny and very angry head. "How dare you impede my progress!" it said. "Replace me instantly. Instantly, fur-covered busy-body!"

Mary obeyed so promptly that the saucer reached the ground rather too quickly for comfort and this and the fact that it was also upside down, made it angrier still.

" Restore my equilibrium, you officious perambulating hay-stack ! " it spluttered furiously.

Mary wasn't at all partial to being called a hay-stack, or any of the other things for the matter of that, but she had never seen anything so small so angry before, so she turned it carefully the right side up and then said, politely, " What are you ? I'm Mary Plain."   And she gave a little bow.

" Anyone can see that," said the saucer rudely.   " *What* am I, indeed ! I presume you mean ' Who ' ! Unmannerly pickthank ! "

" Who, sir," said Mary, still willing to oblige because of its angriness and because of its being right in the middle of the path so she couldn't pass.   " I thought perhaps you were called ' Mr Saucer ' ? "

But at this the saucer went off into such a series of explosions that Mary backed away.

" I'll teach you to make puns about my shape," it said, rising on its hind legs and advancing on Mary threateningly, " you bearded baggage ! "

Mary, in retreat, suddenly couldn't bear to be called a single name more, so she said " Good-afternight," not quite sure, owing to the darkness of the wood, if it was day or night and, taking her courage in her paw, she gave a flying leap for safety.

" Grasshopper ! " she heard it spit, as she passed the danger zone and then " Capering kangaroo ! "

But Mary, safely out of range, ran as fast as she could till, arriving at the end of the wood, she found herself in broad sunshine on the edge of a big green field with more trees beyond.   In the middle of the field stood a red cow and beside it a bucket and stool.   Mary trotted up to it, hoping very

After that there was a long silence

much it would be a friendly cow.   It swung its head slowly
round and looked at her.

" Moo," it said.

" Moo," said Mary back, determined not to offend.

" Moo, moo," said the cow, and " Moo, moo, moo," said
Mary, going one better.

" Moo ? " said the cow enquiringly, but Mary felt she simply
couldn't go on saying ' moo ' so, only too pleased, as always,
to introduce herself, she said, " I'm Mary Plain, an unusual
first-class bear with a white ro— Oh dear ! " she broke off,
suddenly catching sight of the bucket, " I'm so empty."

After that there was a long silence and after the silence Mary
was a completely different shape.

She sat down on the grass for a bit but, almost at once, she
was alarmed by the sound of loud shouts and, turning round,
she saw racing towards her two boys and a man, holding a
rope in his hand.

Now Mary had been lassoed once before, and at sight of that
rope she made off across the field towards the trees.   Wisely
choosing a pine which had no branches near the bottom, she
swarmed up it and a moment later was safely at the top.

The two boys tried to climb up the slippery trunk with no
success while Mary, quite safe and quite full and therefore
quite happy, sat astride a branch and pelted them with fir-cones
from above.   " Baggage ! " she   shouted,   " Hopperoo ! "
enjoying herself mightily and maddening the boys.

In the end their father, saying he'd stay and keep a watch on
her himself, sent them off home and, settling himself at the foot
of the tree, he lighted his pipe.   Mary, remembering the rude
saucer had called her a hay-stack, began picking off some of the

bits of straw sticking to her. That done, she began to look
about for something else to do. But there isn't much you can
do on the top of a pine-tree, so presently she climbed down a
little way and was rewarded by the comforting sound of a
snore. So he was asleep ! " Hurrah," thought Mary, " I'm
off ! " But she determined to run no risks—not with ropes
about. So she crept down a bit further and out along a
branch and, leaning over, gripped the branch below and
began pulling her own down to meet it. Whether she pulled
too hard, we shall never know but, the next instant, Mary was
performing the most wonderful acrobatic feat of her life. For
the under branch cracked and the upper one, released, sprang
back, sending Mary catapulting through the air.

" I believe I've flown again," she said as she landed, a little
breathless, but safe, on quite a different tree. Meanwhile the
man, awakened by the crack, got up, rubbing his eyes. Looking up and seeing no sign of a bear he thought it must, after
all, have been a dream and, picking up his rope, he went off home.

Mary watched him out of sight and then crept cautiously down, dropped to the ground, and set off as fast as she could go in the opposite direction.   Almost at once the trees ended and she found herself standing in a small street with houses on each side.

One house had a car standing outside—a car which reminded her of the Owl Man's. Cars meant travelling and svisits and picking nics and all kinds of nice things. Mary liked cars. She went up to this one and stroked it. No one was inside but there was a large black case strapped on behind, with a label on it.

Labels ! They meant travelling, too. But labels had to have writing on them and this was an empty one. " Labels, cars, travelling, Owl Man," thought Mary to herself. She began to smile and her smile grew bigger and bigger until it almost met behind.   Then she bent down and began searching in the road.   She had found a car and a label all ready for her and now all she wanted was a pencil and she felt quite sure she'd find one ready, too.   She didn't, but a small piece of coal was just as good.   Next she bit the string of the label through, and, kneeling down in the road, she wrote on it in Mary writing,

MISS

GOING  THE

MAN

ENGLAND

As coal isn't as easy to manage as a pencil, a good deal of it that didn't get on to the label got on to Mary. The writing finished, she searched for a place to put it, and, finding her ear seemed the most convenient place for a label, she tied it on there. At first she thought she would sit and wait and see what happened and then she thought it seemed a pity to waste the case, so she climbed up and got inside, but before she closed the lid she stood for a moment and said solemnly, " Mary Plain ! I bet you're going on a svisit after all ! "

CHAPTER FIVE

MARY WINS AGAIN

" STEADY, there, whoa ! Let her down gently, Bill—that's right.
Good ! I think you said you were the owner of this car, sir ? "

" That's right.   My suitcase is inside, but I've nothing to
declare."

" What about the case on the back ? "

" Empty."

" Just let me have a look, please."

The man stepped forward, unfastened the catch, lifted the
lid, gave one loud scream and fell down in a dead faint.

All the people standing on the pier at Dover immediately
rushed forward, talking excitedly, asking each other what had
happened, jostling and pushing towards the black case.   Out
of the case rose Mary, very calm and dignified, in spite of
affectionate bits of straw and a good deal of coal, still.   At sight
of her, all the people who had been pressing forward began

pressing backwards and, in a moment, there was an empty space round the car.

Mary gave a little bow; the label fluttered gaily from her ear.

"It's me," she said. "I'm Mary Plain, an unusual first-class bear from the pits at Berne and I won a white rosette and a gold medal with a picture of myself on it and I have come to svisit the Owl Man and I'm very empty. God save the King," she finished at the salute, remembering it was England.

Now, Mary had, of course, spoken in Swiss, so "God save the King" was the only thing that the crowd had understood, except for one man, who luckily had been to Switzerland and knew a little. Mary repeated, laying her hand with a great deal of feeling on the place, "I'm very empty here."

The man who understood Swiss took a step forward. "Hungry?" he asked.

Mary nodded so hard that she nearly nodded herself out of the case. As this was the very last thing any of them wanted to happen the man said hastily, "You stop there and I'll fetch some milk and buns."

So Mary stopped and when the food arrived she tucked into it, while all the people stared and stared as if they had never seen a bear eat buns and milk before, which they probably hadn't. And while Mary ate and the people stared, all the officials discussed what to do with her.

Those in the Customs' Office were certain that the officials in the Lost Property Office ought to look after her and the Lost Property people felt quite sure it was the Customs' men's job. They were just going to toss for it when the head man suddenly said, "What about her passport? Has she got one? Otherwise she can't be allowed to land—she's not a British subject."

So the interpreter was pushed forward a step or two and he asked, " Have you got a passport ? "

" I don't think I have," said Mary, " but I've got some bathing drawers in Berne, with stripes—red and white."

This information, however, didn't seem to help the officials very much. " She oughtn't to land," said one. " It's against the law."

But Mary had landed and that was that, especially as no one seemed anxious to ask her to un-land.

Just at this point Mary, having finished her meal, stood up and beckoned to the man who had got it for her. Very naturally she looked on him as her greatest friend. The man was quite willing to be interpreter where he was, but he wasn't at all sure he wanted to be confidential close to—not with a bear. However, someone gave him a push again, and he went forward a few steps.

" Please," said Mary, " I'd like a bath."

Now, if she had asked for a bottle of champagne or even a Rolls Royce, it would have been less surprising and more convenient.

" A b–bath ! " stammered the man, turning pale and deciding on the spot that she was not only a loose bear but a mad bear, too.

" Certainly," said Mary, who was quite used to bathing in public. " You see," she continued, leaning confidingly over the edge of the case, " I'm a bit coaly and I don't like being called a hay-stack."

" H–hay-stack ! " repeated the man, more certain than ever that she was mad.

" So please will you get it for me ? " said Mary.

" Hot or cold ? " asked the man.

" Both," said Mary.

" Soap ? " asked the man.

" Pardon ? " said Mary, who didn't know about soap.

" Soap *and* towels ? " asked the man.

" Yes," said Mary, who never believed in saying ' No.'

And there and then, from somewhere, somehow, a tank of water was produced and there and then Mary had her bath in full view of the Dover public for, by this time, the news that there was a live bear loose on the pier had spread and everyone in the town was rushing to see her. As she climbed down from the case, the crowd all melted away behind a fence but, as she got into the water, first one and then another head came popping up to watch till there was a solid row of watching heads all along the fence. The water got blacker and blacker and Mary got cleaner and cleaner and when she had finished she got out and raced round and round to get dry and all the people of Dover were specially glad of the fence.

" What's that she's got on her ear ? " asked one man as Mary flashed past, so, next time she came galloping along, they all craned their necks to see.

" Bless me if it isn't a label ! " said the Head Customs' Officer. " Henry ! Just get it for me, will you ? " he called to the interpreter man.

But Henry didn't see why, just because he knew a little Swiss, he should be expected to get a label off a galloping bear and said so. Here the Officer got exceedingly angry and was just saying he would have to dismiss him for cowardice and shirking his duty, when Mary settled the question by turning a somersault, which loosened the label and sent it fluttering to the ground, close to the fence.

They fished it up with a stick and Henry was quickly called back so as to be able to translate. He stared at the label and scratched his head and said it was all gibberish to him and the Head Officer was just going to dismiss him again when a man pushed his way through the crowd. " Hallo ! " he said, " what's all this about ? "

The Officer handed him the label and the man exclaimed " Good heavens ! If it isn't Mary writing ! " and he read aloud

MISS   🐱   ✈️

GOING   ⏰   THE   🦉   MAN

ENGLAND

and then burst out laughing.

" Where is this bear ? " he asked and a way was cleared and he strode up to the fence and looked over. Mary was standing in the middle of the space looking her best, her fur and herself very sticking out and her pointed ears pricking, as she wondered what to do next.

" Hallo, Mary Plain ! " called the man and he vaulted over the fence, while all the crowd gasped and said, " He's got some nerve ! " " Remember me at all ? " went on the man. Mary trotted up to him and stared. " Weren't you one of the Fur Coat Lady's svisitors, when I went to stay with her ? " she asked.

" That's right ! Bill Smith's my name," said the man and Mary, the excitement of seeing someone she knew going to her head, hastily recited her list.

" I know all that," said Bill, " but look here, I'm off on this next boat in three minutes, and I must fly. I'll give them the Owl Man's address and they'll get hold of him for you. Good-bye, sit tight till he comes."

Mary immediately sat.

" Here, send a wire to this address," said Bill, thrusting a slip of paper into the Head Officer's hand and he rushed away.

Half an hour later the Owl Man who had just come in for a late lunch in a great hurry at his London flat, was handed a telegram.

" Important goods awaiting you here. Please collect at once."

It was signed by the Customs' Officer at Dover.

The Owl Man wired back, " Impossible come. Please seal goods and forward to above address."

But the answer came whizzing back along the wires.

" Impossible seal. Cannot approach. Dangerous. Come immediately."

And the Owl Man, angrily wondering who could have sent him a barrel of gunpowder, climbed into his car and started for Dover.

" This way, please, sir," said the Head Officer, more thankful to see him than he had ever been to see anyone in his life before, for the still growing crowd had blocked all the approaches to the pier and the Cross-Channel services threatened to be held up.   And the Owl Man was led to the pier where Mary Plain was sitting as tightly as ever on exactly the same spot where Bill had left her.

" Gracious Heaven ! " said the Owl Man, standing stock still and staring at Mary as if he couldn't believe his eyes.

" I've come," said Mary, beaming all over.

" So I see ! " said the Owl Man, not beaming at all.

" Please could I stop sitting tight now ? " enquired Mary.

" Stop sitting tight !   What do you mean ? "

" The Bill man said I was to sit tight till you came and I have."

The Owl Man took a deep breath, shook his head, smiled and held out his hand.

" You win, Mary," he said, " as usual."

Mary, a little stiff, scrambled to her feet and tucked her paw into his hand.

" What have I won ? " she asked happily.

" Me," said the Owl Man and then, with a sigh, " as usual."

CHAPTER SIX

WHICH IS VERY MARY

" MORE porridge, Mary ? " asked the Owl Man, for the last time.

" Yes, please," said Mary.

He had quite decided this would be the last time because three times already he had said, " More porridge ? " and Mary had said, " Yes, please."

" That's all, now. You'll be eating me out of house and home, at this rate. To say nothing of getting too fat."

" ' Fat ' or ' flat,' did you say ? " asked Mary.

" ' Fat ! ' " said the Owl Man. " Good gracious me ! Show me any flatness about you, Mary Plain, and I'll give you a lump of sugar."

Mary, being very fond of sugar, stood up in her chair so as to get a good view of herself. The Owl Man had a good view, too—a profile one, against the sunny window and, as he saw it, he decided definitely, it must be two lumps. Mary shook her head sadly. " I'm afraid porridge isn't very flatting," she said, stroking the curve. " Perhaps there's a bit behind somewhere ? " she added hopefully and, climbing down, she presented her back to the Owl Man. " Please look."

The Owl Man looked. " Nothing doing, Mary," he said, " absolutely nothing, so I think you'd better have the sugar as a consolation prize, don't you ? "

" I bet," said Mary, crunching.

" The thing is," went on the Owl Man, " what on earth to do with you—you're immensely inconvenient just now, Mary."

" Is that a nice thing to be ? " enquired Mary.

" It's the sort of thing you very often are," said the Owl Man. " Well, I must be off, anyway. I've got a very important case on just now and I'm fearfully busy."

" Could I get inside ? " asked Mary, who was used to cases.

" It's not that kind," said the Owl Man, laughing. " No, you'll have to amuse yourself, Mary, as best you can, and I'll be back to lunch. Why don't you write to the bears and tell them where you are ? I expect they are all wondering. Look ! Here's some paper and pencils. Good-bye, be good," and off he went.

So Mary wrote :—

Here Mary paused a little to look round. The room was very empty, "There's only me," she thought.

WITH LVV 💥 X X XX X X X
FROM 🐱 PLAIN

After another look round the room she wrote underneath :—

I HOP THE 🐱 🐱 R HAPPIE
WITHOUT M E
MARY

Then she got down.

"I don't like empty rooms," she said and, going to the hall door, she opened it quite easily because the Owl Man had forgotten to lock it, and running down lots of stairs, she found herself in a moment out in the street. That was empty too. "And," said Mary aloud, "I believe I'm beginning to be empty myself."

A sound of approaching music drew her down the street. Round the corner swung a band of ex-soldiers playing *Land of Hope and Glory*, but the next minute they caught sight of Mary and there isn't much glory about soldiers running away.

Next, Mary wandered up some front door steps and there was a nice shiny button there. Now shiny buttons always seemed to say " Please press me " to Mary, so she pressed, and went on pressing till the door was flung open by a very angry parlour-maid.

" Murder ! " she exclaimed, suddenly seeing Mary and slamming the door in her face before Mary got a chance of explaining that she was not ' Murder ' but Mary.

Mary sat down disconsolately on the step to think over how very unfriendly people were, but she didn't sit there long for lots of other things began to arrive on the step too—hair brushes and books and bits of coal.

" This step doesn't seem to want me much," said Mary, getting up.

" Shoo, bear, go away, shoo ! " shouted a voice from above and Mary, looking up and receiving a glass of water full in the face, shooed.

Luckily she shooed back up the street and into the right door and into the lift and directly she shut the doors the lift began to go up, up. Mary stared at the row of shiny buttons on the wall which said 1, 2, 3, 4, 5, 6. " I'm flying again," she thought, " me and the buttons together."

The lift stopped at the landing and Mary got out and found a lady and a little boy there.

First the lady screamed but Mary was used to this, and then she fell on her knees. " Mercy ! " she cried, clasping her hands together. " Take me, but spare, oh ! spare, my little Harry ! Kneel, Harry, kneel ! " and she tried to pull Harry on to his knees.

But little Harry didn't want to kneel, he was far too interested in Mary. Mary stared at the woman and wondered what she was saying and why she was on her knees. Perhaps she had a pain ?

" Never mind," she said kindly, giving her a pat on the head, " you'll be better soon. Try a hot sandbag." And she retired into the lift, and, because the shiny buttons winked at her, Mary pressed and sailed down to the next floor.

" There, ducky ! Just you wait and see what a treat Nannie's got for her Baba this morning. She's going to take her and show—her—"

But no one heard what Baba's treat was to be because just as Nannie arrived at the treat, Mary arrived in the lift. Mary hadn't any idea that anyone carrying a big baby could run so fast—nor had Nannie, either.

Back in the lift, Mary pressed again and this time when she stopped, the doors opened from the outside, so she tucked herself into a corner to see what was going to happen. What did happen was that a very plump old gentleman, shaking his head over all the noise going on above, got in, muttering, " Disgraceful ! Might be a tenement—I shall lodge a complaint."

Mary could see he was very pink in the face. She waited till he had shut the doors and then she untucked her self, and because whenever she talked in Swiss, people seemed to disappear, she gave instead, her friendliest growl.

The old man seemed to turn to stone and then very stiffly and very slowly, he turned round and Mary saw, to her surprise, that his face wasn't pink after all but a kind of pale green. He stood there, staring at Mary with popping eyes, making swallowing noises. Mary, attracted by a large gold chain stretched across his waistcoat, bent forward and stroked it. The next moment the chain with a large gold watch at one end and a bunch of seals at the other, was in Mary's paw.

Meantime a crowd, led by little Harry and his self-sacrificing mother, Baba and Nannie, had collected and were all waiting at the bottom of the stairs for the lift to arrive, all ready to scream if Mary got out.

But she didn't. Instead, very slowly and backwards, came the plump old gentleman in his vest and trousers, while in the lift Mary, who adored dressing-up, was enjoying all the things she had stroked on the way down.

" Help ! " thought the Owl Man, just back for lunch, and recognising a Mary scene at once. But a bit of fur in the lift caught his eye and the next minute he had shot into it, slammed the doors and pressed the button.

He stood with his back to the door and faced Mary. Mary was swamped in the plump old gentleman's shirt, her legs were thrust through the arm-holes of the waistcoat, while the gold watch sat perched on the top ledge of the porridge curve. But the Owl Man didn't seem to notice any of this. He only said grimly, " What next, Mary ? That's what I want to know. For pity's sake, what next ? "

" Dinner, I hope," said Mary.

CHAPTER SEVEN

ABOUT TWINS AND TELEPHONES AND A SHIPWRECK

FOR the next few days nothing very exciting happened, because the Owl Man was always most particular about locking the door before he went out.

In the afternoon he took Mary down to Richmond Park and she galloped about and chatted to the deer and enjoyed herself very much.

But she didn't enjoy the mornings at all. Every morning the flat seemed to get emptier and emptier till at last one morning, when the Owl Man came back, he found Mary so close to the door that he almost stepped on her as he opened it.

" Hallo ! " he said. " What are you up to ? "

But for once Mary wasn't up to anything. Instead she asked, in a very small voice, " Do you think the twins are happy without me ? "

" Oh dear," said the Owl Man, who knew something would have to be done at once.

" You see," said Mary, " there's always two of twins."

The Owl Man patted her head. " Quite right, Mary, but

I'm afraid I can't turn you into a twin, much as I'd like to please you."

" Could you buy me one ? " asked Mary hopefully.

" I'm afraid not, but, come to think of it, I might borrow one—an English one."

" I'd rather have a Swiss twin, please," said Mary.

" No, an English one," said the Owl Man firmly, " and then you'll learn to speak the language. It won't be a bear, of course, but I might find a child who could come and play about with you."

" And be my twin ? " insisted Mary.

" Well, you could always ask," said the Owl Man. " Hallo, that's the telephone."

" What are you talking into that little hole for ? " asked Mary, who had followed him across the room.

" Ssh ! Hallo, Jill, is that you ? What ? I'd love to. Right. I say, hold on a minute, there's a surprise for you here—a friend who wants a word-with you. Here, Mary, it's the Fur-Coat-Lady."

Mary applied her eye to the hole. " It isn't ! " she said reproachfully.

" No, no. You can't see her, only hear. Hold this up to your ear and put your mouth near the hole." Mary held the receiver and breathed heavily into the mouth-piece.

" Go on," urged the Owl Man encouragingly. " Say something."

" Something ! " shouted Mary at the top of her voice.

" Steady, steady," said the Owl Man, " you don't have to shout," while the Fur-Coat-Lady at the other end wondered if her ear was broken.

" Isn't she in Switzerland, then ? " asked Mary.

By this time, and because of her ear, the Fur-Coat-Lady had guessed what the surprise was but, so as not to spoil it, she said, " Who *is* that, please ? " and Mary, hopping up and down with excitement, said, " It's Mary Plain, an unusual first-class bear with a—"

" Here, that'll do," said the Owl Man, removing the receiver. " Did you get that, Jill ? I say, couldn't you come round and have lunch ? Yes, now. Good ! We'll wait for you and afterwards we must have a Mary conference."

Mary sat down on a chair facing the telephone and the Owl Man left her there while he went off to see to something in his room. When he came back, Mary was still there and it was so unlike her to be still in the same place that he was just going to ask her if she was sure she felt quite well, when the doorbell rang.

" That will be the Fur-Coat-Lady, I expect," he said and went off to answer it.

It was, but when they came back Mary was still sitting with her eyes glued to the telephone. " Why doesn't she hurry up ? " she complained. " I'm so tired of her not coming."

" But I'm here ! " said the Fur-Coat-Lady.

Mary swung round and the next minute the Fur-Coat-Lady was getting a real Mary hug which is a particularly nice thing to get.

" But how did you come ? " asked Mary, looking first at the telephone and then at her friend. " I didn't see you come out. Was it a conjuring trick ? " And though they both explained hard, Mary couldn't really understand about telephones.

They had lunch and, as the Owl Man scraped the last of the suet pudding on to Mary's plate, he said, " Mary is a very unwasteful person to have about."

" So I see," said the Fur-Coat-Lady who had not seen Mary for some time and had forgotten about her appetite. " Don't you ever feel anxious ? " she asked.

" Four times a day, terribly ! " said the Owl Man. " I shudder to think what would happen if she should ever get punctured with a pin."

" Get what ? " said Mary.

" Get down and wipe your paws carefully," said the Owl Man.

After lunch they held the Mary conference and it was decided that the first thing to do was to teach Mary English. " And the best way to do that," said the Owl Man, " is to get hold of some child who could be with her. I know. A friend of mine in the flats above has a young god-son staying with him— the very thing. I'll run up now and see if I can arrange anything."

Presently he came back with a small boy. " This is Mark," he said. " He's lonely too, when he's not at school and, what's more, he can understand Swiss a bit, so you ought to get on like a house on fire, Mary."

Mary stared at Mark and Mark stared back, not quite sure whether you shook hands with a bear or not. Mary settled the question by going up to him and giving a little bow. " Will you be my twin when I want one, please ? " she said. And Mark, who knew his manners, bowed back and said he'd do his best.

" Well, as that seems to be satisfactorily settled, I must fly," said the Owl Man and flew.

" How would you like to go and see the boats on the Round Pond, you two ? " suggested the Fur-Coat-Lady.

" Is it a wet kind of pond? " asked Mary, and when they said " Yes," she said she must just go and fetch her luggage.

The luggage had arrived that morning from Berne and was an exceedingly gaily checked bag with a zipp fastener but when Mark asked what was inside, Mary said it was very private luggage. The Fur-Coat-Lady thought she had never seen such un-private luggage in her life, but she didn't say so.

When they reached the Marble Arch they stood waiting to cross by a Belisha beacon and Mark, who didn't know Mary very well, said for fun, " Have an orange ? "

" Yes, please," said Mary, just as the policeman stopped the traffic for them to cross.

" Come on, Mary," said the Fur-Coat-Lady, pulling. But Mary braced her legs and said " After the orange," and the traffic jamb got bigger and bigger and the Fur-Coat-Lady pulled and the policeman shouted and then, just in time, Mark had a clever idea.

" There's some on the other side," he said and then, so as to make a sure thing of it, he added, " Nice big juicy ones," and Mary stopped bracing and crossed at once.

Safely on the other side, Mark explained that he had only been teasing her and Mary didn't like him quite so much as she had at first and, by the time she had climbed up the beacon to see for herself that it was a joke orange, and the policeman had taken the Fur-Coat-Lady's name and address for allowing her to climb the beacon, the usual crowd had collected.

" This won't do," said the Fur-Coat-Lady, rather pink in the face, and she called a taxi and bundled her charges in.

Luckily at the Round Pond there were only a few children, because it was a cold day. One of them was Sandy. Sandy was the Fur-Coat-Lady's nephew and Mary had met him when she was svisiting her.

" Hallo, Mary," he called, while all the other children wished they knew a bear. " These are my two friends, David and Michael."

David and Michael were as like as two peas and Mary looked at them hard and then pulled the Fur-Coat-Lady's arm. She bent her head and Mary whispered " Why are they both the same ? "

" Twins ! " whispered the Fur-Coat-Lady.

" Good morning, both ! " said Mary, politely bowing. " This is my twin," and she pulled Mark forward. Mark, rather red in the face, translated and said, " It's only a game, of course."

The twins looked very envious.

" I wish I could have a little holiday from David and be Mary's twin instead," said Michael.

Among the other children Mary specially liked a small girl in a very blue bonnet and coat with eyes to match, because blue was Mary's ' best ' colour. She was called Ruth.

The small girl had a white steamer with a little wooden captain on board which chugged across the pond, while she

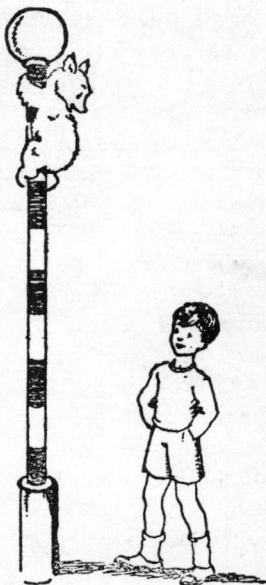

She picked up the captain in her mouth

stood on the edge and shouted " Look at my captain ! Just look at my captain ! "

But, alas, a big battleship ran right into the little white steamer and it was sunk, and the captain went down with his ship. The ship stayed sunk but the captain floated to the top and the small girl wrung her hands and said, " Oh, won't somebody save me my captain ? " And Mary, perhaps because she was so blue, decided she would. Again she pulled at the Fur-Coat-Lady's arm. " Please could you be a tree for a minute," she said, " because there isn't one near ? "

" Certainly," said the Fur-Coat-Lady, standing very stiff and hoping she looked like an elm, while Mary puffed and panted behind her and then came out dressed in her red and white bathing drawers.

She took a running dive into the Pond, and in a few moments, she was out at the scene of the disaster. Here she dived again and again and came up spluttering and there was a lot of splashing and fuss while Mary seemed to be tying herself into knots under the water and then she picked up the captain in her mouth and started for shore.

Mary had gone into the water her usual shape but she landed quite another, and the Fur-Coat-Lady looked at the odd knobbly bulges which stuck out in front and wondered anxiously about bears' appendixes. Anybody who knew Mary wasn't surprised about ordinary bulging but this was different, and a little alarming.

However, the children didn't seem to notice. They stood in two rows and made an arch with their arms and Mary walked underneath, bowing to left and right and thoroughly enjoying the cries of " Well done, Mary Plain ! " which was the kind of English she could understand.   At the end of the arch stood Ruth who flung her arms round Mary's wet neck and cried, " Oh thank you, thank you, brave bear ! "   Being a bear, Mary, of course, couldn't blush, but she did feel very awkward with the small girl fastened round her neck like a necklace and was very glad when someone unfastened her.

She went at once to the Fur-Coat-Lady.   " Please will you be my tree again ? " and once more the Fur-Coat-Lady played at being an elm.   This time there was a good deal of grunting and then a sound of popping elastic and then Mary emerged with the little white steamer in her hand and the right shape in front.   " Thank   goodness," said   the   Fur-Coat-Lady, fervently.

Then Mark climbed up on the railings and shouted, " Let's give her a bear cheer, everybody.   Come on ! "

And all the children cried, " Hip, hip, hoo-Mary !   Hip, hip, hoo-Plain ! " as loud as they could.

CHAPTER EIGHT

MARY SVISITS A DANCING-CLASS

MARY was getting on very nicely with her lessons. Mark went to school in the mornings and then she did lessons alone with the Fur-Coat-Lady, but after lunch Mark very kindly had another lesson with Mary as she seemed to learn much quicker if there was anyone about whom she had a chance of beating. Twice she had been at the top of the class which meant of course at the top of Mark.

Mary's dictations were quite different from Mark's. For instance the Fur-Coat-Lady would say, " The teapot was left in the kitchen."

Mark would write, " The teepot was left in the kittchen," but Mary would write it like this :—

THE WAS LEFT IN THE CHIN

The first morning the Fur-Coat-Lady and Mary had started off cheerfully on arithmetic but, at the end of the lesson, the only one that was cheerful was Mary. The Fur-Coat-Lady had a headache.

293

To start the arithmetic lesson she had emptied a box of matches on to the table. Mary had told her she could count up to 5 backwards or forwards, always, and up to 7 on extra clever days. This first day, however, didn't seem to be an extra clever day, and Mary stuck at 6. After that she said "lots of matches," or "heaps of matches," or just "more matches."

So the Fur-Coat-Lady, who knew Mary rather well, fetched a bowl full of lump sugar. Mary's eyes glistened. "Sugar's *much* easier to count," she said, and the Fur-Coat-Lady congratulated herself on having had such a very good idea.

"Now Mary, come along. One lump of sugar."

"One lump of sugar," repeated Mary as well as she could because of its being the biggest in the dish.

"Yes, this is a very good idea," thought the Fur-Coat-Lady, watching Mary's happy face. "This is the right kind of lesson for bears. When we do geography I shall have a saucer of milk for the seas and sugar for islands. Lessons ought to be fun."

Mary finished the lump carefully before she picked up another and popped that into her mouth. "One lump of sugar," she said again.

"No," said the Fur-Coat-Lady. "Two."

"But it's one," said Mary, "look!"

"That'll do, Mary," said the Fur-Coat-Lady, hastily, wondering if her idea had been such a good one after all. "But it is your second lump," she added.

Mary looked stupid. Mary could look very stupid if she liked and she did like now. She opened her mouth wide.

"That'll do," said the Fur-Coat-Lady again, trying not to see her tonsils.

" But there isn't anything there, is there ? "   And the Fur-Coat-Lady was forced to admit there wasn't.

So Mary picked up another lump and looked at the Fur-Coat-Lady out of the corner of her eye—not a stupid look this time.   " One lump of sugar," she said, as it disappeared.

" And now," said the Fur-Coat-Lady firmly, " we will have some geography," and she removed the sugar-bowl and, at the same time, gave up any idea of a milk Mediterranean because of the expense it would be.

" Perhaps, after all, you'd do better at school," she said, looking doubtfully at Mary.

" Oh, but I like these kind of lessons very much indeed, thank you," said Mary, licking her lips.

So the lessons continued and the Owl Man's sugar bill was enormous and the Fur-Coat-Lady said she was very sorry but he'd better try and teach Mary himself and then he'd see. But the Owl Man didn't a bit want to see and he paid the bill without another word.

Mary got on excellently well with her English, and one day the Fur-Coat-Lady said she was such a good pupil that she would give her a treat and take her to watch Sandy's dancing class.

The class was held in a large empty room and directly they went into it, Mary fell flat on her back.

" Oh dear," said the Fur-Coat-Lady, " it's slippery, like the rooms in my house.   I ought to have warned you."

" You did," said Mary, rubbing her behind.

Now, it is very exciting and a little upsetting when a bear comes to watch you dance for the first time and the forty little girls in frilled skirts and thirty-five little boys in silk shirts, all kept their eyes fixed on Mary instead of on the dancing mistress.

So presently the mistress said that perhaps it would be better if the little visitor came and sat in front, and she pulled up two chairs for Mary and the Fur-Coat-Lady.

Mary gave a little bow before she sat down and the mistress said " Charming ! Now, children, what do little ladies do when a gentleman bows to them ? *All* together ! " And all the rows of little girls in frilled skirts curtsied to the ground. Mary was so impressed that she got off her chair and tried to curtsy back but it wasn't much of a success for somehow she trod on her own paw and fell. The kind mistress picked her up.

" I'm good at bowing," explained Mary, " but I'm not bendy here," and she laid her paw on the place where most people wear their waists.

" Quite," said the mistress helping her to her seat.

" And, please," said Mary, " I aren't a gentleman but a gentle-lady."

" I beg your pardon," said the mistress.

" Certainly," said Mary graciously. " Bears all dress the same, so it's very mixing, isn't it ? "

The mistress agreed and the Fur-Coat-Lady said Mary must really sit still and not interrupt any more. But Mary didn't sit still long, because very soon they started skipping. She got down at once.

" I always win at skipping, so could I try, please ? "

" Mary ! " said the Fur-Coat-Lady, getting very pink because of Mary's boasting but the mistress said, " Never mind,

I understand," and then " Aline and Gervase ! Will you both swing a rope for our little visitor ? "

So Aline and Gervase swung and Mary, her paws tight down at her sides and her ears flying, jumped so high that they could pass the rope three times underneath before she came down.

" She's done the ' treble=through,' " said Aline in awed tones.

" Oh, it's very easy indeed," panted Mary, a little puffed by her jumping but more puffed at her success.

" Oh, Mary ! " said the Fur-Coat-Lady again.

" And now, how would you like to try to do some of the exercises ? " enquired the mistress.

" Please," said Mary, so a space was made in the front line between Aline and Gervase for her.

" Now, children ! First position ! " called the mistress.
All the little girls placed their feet neatly in the first position
—right foot turned outwards. Mary, watching them, did
her utmost to do the same.

The mistress passed along the front row, criticising.
" Well done, Polly ! Good, Felicity ! Excellent, Joy and
June ! "

When she came to Mary and saw her right paw neatly in
the first position, only inwards, she stopped. Mary looked up
at her anxiously. She was trying terribly hard. " It fits
better this way," she said, trying, without success, to see her
own paws. " It's an excellent fit," said the mistress, kindly,
and gave her a pat on the head.

Then came the final march and the mistress said would Mary
care to join in and, of course, Mary cared.

" Let me see," said the mistress, holding Mary by the paw,
" who had she better march with ? I think Jenny would be
the right height. Yes." She clapped her hands. " Will
Jenny please come here ? " And Jenny came, in a white frock
with a blue sash and a blue wreath of flowers round her curls.

" I've got a blue bow at home," said Mary.

" Have you ? " said Jenny, wondering where she wore it.

" I wish it was here," said Mary, looking wistfully at Jenny's
wreath.

Jenny's Nanna rushed to the rescue. " Jenny likes marching
without her wreath, don't you, Jenny ? " she said brightly, and
the next minute the blue wreath was round Mary's neck.
Jenny gave a little sigh but, after all, what was the loss of a
blue wreath and a few curls in the eye compared to marching
with a bear, she told herself.

"Now, Jenny!" said the mistress, "you two shall lead."
("Leading too!" thought Jenny. "Bother the wreath!")
"Take her paw—so! Now, children, point your toes."
Mary, with extreme difficulty, pointed her paw.
"Ready? One, two, three, march!"
And round went all the forty frilled skirts and the thirty-five
silk shirts with Mary and Jenny in front, marching beautifully,
because of both having lots of hair and the same kind of shape.

Just as they got near the door, the Owl Man came in and,
seeing the approaching procession, he tried to slip behind
someone.

But it was very difficult to slip with Mary about. "Hallo!"
she shouted, delightedly, coming to a halt and bringing all the
marching children into a jamb behind her. "Jenny and me's
leading, both of us. Look at my points!"

"Get on, Mary," urged the Owl Man. "Don't stop,
go on!"

But Mary wanted to tell him all about what she had been
doing and the Owl Man, because it was the only thing to do,
took her paw and marched along beside her, very much wishing he had stayed behind with his case.

The music ended, the children crowded round Mary and
the mistress came up and thanked the Owl Man for saving the
situation.

"What's a situation?" asked Mary.

"Well, you ought to know better than most people," said
the Owl Man, putting his hand on Mary's head to stop her
jumping. "Time you came home, Mary. There's altogether
too much bounce about you to-day."

"It's a bouncy kind of day," said Mary.

"*Look at my points!*"

"Most of your's are," said the Owl Man, as he led her away.

"Come again, come again!" shouted all the children, who had found dancing classes with bears far more fun than without.

"All right!" shouted Mary back. "And next time I'll do the ' sixle-through.' "

CHAPTER NINE

MARY GOES TO SCHOOL

THE great day came when Mary was to go to school for the first time with Mark. He went to a senior class, of course, but Mary was to go to the Kindergarten where the very smallest children were.

She had passed the entrance exam with flying colours. One or two of the teachers weren't at all sure that some of Mary's answers were not too flying, but they all agreed that she showed promise. Here are the exam questions, with Mary's answers underneath.

1. *Why do you want to come to school?*
   To get to the top of the class.
2. *What is the difference between a pond and a lake?*
   A pond is wet and a lake is wetter.
3. *How do you spell physic?*
   I don't.

4. *When do you feel happiest ?*
   Eating meringues.
5. *When do you feel saddest ?*
   Finishing meringues.
6. *Name three famous people.*
   Mary Plain, Mary Plain, Mary Plain.
7. *Who is your favourite saint ?*
   St. Bruin.
8. *Name two kinds of wool.*
   Big and Little.
9. *What do the following letters stand for—L.s.d., G.R. ?*
   Because there isn't a chair to sit on.

And the examining mistress had written underneath *Passed on the last answer.*

Mark came down after breakfast to see if Mary was ready.

" Has she got her satchel ? " he asked the Owl Man.

" Rather," said the Owl Man, " time to get ready, is it ? "

" Yes. I'll just run up and get my things on and then I'll come and fetch you, Mary."

" I'll be quite ready," promised Mary, trotting off to her room with the satchel. She was ! When Mark came back, she came trotting back again, looking as pleased as Punch.

" Phew ! " said the Owl Man and " Oh, I *say !* " said Mark, beginning to wonder if he wouldn't rather Mary went to school separately.

" I've been getting my things on too," she said.

" You have ! " said the Owl Man.

For Mary had on her red and white bathing drawers, her blue bow, and her gold medal and chain. Down the back hung the card she had had at the Crystal Palace Show with

"Miss Mary Plain. From the famous Bear Pits at Berne. Shown by the Owl Man," written on it and, as a final touch, she had pinned the white rosette on to the front of the bathing drawers. She held the satchel in her paw.

"There doesn't seem to be any room for this," she said.

"There doesn't, does there," said the Owl Man helplessly, wondering how he could get the things off.

"I must be smart for school," said Mary, preening herself.

"Yes. But not *too* smart," said the Owl Man, seeing Mark's face of growing horror and pulling himself together. "You must just let me explain. You see, Mary, you couldn't possibly wear your medal, for instance, because all the children would want medals too, and bathing drawers are absolutely forbidden in the autumn term, aren't they, Mark?"

"Absolutely," said Mark, firmly.

"And this card," went on the Owl Man, and presently he had explained all the things off and there was only Mary left. She stood, drooping a little, and looking sadly at the pile of things on the table.

"All the smart has gone now," she said and her voice wobbled. "Do you think the twins are happy without me?"

And the Owl Man said, very loudly and cheerfully, "Oh, but we've forgotten her school colours, Mark! She can't possibly go to school without her colours. I've got the ribbon somewhere. Now, where did I put it?" and he went on loudly and cheerfully hunting for the ribbon.

"Would she like my cap, just for to-day?" suggested Mark, feeling sorry for Mary who looked as if she was still thinking about the twins.

So they tried the cap on, first on each ear and then between, but it was no good, Mary just didn't suit caps.

" No, it will have to be a bow," said the Owl Man, " Mary wears a bow very well."

" I'm glad I wear something well," said Mary a trifle bitterly.

" Or what about a belt ? " suggested Mark. " I say, wait a sec." and he fiddled in his pocket and produced a school belt, complete with a snake buckle, " I thought so—the very thing."

" Always providing we find just the right position and that it fits," said the Owl Man, shutting one eye and looking at Mary. After a bad shot or two he found the position but, alas, there were three good inches of Mary between the two ends of the belt—four when she breathed.

The Owl Man shook his head and pursed his lips and did a good deal of fiddling with the belt and tried again and this time there was a most satisfactory little click as the buckle snapped together.

She marched off between them

"Luckily for you it was a very obliging snake," said the Owl Man, mopping his brow and stepping back. "Yes, there's no doubt about it, that was a very good suggestion of yours, Mark. Mary wears a belt exceedingly well—exceedingly well."

"Yes," agreed Mark. "You look terribly smart, Mary. Got your lunch?"

Mary dropped her eyes and looked at the floor.

"Have you, Mary?" asked the Owl Man, suddenly suspicious.

Mary kicked at the floor a bit with her paw and the Owl Man got up and looked inside the satchel. "There were three bananas and two *Petit Beurre* biscuits in this satchel this morning, weren't there, Mary?"

"Yes," said Mary, still kicking at the floor.

"And where are they now?"

"Inside me," said Mary, who was often truthful.

The Owl Man didn't speak but his back view, as he went off to collect a second lunch, was very expressive.

At last Mary was ready, with her satchel strapped on her back, and she marched off between them, one arm stretched very high because of the Owl Man being so tall.

"I'll just come in and introduce you," he said and, when they got to Mary's class-room, they found a nice surprise waiting for them, for the teacher was the lady in the blue hat whom they had met in the Golden Arrow train on Mary's last visit to England.

"Blue is still my best colour," said Mary frankly.

"That's good," said the lady, "because it's still mine, as you see by my jumper."

" Yes," said Mary, wondering if it ever jumped.

" Now, children, this is Mary Plain and you must all be very kind to her because this is her first day at school."

" Yes," said all the children, staring hard at Mary as they sat at their little desks.

" This is your desk, Mary, between Prudence and Nicholas, just behind Richard. Come and sit down." But Mary got rather badly stuck in her effort to sit and then it was discovered that she still had her satchel on. The mistress took it off and wanted to take it away but Mary said " It's mine, it's mine!" and grabbed at it. " Very well," said the teacher sensibly, " we'll put it by your feet and, so it won't get lost, you shall write your own name on a label and stick it on. That will give you something to do while I am correcting these exercises. Look, here are some sticky labels," and she handed Mary a little book of labels. Mary pulled one out, wrote on it and then licked it.

Then she licked her lips. " This is a nice label," she thought. " I'll just see if the next one tastes the same."

When the teacher came back, there were no labels in the little book but Mary's satchel had a white coat on. It looked like this.

" Everyone can see it's mine now, can't they? " said Mary.

" Unless they were quite, quite blind," agreed the teacher, knowing she ought to scold Mary but not doing it because of its being her first morning at school. So instead she fetched out a huge cardboard clock and, hanging it up at the end of the room, she began moving the hands round and asking the children to tell the time.

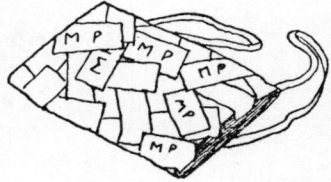

" What's that? " she asked.

" Eleven ! " said one child.

" Quite right ! We all know eleven, Mary, because that is the time we have our lunch." Mary's ears pricked. The next time it pointed to eleven Mary shouted " Banana time ! " and all the children laughed.

When banana time really came, Mary was the centre of a crowd, but she was too busy with her bananas and *Petits Beurres* at first to talk much and when she was ready to talk the bell rang for dictation.

Mary, as usual, did well at the dictation and when they had finished the teacher said that, to end up with, they could each try and write a little poem.

" A pome about what ? " asked Mary.

" Anything you like, as long as it is really interesting," said the teacher.

So Mary wrote :—

> *I dance like a fairy*
> *I'm lovely and hairy*
> *I went in an airy*
> *O plane.*

> *I am a bear*
> *A famous bear*
> *My name is Mar*
> *Y Plain.*

The teacher didn't know what to say when she had read Mary's. It was definitely a boasty poem and she ought not to allow boasty poems but, on the other hand, she couldn't help agreeing with Mary that Mary Plain was a very interesting subject to write about. So she got out of it by saying that the poem was a little unusual and that she would have to take it home and think over how many marks it deserved.

And that evening Mary told the Owl Man that they had been asked to write a poem about something interesting. " And guess what mine was about ! " said Mary, hopping up and down in front of him. " You can have three guesses."

" I shall only need one," said the Owl Man.

CHAPTER TEN

WHICH HAS GOT MARY, MEASLES AND MURPHY IN IT

WHEN Mary had been at school about a fortnight, one of the children in the Kindergarten developed measles.

"We are not going to close the school," the Head Mistress wrote to the Owl Man, "as we hope there will be no further cases, but I would be glad if you would keep an eye on Mary Plain as, of course, she has been exposed to the infection."

So every morning before he went off to his case the Owl Man had a Mary inspection.

"Tongue out," he ordered and Mary hung her tongue out so far that every day it was a fresh surprise to him. "Feel all right?" he would then ask and Mary would say, "Quite, thank you," and the inspection would be over.

But one morning Mary's tongue, though it was just as long, wasn't a nice tongue and when, with a sinking heart, the Owl Man asked her how she felt, she said her throat felt tight. So the Owl Man telephoned at once to a doctor friend of his who had a small children's hospital and explained about Mary and the doctor said he'd better bring her round at once and let him have a look at her ; luckily there was a vacancy in the measles ward, so, if necessary, Mary could be kept there.

On the way down in the lift Mary was so quiet that the Owl Man said " Feeling all right, Mary ? "

" My head hurts," said Mary and the Owl Man wished lifts weren't so slow.

As they got into the car Mary said, " My head hurts more," and the Owl Man drove as fast as he dared till a traffic block held them up and he came to a dead stop.

" I feel sick," said Mary helpfully.

" Well, you can't be sick now, Mary," said the Owl Man, desperately, " not in my new car. You must hang on till you get to the hospital."

" I'll try," said Mary. And the Owl Man put the accelerator down very hard and did all the things one oughtn't to do in London, like cutting in and taking no notice of Belisha crossings, and in five minutes he was at the hospital. It was a tall black house and Mary, after one look, said, " My head is better and my sick has all gone now and if I have to have measles I'd rather have them at home with you, thank you."

" I'm afraid that isn't possible," said the Owl Man. " You see, I'm away at my case all day and bears can't have measles alone in flats—it isn't done. No, if it is measles you'll be far better off here, Mary, and, perhaps, after all, it's not that at all. We'll see ! "

But that was just what the doctor couldn't do.

" I'm afraid we shall have to—well—clear the ground a bit," said Dr. Murphy.

" Quite," said the Owl Man.

So a razor was fetched and a small neat square made on Mary's chest and inside the square they found the measles.

" So that's that ! " said Dr. Murphy. " Now, I must just fill up this card—a mere question of formality." And he did a bit of questioning and the Owl Man did a bit of answering and then the doctor handed over a card on which was written,

> *Name, Christian* Mary.
> *Surname (in block capitals)* PLAIN.
> *Profession* Svisiting spinster.
> *Address* Bear Pits, Berne.
> *Nature of ailment* Measles (mild).

Across the bottom was printed in red letters,
> *Please admit bearer to Sunshine ward, Bed* 27.

" Have I won a prize ? " asked Mary.

" Not this time, old girl," said the Owl Man. " This is just a kind of invitation from Dr. Murphy asking you to svisit him for a little while. He's a great friend of mine and I'm sure he'll be glad to help you if he can. She's never been in hospital before and—well, you understand, Murphy ? "

" Perfectly," said Murphy. " If there's anything you want, Miss Plain, just let me know. And now, if you'll take her up to the ward—third floor and the lift's at the end of the passage —I'll be up presently to have a look at her." Mary went off, holding very tightly to the Owl Man's hand.

Sunshine Ward was full of measly children. Some extremely measly, some only a little, but none too measly to be interested in Mary's arrival. A nice young nurse came smiling to the door.

" I'm afraid I can't let you come any further," she said to

the Owl Man. " You see, this is an infectious ward. She is to have the bed in the corner—I'll just turn back the cover."

The nurse went off and the Owl Man looked down at Mary. She looked very small and clung to his hand more tightly than ever.

" Well, Mary," he said, in an extra cheerful voice, " I must be off."

" Please," said Mary, earnestly, " I'm quite sure the measle has gone now. Just you look."

The Owl Man bent and examined the square. Then he shook his head. " Afraid not, Mary. But cheer up, you'll be so happy here, you won't want to leave when the time comes ! Here comes your nurse. Do you see she has a blue dress on ? Specially for you, I expect," he whispered encouragingly.

But Mary wouldn't be encouraged. " I wish it was pink," she said unreasonably and holding on to him with both paws. Luckily, the Owl Man hadn't been Mary's friend for a year for nothing. Just as the nurse came back, he whipped a little parcel out of his pocket and slipped it into her paw.

" There ! " he said. " That's to open when you're in bed," and before Mary could say another word he had disappeared.

Five minutes later Mary was sitting up in bed, in a red flannel bed-jacket a size too big for her, eating a bowl of bread and milk and opening the parcel between the mouthfuls. Presently Dr. Murphy came along and got out his stethoscope to listen to her chest.

" Why are you telephoning me for ? " asked Mary.

" Because there are one or two things I want to ask you," said the doctor. " You've got a headache, you said. Is that all ? "

" I feel prickly," said Mary. " It prickles me to sit."

" H'm. Any other symptoms ? "

" Symp—what ? " said Mary.

" Toms," said the doctor. " Feelings, I mean."

" Oh yes," said Mary, " I feel quite sure I'd be better at once if I could go home to the Owl Man."

" Well, I didn't quite mean that," said the doctor kindly, " I meant aches or pains."

" I feel achy here," said Mary, pointing to her left side.

" Yes, that's a very usual sort of ache to have on the first day," said Dr. Murphy, " and, luckily, one I'm sure we can quickly cure. Well, good-night to you, Miss Plain. Remember, if there's anything you want, you have only to ask."

Mary asked for a good deal before the nurse got her settled

for the night.   She asked three times more for bread and milk
and the nurse, who had never nursed a bear before, got it
for her and then she asked for a basin and the nurse said she
wasn't at all surprised.   At seven o'clock nurse went off duty
and left all the children tucked up for the night.   Each had
a little bell beside their bed ; she said she hoped they wouldn't
use it but it was for the night nurse—just in case.

In Mary's case it was most useful.   The bell got little rest
that night, nor did the nurse.

The first time Mary rang it because she wanted to hear
what kind of noise it made.

The second time she rang it she asked for bread and milk.

The nurse was firm—no bread and milk till morning.

Mary bore it for half-an-hour and then she rang again, this
time keeping her paw on the bell till the nurse appeared.

" I want Dr. Murphy," said Mary, sitting up in bed, with a
ruffled head and forgetting to say ' please.'

The nurse argued and Mary argued and Mary won.   In
ten minutes Dr. Murphy appeared in pyjamas with an overcoat
on top.   He looked very sleepy and not quite so kind as before.

" Hallo ! " he said.   " What's all this about ? "

"Do you think the twins are happy without me ? " said Mary.

" Bless my soul ! " said Dr. Murphy, sitting down rather
suddenly.   " Do you mean to say that you've got me out of
my bed to ask me that ? Who are the twins, anyway ? "
Mary explained and the doctor did his best to forget about his
bed and to pacify her, remembering what the Owl Man had
said about its being her first visit to a hospital.   He left her
with a pat on the head and an injunction to sleep tight till
the morning.

Mary fell asleep for an hour. Directly she woke, she rang the bell. The nurse appeared.

" I want Dr. Murphy," said Mary.

" Oh no you don't," said the nurse, trying to forget what Dr. Murphy had said the last time she had woken him up.

But Mary won again. Back came the doctor, looking less kind than ever.

" Look here, Miss Plain," he said, " I've had about enough of this."

" So have I," said Mary. " I want the twins and the Owl Man and the Fur-Coat-Lady and my luggage and I've got a hurt in my head and my measles keeps waking me up and I'm not allowed any bread and milk and—"

" Oh, give her a bucket of bread and milk !" said Dr. Murphy and went back to bed.

CHAPTER ELEVEN

THE FIRE THAT WASN'T

THE next two days were very miserable ones for Mary. They moved her into a ward by herself. She tossed about in bed and her head ached and her body prickled; she even turned away from bread and milk, which was the worst sign of all.

But after a few days there was a distinct change for the better and she was able to sit up and take notice again. She listened in to the Children's Hour and very much enjoyed it.

" I'll give you a nice blanket bath," said nurse that evening. " It will make you feel clean and fresh." So she fetched a big basin of hot soapy water and put it by Mary's bed and then covered her up with blankets while she ran off to fetch a towel.

She seemed to be gone rather a long time and Mary, looking at the basin, thought it seemed a pity to waste any more minutes, so she threw off the blankets and climbing on to the table, got into the basin. It was a full basin and there wasn't room in it for Mary and the water so most of the water went on to the table and the floor. Mary started rubbing herself with what was left and made such a lovely lather that when the nurse came back she looked like a picture of a small polar bear, sitting in a lake.

" Gracious goodness ! " said the nurse, angry about the wetness, but at the same time thinking how becoming the soap was to Mary. " Whatever are you doing, Mary ? "

" Just helping you to bath me," explained Mary, blowing a soap bubble off the tip of her nose. " Wasn't it kind of me ? "

The nurse didn't answer but she looked a lot. She finished Mary off and got her back to bed as quickly as she could.

" Now," she said, " I'll take your temperature and then you can have a bowl of bread and milk. Not that you deserve it," she added. She tucked the thermometer under Mary's arm, and at the same time placed a steaming bowl by the bedside.

" Don't you dare move for three minutes," she cautioned Mary as she went off.

Mary lay and sniffed at the bread and milk. Some sifted sugar lay on the top. It seemed a pity to leave it lying on the top because it would taste better mixed. But nurse had forgotten the spoon. " Never mind," thought Mary, " I'll give it a mix with my 'mometer and then it'll be ready when I want it." So she did.

Back came nurse and whipped out the thermometer from under her arm. " Gracious goodness ! " she said again, for Mary's temperature was about as high as it could go, and she sat down rather suddenly on the bed and went the same colour that the old plump man in the lift had gone. " Don't move, Mary, don't move an eyelid, till I fetch Doctor Murphy." She rushed off and Mary lay as still as a mouse, managing the eyelids very well but not so successful over her nose which would keep twitching because of the nearness of the milk.

Dr. Murphy came running. He felt Mary's pulse, looked at her tongue, telephoned her chest and pummelled her tummy.

"And now can I have my bread and milk, please?" asked Mary. The doctor looked at the bread and milk, then at Mary and then at the thermometer and took a deep breath. "Only I haven't got a spoon," said Mary.

"So I see," said the doctor shortly. "So ought anyone to to see," he added, glaring at the nurse, whose face was now scarlet, "but some people don't use their eyes or their brains," and he stumped off angrily.

"Why did he look like that for?" enquired Mary.

"Oh, why did you get measles for?" answered the nurse impatiently.

"Not on purpose," said Mary trying to look offended and eat her bread and milk at the same time and not succeeding very well.

The supper finished, nurse tucked her up for the night.

"You just go to sleep and stay there, Mary Plain," she said, "we don't want to hear another sound from you till morning. Don't you forget it."

So when Mary woke up in the middle of the night and felt bored, she didn't ring her bell as usual but got out of bed, instead.

"I'll just have a bit of explore," she said, "and see what I can find."

She crept out of the room and into the big ward where she had been the first night. All the children were asleep, making soft breathing noises, not a bit like the bears' night noises. One little boy was lying on his back with his mouth wide open.

"Poor little boy," said Mary to herself, "he looks so thirsty," and picking up a glass of water, she emptied it into his mouth.

The boy sat up making loud spluttering and choking noises and the nurse came rushing through the door. Mary popped under the bed. "Perhaps it wasn't water he wanted," she thought, edging away from nurse's feet which kept poking under the bed and hoping she didn't show the other side.

"Must have dreamt you were thirsty, I should think!" said the nurse, as she bustled the boy into dry pyjamas while Mary, underneath, held her breath till she nearly burst.

At last all was quiet and Mary, rather stiff from her cramped position, crept out and tip-toed to the further door. It had been cold on the floor—linoleum isn't at all comforting to sit on. Mary shivered a little and looked back at the ward grate which was mostly grey ashes now with just a few little sparks left in one corner. " I wish I had a fire," she said disconsolately and, turning round, found the answer to her wish. For, hanging on the wall, just above her head, was a beautiful brass fire-helmet and underneath was a handle which said " Fire ! Pull ! "

So Mary pulled.

There was a loud whirr and then all through the hospital a deafening sound of electric bells, a sound that went on loudly and without stopping. It didn't even stop when four doctors, eleven nurses and nine maids came rushing up the stairs, carrying buckets of water and sand and all shouting different orders. " Where is the fire ? Someone locate the fire ! Clear the wards ! Women and children first ! "

Dr. Murphy sprang on to a chair and shouted through a megaphone. " Steady now, remember the children ! Half of you go down to the next floor and clear those wards. We must not let one little life be lost. Their safety comes first ! Open that window ! Let down the ladder escape ! Now, all of you, follow me ! " And picking up a measly child and flinging it, wrapped in a blanket, over his shoulder, the brave man sprang to the open window. Out on the sill he turned and shouted, " Don't spare the water. Remember, anything that's really wet has less chance of catching fire." Mary immediately emptied a bucket of water over the nearest nurse and then, as everyone seemed to be too busy rescuing children

to follow the doctor's orders, she methodically emptied a
bucket of water over each bed.

In a few moments she was alone in the ward, still working
steadily. Going into the hall to fetch another bucket, her
eyes fell on the brass fire-helmet, still hanging on the wall,
all shiny and inviting. Climbing up, she got it unhooked just
as a sort of roar went up from the yard outside, where all the
rescued children and their rescuers were standing in different
stages of shiver.

Mary listened. Whatever could they be shouting? Something about "volunteers" it sounded like. She ran back
into the ward; her eye caught a little flicker still in the grate
—mustn't leave that. Half of the bucket put it out and she
didn't need the second half. It was the matter of a moment
to empty it out of the window.

Screams and yells were now added to the shouting and some
of the shouts seemed to be about "Mary Plain." It was time
she went. She climbed out of the window. It was a little

A bit wobbly, because of the helmet

difficult to see as the brass helmet fitted her like an extinguisher. A roar greeted her appearance, she waved her paw airily. " It's all right," she called, " I've just put the fire out."

A second and louder roar greeted this remark and was continued while Mary descended the ladder (a bit wobbly because of the helmet being so much heavier than she was). At the bottom she was surrounded, patted, kissed, thumped on the back and carried shoulder high round the yard.

Half an hour later, seated on top of Dr. Murphy's desk, still in the helmet with two paws dangling and the other two busy with very sugary bread and milk, she gave a big contented sigh.

" We really are most deeply indebted to you, Miss Plain," said Dr. Murphy, as he handed her the sugar-bowl for the third time.

" In—what ? " asked Mary.

" Indebted—grateful."

" Oh, but it wasn't full," said Mary, " half a bucket was enough to put it out."

Dr. Murphy looked at her a little anxiously. " I hope the strain has not been too excessive ? " he said. " Perhaps you had better go to bed now ? "

" Perhaps I better had," agreed Mary, " me and the sugar-bowl. That's tired, too."

CHAPTER TWELVE

MARY GOES TO THE CINEMA

ON the day after she got back from the hospital, Mary was to give a welcome home party to which the Fur-Coat-Lady was to come. The Owl Man went off to his case as usual, a little uneasy about leaving Mary alone.

" You quite understand, Mary, that you will only have the party if you are very good ? " he said. " It's a pity that it's a Saturday and there's no school. What will you do all the morning ? "

" Oh, I've got lots to do," said Mary, " I shall be very busy being glad about getting home again."

The Owl Man laughed and patting her on the head went off, carefully locking the door behind him. Just after he had gone, the telephone bell rang. Mary went across the room and looked at it and then, as it still went on ringing, she picked up the receiver, rather gingerly.

" It's me," she said.

" This is the Ideal Bakery speaking. We understand that there is to be a party at your flat this afternoon and as the boy is just off with the bread, I thought I would ring and ask if you needed anything else sent along by him ? "

" What kind of things ? " enquired Mary.

" Well, scones or cakes or things in that line."

" Just the line I like," said Mary.

" Would you care for some cream buns ? They're nice and fresh this morning." Mary licked her lips.

" Yes, please," she said.

" How many dozen shall I send ? " enquired the woman. " Eight," said Mary, who had no idea what dozen meant.

" Eight dozen cream buns," said the woman, writing it down on her pad. " And some big cakes ? Lemon—coffee —orange—chocolate ? "

" Yes, especially chocolate," said Mary.

" Any éclairs ? "

Mary dribbled a little into the telephone. " Oh, yes, plenty of éclairs."

" Four dozen éclairs," wrote the woman. " And how about meringues ? "

" Oh, yes, please, more of meringues than anything else, please," said Mary.

" Ten dozen meringues," wrote the woman.

Some time later a bell rang again. It was the front door this time and the front door was locked so Mary could do nothing about it.

" I can't open it, it's locked, whoever you are," she shouted.

" It's the things from the bakery—shall I leave them outside ? "

" Yes, please," said Mary. How terrible not to have a key !

" I'll put the meringues down and go back for the rest," said the boy.

Mary bent down and sniffed through the keyhole. The boy came back several times and each time Mary heard exciting paper-rustling noises and said to herself " Éclairs, chocolate cake, cream buns, and no key ! Oh *dear !* "

The Owl Man could hardly reach the door when he got back—it was covered with paper bags. He had to wade knee deep through the pile to reach the keyhole. As he opened the door Mary fell out, right on to a bag of meringues which went off with a pop.

" What does this mean ? " asked the Owl Man angrily.

" What ? " asked Mary getting up with a good deal of burst meringue on her front which she proceeded to lick off.

" This—this—sea of confectionery."

" I don't see any sea," said Mary, " I can only see things for tea."

" Things for tea ! Who ordered them—how did they get here ? "

" The woman asked and I said ' Yes ' and the boy came," said Mary, going on licking.

The Owl Man strode to the telephone. Mary stayed behind, tidying up the meringues, so she didn't hear what he said but in a few moments the boy came running up the stairs very quickly and removed all the bags except three.

" Hallo, there's a bag of meringues missing," he exclaimed.

Mary tucked her paw, in which was a screwed up paper bag, behind her back.

"Meringues?" she said innocently. "What are they like?"

"White and crisp and—well—kind of full of cream," explained the boy.

"Well, I don't see any about, do you?" asked Mary.

"Not exactly," said the boy, looking suspiciously at a damp spot on Mary's chest.

"So good-morning," said Mary, not liking the look, and she shut the door in his face.

The tea-party went off very well and afterwards the Owl Man said, "How about a cinema? There's a rather primitive one round the corner but it's got the *Three Little Pigs* on and a couple of stars in something after."

Both the Fur-Coat-Lady and Mary said they'd like to go, so after tea they set off, Mary hopping a good deal because of never having been to a cinema before. There was some difficulty in getting her through the turnstile and finally the man kindly lifted her over the top.

It was quite dark in the theatre and they followed the attendant's flash lamp which guided them to their seats.

"Is that one of the stars we've come to see?" whispered Mary, who had been told she mustn't talk out loud.

"No," said the Owl Man, fumbling in the dark. "Here, sit down, Mary, and be careful because it's a spring seat."

They had got there in such good time that it was the tail-end of the performance before and in a few moments the King's head appeared on the screen. Mary sprang to her feet.

"God save the King," she said, at the salute.

"Sit down, Mary," said the Owl Man, wishing Mary was not quite so patriotic. Mary sat, with a bump.

"Ow!" she said, "my seat's not there."

The Owl Man lifted her back. "Now, for goodness sake, keep still, will you?" And for a bit Mary did sit quite still, making whispered remarks about everything on the screen. The Fur-Coat-Lady decided that she had quite the loudest whisper of anyone she knew.

Some advertisements were shown. A young lady tripped on to the screen and said, "Have you tried Clenolux? Makes white things whiter still. May one of our assistants call on you and show you her Clenoluxed blouse?"

Nobody answered so Mary, who felt rather sorry for the girl, called, " Do ! I'm always back from school by one."

" Shut up, Mary," said the Owl Man.

Next a man in a very waisted coat and patent leather hair stepped forward, holding a banner in his right hand on which was written *Worth & Co. General Furnishers. Established 1885. Worth we are and worth we supply.*

" Does anyone here want a free gift ? " he asked.

" I do," said Mary, quickly.

" Because if they do," continued the man, who didn't seem to have heard Mary, " come to our Jubilee party on Wednesday next. This is a Jubilee year. All tastes catered for, at all prices. Come and see."

" I will," promised Mary.

Then came a picture of a very fat man under which was written *January*, 1934, followed almost immediately by one of the same man, looking beautifully flat and labelled *January*, 1935. Underneath was written in scarlet letters. *Try our Fitite belt.*

" That might suit you, Mary," whispered the Owl Man, giving Mary a nudge.

" But I've got a belt already," objected Mary, not seeing the joke.

Chocolates and ices will be served in the interval, said the screen.

" Where's the interval ? " asked Mary, pulling the Owl Man's arm and preparing to get up.

" It's here," said the Owl Man. " If you sit tight and keep quiet, it won't be long."

But you might just as well ask Niagara to stop Niagging.

From then on Mary's conversation was something like this. " Has the interval come yet ?   Why has he got black hair on his chin ?   What kind of ices will they be ?   I like pink ones best.   Why is she taking her dress off ?   Who's that in the bath ?   Wouldn't it be lovely to have a bath of ice-cream ? Why is he squeezing her neck like that for and why is he putting her into a trunk ? "   The Owl Man gave up saying ' Hush ', it just wasn't any good.

At last the interval came and the attendant came along with a tray of ices.   The interval was the only time that Mary was silent.   Luckily, there weren't many people in the cinema and none of them seemed to mind Mary except one bald man who made hissing noises through his teeth from time to time.

The *Three Little Pigs* came next and when they cried, " Whose afraid of the Big Bad Wolf ? "   Mary shouted, " I'm not," but when the Big Black Wolf came galloping towards them, growing bigger and bigger till he burst off the screen at them, Mary disappeared under the Owl Man's chair and there she remained, gripping each ankle, which was very inconvenient for him and rather tickling.

" Come along, Mary," he said, hoping there wouldn't be a fire, so he'd need his ankles.

" I like it best here," said Mary, and there she stayed till half-way through *Golden River* when the Owl Man came to the conclusion he couldn't bear a moment's more tickling and they all went home.

As he was tucking Mary up in bed that night, she said, " What does ' Jubilee ' mean ? "

" It means a kind of special birthday.   The King is having one this year to celebrate his twenty-five years' reign."

"Did he come to the cinema especially to see me this afternoon?"

"Very likely," said the Owl Man.

"How did he know I was there?" asked Mary.

"Must have guessed," said the Owl Man. "They say he's very unusual."

"That makes two unusual people in one cinema," said Mary, drowsily. "Me and the King."

CHAPTER THIRTEEN

IN WHICH MARY GOES JUBILEEING

For weeks Mary had been talking about the Jubilee and when the day actually came she was up and dressed and calling the Owl Man by six o'clock.

"But you aren't going bathing, Mary," he expostulated, for Mary had on her bathing drawers and her blue bow.

"Red, white and blue," said Mary pointing. "I'm jubileeing to-day."

"You are!" said the Owl Man. "But most people go jubileeing in rosettes and if you wear those drawers I shan't get you a rosette. Just as you like, of course, but it must be the drawers or the rosette—not both."

"What kind of a rosette?" enquired Mary, cautiously.

"Large and frilly, made of silk," said the Owl Man. "Perhaps a flag, too."

"I unchoose my bathing drawers," said Mary.

Mark joined them after breakfast and they set out for their stand in the Green Park, looking very gay with their rosettes and Jubilee expressions.

" Do I say ' Hurray ' or ' Hurrah ' to the King ? " asked Mary, anxiously.

" Now, that's a very serious question to settle," said the Owl Man. " We don't want to go and spoil the King's whole day by saying the wrong thing. What do you think, Mark ? "

But Mark was in explosions of laughter and was no good at all.

" I'll say both," decided Mary. " What are their names ? Just King and Queen ? "

" King George and Queen Mary," said Mark.

" *Mary !* Oh dear," and Mary gave a huge sigh. " Aren't I a lucky bear ? "

" Why ? " asked Mark.

" Having a Queen for my twin, of course," said Mary. " Now I've got two twins."

" Now," said the Owl Man, as they got out of their taxi at Hyde Park Corner, " hang on to me, and if either of you get lost, ask for Stand Twenty-Two."

The crowd was immense and Mary was small and halfway across the road she got swept away from the others.

For a moment they tried to find her and called her name but the jamb was terrific and finally the Owl Man said it was quite hopeless—they'd better go to the stand and wait ; Mary knew what to do and she had a lot of sense.   All the same, he looked more and more anxious as the moments passed and no Mary appeared and, when the streets were cleared from traffic and

The seven policemen stood around at the bottom

the distant sound of music told of the arrival of the troops to line the route, he felt quite frantic.

" I'd go and look for her but you might as well look for a needle in a hay-stack," he said, " I've a better chance of spotting her from here. I must just wait."

He didn't have to wait long. Round the corner of Constitution Hill in close formation swung the Guards, looking in their smart red coats as if someone had just cut the string and let them out of their box. Cheers greeted their progress but suddenly there was a difference in the cheering—a kind of a shout and a whoop which made everybody crane their heads to look at the cause.

The cause was Mary, marching a couple of yards in front of the band with a paw held stiffly to attention.

" Jehoshaphat ! " murmured the Owl Man, too paralysed to move.

But someone else moved. A large policeman followed by six others started to run towards her. Seeing them, Mary took sudden fright, sped across the open space towards an island, and in a moment she had swarmed to the top of the lamp-post. The seven policemen stood around the bottom and looked up at her, shaking their fists, while Mary, safe, and therefore quite unconcerned, looked over their heads and enjoyed a better view of the crowds and decorations than anyone else.

" They'll never get her to come down," said the Owl Man, who still seemed to be rooted to the spot and unable to move.

" Hadn't you better go ? " suggested Mark and then, " Hallo, here comes the fire-engine, how thrilling ! "

Sure enough, up Piccadilly came thundering an engine with bell clanging and great folded red ladders. Everyone began to look about for the fire when, to their amazement, the engine drew up under Mary's lamp-post and a great roar went up as the crowd realised it had come to rescue her. To an accompaniment of shouts and hoots the ladder was unfolded to its full length and a shy and rather unwilling fireman started to climb up towards Mary.

It took a good ten minutes to persuade her to come down and during that ten minutes the Owl Man fought and pushed his way through the crowd and arrived underneath the lamp-post just as Mary reached the bottom. At first the seven policemen wanted to arrest her but the Owl Man pointed out that she had done no harm and, being a foreign bear, she could hardly be expected to know lamp-post climbing was forbidden —especially at Jubilees. As it was getting very late, the policemen let her go and the Owl Man, amid friendly jeers from the crowd, got her back to the stand just as the Procession was due.

" Phew ! " he said sitting down and mopping his forehead with his handkerchief.

" That was a pretty near shave," said a man sitting on Mary's other side. She turned and looked at him. He had the kind of face she liked.

" Did you see me marching ? " she enquired pleasantly.

" I did," said the man, " and I liked the way you climbed that lamp-post, too."

" The policemen didn't," said Mary.

" No, they wouldn't be likely to," said the man. " They never like anything unusual, I've noticed."

Mary beamed. " I can't help being unusual sometimes because, you see, I am an unusual first-class bear with a white rosette and a gold medal with a picture of myself on it, and, and—"

" Oh, shut up, Mary," growled the Owl Man who was still too hot to bear Mary's list.

" And," finished Mary, " I do like Jubilees."

" Well, you'd better enjoy this one as much as you can," said the Owl Man, " because it'll be your last."

" Why ? " asked Mary, but the Owl Man never answered as just then the Procession began.

Because of their being in the back row and the shortness of Mary's legs she couldn't see, so the two men lifted her up on to the bar behind them and there, with a paw on each of their shoulders to steady her, she had an excellent view. She lurched rather dangerously as the two little Princesses passed, as it is difficult to wave and balance at the same time.

" Steady there, Mary," warned the Owl Man. " Here comes the Prince of Wales."

" Why has he got a fur head ? " enquired Mary, between her cheers. But the answer was drowned in the growing roar of sound which told them that the great moment had come and along came the exciting trotting Horse Guards and behind them, most exciting of all, the King and Queen.

" Hurrah, King ! Hurray, King ! " yelled Mary. " Hurrah, Queen-twin ! " and waving wildly with both paws, she lost her balance and dived head foremost into the people two rows ahead. There she remained till the King and Queen passed out of sight, her head wedged and two furry legs kicking frantically. The Owl Man climbed over the row between and, catching her by one leg, gave a pull.

" Ow," said Mary and " Really ! " said the people, who, now that the Procession had gone, had time to be annoyed at being dived into by a strange bear. The lamp-post episode

had been amusing but when it came to being dived into—
well, there were some things one didn't do at Processions.

"I'm terribly sorry," apologised the harassed Owl Man.
"She over-balanced."

"I over-hurrahed myself off the bar," explained Mary,
rubbing her head ruefully and looking a bit glum.

Back in their own row her new friend looked at her with
rather a twinkle.

"Well," he said, "lots of people got terribly excited but I
don't believe anyone else actually stood on their heads while
the King and Queen passed. Have some chocolate to refresh
you."

"Thank you," said Mary. What a particularly nice man
this was! "I like chocolate—it's one of my favourite eats."

"She's a friendly cub," said the man to the Owl Man.

"I like being friendly," said Mary, finishing his last slab
of chocolate. "I like lots of things."

"Do you, now? What kind of things?"

"Well, meringues and Kings and winning things and labels
and twins and school colours and letters and—and—"

"Talking," put in the Owl Man.

The other man laughed and got up. "Well, I must be

getting along," he said. "But, look here, you write to me and tell me the rest, will you?"

"But you couldn't read my writing," said Mary. "it's very special."

"I bet I could," said the man. "Just you try me. Here's my address," and he scribbled on a scrap of paper and gave it to Mary and waving his hand, went off.

"Come on, Mary," said the Owl Man, "we must go, too."

"But what a little address," said Mary. "Look!"

The Owl Man looked. "Hallo!" he said. "Hallo!" For on the card was written, *Mac. B.B.C.*

"Do you know who you've been talking to, Mary?"

"Who?" asked Mary.

"Why your friend Uncle Mac."

"Him what's on the wire-phone?" asked Mary excitedly.

"None other," said the Owl Man, while Mark sighed and said, "Mary *does* have luck, doesn't she?"

CHAPTER FOURTEEN

MARY GOES TO THE B.B.C.

MARY did not forget to write her letter to Uncle Mac. She sent him quite a long list of things she liked that she hadn't had time to tell him about at the Jubilee, ending with, " I like all the voices what talk but specially yours because now I know what kind of face it lives in. I like it too, when it's the *Teddy Bears' Picnic* because that's about me and I like things about me."

Next day a letter arrived addressed to Miss Mary Plain, G.M.

" What's the G.M. for ? " asked Mary.

" I can't think," said the Owl Man. " Gracious me, or Good Mary—it might be anything. Look inside."

Inside was written,

Dear Miss Plain,

Thank you for your letter. I am so glad you enjoy the Children's Hour. I wonder if you would come along on Friday evening and give the children a little talk? It would be a delightful addition to our programme and I am sure you would do it charmingly.

Yours sincerely,

Uncle Mac.

Mary looked up with her eyes shining. "Isn't he kind?" she said.

"Almost too kind, I think," said the Owl Man, who often wished Mary was a less public character.

All the same he got home on Friday in good time to give her a good brushing and get her ready for her visit.

They went in a taxi. The driver politely opened the door.

"I'm going to the A.B.C.," Mary told him, "to give a talk."

"Really!" said the man, wondering if it was a lecture on penny buns.

"To the B.B.C." corrected the Owl Man, as he got in after her.

All the way in the taxi Mary had guesses about what G.M. meant. The inside of the B.B.C. was rather like a hospital and Mary clung to the Owl Man's hand. "I haven't got measles again," she said uneasily, "I don't prickle anywhere."

"Don't be a silly little goose," said the Owl Man.

Uncle Mac was waiting for them in the studio. He held a small girl by the hand who kept hopping up and down.

"What's the G.M.?" asked Mary at once.

" Why, Gold Medallist, of course," said Uncle Mac surprised. " I naturally thought you would wish to have your full title on your letters."

" Oh yes, I always do," said Mary hastily, while the Owl Man cleared his throat in the background.

" Does she ever stop ? " asked Mary, pointing at the little girl.

" Stop what ? "

" Hopping. Does she just hop because she feels hoppy ? "

" Well, you see, it is rather exciting to meet a bear for the first time."

" Especially an unusual one," said Mary, gravely.

" Exactly. Now, Judith, you stop hopping and shake hands with Miss Plain." So Judith stopped for just long enough to say how do you do.

" I expect you have often heard Elisabeth and Barbara talk," went on Uncle Mac, " and here they are."

" It's very exciting to meet voices," said Mary.

" It's very exciting for us to meet ears," said Elisabeth.

" Ears ? " said Mary. " How do you mean, ears ? "

" Well, if we're the voices that talk, you're the ears that listen, do you see ? "

" Yes," said Mary, who didn't.

Uncle Mac clapped his hands. " Now, when that light there goes on, everybody must stop talking," he said.

The light went on and Uncle Mac and Elisabeth and Barbara all stepped up to the microphone.

" Good evening, children," said Uncle Mac.

" Good evening, children," said Elisabeth.

" Good evening, children," said Barbara.

" There's a—" said Mary.

" Ssh ! " said everybody—at Mary.

" Now, this evening, children," said Uncle Mac, " we are starting our programme with a—"

" I say, there's a—" began Mary again, and " Ssh ! " said everybody very sternly.

"With a few songs which have been especially written for the Children's Hour. The first is called—"

" There's a— " began Mary.

" *Bluebell growing in my garden* ! " finished Uncle Mac neatly. " Now, Miss Black, if you will begin ! " He crossed to where Mary was sitting and shook his head at her.

" Look here," he whispered, " you mustn't talk in here, you know."

" I only wanted to tell them there's a bear in the studio

tonight," said Mary, reproachfully. " Why didn't you let me ? "

" Because it wasn't the right moment," answered Uncle Mac. " All speakers have to be introduced properly."

" Am I one then ? "

" One what ? "

" One squeaker ? "

" *Speaker*, I said."

" So did I " lied Mary quickly.

" Of course you are," said Uncle Mac.

" Is it an important thing to be ? " asked Mary next in a hoarse whisper.

" Very," said Uncle Mac.

And because importance was one of her favourite things and she loved introductions, when she was the one that was being introduced, Mary said no more.

" I say," whispered Uncle Mac after a few moments," have you thought of what you are going to say yet ? "

" Not yet," said Mary. " I've been too busy. I can't listen and think all together."

" Well, I'll leave you to think quietly," said Uncle Mac, " because in ten minutes it will be time for you to begin."

During those ten minutes Barbara read a rather thrilling story about a porcupine and Mary listened enthralled and never remembered about the thinking till she saw Uncle Mac coming towards her again. Then she got suddenly frightened. What was she going to say ? She didn't want to talk into the wire-phone. She'd rather stay safely with the Owl Man. Why had she left the nice safe pits ! She tugged at the Owl

Man's arm. " Do you think the twins are happy without me ? " she asked.

The Owl Man sprang to the rescue. " You bet they are ! " he said. " Think how jealous they'll be when they hear you've been broadcasting. Why ! Friska would give her eyes to have such an exciting chance."

Friska's eyes did the trick. Mary consented to be helped up on to a tall chair opposite the microphone while Uncle Mac, remembering her Jubilee dive, put his arm as far round her middle as it would go.

And this is what the children at the other end heard.*

U. Mac. : " Now, children, our next item is to be a surprise talk from a surprise visitor—"

Mary : (" S'visitor.")

U. Mac. : " S'visitor. (Sorry). She has come from the bear-pits at Berne and I am sure what she is going to say will interest you very much."

Mary : (" Yes—I'll tell them lots of exciting things.")

U. Mac. : (" What about ? ")

Mary : (" About me and Mary and Mary Plain—all of us. What's the Owl Man making that funny noise in his throat for ? Has he got a cold ? ")

U. Mac. : (" No, he's all right.) Now, children, I want to introduce Miss Mary Plain."

Mary : (" Have they guessed I'm a bear ? ")

U. Mac. : (" I expect so, because of the address.")

Mary : (" ' Bear-pits ' is a very beary address, isn't it ? ")

U. Mac. : (" It is.) Now, Miss Mary Plain."

Mary : (" Do I begin now ? ")

* All conversation in brackets to be spoken in a loud whisper.

U. Mac. : (" Please.")

Mary : (" Introduce me again, please, I wasn't quite ready.")

U. Mac. : " Miss—Mary—Plain."

Mary : " An unusual first-class bear from the bear-pits at Berne, with a white rosette and a gold medal with a picture of me on it. (They'll know now, won't they ?) "

U. Mac. : (" They will.) Tell me, Miss Plain, do you ever feel homesick at all ? "

Mary : " Pit-sick, do you mean ? "

U. Mac. : " I suppose I do."

Mary : " No, but I sometimes feel twin-sick because of playing with them. But I don't ever feel even a tiny bit Friska-sick."

U. Mac. : " And who is Friska ? "

Mary : " She's my aunt—a very aunty aunt what gives us lessons."

U. Mac. : " I see—and what other bears are there in the pits ? "

Mary : " Well, there's Bunch. He sits on the tree and catches the biggest carrots—he's a very greedy kind of bear, is Bunch. (I think the Owl Man has got a cold. Bet I put a hot sandbag on him to-night ?")

U. Mac. : (" Don't you worry about him, he's quite all right.) And is that all the bears there are ? "

Mary : " Oh, no, there's Forget-me-not and Plum, only they're too little to matter and there's Big Wool ; she's very strict and un-playey, and there used to be Harrods."

U. Mac. : " Where is Harrods now ? "

Mary : " She's gone to live with St. Bruin because he wanted her. We didn't."

U. Mac. : " Didn't you like her ? "

Mary : " No, she was very cross and both her eyes looked at her nose. And then, of course there's Alpha and Lady Grizzle."

U. Mac. : " Who are they ? "

Mary : " They're very old and special and when we go and svisit them we say a pome. Shall I say it now ? "

U. Mac. : " Please."

Mary : " *Many happy years we wish to you*
May carrots and dried figs your pit-floor strew,
We hope that happiness will with you stay,
Till we all meet on next St. Bruin's Day.

By FRISKA."

U. Mac. : " Thank you very much. It's a beautiful poem. And now, Miss Plain, I am afraid your time is up."

Mary : " Oh, but I haven't begun yet."

U. Mac. : " I'm awfully sorry. You must come again one day soon and then—"

Mary : " Then I'll be able to tell them some things about me next time, about my being unusual and first-class and having a white rose—"

U. Mac. : " Quite. Now, children, I am sure we are all most grateful to Miss Plain for coming and as this is her first visit—"

Mary : (" Svisit.")

U. Mac. : " Svisit (Sorry), to the B.B.C. let's all give her a real good send off. We here in the Studio are all joining hands in a circle and Miss Plain is standing on a chair in the middle and I believe she's wondering what we're going to sing. Now, you can't join in our circle, children, but

you can join in the song, wherever you are, so altogether—"
And all over England, all the children sang as loud as they could,

> *For she's a jolly good fellow*
> *For she's a jolly good fellow*
> *For she's a jolly good fellow*
> *And so say all of us !*
> *And so say all of us,*
> *And so say all of us !*
> *For she's a jolly good fellow*
> *And so say all of us !*

Elisabeth : " Good-night, children."
Barbara : " Good-night, children."
Uncle Mac. : " Good-night, children."
Mary : " Good-night, children.   (That's me—Mary Plain ! ")

MARY PLAIN ON HOLIDAY

CONTENTS

CHAPTER ONE

IN WHICH MARY DOES A BIT OF MARYING

" Is Christmas the same as St. Bruin's Day ? " enquired Mary.

She sat drumming her feet against the bars of her chair after a particularly large bowl of bread and milk. A bit of the bread had very becomingly got left behind on the tip of her nose.

" Stop that drumming, Mary," said the Owl Man, as patiently as he could because it was the fifth time, " and wipe your nose."

Mary extended a surprisingly long pink tongue and removed the bread. The Owl Man shook his head. " How often have I had to tell you—"

" About Christmas," nipped in Mary quickly, " about its being like St. Bruin's Day ? "

" But it isn't," said the Owl Man, " not really. You see, Christmas belongs to people like the Fur-Coat-Lady, and me and—Mrs Orchard, whereas St. Bruin's Day is specially, specially—"

" Beary ? " suggested Mary helpfully.

" Exactly," said the Owl Man.

Mary sat and drummed again without thinking and wondered if she'd really care much about Christmas if it belonged to Mrs Orchard as well. She didn't like Mrs Orchard much, mostly because she didn't believe in eating between meals. Nor did Mrs Orchard like Mary. She didn't hold with cluttering young bears about the house. So altogether they didn't get on very well. Very often Mary, drawn irresistibly along the passage by a lovely smell, would stand, with one paw tucked round the other and a paw to her mouth, rather wistfully and sniffingly in the kitchen door-way. Mrs Orchard, up to the elbows in flour, would scowl at her and say, "No buns, now! Not till your proper eats—they're ruination to the digestion at other times, are buns. Get along with you."

Mary got. She didn't know or care what "digestion" or "ruination" meant. She only knew she wanted the bun dreadfully. She decided she hated all no-bun people and especially Mrs Orchard.

" What's Christmas for ? " she asked next.

" For ? It's for presents and puddings and parties and you hang up your stocking——"

" But I haven't got a stocking," interrupted Mary, " only drawers."

" Well your bathing drawers would do just as well—or a pillow-case."

" But what do I hang them up for ? " asked Mary.

" To find them full in the morning, of course."

" Full of leg ? " enquired Mary, being rather stupid.

" Don't be ridiculous, Mary, full of presents."

" For me ? "

The Owl Man nodded.   Mary scrambled down from her seat.

" Might I go and hang them up now ? "

" Certainly not ; not till the night before Christmas. First you have to write a letter to Santa Claus and tell him what you want."

" Who's Santa Claus ? " asked Mary.

" He's the very kind gentleman who drives all over the world in a sleigh the night before Christmas.   The sleigh is drawn by eight reindeer and it is full of presents for the children—and bears—who have hung up their stockings."

" Or drawers."

" Or drawers, of course.   He comes creeping down the chimney when it's dark."

" Am I asleep ? " asked Mary, a little anxiously.

" Rather—or he wouldn't come.   Now, you settle down and write that letter and then we can post it up the chimney.   And after you've finished it you must go and rest so as to be ready for the afternoon.   It's most important that you should do your very best at this show."

" Because I am very important, aren't I ? " asked Mary.

The Owl Man didn't answer.   He knew he ought to sit on Mary but it just wasn't any good.   It was like sitting on a bouncing india-rubber ball.   So, instead, he sighed as he took his hat down from the rack and wished

Mary's school hadn't broken up quite so soon. It might at least have kept open till the day of this Christmas performance in which Mary was taking part in a sort of nursery ballet. Except for the daily rehearsals he'd had to leave Mary a lot alone and Mary wasn't the sort of cub you left alone in a flat with an easy mind. He'd be very glad when next week came and he'd be less busy and have more time for her.

"Good-bye!" he called. "Be good. Mrs Orchard will be here presently and the letter will keep you busy till then."

It did. Mary sat thoughtfully sucking her pencil, which she was forbidden to do, and drumming, which she was also forbidden to do. It just showed how little good forbidding did to Mary. She wrote as follows :—

DE MR SANTA
ARI SO GAINO
ABOVE J G THESE R THE I
WANT PLEASE. A FULL OF ECLARES
CHOCOLATE IS G A NU WITH A
OIN IT G A SPESHULLY SQUEAKY
D.CAUSE THE DORENT LIKE
IT G A LOT OF WITH XTRA

PLESE 6 ½ MERANGS THE LARGEST SIZE
IF ONLY. ME 6 A ⌐ LIKE I WOREAT
THE 🌿 6 A HUGE XMAS 🎂 WITH
MARY ⚟ PRINT ON IT AND O PLESE
DONT BUMP CUMING DOWN THE ⬜
🐝 COS I DONT WANT I WAKE UP THANKU
WITH A BIG HUG FROM 🐱 PLAIN
PS. IT WILL B A ◇ SO T WILL BEE
LOTS OF RUUM P.S.S. 6 🐝 II. M P.

" Cream buns ! " thought Mary, giving a little skip
of joy.   " Eclairs ! ! " she cried, as she jumped over the
stool and " Meringues ! ! ! " she shouted, taking a flying
leap on to the sofa.   Standing there on her head, she
wondered what to do next.   It never took her long to
decide.   " I'm thirsty," she thought ; " writing letters
makes me thirsty."

Crossing to the sideboard she stared at a soda-syphon
on it.   She had seen the Owl Man use it but had never
done so herself.   Tilting it a little she pressed the handle
at the side to see what would happen.

" Oh ! " gasped Mary, as what would happen, did, and

the cold water poured down, soaking her fur. For a minute she was so taken aback that she went on pressing and the soda went on syphoning at her while she went on saying " Ow ! " Then her paw luckily slipped off the handle, and just as she was standing there forlornly, feeling wet and miserable, she heard a scrapey noise in the hall. " Mrs Orchard," thought Mary, " no-buns ! "

She smiled a most wicked smile and, seizing the syphon, she padded to the front door. As it opened she shouted " Good morning, Mrs No-buns ! " and scored a bull's eye, hitting Mrs Orchard full in the face.

Mrs Orchard spluttered and spat and spat and spluttered. Always a bit angry with Mary, she was now angrier than ever. " Just you wait ! " she gasped between the spits. " I'll larn you. Don't I just itch to larn you ! " And she made a dive at Mary.

But Mary hadn't the slightest intention of being larned. She darted away and flew all over the flat, while Mrs Orchard, too fat to fly, puffed behind in full chase. At first it was quite easy to keep just out of her reach, but at last Mary made a mistake and found herself in an exceedingly uncomfortable position backed against the wall, with a puffing and itching Mrs Orchard approaching her in a half-crouching position.

Mary did the only thing possible. She dropped on all fours and, growling furiously, approached Mrs Orchard back. Mrs Orchard turned and fled into the kitchen, slamming the door behind her. Mary, following, calmly locked it on the outside and then went and sat by the dining-room fire to dry her wet chest.

Mrs. Orchard turned and fled into the kitchen

The Owl Man found her there when he came home unexpectedly early, sitting with her paws crossed over her chest to hide the damp and looking as if butter wouldn't, and hadn't ever, melted in her mouth. But a little pool at her feet gave her away.

" What in the world. . . ." he began, staring at it and then he bent down and pulled away Mary's paws, " Why, Mary, you're soaking—*whatever's* happened now ? "

" Nothing," said Mary and then, to hide a funny murmur of sound which came floating down the passage, she repeated very loudly, " Nothing—nothing at all ! "

But the Owl Man took no notice. He was standing with his head bent, listening. Then, as the murmur got louder and seemed to be accompanied by bangs, he strode off down the passage.

Presently he strode back. Very carefully he folded a

newspaper into a long flat packet and called Mary to him.
A few moments later Mary went off for her rest.

She lay on her face.

CHAPTER TWO

BECAUSE Mary behaved extra specially well and because
Mrs Orchard had promised not to leave after all, the
Owl Man got less and less angry during lunch. All the
same Mary could see from his face that he wasn't feeling
very fond of her, so although as usual he was full of
things to say, she managed to keep quiet until the cheese.
By that time she felt like bursting and couldn't wait
another minute. " Could-I-post-my-letter-to-Santa-
Claus-please ? " she said in a rush.

" All right," said the Owl Man. " Come and kneel
down by the fire."

" But I can't," said Mary, whose legs weren't made that
way.

" Lean then," said the Owl Man, rather kindly, because
he was always forgetting about Mary's legs. " Now,
throw it up the chimney and say after me :—

362

Off you go up the flue
All my wishes go with you
Send me back at least a few."

" But I want them all," objected Mary, trying to see where the letter had gone and get it back again.

" It's gone now, old girl, you must just hope for the best," said the Owl Man and looking at his watch he added, " By Jove, we must be off or we'll be late. Cut along, Mary."

Half way to the school Mary stood up in the car and clutched frantically at the Owl Man's arm. " Stop, stop ! " she shrieked. " I must go back, I've forgotten them. Stop ! "

The Owl Man grabbed at her and pushing her back into the seat he pinned her there with his elbow while he slowed up and finally drew up at the kerb.

" Forgotten what ? " he asked, nearly cross again, for he hated pulling up suddenly.

" My bathing drawers," wailed Mary, trying to open the door.

" *Bathing drawers* ! " exclaimed the Owl Man, pushing Mary back into her seat and holding her with both hands. " Am I crazy or did you say ' bathing drawers ' ? "

" Yes, yes, for the ballet," said Mary, wriggling to get free.

" Steady, steady, Mary," said the Owl Man. " You don't wear drawers at a ballet."

" What do I wear then ?   Just me ? "

" A ballet skirt."

" What's a skirt ? "

"It's—well, it's a skirt. You wear it round your waist."

"Where's my waist?" enquired Mary.

The Owl Man shot his lever into gear and gave Mary a quick look, "I don't know, Mary," he said. "Quite honestly, I don't know."

Very soon they arrived at the school. There they found all the small performers busily getting dressed and having their hair curled. Of course there was no question of curling Mary, but it took the mistress, Miss Anderson, and the Owl Man quite a long time to get her skirt fixed. Mary didn't seem to fit ballet skirts awfully well. They tried it up, they tried it down and at last Miss Anderson said, "There! Don't touch it again, it's just exactly right."

"It still tips a bit in the front," said the Owl Man anxiously.

" Never mind—tips are worn this season," said Miss Anderson, cheerfully. " Now this bunch of grapes— just behind the right ear, don't you think ? "

Mary surveyed herself in the glass and then turned round.

" It *is* me, isn't it ? " she asked.

" Yes, it's you all right. Pleased with yourself ? "

Mary gave a deep sigh. That was her, Mary Plain, with that beautiful pink stuff sticking out all round her. She turned round and looked over her shoulder. Yes, it still stuck out behind ; not quite so much, of course, but it stuck. Grapes, too. " Are they real ? " wondered Mary. All the little girls and boys chattered and all the mothers and aunts patted and curled and fussed and then suddenly, " Now, children, are you all ready ? Ann ! Quite ready, dear ? Point your toe and don't forget *two* chassés before the turn. In a minute you'll hear the orchestra begin your tune. There ! On you go ! "

Ann was swallowed up behind the big curtain and the mistress hurried over to where Mary was standing alone. The Owl Man had gone round to sit in the audience. " You next, Mary. Why ! " she exclaimed, " you've lost your grapes ! "

" Yes," said Mary, " isn't it sad ? And I did like them so," she added with much feeling.

" How did it happen ? "

" Well, sometimes I do lose things," explained Mary.

" Well, never mind, now," whispered Miss Anderson, " I'll give you a rose instead." She hastily tucked a pink rose where the grapes had been. " Ann's nearly done now and I must go and see to the curtain. You stand just here and I'll wave when it's time for you to go on. See ? "

Mary nodded. She was beginning to feel rather frightened. What was on the other side of the curtain, she wondered? This side was dark and empty ; she hoped it would be better in front. She wasn't sure she wanted to do her dance, anyway. She began to think about her twin cousins left behind at Berne. " I do wonder if they're happy without me," she said to herself. " I wish I'd got them here. One on each side and me safe in the middle. I don't think—"

A burst of clapping interrupted her thoughts. Ann came through the slit in the curtain, looking very pink and pleased. Mary watched her disappear and come out again. Miss Anderson waved.

Mary stood still.

" Go on, Mary, go on," whispered Miss Anderson, giving frantic little waves in the direction of the curtain. But Mary still stood.

The curtain came down with a rattle and Miss Anderson rushed across to her. " Whatever's the matter with you, Mary ? I told you to go on when I waved and now I've had to let the curtain down again." She looked very worried and the Owl Man in the front was thinking to himself, " Mary again ! "

" I feel sick," announced Mary.

" Nonsense," said Miss Anderson, who had suffered from stage fright herself.

" Do you think the twins are happy without me ? " asked Mary. Miss Anderson, in the dark, couldn't see how miserable she looked. Not having the slightest idea who the twins were, she said briskly, " I'm quite certain they'd be ashamed of you if they knew you were behaving like a little coward."

" I'll go now," said Mary in a small voice.

" Good. Just give me time to pull up the curtain," and Miss Anderson hurried back to the other side. " Now ! "

" Now," thought Mary, " and no twins—only Mary Plain and me."

Very reluctantly she pulled back the side curtain. The people in the audience saw first a paw, then a pink frill and then the rest of Mary come through and, as she appeared, they all clapped loudly. " Thank Heaven," said the Owl Man to himself.

Mary advanced to the middle of the stage. She couldn't remember ever having felt so tiny before. The lights were dazzling but the clapping helped. Mary liked clapping, especially when it was for her. Slowly she took up her position, feet together and arms outstretched. Bang went the music and whizz went Mary, spinning round on one foot with the other tucked as far under her ballet skirt as it could get. More clapping and Mary felt better and forgot about the twins. Crash went the music and up shot Mary into the air, crossing her feet three times before she came down. More clapping ! Mary was completely happy again and completely the right size. " It's me they're clapping," she

MARY PLAIN ON HOLIDAY

thought as she whirled round the stage, " because I'm so clever and important." More spins, more jumps, all accompanied by most satisfactory applause and then her final pose came. Poised on one foot, her arms out-stretched, she slowly raised the other till it was on a level with her shoulder. Her eyes were fixed on the audience. She'd got used to the lights now and could see all the people down there watching. Suddenly she caught sight of the Owl Man, sitting in the second row and looking very proud.

" Hallo, Owl Man ! " she called cheerfully, still retaining her pose. " I see you." So, suddenly, did everybody else and the Owl Man immediately stopped looking proud and got very red. He didn't answer Mary.

" ' I see you,' I said," called Mary, still posed. " Aren't I clever, all on one paw ? "

The Owl Man still didn't answer.

" And I've got a rose instead of grapes," continued Mary conversationally, but by this time the Owl Man, climbing over people's knees and treading on their toes, had disappeared.

Mary, in response to urgent whispers from Miss Anderson from behind the curtain, finally finished her dance. Prolonged clapping followed her bow and twice she had to re-appear. The second time she came right forward to the front of the stage, and someone in the audience cried, " Speech, speech ! "

" I'm glad you liked me," began Mary smoothing her pink frill, " you see, I am an unusual first-class bear with a white ro—"

" Let down that curtain ! " hissed the Owl Man into Miss Anderson's ear.

" —sette, and a gold medal with a picture of myself on it," shouted Mary from behind.

CHAPTER THREE

MARY SVISITS HARRIDGES

PLOP came the letters through the slit in the door and lay scattered on the hall floor.

" That's the post, Mary. Run and get the letters, there's a good cub," said the Owl Man who was sitting by the dining-room fire and enjoying an after-breakfast pipe. Mary ran off and collected the letters. She stood at the Owl Man's knee as he opened them.

" I never get none, do I ? " she said.

" Suppose not," muttered the Owl Man, who was much more interested in the post than in Mary.

" Hallo," he said suddenly, " here's one that will interest you, Mary; it's for us both really, from Bill Smith. Remember when he met you at Dover ? "

Mary nodded.

" He says, *I have been thinking about Christmas. I hate Christmassing alone so it would be great fun if you and Mary would come and spend it with me. The cottage is pretty small but if you don't mind having Mary in a cot in your room we can just squeeze in. I'm asking Jill, too.* That's the Fur-Coat-Lady, Mary. How's that for an invitation ? "

Mary was jumping up and down with excitement. The Fur-Coat-Lady was a very special friend and she hadn't seen her for some time.

" Oh ! " she said, hopping some more.

" Yes," said the Owl Man with a grin. " I guess you and I are needed to do some chaperoning, Mary Plain. Well, we must get busy about our shopping. In fact we'll start at once if you could oblige by stopping that hopping, Mary."

Mary obliged at once.

" Come along and get the car. We'll try Harridges first."

Harridges was very big and very full of people and Mary clung tightly to the Owl Man's hand. They went first to the leather department where Mary helped choose a present to give the Fur-Coat-Lady then, while the Owl Man bought more things, Mary sat on a high chair, drumming, and all the people who weren't used to bears shopping, stared, which Mary thoroughly enjoyed.

Next they went to the silk handkerchief counter. Here Mary got bored and began playing with the handkerchiefs on a stand. Every design and colour you could imagine were there. " I think I'll try this one," decided Mary and draped a bright bandana over her head. By the time the Owl Man turned round you couldn't see Mary for handkerchiefs.

" Really, Mary," he exclaimed, " you're for ever in mischief ! "

"I'm in handkerchiefs now," said Mary.

"I'm so sorry," apologised the Owl Man, handing them all back to the assistant.

"Not at all," said the man, "it's not often we have the pleasure of serving so unusual a customer." Mary beamed.

"Yes," she began, "you see, I am an unusual bear with a white ro—"

"Come along, Mary," said the Owl Man grimly, pulling her almost too quickly off her chair. "Gramophones next. We'll go up in the lift."

The lift was fun because it was very full of people all interested in Mary, but the gramophones were dull. So, after the Owl Man had said "Enter the records to me, please," which Mary had decided was a part of shopping because he'd said it at every counter, he suggested they should go up to the Restaurant and have a bun, just to keep Mary going.

"Yes, please," said Mary, who loved being kept going.

There was a slight argument as to how many buns it took to do this. Mary thought six but the Owl Man said two and a bowl of milk was ample. Then they went to the toys and Mary gasped. Could all these houses and trains and games be true?

"You have a look round, Mary, while I get some things, but don't go far, mind."

Mary wandered off, paws behind her back. First she passed a crowd of dolls. One, dressed like a little girl with long golden curls, nodded at her and said, "Mamma." Mary nodded gravely back. "Papa,"

said the doll next, but Mary was hurrying towards something exciting which she had seen at the end of the row.
It was a slide with steps leading up to it. Mary scrambled
up the steps to explore. At the top she found a mat
with PLEASE SIT on it.   Mary sat.

The Owl Man, looking up from examining a toy
engine, was just in time to see her whizzing down the
chute with ears on end. He met her at the bottom.
" Look here, Mary," he said, " you mustn't go doing
things like this unless you're asked, you know."

Mary got up and pointed to the mat with PLEASE
SIT on it. " You see ? " she said.

The Owl Man saw, of course, and so did the assistant who was serving him. " She's all right," she said, " it isn't often we get such a—"

" Quite," interrupted the Owl Man, " and now, about these engines," and he hurried the girl away.

After several slides more, Mary decided to look further. Round a corner she stood stock still before a lot of Bruins. " Bears ! " she exclaimed excitedly, " lots of them with drawers on like mine." Eagerly she began to speak to one after the other but none of them answered. Very disappointed, Mary sat down beside the largest and thought how sad it was that it wasn't one of her twin cousins, Marionetta or Little Wool. She sat so still that a lady, passing with a little girl, mistook her for a Bruin.

" This is the one I choose," said the little girl, giving Mary a poke.

" Don't ! " said Mary, indignantly. " That's me ! "

" Mummie ! It's alive, it's alive ! Oh, do please let's buy it ! " cried the child.

" Are you for sale ? " enquired her mother.

" For what ? " asked Mary, cautiously.

" For sale."

" I think so," said Mary, wondering what " sale " meant.

" Good, then come along with us and we'll pay," said the lady, looking very pleased.

Mary trotted off between them. Arrived at the desk, the woman turned to an assistant standing by and said, " Please enter this bear to my account," and gave her address.

The assistant was new to her job and rather stupid,

but she had been told that she must tie up all parcels before they were taken away.

" Shall I wrap her up for you, Moddam ? " she asked, looking doubtfully at Mary.   " A paper bag, perhaps ? "

So the largest paper bag in stock was fetched.

" I'm not a bun," said Mary, highly offended, as they pushed and forced her head into the bag.   Luckily, it split and Mary came out almost at once.

" Never mind," said the purchaser, " I'll take her as she is.   Come along, bear." And she took hold of Mary's paw.

" Oh, but I'm not coming with you," said Mary, trying to get her paw away.

" Oh, but you are," said the lady.   " You're mine now —you're entered, remember."

" I won't be entered, I won't be entered," cried Mary, bracing the legs she had free.

" Don't make a scene, now, or I'll smack you," said the lady, pulling.   Unluckily for Mary, she pulled her on to a slippery bit of floor and, try as she might, Mary couldn't stop herself from sliding horribly quickly towards the lift.

Then Mary raised her voice and shrieked, " Owl Man, Owl Man ! I've been entered—come quick ! Oh, do come ! "

The Owl Man dropped the boat he was buying and ran as fast as he could.   He arrived just in time to see the lady backing into the lift, dragging Mary after her. The Owl Man, scarlet in the face, gripped Mary round her waist.

" Let go of this bear immediately, please," he said in a tight voice. " You're mistaken—she's not for sale."

" Oh, but I've entered her," said the lady, scarlet too.

" Then you must un-enter her," said the Owl Man, " she's not for sale, she's a private bear."

By this time the usual Mary crowd had collected and the Owl Man began to feel a bit desperate. He tightened his hold on Mary. Mary squealed.

" If you don't let go of this bear," he said, "I'll send for the manager."

The woman held on.

" If you don't let go at once," said the Owl Man, " I'll send for the police."

The woman still hung on.

" Very well. If you don't let go this minute," continued the Owl Man, " Mary shall bite you."

The woman let go so suddenly that she shot backwards into the lift and the Owl Man and Mary shot backwards into the crowd. Mary rubbed her arm and her waist. She was trembling all over.

" I'm very pulled," she said plaintively.

It didn't take the Owl Man long to get her home and into bed with a bowl of hot bread and milk.

" Now, you have a good sleep," he said when she had finished, " and forget all about this horrid affair."

" But I aren't entered, are I ? " said Mary, lying down and closing one eye.

" Of course not."

" Nor I aren't a bun neither, are I ? " closing the other.

" Of course not," said the Owl Man again.

CHAPTER FOUR

MARY JOURNEYS TO KENT

ON Tuesday afternoon the Owl Man and Mary were to start for the country by car after an early lunch. The lunch was finished and the Owl Man's suit cases were all ready in the hall, with Mary's brilliantly striped canvas, zipp-fastened bag beside them. "Mary travels light but bright," thought the Owl Man, his eyes dazzled by her luggage.

Just then the telephone bell rang and he went off to answer it. "Hallo?" A pause. "Oh, hang the magneto. Can't you fix me up with another? Well, it's about the most confounded piece of luck I've had for many a day. What? But that's not the slightest good to me. I'm leaving now, my good fellow, for Kent—at once. All right—but get her ready for me by Monday without fail, will you? Goodbye," and he jammed the receiver down so hard that Mary felt glad she wasn't the little black box it sat on. Then he ran his hand through his hair in a worried way.

"Is the motor broken?" enquired Mary.

"It is," he answered. "We shall have to go by train, Mary." And he started hunting through a drawer.

"I like going in tr—"

"Diaoul!" said the Owl Man, as he shut his finger in the drawer. "Where is that blessed *A.B.C.*?"

"You pu—"

"Shut up, Mary,"

"I saw you put —"

"Shut *up*," shouted the Owl Man, sucking his pinched finger.

Mary shut.

After another hunt the Owl Man sat down on a chair and, running his hand through his hair again, said they just couldn't go, that was all. He knew the only decent train to Riverhurst went somewhere about two o'clock and they'd missed it already. "So you may as well unpack, Mary," he finished.

But Mary had disappeared and returned just then with the *A.B.C.* clasped against her chest.

"Why in the world didn't you—" began the Owl Man.

"I did try," said Mary.

While the Owl Man turned over the leaves with one hand, he patted Mary on the head with the other. "Sorry, Mary, to be such a boor, but pinches do hurt. Here we are," and he ran his finger down a page, "Charing Cross, 2.58. Ring for the lift, quick, while I telephone for a taxi."

The lift was worked by a nice man called Higgins. He helped them put the luggage in the taxi. " Charing Cross and no time to spare," he shouted and off they went. They were lucky with the traffic lights all through and arrived at the station with a good fifteen minutes to spare. The Owl Man went to an empty carriage right up at the front and settled Mary in a corner seat. He sat down himself opposite and, taking off his hat, was just making himself comfortable when a distracted figure rushed up to the door. It was Higgins.

" Thank goodness I've found you, sir," he panted. " An urgent message from the office to say will you please go round immediately."

" But it's impossible," said the Owl Man, " I'm going away, I've almost gone."

" I know, sir, I told them so, but they said I must take a taxi and stop you at all costs—so I did."

The Owl Man thought and thought. How could he take Mary to the office ? And if he sent her back with Higgins, there'd be no one to bring her back to the station to meet him for the slow train he'd have to take later on. Mrs Orchard had left for the day. He'd just have to put her in charge of the guard and risk it. Higgins found the guard for him while the Owl Man found half-a-crown for the guard.

" Look here," he said, " I've been called back suddenly and can't travel by this train. Would you be awfully kind and keep an eye on this young cub ? She'll be met at Riverhurst ; I'll telephone and arrange it."

" Certainly, sir, if you'd kindly introduce us."

" Miss Mary Plain, the guard. The guard, Miss Mary Plain,"said the Owl Man gravely. Both bowed. The guard pinned a big ENGAGED above Mary's seat. Higgins touched the Owl Man's sleeve. " They said to be quick, sir."

" All right. Now, Mary, you'll be particularly good, old girl, won't you ? Sit very still and look out of the window and the guard will tell you when to get out. Here, I'll put my suitcase on the seat so you can sit a bit higher and look out of the window." Mary sat perched and felt very sorry that the Owl Man was being left behind. " You'll come soon ? " she said. " I like svisiting with you best."

" I'll be there before you're in bed," promised the Owl Man and, as the train moved, he waved till Mary, with her nose pressed flat as a button against the glass, couldn't see him any more.

At first Mary looked out of the window, but after she had watched a great many chimneys go by she did a bit of exploring. It was when she was up on the rack that the train stopped with a jerk at a station. The door was flung open and a bunch of children scrambled in followed by a large mother, carrying a basket and an umbrella.

" Good-bye, Alf ! Give my love to Auntie ! " she cried as the train started.

Mary lay very still, watching.

" Look here," said one boy, " this seat's engaged. See, Liz ? "

" Coo ! " said his sister. " Why's it empty, then ? "

" T'aint now," retorted her brother, seating himself
on the suitcase.

" Look at Freddy, Ma ! " cried Liz.

" It can't do no 'arm for Freddy to sit there till she
or 'e comes," said Ma. (" Can't it ! " thought Mary).
" And no one can't want it till the next station."
(" Can't they ! " thought Mary, wriggling to the edge
of the rack).   But any further thinking on her part was
interrupted by a piercing shriek from Freddy who had
suddenly caught sight of a furry leg hanging over the
edge of the rack.

" Look ! " he gasped.   " An animal !   Oh, Ma, a
wild animal !   Will he bite ? "

" Ow, Ow," shrieked all his brothers and sisters,
stampeding towards Ma.

Ma was beyond shrieking.   Gathering as many of the
children as possible into her arms she sat, thinking wildly
" It isn't an 'e or an 'er, it's an it."   Escape, how to
escape ?   But you couldn't escape from a non-corridor
railway carriage going at fifty miles an hour.   All she
could do was to die for her children, she decided,
jamming them all behind her against the door furthest
from Mary and acting as a barricade with arms out-
stretched in front.

The children too were now far beyond screaming.
Seven lots of eyes gazed with frightened fascination at
Mary's back view.   Mary's back view wasn't being very
dignified.   It was hanging half on and half off the rack.
She wasn't finding getting down as easy as getting up.
At last, with a final wriggle, she dropped on to the floor.

A hiss of seven in-taken breaths greeted her arrival. She picked herself up and bowed politely.

"I'm Mary Plain," she announced, "an unusual first-class bear from the bear-pits at Berne and I've got a white rosette and a gold medal with a picture of myself on it." She drew a deep breath; how lovely not to be interrupted. Ma relaxed a bit though she was too frightened to have heard a word of what Mary said. Still, it seemed a quiet-spoken bear—much smaller than she thought too. But you couldn't always trust appearances. She wondered if she couldn't fetch it one over its head with her umbrella but before she could remember where her umbrella was, Mary said graciously, "Shall we sit?"

They sat—Ma and the batch of children still huddled at the farther end and Mary in a position of great advantage on the Owl Man's suitcase.

"Well, well," said Mary, crossing her legs, "this is a nice kind of train, isn't it?"

Ma and the batch nodded as one man. ("Always humour wild animals," thought Ma, "like lunatics.")

" What's your name ? " enquired Mary, pointing directly at her.

" Eliza. Eliza Maud, after me Grandma," answered Ma a little wildly, wishing Mary would put her paw down.

" And yours ? " pointing to the largest boy.

" Peregrine, please sir—miss," said the boy, anxious to please.

" What kind of a grine ? "

" Pere," answered Peregrine, while Ma wished they had christened him Tom.

For the next few minutes Mary stared out of the window and seemed absorbed by the passing landscape. The batch unhuddled a bit and breathed more freely, and at last the youngest and bravest found courage to whisper hoarsely. " Got a bun, Ma ? "

Mary immediately became unabsorbed and turned round. " Bun, did you say ? " she asked sweetly.

" Yes," said Ma hastily. " Will you 'ave one ? " and she held out a paper bag, rather gingerly.

" Thank you," said Mary, taking two. Nor did she refuse a second helping. By the time she had eaten Dot's buns and Peregrine's apples, and Liz's bull's-eyes, she felt exceedingly comfortable inside, and after she had told Ma and the children all about the show at the Crystal Palace and the Jubilee and the Ballet, they were fast friends.

Several times the train stopped at a station and each time Mary shook hands all round and got out and the guard pushed her in again. At last Riverhurst was reached and Mary had a final shake all round and got out.

"Good-bye," she waved, as the train began to move off.

"Well, there's bears and bears," said Ma to the batch.

CHAPTER FIVE

MARY ARRIVES IN KENT

MARY remained on the platform for exactly two seconds. Then, with a yell, she hurled herself on to the footboard and, scrambling up to the window of the carriage in which she had travelled, she shrieked, " My luggage ! Oh, my luggage ! "

It all happened so suddenly that before the engine driver could stop the train and before the shouting porters could grab hold of Mary, Ma had stuffed the bag through the window and Mary, taking a sideways jump, had landed neatly in the station-master's arms, just as the train began to disappear into a tunnel.

" Pardon ! " said Mary.

" Bless my soul ! " exclaimed the station-master, taken aback at finding his arms so very unexpectedly full of bear and the brightest bag he had ever seen. " Bless my soul ! " he repeated. " And who might you be ? "

" I'm Mary Plain," explained Mary, perched on his arm, " from the bear-pits— Hullo, oh hullo ! " she cried and wriggling down she hurled herself at a lady who came hurrying up to them, dressed in a fur coat.

" Pardon !" said Mary

" I've arriven ! " cried Mary, hugging her friend.

" So I guessed," said the Fur-Coat-Lady, hugging her back, " and I'm so glad.   You remember Mr Smith ? "
Mary shook hands solemnly.   " Of course," she said.

" Good ! " said Bill.   " Delighted to meet you again, Miss Plain."   Mary shook hands again.   Bill turned to the station-master.   " So sorry, Edwards.   I don't quite know what happened ? "

" Seems as if the porter had missed this piece of luggage," he answered, holding up Mary's bag.   Two or three people collected, fascinated by the brilliant stripes.

" It hardly seems possible, does it ? " said Bill, blinking a little.   " I mean—to miss it."   He glanced round at the rapidly growing Mary crowd.   " Thanks awfully, Edwards.   Come on, Jill," he said hastily and, seizing the luggage and Mary's paw, he hurried out to the car.

But the crowd came too, and grew and grew while Bill, perspiring with hurry and rage, strapped the Owl Man's suitcase on behind.   " We're not a bloomin' zoo," he muttered, climbing into the driver's seat.

" Good-bye ! " called Mary, the tip of whose nose just reached the window ledge.   " Good-bye, all ! " And she waved the dazzling bag out of the window.

" Umph ! " grunted Bill, stepping on the accelerator, and " Oh dear ! " sighed the Fur-Coat-Lady, throwing open her fur coat and " Isn't it nice being svisitors together ? " said Mary sweetly.

The Owl Man didn't arrive till after dark.   He came

in stamping his feet and shaking snow-flakes off his hat. Mary flew to the door to meet him, a large bib tied under her chin.   The Owl Man seemed extraordinarily relieved to see Mary.

" Why are you all white ? " asked Mary.

" Because it's snowing," he answered, patting her on the head as he shook hands with the others.

" So she arrived, all right, Bill ? "

" Umph ! " said Bill.   " Ask Jill."

" I'll tell you later," said the Fur-Coat-Lady, hastily. " She arrived, that's the main thing, isn't it Mary ? "

" And now we're three svisitors," said Mary, gaily, tucking a paw under their arms and swinging herself backwards and forwards between them.

" How about Mary showing you your room and taking herself to bed at the same time ? " suggested Bill. " It's nearly dinner-time and you'll want to wash."

" Dinner-time, did you say ? " asked Mary, who was of a hopeful nature.

" Yes, dinner-time—for us.   Not supper-time for you, Mary Plain," said the Owl Man, leading her firmly up the stairs.

Bill's house was old and full of oak beams and odd corners.   Mary's cot was tucked away in an alcove. From it she could see the fire-place where a bright fire burned, but not the Owl Man's bed.

" I'm rather a long way off, aren't I ? " she asked, as the Owl Man pulled down the blankets.

" Nonsense ! " he said.   " Why, in London you have a room of your own.   Now, come and help me hang up your drawers—that's right. And now, good-night! You must hurry and pop off to sleep before Santa Claus comes."

But Mary couldn't pop. She lay and looked at the fire spluttering up the chimney and then at her bathing drawers hanging at the end of her cot. "They couldn't get in," she decided. "Not all those meringues, not nearly enough room. What was it the Owl Man had said? A pillow case, of course."

Mary had two pillow cases on her cot and the Owl Man had three. Presently they were all hanging off the end of Mary's cot. "That's better," she thought, as she climbed in again. She wondered uneasily how soon Santa Claus would come. Not till the fire was out and she was asleep the Owl Man had said. But supposing she couldn't go to sleep? She lay down and tried very hard. The door opened softly and Mary shot up in bed, her hair all on end with fright.

" You can't come in," she shouted, " I'm not asleep and the fire's not—"

" Bad dreams, Mary ? " said the Fur-Coat-Lady, switching on the light. Mary scrambled to the bottom of her cot and looked at her over the hedge of pillow slips. She felt exceedingly glad to see her.

" Hallo ! What are all these for ? " asked the Fur-Coat-Lady.

" My list," said Mary, " but he doesn't come till the fire's out, does he ? "

" Of course not. And not till you're tight asleep. Look here, I've brought up a present for you to give the Owl Man in the morning."

" Does everyone have presents, then ? " enquired Mary, surprised.

" Of course, at Christmas. Now, I'll hide it under your bed so it will be safe till morning."

Which showed that the Fur-Coat-Lady didn't know Mary quite as well as the Owl Man did. Almost before the door closed, Mary was under the bed tugging at the string. She pulled out a rather gaily coloured woollen scarf and wound it round her neck just to see how many times it would go round. " Five ! " she murmured and, lying down, wondered what she could give Bill for a present. After a good think she got up and crept to where she could hear a rather loud ticking and, feeling about, found a clock. " Just the very thing," thought Mary. " He'll like a clock to tell when it's dinner-time." And she carefully wrapped it up in the

paper which had come off the Owl Man's scarf and pushed
it under the bed.

" I must try and pop off now," she said, lying down
and closing her eyes so tight that little stars danced up
and down in front.   A few minutes later she really was
beginning to feel sleepy when a large piece of coal
dropped on to the hearth.

Mary started up, bristling.   It was him, Santa Claus,
coming down the chimney while she was still awake.
They'd made a mistake—he didn't wait till you were
asleep after all, and the fire was . . .   Another coal fell
and Mary took a flying leap over the pillow-cases and
landed on all fours in the middle of the room, her heart
hammering.   Fumbling for the handle she got the door
open and flew along the passage and down the stairs,
stumbling every few steps over the scarf which had
begun to come unwound.

The sitting room door was half open and all three
grown-ups sprang to their feet as Mary appeared.

" Coming ! Chimney ! Couldn't pop ! Meringues !"
she gasped and, catching her paw in the scarf, fell flat
at the Owl Man's feet.

He picked her up but, by this time, Mary and the scarf
had become so mixed up that it was a little difficult to
tell which was which.

" And now," said the Owl Man, holding Mary with
one hand and the scarf with the other, " now that I've
disentangled you—what's it all about, Mary, and what
is this ? "

He waved the scarf in the air and the Fur-Coat-Lady

sprang forward. " You're not supposed to know about that," she cried, " shut your eyes ! "

The Owl Man obediently shut his eyes while she put the scarf into a drawer. Mary pushed herself between his knees. " Please," she said, glancing fearfully over her shoulder at the door. " Please, Owl Man."

" It looks as if you'll have to go to bed as well, Owl Man," suggested the Fur-Coat-Lady.

So the Owl Man went up, with Mary, very safe, on his shoulder. " There ! " he said, plumping her on to the cot. " Aren't you a little goose ? A bright fire, empty drawers and by Jove, *how* many pillow slips ? And that's all. You ought to feel ashamed of yourself."

" Yes," agreed Mary, " but I like it best with you here."

Very soon the Owl Man was in bed, too. " Good-night, old girl," he called.

" Good-night," called Mary from her corner.

The Owl Man closed his eyes.

" But I'm a long way off, aren't I ? " came plaintively from the cot.

" Nonsense ! " said the Owl Man, sleepily.

" But he doesn't never—not till the fire's out, does he ? "

No answer. A coal fell in the grate. Presently the Owl Man turned over in bed and murmured, " Hang Annie ! I told her I didn't want a hot-water bottle ! "

" But I'm not," said the " hot-water-bottle " and snuggled closer.

CHAPTER SIX

MARY AND CHRISTMAS

CHURCH bells ringing! Christmas morning!

The Owl Man rolled out of bed, stretching his arms above his head and yawning enormous yawns. "Mary still asleep, I suppose," he thought and walked round to her corner to have a look. But there wasn't a sign o Mary. Five fat pillow cases and a pair of bathing drawe with a trumpet sticking out of the top, but no Mary. The Owl Man scratched his head. Just at that moment the door behind him opened and Bill poked his head in.

"Merry Christmas, Owl Man," he said. "Merry Christmas, Mary!" He came into the room. "But where is Mary?"

"Gone," said the Owl Man, "not even a footprint to be seen."

"But really," began Bill, "wherever can she be?"

"Here!" said Mary, appearing, very ruffled, from the wrong end of the Owl Man's bed.

"I'll be blowed!" exclaimed the Owl Man. "Do you mean to say you've been there all night?"

"Yes," said Mary, "but I only took a little room. Is it Christmas and has he come?"

"It is and he has," said the Owl Man. Mary tumbled out of bed and pattered round to her cot. "Oh!" she said, a paw up to her mouth. "Oh!"

And really there was plenty for Mary to "Oh" about for there were the five pillow cases and the bathing drawers, all bulging.

There were several balloons, a huge rubber ball, a slate and pencil, a busman's outfit, odd boxes with meringues and figs and sweets and lots of other things. Mary gave little shrieks of delight as she opened them all and after, when the room was knee-deep in paper and boxes, she perched on the end of the Owl Man's bed and ate meringues while he had his early morning tea.

"How you *can*, Mary!" he said, not enjoying his cup of tea as much as usual.

"Can what?" asked Mary, carefully rescuing some whipped cream off her chest.

"Eat those at this time of the morning."

Mary looked very surprised. "I think it's the best time," she said, "because then there's lots of time left for more."

The Owl Man groaned and gave it up—also his tea. Next to the meringues Mary liked the busman's outfit best. The hat, worn at a slight tilt, was very becoming and the belt fitted excellently when it had an extra piece of string attached to it. By the time the Owl Man had shaved and dressed he had travelled so many times

from **Kensington** to Hornsey Rise that he felt extremely
tired.

"Now this ends it, Mary," he said firmly. "No
more travelling till after breakfast. I'm worn out,"
and he led her along the passage to the bathroom where
she was washed and combed.

Looking her very best, sleek and clean, Mary went
down to breakfast. Under one arm she clasped an untidy
and loudly ticking parcel.

"No present giving till after breakfast," said Bill but
Mary refused to be parted from her parcel which was
finally placed on a chair beside her while everybody
pretended not to hear the ticks. When they had
finished Mary got down and presented it to Bill Smith.

"From me to you," she said, graciously.

Bill opened it. "Why, it's just exactly what I
wanted, Miss Plain," he said, a little surprised at seeing
his own clock. "How clever of you to guess!"

Mary beamed.

" And this is for you, with all my best wishes," said Bill, handing Mary a long flat parcel. It was a nurse's outfit.

" I'm off ! " said the Owl Man, making for the door. " I've already spent hours bussing to the Elephant and Castle and I'm blessed if I'm going to have my temperature taken all the morning."

So the Fur-Coat-Lady very kindly and promptly had an attack of measles and Mary nursed her well again. Later on, the grown-ups went to church while Mary played in the garden with James the house-boy. When they came back Bill fetched two toboggans from the barn, a big one for three and a baby one for Mary, and they dragged them up to the top of a steep field.

" Now, Miss Plain," said Bill. " Just lie down quite flat on your front, hang on tight, push with your back paws and you're off."

Mary was, but not with the toboggan. For one of the things that Mary just couldn't do was to lie quite, or even rather, flat.

" Really, Mary," said the Owl Man, as he collected them both, " you're no good ! "

" Oh, I am," said Mary trying again and this time pitching head foremost into the snow.

" You see ! " said the Owl Man, which was just what Mary couldn't do, upside down.

But the next moment she was sailing down the field yelling, " I'm off ! I'm off ! " The others were talking and so they did not see Mary overturn on a hillock and go flying through the air, right into a tree.

" I've flown again," gasped Mary, hugging the branch on which she landed.

There were cries of dismay when the others, shooting down the hill, passed the overturned toboggan. They rushed back and searched all round it. Mary kept very quiet.

" But she can't have disappeared into thin air," exclaimed the Owl Man.

" One never knows with Mary," said the Fur-Coat-Lady.

" I'll have a look from this tree," said the Owl Man. " I can see further afield," and he swung himself onto the first branch.

" Hallo ! " said Mary. " I got here first—I flew."

" The dickens you did ! " said the Owl Man and he dropped down pulling Mary after him and rolled her in the snow.

" That'll larn you," he said.

" Larn me some more ! " cried Mary, looking just like a snowman. But it was time for lunch and they all went in with quite enormous appetites.

To everybody's astonishment, when the plum pudding was brought in, blazing fiercely, Mary disappeared under the table. It took quite a few moments to get her out again. " It'll frizzle me inside ! " she said, gazing fearfully at the helping on her plate. " I know it will."

" Don't be silly, Mary," said the Owl Man. " Jus' you poke it a bit and perhaps you'll find something."

So Mary poked and found first a sixpence and then a silver pig and after that she liked plum pudding. Bill laughed a lot when the Fur-Coat-Lady found the ring but when he himself found the batchelor's button he was not at all amused.

The day ended with a game of hide-and-seek. "Whoever thinks of the best place to hide gets a box of sweets," said Bill. Mary hid first but they soon found her for she kept shouting "Cuckoo" till they did. The Fur-Coat-Lady explained that it was far cleverer to hide quietly and not be found. "I'll go now," she said, "and you'll see."

Sure enough, after one "Cuckoo" she never made a sound and they took quite five minutes before they found her in the airing-cupboard, among the linen.

"Thank goodness I wasn't born a sheet," she exclaimed, "the heat's terrific!"

After both the men had hidden it was Mary's turn again. "Only one 'Cuckoo' remember," said the Owl Man.

They waited a good while for her "Cuckoo" and when it came it sounded very muffled and far away.

"Oh dear," said the Fur-Coat-Lady, "I hope she isn't anywhere impossible."

"More likely exceedingly possible," said the Owl Man.

But they couldn't find Mary. They hunted upstairs and downstairs and under the stairs and still no sign of her. James and Annie helped too.

"All your fault for telling her only to cuckoo once, Richard," grumbled Bill.

"I know, I know," said the Owl Man, who was beginning to look worried. "Mary! Call 'Cuckoo' again," he shouted, for the twentieth time.

Dead silence.

They were all standing in the hall facing the front door except Annie, who was standing with her back to it and close to the row of coat-hooks where all the overcoats and mackintoshes were hung. Among them was the Fur-Coat-Lady's coat and this now slowly stretched out two furry arms and placed them affectionately round Annie's neck.

The sight of James's face opposite first frightened Annie but, at the feel of the fur arms round her neck, she fell in a faint on the floor.

"Brandy! Quick!" cried the Fur-Coat-Lady.

Mary stepped out of the coat and over the body.

"I've won, haven't I?" she asked.

"You have!" said Bill grimly.

The brandy did the trick and presently Annie went off to the kitchen, looking a little shaken.

"You really don't deserve them, you know, Miss Plain," said Bill, "but I don't expect that will stop you from enjoying them."

"No," said Mary, "I've enjoyed every single one."

CHAPTER SEVEN

MARY IS EXTRA BRAVE

THE next evening Bill and his guests had been invited to a big ball at Lady Ex's.

" Taking the car ? " asked the Owl Man.

" May as well," said Bill, " for though it's very near, it will save snow-boots and goloshes."

" I like balls, too," said Mary, hopefully, drumming with her paws.

" Not this kind," said the Owl Man tweaking her ear. " And stop that drumming, Mary ; it's so interruptive. Go on, Bill, tell us some more about the burglar."

" Well, it appears he chose exactly the ten minutes when the Macleans and staff were all at family prayers to empty their safe. Hang, there's the telephone," and he went off to answer it.

" What's a bugglar ? " enquired Mary.

" A burglar ? He's a naughty man who gets into people's houses and steals things."

" Without asking ? "

" Yes, I don't believe I ever heard of a burglar who asked," said the Owl Man, laughing.

" What does he steal ? "

" Well, anything of value."

" What's value mean ? "

" It means—well—things people specially care about like—"

" Cream buns ? "

" No, *no*, Mary. Not everyone is as bun-minded as you. It means things like silver and jewellery. Hallo, Bill, what's up ? "

" I say," said Bill, " this is getting beyond a joke— he's been to Lady Ex's and pinched the famous diamond necklace and rings ! "

The Owl Man whistled.

" I hope he doesn't come here," said the Fur-Coat-Lady with a little shiver.

" He won't find much if he does," said Bill.

" He'll find me," put in Mary, but nobody took any notice.

" But didn't you say you had a safe somewhere, Bill ? "

" Yes, in the sitting room. I'll show you," and he led the way there and showed them a door in the wall. He took out a bunch of keys from his pocket and the heavy door swung open. Mary peeped in. " What a nice little room," she said. "It would just fit me nicely."

"By the way," said Bill. "I suppose it will be alright leaving a certain person alone to-night? You know Annie and James sleep out?"

"Quite," said the Owl Man. "Once asleep she stays asleep."

That night before they left, however, he tip-toed upstairs to be quite certain Mary was asleep. She was, fast. "Good," thought the Owl Man, "she's safe till morning," and he tip-toed away to the ball.

But some hours later Mary was awakened by a strange noise under her window. She sat up in bed and pricked her ears. There it was again—the kind of noise a window makes when it's being pushed up. Perhaps they'd come back from the ball? She'd better have a look. She slipped out of bed and padded across to the open window. The moon was shining brightly and, leaning out, Mary was just in time to see a back disappearing over the window-sill of the room below hers. And it wasn't the Owl Man's back nor Bill's and certainly not the Fur-Coat-Lady's. Mary stood still and decided she didn't much care for backs at night—not strange ones and not when one was quite alone in a house.

A slight noise in the room below sent her back into bed. "Me and a back and no one else, poor Mary Plain," she thought and drew the blankets well up over her head. After a bit her nose re-appeared and gradually her whole head. She sat up in bed and cocked her ears, listening.   Perhaps she ought to go down and see if that back had gone ?   She put one paw softly on the floor.   Perhaps he was a bugglar stealing things ?   The second paw reached the floor.   Perhaps he'd steal all there was to eat in the house ?   Mary stood up, still not feeling awfully brave.

"Come along, Mary Plain," she said.   "You aren't frightened, are you ? "

"No," said Mary Plain, in a tiny voice.

"Not of a back ! " said Mary, encouragingly.

"No," answered Mary Plain in a tinier voice still.

So there wasn't much help to be got from Mary Plain. She'd have to go alone.   Mary took a deep brave breath and crept to the door, opened it and stole down the stairs.   So quietly did she move on her padded paws that she reached the door of the sitting-room without making a sound.   Her heart was going pit-a-pat, pit-a-pat.   "Come along, Mary Plain ! " she said to herself.   "Come along ! "   and she gave the door a push.   Unfortunately, James hadn't oiled the hinges lately and it gave a little squeak as it opened.   A man standing by the open safe swung round and, seeing Mary, his mouth fell open and he stood transfixed, staring at her in horror.

Mary, rather frightened herself inside but very brave outside, bared her teeth and said, " Grrrrr ! "

The man took a frightened step backwards.

"Grrrr, grrrr," said Mary, feeling encouraged and advancing slowly.

At each growl the man retreated.   "In a minute, if

he goes back just a little more I can reach the door,"
thought Mary and, rising on her hind legs, she pawed
the air with her claws all out and made the growliest
growls she'd ever made. Terrified, the man backed
right into the safe and Mary, with a quick spring,
caught the door and slammed it shut.

Then she sat down rather suddenly on the floor,
feeling very breathless. All that growling and shutting
bugglars into little rooms made your heart bang. " What
I need is a nice cream—hallo ! " exclaimed Mary,
catching sight of an open black bag with things tumbling
out of it. She scrambled up and had a look inside and a
bright sparkle caught her eye. Out of an inside pocket
she drew a long bright chain. " Stars ! " thought Mary
who had never seen diamonds before. " A string of
stars." She hung them round her neck and then
suddenly she remembered what Bill Smith had said
about a necklace being lost—the bugglar had taken it.
She took it off and had a look. Perhaps this string was
called a necklace ? " Nice, shiny, stars," she thought,
swinging them round and round her head to see them
glitter.

But what else was it Bill had said the bugglar had
taken ? Mary scratched her head thoughtfully with the
biggest diamond. Rings ! Of course. She dived again
into the bag and found some sparkling rings. A dull
thud came from inside the safe and Mary looked uneasily over her shoulder.

" He might get out," she thought, " and I don't like
backs—not when they're bugglars in front. I'll take

the string to the Owl Man—that's a good idea." But how to carry the rings? Mary looked sadly at her plump paw but she was full of good ideas that night. She opened her mouth very wide and presently she set off across the garden with thousands of pounds worth hung round her neck and a diamond smile.

The house was easy to find because it was the only one near-by and light streamed from all its windows. "It's saying, 'Come along, Mary Plain,'" said Mary, encouraging herself through the darkness of the shrubbery.

Mary arrived just at the end of a waltz and through a window, into the ball room. A girl's scream greeted her arrival and then pandemonium reigned. The women shrieked, the men shouted and made for Mary, while Mary made for the Owl Man, whose head she had seen over the top of the crowd. "Here's the thief—catch him—don't let him go—trip him up—lay him out!" shouted the excited men, closing in on Mary.

How Mary got through she never knew but somehow she reached the Owl Man and a moment later was safely in his arms.

" What the—" he began, but words failed him.

Mary, still panting, smiled her diamond smile and then spat the rings neatly into his hand. " The bugglar's in the little room," she announced between pants, " and I've brought you these. Don't you like the string, Owl Man ? "

The Owl Man gasped. " I do," he said, " but I know someone who'll like it even more than I do. You cut along and take them to Lady Ex, Mary, while I see to the burglar. I'll wrap the rings up in my handkerchief, like this."

By this time every guest and servant and gardener and chauffeur on the place had collected into a Mary crowd. It took quite a few minutes to clear a passage between Mary and Lady Ex. Mary walked up it slowly, bowing to right and left, while the guests yelled and clapped and shouted and stamped. She found Lady Ex at the end—in tears.

" There ! " she said, emptying the diamonds into her lap. Then, seeing her tears, she added uncertainly, " Didn't you want them then ? "

" I did, oh I did ! " said Lady Ex, crying some more and laughing at the same time and then and there, before the whole company and though it was the first time she'd ever seen her, she hugged Mary Plain as hard as she could. " Isn't there *anything* I could do in return ? " she asked. " Anything at all you'd like ? "

" I'd love a meringue," said Mary.

CHAPTER EIGHT

MARY HAS ANOTHER MARY IDEA

MARY woke up extra early the next day. At first she lay in her cot and listened to the Owl Man sleeping which was fun, because first he went " rrrch " and then he went " phrrr." But after about five minutes it stopped being fun, so Mary decided to get up. She did this very quietly because she knew the Owl Man didn't like being wakened up before his tea came and it couldn't be early tea time yet because it was still quite dark. So Mary crept to the door and opened it softly. Once out in the passage she stood on tip-paw and, reaching for the switch, turned on the light. No-one about.

The banisters looked flat and shiny and very inviting. Of course, they hadn't got " Please sit " on them but Mary felt they were saying " Please slide " so she did, landing with a soft thud on a fur rug which lay at the bottom of the stairs. " Fun ! " thought Mary, scrambling softly up the stairs and doing it again.

The third slide she whizzed a little faster than usual

so that her thud was a little louder, too, and a moment later a door opened above. Quicker than winking, Mary slid herself under the mat and kept as still as a mouse. Luckily, there was shadow at the bottom of the stairs so perhaps whoever it was wouldn't notice that the rug had suddenly developed a large round hump.

" Anyone there ? " asked a voice.

" No," said Mary, losing her head. Luckily the rug was thick so the voice didn't hear and a moment later the light was turned out and a door closed above.

Mary slid out from her hiding place and, feeling her way along the wall, she came to a door. Inside she found the kitchen. She knew it was the kitchen because it smelt of bun. Mary's nose twitched and she had an explore but couldn't find where the buns lived. Next she climbed on to a table by the window. It was getting a little lighter now and, peeping out, Mary saw something which made her nose twitch more than ever. Sitting on the table she did a bit of thinking.

Five minutes later a bell pealed loudly through the house. Bill and the Owl Man and the Fur-Coat-Lady all tumbled out of bed.

" It must be a fire," said the Owl Man, appearing with his jug of water.

" Or an accident," cried the Fur-Coat-Lady, rushing for a towel.

" Whatever it is, it's pretty serious," said Bill as he hurried downstairs, " the bell's not stopped for an instant yet."

The reason it hadn't stopped was because whoever

" Milko !" *said a cheerful voice*

was ringing it hadn't taken their finger off the button.

"No one here," said Bill, opening and shutting the front door, "must be at the back," and he raced through to the kitchen.

By this time the Owl Man and the Fur-Coat-Lady had rushed downstairs and were just behind Bill as he flung open the back door.

The bell stopped suddenly and all three stood stock still, staring.

"Milko!" said a cheerful voice from under the Owl Man's felt hat. There was so much hat that for a moment it was all they could see. Then in the half dark they saw a pair of furry legs and a milk-can swinging on a paw.

"Mary!" exclaimed Bill.

"Mary!" exclaimed the Owl Man.

"Mary!" echoed the Fur-Coat-Lady.

"I'm Milko," announced Mary, trying hard to see them but only seeing hat. "I've brought your milk nice and early for your morning tea."

"I'll milko you," said the Owl Man, starting to laugh. Both the others laughed, too. There was nothing else to do.

"Come in, Mary, and hurry up—we're all shivering. Be careful not to spill the milk, now."

Mary hurried, but because she could only see hat she didn't see the doorstep and the next minute she and the milk-can were scattered on the kitchen floor.

"Oh," wailed the Fur-Coat-Lady, "there goes our milk."

But it didn't, for the simple reason that there wasn't any milk to go.

All three stopped laughing suddenly.

"And the nearest farm's two miles away," said Bill gloomily.

"Mary shall be punished," said the Owl Man.

"That won't give us back our milk," said the Fur-Coat-Lady sadly.

"Aren't you ashamed of yourself, Mary?" asked the Owl Man.

Mary was still in the hat. Perhaps because it fitted her so far down, it hadn't come off when she fell. "No," she said, from the inside.

The Owl Man removed the hat.

"Did you hear what I said, Mary?" he asked.

"No," said Mary, from the outside, kicking at the floor with her paw, and then in a wobbly voice, "Do you think the twins are happy without me?"

The Owl Man lifted Mary on to the table while Bill and the Fur-Coat-Lady tactfully disappeared.

"Look here, Mary," he said, "you've been a greedy little cub. You know you oughtn't to have drunk all that milk, don't you?"

Mary nodded.

"Then why did you do it?"

"Because I wanted it, very badly, here," said Mary, stroking her front.

"Well, you mustn't do things like that," said the Owl Man, "because it's naughty, and to make you remember not to, I shall punish you."

This he did by not letting Mary have any milk with her bread for breakfast, but, as she was still comfortably full of the two quarts she'd had at seven, Mary made no fuss.   Nor did she much mind when she wasn't allowed any cream for lunch.

" This tart reminds me of the time you made me an apple-pie bed at school, Bill," said the Owl Man.

Bill grinned.   " Weren't you pleased ! " he said.

In the afternoon they all went tobogganing again and after a large tea they played Snap.   Mary was so afraid of losing a chance that she said " Snap " without stopping and very soon the Owl Man told her to run off to bed.

Mary ran off, but not straight to bed.   Anyone coming down the stairs five minutes later would have met Mary staggering up them with her arms very full.   She could only manage one foot at a time and she panted a lot.   But, by the time the Owl Man ran up to tuck her up as usual, she was safely in her cot. He sat down on the edge of it. Mary looked up at him with bright eyes and he couldn't help wishing Mary wasn't so very full of Mary ideas always.

" Would you like a nice surprise ? " she asked.

" Very much, if it's nice," said the Owl Man. " What would it be ? "

" But you mustn't tell about surprises," said Mary, " must you ? "

" I suppose not," said the Owl Man.

So Mary didn't. She was very busy for the next three hours keeping awake. She kept pinching herself to be sure she hadn't popped off by mistake. At last she was rewarded by seeing the Owl Man creep up to bed. Mary shut her eyes tight. He was always very quiet so as not to wake her. After a few minutes she opened one, just in time to see the Owl Man jump into bed.

" Great guns ! " he shouted, jumping out again and forgetting all about waking Mary. " What's all this beastly mess—wet and soft and—ugh ! "

" Apple," said Mary, " out of your pie."

" My *pie* ! " exclaimed the Owl Man, sitting down on the bed rather suddenly.

" Yes," said Mary, " Mr Bill Smith said you were pleased with the apple-pie bed he made you and I wanted you to be pleased, too. Aren't you ? "

The Owl Man sat and stared at his appley feet.

" Aren't you ? " asked Mary again.

The Owl Man looked at Mary. She was sitting up in

bed, beaming, with a ruffled head and cocked ears.

"But—" he began—"you see, Mary, it's not—" and then he gave it up. He just couldn't un-cock Mary's ears even if his bed was in a fearful mess. It was only another Mary idea, after all.

"It certainly was a surprise," he said, "but surprises must only happen once, you know, Mary; it wouldn't be a surprise if you did it again."

"No," said Mary, and, with a final beam, she dropped off to sleep while the Owl Man wearily reached for his towel.

CHAPTER NINE

IN WHICH MARY IS BRAVER STILL

" There was a sharp frost last night, let's go and see if the pond is bearing," suggested Bill, next morning.

" Whatting ? " asked Mary.

" Bearing," said Bill.

" Do let's ! " said the others and " Oh yes, oh yes, do let's, *do* let's ! " said Mary, in such an excited way that they all stared at her.

On the way there through the little wood and across a big field Mary kept running on ahead and then running back to the grown-ups. " Hurry up, oh do hurry up," she cried, once or twice.

" You must remember we've only two legs to walk on, Miss Plain," said Bill. " And snow-boots aren't as useful as pads in the snow, you know. You have a look."

Mary did, and because it isn't easy to examine your hind pads when you are on a path all slippery with snow, she landed on her back. The Owl Man seized the opportunity to give her a roll and she got up looking exactly like a small white bear.

" You've gone Polar, Mary," said the Owl Man. " Hullo, there's the pond, we're nearly there." Mary flew on ahead but, when she had reached the pond, she stopped dead.

"It isn't," she said, looking very disappointed.

"Isn't what?"

"Bearing," said Mary.

"We haven't tried yet," said Bill.

"But I can see," persisted Mary. She turned to the Owl Man, her ears drooping. "It isn't Little Wooling or Marionetting," she said, sadly, "not even Friska-ing. I thought they'd all be here when he said it was bearing."

As we know, the Owl Man hated to see Mary's ears droop. He glared at Bill, who had begun to laugh and stepped on the Fur-Coat-Lady's toe, because she had begun to smile.

"It's not that kind of bearing," he explained kindly, "it means—"

But luckily Mary's attention was suddenly drawn to two small boys, who, with a still smaller sister in a bright red coat, were throwing stones across the pond; partly to try and hit a bit of blue paper, which, fluttering on a twig sticking up out of the water, made an excellent target, but mostly because the stones, skimming across the ice, made a lovely whirring sound.

"Pretty, pretty," said the baby, stretching her fat fingers towards the fluttering paper.

"Hi!" called Bill. "Stop that, you young ruffians; you'll ruin the ice."

The young ruffians stopped at once and watched interestedly while Bill stepped cautiously on to the edge of the ice. A squeaking crack ran right across the pond and he got off, shaking his head.

" Not safe," he said, " needs another couple of days at least ; then we shall get some good skating if only we can keep it clear of stones." He turned to the two boys. " Look here, you two, if I give you each a penny will you promise not to throw any more stones and go and buy some sweets instead ? "

Two small heads nodded hard. " I'll promise, too," said Mary quickly, but Bill took no notice. " All right," he said, " here are two silver pennies," and he handed two sixpences to the largest boy.

Now, whether his brother thought he wasn't going to get his, no one ever knew but what everyone did know was, that the next minute the two boys were fighting like two little wild cats. The grown-ups rushed to separate them and so nobody heard the baby say " Pretty, pretty," again nor saw her start across the ice towards the blue paper. One, two, yes, twelve steps she took before, out of reach of the bank, her feet slipped, and with a cry she disappeared through the ice. Luckily, Mary's sharp ears heard the cry and she turned round just in time to see the red coat disappear into the pond, leaving a dark round hole in the ice.

" Quick ! " shrieked Mary, " the baby's gone—it's in the water, quick ! "

Horrified, the grown-ups rushed to the edge of the pond and saw the jagged hole. Bill, on his hands and knees, started to crawl towards it but, within a couple of feet, the ice gave way.

"... _then only a black hole_" _thought Mary_

Quick as lightning, the Owl Man seized the belt off his mackintosh, off Bill's, off the Fur-Coat-Lady's. And as he knotted them together he talked rapidly to Mary.

" I'll fix this on you, Mary, and you crawl out carefully, drop into the hole and dive for the baby—it's the only chance. Understand ? Just as quick as you can."

Mary nodded. She felt too choky to speak. She kept her eyes fixed on the black hole. The next instant the belt was fastened and she was out on the ice. " First a baby and a red coat and then only a black hole," thought Mary, crawling carefully but rapidly towards the spot and trying not to notice the frightening way the cracks spread like stars beneath her weight.

The people watching held their breath. " It'll just bear her," said the Owl Man, " only just."

Ten seconds and she was half-way, twenty and she was nearer, thirty and she was there. Taking a deep breath, Mary half slid and half dived into the hole.

The Owl Man, standing up to his waist in water, was holding the other end of the belts with an arm stretched as far as he could reach. His face was very white.

" If she doesn't come up in another second I shall pull," he said. " One, two, ah, thank *heaven !* "

A bit of fur appeared on the surface of the pool— a glimpse of red. Then Mary's face popped up for a moment. She gave a gasping breath and disappeared again.

" She can't make it," said the Owl Man, " the child's unconscious and too heavy," and he began pulling on the belts.

Mary's head appeared again.

"Good Mary, good girl—hang on to her, Mary,"
he shouted. "Just a minute longer and you'll be all right.
I'm pulling you in. Stick to it, Mary."

Mary heard. Struggling to keep her head above the
water, her mouth half full of red coat and half full of
pond water, Mary hung on. The Owl Man pulled and
their combined weights broke the ice and in another
minute they were within reach and eager hands pulled
them out on to the bank.

Mary, half blinded with wet and tiredness, was first
very sick and then lay down on the ground, too tired
for once to hear the cries of " Well done, Mary ! Well
done, Miss Plain ! "

" She'll be all right for the present," said the Owl
Man, lifting her on to a coat with the belts still round
her and covering her up. " She's asleep already."

They all bent over the wet baby. The Fur-Coat-
Lady on her hands and knees chafed the small cold feet
and hands while Bill worked her arms up and down.
Presently, it gave a little cry.

" Thank Heaven," said Bill, " she's saved ! " They
stripped off the red coat and wrapped her in a jersey
and Bill stood up with the bundle in his arms.

All this time the boys had been standing staring
and staring, hand in hand. Now that their sister was
safe they began to cry from over-excitement.

" Now, now," said Bill, " no tears, please. We're
all wet enough already. You trot ahead and show me

the way home for we must get this young lady into a hot bath as soon as possible."

"And this one," said the Owl Man, turning to where Mary lay. He and the Fur-Coat-Lady took the corners of the coat and, lifting it gently, carried Mary home between them.

They had to shake her awake before they gave her a good hot bath and after that she sat tucked up on the sitting-room sofa which was drawn up to the fire, while the Fur-Coat-Lady and the Owl Man waited on her, hand and foot.

"More, please," said Mary, stretching out her empty bowl. She was taking dreadful advantage. The Fur-Coat-Lady gave the Owl Man a look as she filled it for the third time.

"Six lumps, please," said Mary, calmly. "Big ones."

Six big lumps were dropped in.

"I ought to have six, oughtn't I," she continued, watching the Owl Man over the rim of her bowl, "because I'm a first-class bear with a white rosette and a gold medal with a picture of myself on it?"

The Owl Man never said a word.

CHAPTER TEN

THE following morning Bill said he was going over to see if the baby was none the worse for its adventure, "and", he added, "I'm going with the Fur-Coat-Lady, quite alone."

"Not me, then?" said Mary.

"Not you, then, Miss Plain," said Bill, politely but very firmly. "Not this morning."

"Oh," said Mary, taken aback. "Are you going out, too, Owl Man, quite alone?"

The Owl Man chuckled and looked at the Fur-Coat-Lady. "No such luck," he said, "I've got lots of letters to write."

"And I've got toothache," said Mary, suddenly.

"Nonsense!" said the Owl Man. "You cut along and ask Annie if she can give you something to do."

Annie could. She wanted the laundry basket fetched home from her mother's cottage down the lane.

423

" It's got a handle and it's not big," she said, " so you can manage it all right but don't crush it, don't drop it and, for goodness sake, don't forget to bring back Mr Smith's new py-jamas or you'll get into trouble."

" Don't drop, don't crush, py-jama," said Mary to herself all the way down the drive. When she got to the corner of the lane a sharp wind came rushing along and made her tooth ache again. " Oh, dear," said Mary, giving her face a rub, " don't drop, don't crush, oh, dear, py-jama."

Annie's mother handed over the basket, staring very hard at Mary and her bathing drawers, which she was wearing for a treat. She wasn't used to bears in drawers, or out of them, for that matter.

Mary started back, carrying the basket carefully. All went well till she got to the same corner where the wind was waiting for her again and, before she could stop it, the leg half of Mr Smith's bright blue pyjamas flew out

of the basket and on to the hedge.   With great presence of mind, Mary threw herself on to the basket just in time to prevent the jacket of the pyjamas following the legs.

A great battle ensued.   No pyjama jacket is going to lie down quietly in a basket when its legs are waving gaily on a hedge and certainly not the new one belonging to Mr Smith.   It folded itself round Mary, it flapped in her face, and finally it threw itself right over her head just as a motor-car came round the corner and pulled up with screeching brakes within a foot of the fight.

Hearing the car, Mary made a frantic effort to free herself but with no success.   The next moment a voice said, " Allow me," and the coat was whisked off. Though hot and dishevelled, Mary remembered her manners and bowed to her rescuer.   The bow made the basket rock dangerously.

" Allow me," said her rescuer again steadying the basket, and then, " But—surely we met at Lady Ex's ? Isn't this Miss Mary Plain ? "

" It is," said Mary, graciously extending a paw.

The man shook it gravely and then Mary explained what had happened and why she was sitting in a basket in the middle of the lane.   " You see," she finished, " Annie said I'd get into trouble if I lost any, so I got into the basket instead."

" Excellent idea," said her rescuer, handing her the coat neatly folded.

" Thanks," said Mary.   " This is the py.   The jama's on the hedge.   Could you get it ? "

This he did and then lifted Mary and the basket bodily into the car and drove them home.

"Well," said Bill, when he and the Fur-Coat-Lady got back, "the child's all right—no worse for its ducking."

But Mary was. Her face was now definitely swollen and nothing interested her. So after lunch the Owl Man had a private talk with Bill and Bill rang up Mr Grinds, the dentist, and almost at once Mary and the Owl Man set off in Bill's car.

"Where are we going?" asked Mary.

"To see a kind man who will make your tooth well."

"But he won't touch it?" said Mary, quickly. "I shan't open my mouth," she added, through her teeth. So they sat in Mr Grind's waiting-room and the Owl Man looked at a paper while Mary stood close up against his knee and said, "I shan't open my mouth," every now and then, still through her teeth. The Owl Man took no notice but hummed a little tune. The kind of cheerful little tune you would hum to a bear who is waiting to see a dentist.

"Miss Plain, please," said the attendant, opening a door. Holding tightly to the Owl Man's hand, Mary went through and met Mr Grinds. He was kind and fat and he wore a white coat.

"This is Miss Plain," said the Owl Man speaking in the same kind of cheerful dentisty voice he'd hummed in.

"How do you do, Miss Plain," said Mr Grinds, holding out his hand.

" Shan't open my mouth," said Mary, clenching her teeth tight and putting her paw behind her back. Which was very rude. The Owl Man said so but Mary stayed clenched.

So Mr Grinds took no further notice of Mary but turned to the Owl Man and said, " I know *you'd* like to have a ride in my nice new chair ? "

" Rather ! " said the Owl Man, enthusiastically. So Mr Grinds bicycled with one foot on a pedal behind and the Owl Man went up and down, feeling extremely foolish.

" Lovely, isn't it ? " asked Mr Grinds, bicycling hard.

" Wonderful," said the Owl Man, hating each up and each down.

Mary came a little nearer.

" Another ride ? " asked Mr Grinds, hoping the Owl Man would say " No " because all this bicycling was making him uncomfortably hot.

" Mary's turn now," said the Owl Man, brightly, hopping out.

But Mary shook her head and backed. She backed straight into a small table of instruments and upset them all.

" Really, Mary ! " said the Owl Man.

" Never mind, never mind," said Mr Grinds, who evidently did, " accidents will happen. Now Miss Plain, just you let me have a peep inside that mouth of yours—there's a good boy—I mean gir—"

" Bear," said Mary, coldly. But she let Mr Grinds

have a peep and though it was only a small one it showed him where the trouble was.

"It's just a small hole in one of the baby molars that she seems to have got a slight cold in. It only needs a small filling, if you would persuade her to try the chair?"

But the Owl Man didn't try persuading. He lifted Mary firmly into the chair and the next minute she, too, was having a nice ride.

Directly it stopped, she said, "Thank you," very politely and stepped out.

But the Owl Man had come to the end of his patience. He plumped her straight back again and said, in his sternest voice, "You don't want me to be thoroughly ashamed of you, Mary, do you? Now, open your mouth wide, at once, and let Mr Grinds see your tooth."

Mary's mouth opened about a quarter of an inch.

"Very well," said the Owl Man. "I'd been meaning to take you round to the Creamery after, but—"

The next minute Mr Grinds was trying not to see Mary's inside and within five minutes her tooth was stopped and she was out of the chair.

"There!" he said, quite as pleased as Mary that the job was over. "Not too bad, was it? Want another ride?"

"No, thank you," said Mary. "Would you, Owl Man?"

"I think not," said the Owl Man hastily. "Goodbye, Mr Grinds, thank you very much. I am sure we're much obliged aren't we, Mary?"

" Much," said Mary, also shaking hands with Mr Grinds.

All the way to the Creamery Mary hopped.

" It's a case of hop, skip and a jump with you, Mary," said the Owl Man.

" Yes," said Mary.   " I've lost my ache."

" But not your appetite," murmured the Owl Man a few minutes later as Mary's bright eyes looked at him over the top of a bowl of cream.   " The Creamery's a nice place, isn't it ? "

Mary put down her bowl with a sigh.

" Yes," she said, " but I wish it were a bunnery, too."

CHAPTER ELEVEN

MARY MEETS MR LYONS

"WE'VE got some very exciting news to tell you," said Bill next morning. "Can you guess what it is?"

The Owl Man promptly got up and kissed the Fur-Coat-Lady and wrung Bill's hand. The Fur-Coat-Lady looked rather pink and very smiling and Bill was smiling, but without the pinkness. Mary, looking very surprised, got up, too, and hugged the Fur-Coat-Lady and shook hands with Bill and the Owl Man and then asked what the exciting news was.

Everybody laughed and Bill explained that the Fur-Coat-Lady had promised to marry him.

"Oh," said Mary, "what for?"

"Well," said the Fur-Coat-Lady, "mostly because I like him."

"But don't you like the Owl Man best?" asked Mary, more surprised than ever.

The Fur-Coat-Lady shook her head. "I'm afraid not," she said.

"I do," said Mary, going and tucking her paw under his arm and the Owl Man ruffled her head and said he was glad somebody did.

Just then the telephone bell rang. It was Lady Ex to say she was having a little fancy-dress tea-party for her grandchildren the next afternoon and would Mary like to come?

"Would you, Mary?" asked the Owl Man.

"Yes, please," said Mary, who couldn't imagine saying "No" to a party. "What's 'fancy-dress' mean?"

"It means to dress up."

"Oh," said Mary, looking very pleased and disappearing at once.

But not for long. In fact the grown-ups, who wanted to talk about the wedding, spent most of the morning playing a hissing and clapping game with Mary, instead.

She appeared first, wearing her ballet-skirt and a beaming smile, and did a spin.

"Sssss!" said all the grown-ups.

Next came the busman's outfit, with rather less smile but just as much hiss. The bathing drawers and nurse's uniform went the same way and finally Mary appeared, a bit droopy about the ears, as herself.

"Do you think the twins—" she began, but loud clapping interrupted her. Her ears pricked with astonishment. "But—but—this is just me, Mary Plain," she said.

"Exactly," said the Owl Man. "If you go as just Mary Plain you'll be the success of the party, won't she, Bill?"

"She will," said Bill. "You take our advice, Miss Plain, and—how about some elevens's?"

"Thank you," said Mary and found that advice and bananas went very well together.

That afternoon they went into the small town about eight miles away to do some shopping. Their first stop was at an old curiosity shop where they were going to choose a wedding present for the Fur-Coat-Lady. As the shop was full of valuable china and glass the Owl Man said Mary had better wait in the car.

"What's that shop," she asked as they were getting out, "with a window full of faces?"

"That's Mr Lyons' shop—he's a photographer," said the Owl Man. "Some day, if you're good, I'll take you to have your picture done, Mary."

Mary sat and drummed her paws against Mr Bill Smith's best paint and found it very dull. What ages and ages they were. "Oh dear, oh dear," sighed Mary, yawning an enormous yawn. And then she suddenly had one of her bright ideas. The Owl Man had said he'd take her to have her picture done one day, if she was good. She had been good, extra good, so why wait for one day, or any days? Why not go and have it taken now? It would save him the bother of taking her and what a nice surprise for Mr Lyons it would be.

It was. He met her at the top of the stairs leading to the studio but Mary didn't believe she'd ever seen anyone disappear as quickly. It was like a conjuring trick. She hurried up the last few steps to see if she could find him. The studio door was open and yes, there he was, sitting on the top of a ladder on wheels, and his eyes looked like glass balls.

"Hallo!" said Mary. "Are you Mr Lyons?"

Mr Lyons nodded. It was all he could do.

Memories of a svisit to the Zoo came floating into Mary's mind. "Why aren't you at the Zoo?" she enquired next.

"B-b-because I'm h-h-here," stammered Mr Lyons, wishing to goodness he weren't.

"Where's your tail?" asked Mary next. "Turn round."

Mr Lyons turned. He would have done anything Mary asked him to, but because it is almost impossible to turn on a high ladder *without* a bear watching and quite impossible *with*, Mr Lyons missed his footing and came shooting down, landing at Mary's feet. He lay without moving, hardly breathing, and looking so terrified that Mary bent down and patted him kindly on the head. Then she walked round him slowly.

"You haven't got one, have you?" she said. "Never mind, upsy daisy!"

Mr Lyons got slowly to his feet; his eyes, still glassy, were fixed on Mary.

"I'm Mary Plain," she explained. "An unusual first-class bear from the bear-pits at Berne with a white rosette and a gold medal with a picture of myself on it and I want you to do me a picture of me now."

Mr Lyons drew a deep breath. She wasn't the biting kind evidently. All the same, he'd always heard the thing to do was to out-stare a wild animal. But what was that she had said? Mr Lyons took another deep breath and said, all in a rush, " The famous bear who behaved with such wonderful bravery in the matter of the burglary of the famous Ex family jewels? *Not*— but no, you couldn't possibly be *that* Miss Plain ? "

Mary beamed and put out her paw. " Yes," she said, " that's me."

Mr Lyons bent low and kissed the paw reverently. " Madam ! " he said, and choked a little.

Mary had never been called " Madam " before—nor had she had her paw kissed. She was a little uncertain what to do so she gave a little cough and patted Mr Lyons head again. " And now will you picture me ? " she said.

" With all my heart," said Mr Lyons.

But in spite of Mr Lyon's heart he found it extra-ordinarily difficult to take a photo of Mary, because every time he'd got settled under his black cloth and said " See the birdie ! " Mary got down and joined him under the cloth to see it, too.

It took quite half-an-hour before he got Mary posed, her left paw a little forward and out and an anchor clasped under the other arm against a back-cloth of waves and cliff. He took several others including a " God Save the King " one, with Mary at the salute, draped in a Union Jack, but the one Mary liked the best, was one in which only her head and shoulders appeared out of a cloud of tulle.

They were the best of friends by the time the last picture was taken and Mr Lyons bowed Mary down the stairs and out of his door. He promised to post her the pictures as soon as they were ready.

There was still no sign of the others so Mary climbed back into the car. It was dull there by herself and she soon began to look for something to do and caught sight of a little square window in the roof. " I wonder if I could reach that ? " thought Mary, who enjoyed reach-ing things. So she climbed on to the back of one of the front seats and found she was just tall enough. It needed rather a lot of push to get ·her head through but, just as she was going to give it up, it went through with a pop.

She could only see exactly the same as from inside the car and after a look round she decided to go in again.

But she found that, in some extraordinary way, her head had suddenly grown too big and, struggle as she might, she was completely stuck—the little window had her by the neck.

Her shrieks reached the Owl Man almost at once but they reached a lot of other people as well and, by the time he got to the shop door, he had to look over a lot of people's heads before he saw the car with Mary's frantic head popping through the roof. Her mouth was wide open and she was shrieking, " My head's come off. Oh, my head. Let me out, let me out ! "

It took quite a lot of men quite a little time to do this. It was no good the Owl Man saying, in an extra firm, quiet voice, " She got through so she *must* get back." The window was just as firm and it had got Mary.

Bill climbed on to the roof to see if pressing on her head would be better than pulling from below, but it wasn't.

Finally, just as they were sending for a carpenter to saw her out, Mary's head slipped through, quite easily.

" Oo," she said, feeling it all over. " Oh I *am* glad it's come back."

" So are we," said the Owl Man, who sounded tired.

" I'll keep it now," said Mary.

" Please," said the Owl Man, " or I'll go off mine."

CHAPTER TWELVE

MARY ATTENDS A PARTY

WHEN they arrived at the party the children were in the middle of a galop.

" Just to get them warmed up," explained Lady Ex " Here, Millicent, you dance with Mary."

Millicent did. She was dressed as a white rabbit and her face got redder and redder as the dance went on.

Directly it was over she pulled Mary into a cool-looking corner and sat down.

" Phew ! " she said. " I *am* hot. Do unbutton me."

Mary fumbled with her fastenings. " I'm hot, too," she said.

" Now I'll unbutton you," said the child, turning to her.

" I don't unbutton," said Mary, in a freezing voice.

" Zipp, then," suggested Millicent.

" Nor zipp, neither," said Mary. " I'm me."

" You aren't—but—I thought—Mummie," shrieked Millicent, " this is a bear—a real alive bear ! "

" Yes," said Mary, " I'm a first-class bear, too, with a white rosette and a gold medal with a picture of myself on it, so there ! "

" Come along to tea, all of you," cried Lady Ex and Mary, at the welcome words, stopped being offended and trotted off after the others.

Tea was in the big nursery so they all trooped upstairs.

" She won't mind if you leave her and come down to your own tea, will she ? " Lady Ex asked the Owl Man when all the bibs were tied on and everybody seated.

" Rather not," said the Owl Man. " You'll be all right, won't you, Mary ? "

" Oh yes," said Mary, " there's lots to do," and she gave a deep sigh of happiness as she looked at the plates piled with food.

Her late partner who, besides being a white rabbit was also Lady Ex's grandchild, sat at the head of the table and insisted on having Mary beside her. Mary didn't care two hoots where she sat as long as they began to eat.

" Shall we say grace ? " asked Millicent's Nannie. " And then we can begin."

" Grace," said Mary.

" Sssh ! " said all the shocked Nannies. Mary stared while all the little girls and boys folded their hands and closed their eyes. Mary didn't shut hers because there was far too much to look at and during grace she grew particularly fond of a sugar motor which stood between her and Millicent's plates. All the plates had a sugar toy in front of them but the motor was the biggest and by the time " Amen " was said Mary had decided it was hers.

All went well till, after her third piece of bread and jam, Millicent put out her hand and stroked the motor.

" That's mine ! " said Mary, as soon as she could speak for bun. (Mary had already reached the bun stage.)

Now, Millicent hadn't specially wanted the motor, but when Mary spoke she suddenly did and seizing hold of it, cried, " T'isn't, it's mine ! "

" Shame, Millicent," said her Nannie, " that's not the way a little lady speaks and I hope we're all little ladies here."

By this time Mary has got hold of the motor and, to make sure of keeping it, she sat on it. Before her Nannie could stop her, Millicent leant forward and, with her fist clenched, gave Mary a hard biff on the nose.

" Grrrr," said Mary.

There wasn't much " little ladies " about the children who ran shrieking from the room nor about the Nannies who ran screaming after them. In about one minute Mary was left in sole possession of the tea-table. First she rubbed her sore nose and said " Ow " several times and then she rescued the sugar motor, not too melted, and put it on the table. Then, standing on her chair, she pulled as many plates as she could within reach.

She was just starting on a particularly creamy brandy-snap when the door opened and the Owl Man strode in, wearing his angry face.

" What's this I hear, Mary ? " he said.

Mary didn't answer. Instead, she bit the wrong end of the brandy-snap and it exploded on to her chest and face and some of the cream went up her poor nose.

" Did you hear what I said ? " asked the Owl Man.

" Tischsu ! " answered Mary and, as she sneezed, blood suddenly poured out of her nose.

" Great Scott ! " said the Owl Man who, having come up prepared to spank Mary now found himself on his knees beside her, holding his best silk handkerchief to her streaming nose and feeling terribly sorry for her.

Mary's eyes, very frightened, looked at him over the top. " That girl hit my nose," she said. " Am I blooding ? "

" You are l " said the Owl Man, grimly, as he mopped and mopped and wondered if bears' noses ever stopped bleeding once they'd begun. " Ah ! " He turned his head in relief as Lady Ex hurried into the room, looking rather upset.

" Her nose is bleeding like the dickens. What does one do ? "

Lady Ex stopped looking upset at once.

" Lie her flat and drop a key between her back and her clothes," she said, capably. But as there weren't any clothes to drop anything down that was no good.

" I know ! " exclaimed Lady Ex. " A cold sponge." And she rushed away to fetch one.

But the sponge wasn't any good, either.

" What can we do—had I better telephone to the— Oh, *I* know ! " said Lady Ex again.

The Owl Man didn't feel much cheered when she said " I know " again for she'd said it three times already and she hadn't, for here was Mary still lying with her eyes closed, with her nose still bleeding.

This time, however, Lady Ex went to the side-table and, filling a large spoon full of strawberry ice-cream, she plonked it on to Mary's forehead. A little of it trickled down her nose. Mary's eye-lashes fluttered and a tip of pink tongue appeared.

The Owl Man was absurdly pleased at the sight of that tip because Mary had lain so still he'd begun to feel a bit desperate. Still, the ice certainly seemed to be doing the trick for the bleeding was already less.

" Fetch the whole pail ! " ordered Lady Ex, settling herself on the floor beside Mary. While the Owl Man held the pail, she ladled alternatively on to Mary's forehead and into her mouth until the bleeding and the ice-cream both stopped. During this time the Owl Man told her what had happened and though, as he said, there was little excuse for Mary so far forgetting her manners as to growl, the biff had undoubtedly been a hard one.

" I know, I know—dreadful ! " exclaimed Lady Ex. " That little pig Millicent—I'll give her a talking-to to-night, trust me ! Now, do you think Mary could sit up or do you think it might start it off again ? "

But Mary wasn't taking any risks of all that beginning over again. Nothing would induce her to budge and she remained, straight and stiff, with closed eyes.

"Poor old Mary," said the Owl Man, hoping to rouse her. "Your nose looks about the size of two."

Mary immediately begged him to put his handkerchief over her face.

"She can't have that soiled thing over her," said Lady Ex, whisking it off again.

Mary opened her eyes and looked at the Owl Man.

"Do you think the twins are happy without me?"

"Perhaps you could kindly lend her a clean one?" he asked Lady Ex. "And then I think we'd better get home—the children will be wanting their tea."

"Bother their tea!" said Lady Ex and fetched a beautiful pale blue silk square which she laid gently over Mary's face.

"Perhaps your man would give me a hand with her?" suggested the Owl Man. So a slightly timid butler presently tip-toed into the room, carrying a flat table-top to act as stretcher.

"What about my tea?" murmured Mary.

"I'll see to that," promised Lady Ex, while the Owl Man decided Mary was definitely better.

Still stiff as a ram-rod she was lifted carefully on to the stretcher and they started downstairs.

The children were all in the hall talking excitedly, but when the little procession appeared at the top of the stairs, a sudden silence fell.

First came the two men, carrying the stretcher rather high so as to see the steps as they came down, and behind came Lady Ex bearing a tray piled high with meringues

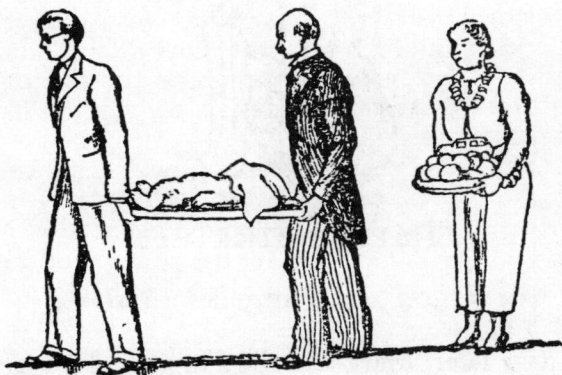

and cakes and êclairs on the top of which was perched the sugar motor-car.

When they reached the hall and lowered the stretcher all the children gazed in frightened fascination at the still, furry figure with its face covered up.

" Oh, is she very hurt ? " exclaimed one frightened voice and Mary, recognizing it for Millicent's, said clearly, " Yes.   I'm dead."

CHAPTER THIRTEEN

IN WHICH MARY RETURNS TO TOWN

A FEW days later, Mary and the Fur-Coat-Lady and the Owl Man travelled back to London. The Owl Man hoped very much they would get a carriage to themselves but the train was so full that they could only find seats in a Pullman Smoker, full of elderly gentlemen behind newspapers.

" Are they playing houses ? " asked Mary, in a loud whisper.

All the old gentlemen immediately came out from behind their papers, rustled them, frowned at Mary and disappeared again.

" Or hide-and-seek ? " she suggested, in a louder whisper.

" Shut up ! " said the Owl Man, who was busy getting his coat off, settling their cases in the rack and trying to cover up Mary's bright bag with a rug.

But Mary had her eyes fixed on a man in the corner seat who, bit by bit, was again lowering his newspaper.

She waited till his eyes appeared over the top and then
called " Boo ! "

Down came all the other papers and there was a lot
of angry rustling and clearing of throats. Mary felt
herself lifted and placed in the corner seat with her back
to the rest of the compartment.

" Sit there and keep quiet and look at this paper,"
said the Owl Man in what was almost a hiss. He was
thinking to himself " Really, how dreadful, if Mary's
beginning already and it's two hours to London ! "

Mary held her paper up like a house, too, but it was
very dull inside and she couldn't turn over the pages
because her paws didn't seem able to manage very well.
So, seeing the Owl Man and the Fur-Coat-Lady were
both safely behind theirs, she slipped on to the floor
and, spreading the paper flat, found she could see
beautifully.

But the restaurant waiter, hurrying in with a tray of
coffee, couldn't see beautifully, in fact he didn't see Mary
at all till he and the coffee had joined her on the floor.

For a few minutes Mary and the waiter and the paper
all seemed to be mixed up together and, when they had
been sorted out, there was a good deal of coffee on Mary.
The Owl Man mopped her a bit with his handkerchief
and Mary was just going to suggest cleaning her chest up
herself, when she caught sight of his face and changed
her mind. Instead, she went and tucked herself away
in the corner and left him to deal with the waiter. Peeping from under her lashes she saw all the elderly gentlemen were out of their houses and whispering together.

Some of them were such loud whispers that they were almost out-louds, and they reached the Owl Man where he was standing, trying to apologize and explain to the waiter about bears travelling and handing him something that chinked. Presently, rather red in the face, he sat down in his seat and picked up his paper. Mary kept wonderfully still for Mary, for about five minutes, and then she nudged the Fur-Coat-Lady and said she felt hungry.

The Fur-Coat-Lady leant forward and touched the Owl Man's hand. He let down his paper.

" Mary's hungry," said the Fur-Coat-Lady.

" Then she can stay hungry," said the Owl Man and disappeared again.

Mary sighed and then, by great good fortune, fell asleep. When she woke up the train was much nearer London but it was rocking a good deal.

" I feel sick," announced Mary, " I think I'm going to be untidy."

The Owl Man got up quickly and gripping Mary's paw, led her past the old gentlemen and out into the corridor where he opened a window wide and made Mary put her head out.

Mary immediately got a cinder in her eye and came in again. " Ow ! " she said, " my eye prickles me— Ow ! "

The Owl Man had a look. Sure enough, there was the cinder right in the corner. He sighed deeply, produced a handkerchief and knelt down.

" I beg your pardon—I wish to pass," said a voice

behind.   As the Owl Man stumbled to his feet, one of the elderly gentlemen pushed past.

Again the Owl Man got down but had no success, so he fetched the Fur-Coat-Lady.

"It's almost impossible, jerking about like this," she said, "but I'll have a try."

The Owl Man held Mary between his knees to keep her as steady as possible and the Fur-Coat-Lady knelt down.

"Pardon me," and the elderly gentleman squeezed past again.

The Owl Man glared at his back before they got into position again and had another shot at Mary's cinder.

"I'm terribly sorry, but it just can't be done," said the Fur-Coat-Lady.   "Not till the train stops."

So the Owl Man got out his handkerchief and bound it over Mary's eye, once more finding himself being sorry for her when he ought to be being angry.   When they got back to the Pullman, several of the old gentlemen were whispering excitedly together and pointing at their newspapers.   Directly Mary appeared they stopped and, amid a dead silence, the three returned to their seats.

The Owl Man picked up another paper, turned a page and gave a great start.   "Great Caesar Augustus's ghost !" he exclaimed.   "But—but—"

By this time both Mary and the Fur-Coat-Lady were beside him and looking at the paper, too.

"Why !" said Mary in a delighted voice, "Mr Lyons has been quick."

"'Mr Lyons ?' 'Quick ?' Mary, would you

kindly explain ? " said the Owl Man, helplessly. He might be mad, of course, but here, in the *Riverhurst Chronicle* was undoubtedly a picture of Mary, clasping an anchor, by the sea. And when had Mary ever been at the sea, far less clasped an anchor ?

So Mary explained, while all the old gentlemen who had also seen the picture in their own *Riverhurst Chronicle*, craned forward with their hands behind their ears and listened hard.

" And there's others, too," finished Mary ; " I like me in a cloud best."

" But why on earth didn't you tell us ? " asked the Owl Man.

" Because it was to be a surprise," answered Mary. " And we never saw the birdie, after all," she added.

" One usually doesn't," murmured the Owl Man. " And now, Mary, do you think you could go and sit in that seat in the corner and keep quite still for a little ? I feel I need a rest."

Mary went at once. She also sat, but not for long. There were quite a lot of things to explore—the rack, and the window straps and a chain near the ceiling. " A funny little chain," thought Mary, getting up to have a look at it.

The next moment everyone was thrown violently forward as, with a screeching and grinding of brakes, the train was brought to a standstill with a terrific jerk.

" Accident ! " said one old man, making for the door.

" Fire ! " said another and the next moment they were

all jammed in the doorway, fighting to get out. Mary scrambled back to the others as quickly as she could.

" This way," said the Owl Man, quietly, and, tucking Mary under his arm and holding the Fur-Coat-Lady by the elbow, he led them to the further door away from the mass of struggling old gentlemen. Having deposited his party on the side of the track, the Owl Man went back and collected their luggage and piled it beside them and then sat Mary on top of it.

The guard and the engine-driver and the stoker and the ticket-collector and all the waiters were rushing along the train searching in every carriage, poking under seats with sticks, but they couldn't find a sign of fire or accident anywhere.

The guard cupped his mouth in his hands and shouted, " How about the roof ? " and, in an instant, the men swarmed up and over the tops of the carriages, hunting hard but still not finding anything.

Mary, perched on the luggage, trying to see from under her bandage, remembered what the Fur-Coat-Lady had said. " Couldn't you mend my eye, please ? " she said, plaintively.

" Poor old Mary, of course we can," said the Owl Man, lifting her down and again the Fur-Coat-Lady got out her handkerchief and again she knelt before Mary. And this time, almost at once, out came the horrid little cinder.

" Hurrah ! " she cried.

" Oh, thank you," said Mary, " it doesn't prickle me any more and now I can see with the both of my eyes. What's that man doing?" she enquired, pointing to a man who was wriggling himself under the train on all fours.

"Well," said the Owl Man, "you see, they're trying to find the person who pulled the communication chain and stopped the train."

"But why do they want the person?" asked Mary.

"To make him pay five pounds or pop him into prison," said the Owl Man, grimly.

Mary slid her hand into his and stood very close against his side. She opened her mouth to speak.

"But I don't think there's a chance of finding him," added the Owl Man.

"Nor do I," said the Fur-Coat-Lady.

Mary shut her mouth again.

"What do you think, Mary?" said the Owl Man.

Mary drew a deep breath. "I know they won't," she said.

CHAPTER FOURTEEN

THE WEDDING

THE day of the wedding had come at last. There had been a lot of discussion about the plans beforehand. The Fur-Coat-Lady had said she wouldn't have any bridesmaids.

" What are they for ? " enquired Mary.

" Well, they follow the bride in a kind of procession."

" Wouldn't you like a brides-bear ? " suggested Mary, who adored processions.

The Fur-Coat-Lady looked at the Owl Man for help.

" How about having a brides-bear's procession just to carry your train from the door to the drawing-room ? " he suggested. " How would that be ? "

" But I wasn't going to have a procession," said the Fur-Coat-Lady, feebly, " nor a train."

Mary's ears drooped.

" Well, just a little train," said the Owl Man, encouragingly, watching Mary's ears. " Just enough for

451

The Owl Man . . . would walk patiently up and down

Mary to carry, and she could be the procession by herself, couldn't you, Mary ? "

" Oh yes ! " said Mary, ears up in points. And ever
since, she had been practising hard.

Sometimes the Fur-Coat-Lady came to tea and, as
soon as she had swallowed it, they'd have a rehearsal,
but oftener it was the Owl Man who, draped in a sheet,
would walk patiently up and down, while Mary, breathing heavily, gripped the other end and tried her hardest
to learn how not to step on the back of his heels

Unfortunately she had seen a picture of a bridesmaid
and she had asked every day and several times a day
what she was to wear. It was no good telling her she'd
be more unusual as a bear—Mary wasn't having any.

So at last they decided on pale blue net with no lining,
a blue sash and bows on the shoulders. And, of course,
a wreath.

She'd wanted a train as well but the Owl Man had
said only brides had them and who did she think would
carry it, anyway ?

" You," said Mary, promptly, but this time it was the
Owl Man who wasn't having any.

And now, here she was, bows and all, watching from
a window of the house where the reception was to be
held, for the bride to arrive. In one paw she had a
bouquet of forget-me-nots with four long streamers
but they didn't stay streamers for long as Mary decided
they'd better be bows on her ankles instead.

At last the car drew up at the strip of red carpet and
Mary flew down the steps.

" Goo ! look at that ! " cried the people who had collected to see the bride.   " Who are you ? "

" I'm the procession," said Mary, " and I'm the brides-bear too and—" but here Mary stopped for the Fur-Coat-Lady and Bill were out of the car and her duties began.

It took a good while getting up the stairs because Mary hadn't practised steps before.   When they finally reached the drawing-room the wreath had landed on her nose. The Fur-Coat-Lady straightened it and said the first hug must be for the brides-bear and Mary, seeing her all white and shining, hugged her specially hard.

Bill then said he had great pleasure in presenting their charming attendant, Miss Plain (here he shook Mary warmly by the paw) with a brides-bear's present.   It was a lovely soft blue rug with a wool picture of a bear in each corner.

" Four me ! " said Mary, highly delighted, and she insisted on going to bed in it there and then, which was rather upsetting for the guests who were arriving through the door and on to Mary.

So the Owl Man removed her and the rug and took her to see the presents.   But Mary had no eyes for anything but the tea-basket she had herself given the bride. It was a specially nice one with a gay orange label tied to each fitting, all with Mary writing on them.   The best label was on the handle and that said—

W🐦 THIS ∪ 🚗RY TH🔑 OF 🐱

which Mary thought was a beautiful " pome."

Presently she wandered off into a small room at the back and just as she was deciding it was a dull room a bell rang. " Telephone " thought Mary. Yes, there it was on a corner table. Mary picked up the receiver but at first she couldn't hear who it was because she never stopped saying " Hallo " herself. At last, however, she heard a voice saying something about " a few questions about the bridesmaids."

" Pardon ? " said Mary.

" Could you tell me anything about the bridesmaids' dresses ? " asked the voice.

" There's only a brides-bear and that's me," said Mary, but there was some buzzing on the line and the man only heard " that's me."

" Excellent ! " said the voice. " Could you kindly tell me about your dress ? "

" It's blue," said Mary, " and I've got (a pause while Mary counted) seven bows."

" Bows ? " said the voice.

" Yes," said Mary, " on my shoulders and at the back of me and on all my ankles."

" Pardon ! " said the voice.

" I said on all my ankles," said Mary, calmly, " all four of them."

" I *beg* your pardon ! " exclaimed the voice. "I am afraid there must be something wrong with this line."

But the voice made one more effort. " Could you," it asked, " tell me how the dress is made—long or short ? "

"Long," said Mary, "but it doesn't matter because you can see my legs through nicely."

"Legs! Did I hear you say *legs*, Madam?"

"Yes," said Mary cheerfully (a pause while she looked) "and all the rest of me, too."

The voice rang off.

Presently in the dining-room, they drank the bride and bridegroom's health.

The Owl Man got up on a stool and raised his glass. "As best man," he said, "I know I am speaking for you all when I offer the bridal couple our very affectionate good wishes for all possible good luck. Will you join me in drinking the toast of—Mr and Mrs Bill Smith!"

Mary tugged at his trouser-leg which was all she could reach and said she couldn't drink toast but she'd like some to eat, please—with jam.

The Owl Man laughed and went off and collected some.

"And which is Mrs Bill Smith?" asked Mary, which showed she didn't understand much about weddings.

"This!" said the Owl Man, laughing again as he pulled forward the Fur-Coat-Lady.

But Mary didn't laugh. She buried her head against the Owl Man's knees and said in a muffled voice, "But I don't want her to be Mrs Bill Smith—I want her to be my Fur-Coat-Lady."

"Oh dear, but I *am* your Fur-Coat-Lady," cried the bride, throwing herself on her white satin knees in front of Mary, "I'm still just the same—really, Mary."

Mary raised her head an inch. "But you can't be both," she said.

"Oh, yes, I can—quite easily. Do please drink—I mean, eat my toast, Mary," she coaxed. "Or would you rather eat it in ice-cream?" And Mary did.

At last it was time for the bride and bridegroom to leave. The guests lined up in the hall and Mary went and stood by the car door so as to see the very last of them. One of the women in the crowd held a handful of rose-petals. "I shall throw these for luck," she said.

"Oh dear, I wish I had some luck to throw," said Mary. All the onlookers laughed.

"Here you are, duck," said one, good naturedly. "Here's an envelope full of luck—you can throw that."

Mary peeped inside the bag and saw hundreds of little coloured rounds. But she had no time to examine them as just then out came the Fur-Coat-Lady and, giving Mary a quick hug, she jumped into the car and Bill after her.

"Oh, the luck, the luck!" cried Mary, and threw the confetti at the car door. Unfortunately, the Owl Man was just shutting it and most of it went down his neck.

But it was too exciting even to bother much about confetti down the neck, for everyone was shouting and cheering and all the people there heard for the first time a real bear cheer as Mary yelled, "Hip, hip, hoo-Fur-Coat! Hip, hip hoo-Lady!"

As the car rounded the corner the Owl Man ran back up the steps. At the top he turned to see if Mary had followed him.

But she hadn't. She was standing on the pavement, surrounded by a circle of kneeling newspaper reporters who, propping their pads on one knee, were scribbling hard.

The Owl Man bent his head and listened. " I thought so," he murmured, as the familiar words floated up to him and, in spite of the confetti, he smiled a very kind smile.

" And a gold medal with a picture of myself on it," finished Mary, turning to mount the steps.

" And the name, please," urged the reporters, wriggling after her on their knees.

Mary walked slowly to the top. There she turned, straightened her wreath, bowed her best bow and said, " Me, of course, Mary Plain."